LADIES OF THE BOROBUDUR

To Joan
my water buddy

Barbara Homier Howett

LADIES OF THE BOROBUDUR
A Mosaic of Interrelated Stories

BARBARA HAINES HOWETT

CREATIVE ARTS BOOK COMPANY
Berkeley • California

For information contact:
Creative Arts Book Company
833 Bancroft Way
Berkeley, California 94710
1-800-848-7789

Acknowledgments

Writing this book has been a journey with many stops and starts along the way. I
would like to acknowledge those who got me running and back on the road on
various legs of the trip.

Bharati Mukherjee, Christopher Tighleman, Dewitt Henry, Linda Nelson,
Mary Jane Zonin, Martha E. Hughes, Ragdale Foundation,
Virginia Center for the Creative Arts, Hedgebrook,
Squaw Valley Community of Writers, Pennsylvania Council for the Arts,
Department of Indonesia Studies, Cornell University
The Bobst Library, New York University.

"We've Only Just Begun"
Words and Music by Roger Nichols, Paul Williams
©Copyright 1970 Irving Music, Inc. (BMI)
International Copyright Secured All Rights Reserved

"Never, Never, Never"
Norman Newell (English words) and Tony Renis
Copyright © 1972 by Peer Edizioni Musicali SRL
Administered by Peermusic (UK) Ltd.
Used by Permission. All Rights Reserved.

"The Last Farewell"
Ron Webster and Roger Whitaker
All Rights o/b/o BMG Music Publishing Ltd. (PRS) and Tembo
Music Ltd. administered by BMG Songs, Inc. (ASCAP)
All rights reserved. Used by permission

ISBN 0-88739-349-7
Library of Congress Catalog Number 2001095291

This book is dedicated
to the memory of Jack Howett.
Wherever he is, may he know that without him
this book would not have been possible.

CONTENTS

LADIES OF THE BOROBUDUR

PROLOGUE

I AM NELIA, BORN OF INDIAN PARENTS IN INDONESIA, AN ARCHIPELAGO OF many islands washed by the waters of the Pacific and Indian Oceans. I absorbed tolerance for the white man's world in a Methodist orphanage on Sumatra. But it is on Java I live now, and it is here I am content, studying *Wayang Kulit*, shadow plays of puppetry that tell Hindu epics thought to have been brought here by my forebears and passed down through centuries of change in this, my adopted country.

In Jakarta I ply my trade, singing and playing the piano in the Pendopo Lounge of the Hotel Borobudur, a way to support those studies. This capital city of seven million people sets the business and social standards of Indonesia. To it have come many foreigners—to exploit us, and to teach us modern technology, and accidentally, new ways of living. But it is the Western women who fascinate me.

When they arrive, they are scared, defiant, preoccupied with one another. Some are physically ill until their bodies adjust to our heat and light, food and drink. And they do not know us. We are as strange a fruit to them as that in the baskets placed every week in their elegant hotel rooms, where, insulated, they are lulled to believe they are somewhere familiar, somewhere they recognize themselves. They share a fantasy of their previous life as a perfect one in a perfect place that will be the same the minute they return home.

In the *Wayang* philosophy, using the mythical worlds of the *Mahabbharata* and *Ramayana*, everyone has a different role to play in society and must know that role. Queens behave as queens, clowns behave as clowns, just as expatriates behave as expatriates and Indonesians as Indonesians. The ladies of the Borobudur struggle with problems they brought with them while my fellow citizens grapple with puzzlements presented by the foreigners—situations neither would have encountered had they been somewhere else.

i

I am only the musical background to their life, but I watch and listen, feeling their pain, seeing them entangled in problems of choice not easy to call good or evil; for choice is central to the shadow play's encyclopedia of human problems—misery or hope, joy or sorrow, defeat or triumph, love or hate. And in the depth of these shadows, as well, are predjudice, lust, greed, envy, compulsion—things we can see but cannot touch, at once real, yet unreal.

To understand it all, as well as the warring cultures inside myself, I would that it were something as familiar to me as a performance of the Wayang. But, alas, the stories are all in the process of being invented. But perhaps the dalang knows, for he is part playwright, part director, part actor. More than that—he is a man of magic, who can speak for everyone.

Not only is the dalang the puppeteer and the narrator, he is also the conscience of his audience. In the course of a performance, traditionally from nine at night until six in the morning, he will manipulate half a hundred puppets made from water buffalo leather; he will sing songs; and he will cue both the requisite female singer and the traditional orchestra, the gamelan. All this he does by tapping signals with wooden knockers and metal rappers on the puppet box. In due course, he will make his audience laugh and cry while teaching them great truths without moralizing.

Imagine then—a setting for the Wayang. All that is needed for this art are a screen, an oil lamp for casting shadows, the chest in which the characters not in use are stored, and a display of puppets, ranging from the largest to the smallest, whose manipulation sticks are thrust into the soft wood of a banana tree log. And of course—the dalang.

Listen now as he raps the puppet box with a heavy mallet. Ndhog-ndhog-ndhog. A great gong resounds. Seat yourself well. If you choose a place in front, you will see only the shadows as do the masses who see things superficially. But if you view the screen from behind, as do the privileged few, you will see how the dalang operates—and thus gain a deeper understanding.

And so—the gamelan begins to play. The dalang seats himself cross-legged before a long white screen with a red border, a bright light suspended above his head. Ndhog-ndhog-ndhog. The music swells. With grace and ease, he flutters the players into position for stories of good and evil, darkness and light, and all the shades of human frailty in-between.

Come, let us listen together as the dalang imitates many voices.

LADIES OF THE BOROBUDUR

CEREMONIES:
Lisa

THE THICK, HOT BREATH OF INDONESIA SUFFOCATED LISA THE MOMENT she walked off the jet into the Jakarta night. She shifted the carryon bag to her other shoulder, blew a strand of hair from her eyes, and tried to keep up with David's lope across the tarmac. After all, she'd come because she loved him too much to deny him what he wanted so badly, but she wasn't giving up any more of her independence. She'd be her own woman here no matter what.

Then a rush of adrenaline. Men with guns surrounded them. She couldn't breathe, couldn't think. For God's sake, guns! She knew it was a military government, but she'd never anticipated—

"*Masuk! Masuk!*" rang in her ears as brown-faced soldiers nudged the passengers inside to a steamy nightmare, a polyglot of raised voices. The air was fetid, the chaotic line she stumbled along endless. Loudest of all were the soldiers, barking orders, scolding laggards. She turned to David for reassurance just as he was pulled out of line. An officer pointed to a sign she couldn't read.

"Evidently, we do health cards first," David said. They stepped to the end of the string of people the officer indicated.

On the plane Lisa had met an Indonesian woman who was returning home after twelve years in the States. Srikandi told her that Indonesians had been inspired by the American Revolution in their own fight for independence. She called freedom—*Merdeka*. Lisa allowed it to roll over her lips—*Mare-dak-ah*. She liked that 'freedom,' the soul of her own country, was her first Indonesian word. If she'd been born here, she'd have been a revolutionary, one of the Indonesian women fighting side by side with the

1

men for freedom from Dutch Colonialism, enduring the Japanese occupation, and putting down the Communists in '65.

At home, she'd taught the privileges of US citizenship to junior high
school civics students. After conscientious deliberation, she'd finally decided to put off going to grad school, not only because she couldn't bear the
thought of David being where she wasn't, but also for the sake of learning
firsthand how freedom worked on the other side of the world—something
she could share with future students.

In the *Immigrasi* line once again, she pushed her bag along the floor
with her foot as they inched forward. The noise, the bright lights ... if only
there were more white faces. If only she could have a drink of water. If only
David didn't have that silly, bemused look on his face. Her fear forced the
angry words. "What kind of a country are they running here anyway?"

David gave her a warning pinch, for now an officious man, standing in
a glass box, beckoned her forward. Dainty hands with a heavy gold ring
took her passport. "*Amerikan*," he grunted, but she didn't see any welcome
in his bored eyes. "*Tourisma*? How long you stay?" She couldn't take her
eyes from the armed guard, slouched against the wall nearby. Unable to
muster up any bravado, she allowed David to answer for both of them.

"Yesssss," the official said, "CAMCO. Joint venture with our great
Pertamina Oil." He smiled. His rubber stamp thudded against their papers.
For a moment she was disappointed, realizing she'd half-hoped they
wouldn't get in, half-hoped she might not miss the grand celebration at
home, the Bicentennial, after all.

But it seemed to her he reluctantly returned her passport, and that his
stare was a question into her eyes, into her heart. Could he discern the lie
they'd told? Did he know they weren't married? But so what? It was the
Seventies for heaven's sake, and women were beginning to do what they
wanted, just like men.

Then they were in a barn-like room piled high with baggage. Officials
motioned them to place their luggage on a low table. Boys lounged nearby,
waiting to carry the bags outside, and just beyond them spectators ogled
them from the other side of a glass wall. Lisa felt like a fish in an aquari-
um. Two white couples tapped on the window and gestured at them.

"Wave, honey," David said. "Someone's come to meet us." She waved.
"This is what we both want, right?" he reminded. She made her wave a little more enthusiastic, although her makeup was running down her face,
although all she could think about was a bed in an air-conditioned room.

They counted their luggage to be sure it was all there, and then a numb
Lisa tried not to care that strangers were pawing her things. Finally, offi-

cials marked their bags with chalk, and they were out in the tropic night, fighting through jostling Indonesians and hustling taxi drivers. The two smiling couples took them in tow. Fighting her disorientation, Lisa tried to smile back.

"We always meet our husbands' new people," said the tall, anorexic one, who introduced herself as Mrs. Sheetz—with a "Z."

"Mrs. Walburton, dear, that's who I am," said the one who looked like a well-stuffed pillow.

Faintly, she heard that the women were going in the car, the men in the van with the baggage. She found herself in the back seat with Mrs. Walburton, who said, "Why you don't get the air conditioning fixed in your car, Edythe, I'll never know." She reached over and rolled down Lisa's window.

As the car sped over the dark road, Lisa relaxed into the upholstery, shutting out Mrs. Sheetz's babble that the two seasons here were rainy and rainier. She slept, dreaming this was all a dream and actually she was teaching her class, who turned out to be Japanese. She woke abruptly with the sibilant Mare-dak-ah echoing in her head—a magic word surely, promising much for Lisa's stay here. The open road soon became city streets that made her anxious and ill at ease. All kinds of shops on wheels competed with cars and trucks for the thoroughfare. Kerosene lamps cast eerie shadows over tables, lining the roadside, loaded with bright fabrics, pots and pans, and odd-looking brooms. A perfume of coconut and oil and grilling meat, and something very sweet, a redolence she'd never experienced before, wafted through the window from cooking stalls.

The car crept along the road that thronged with people in strange dress, past motorcycles and odd three-wheeled conveyances, pedaled by men. The soft lilt of voices lulled her. "AAAOOO" a peddler called. "NYAK, NYAK" called another. Then Sheetz and Pillowcase were talking to her and the spell was broken.

"You young people are so lucky. The entire office has been invited to this grand event."

"A great honor, indeed. They seldom ask us to any of their ceremonies. And these are people very high up—yes, very high."

"It's like going to a funeral in Bali."

"Or seeing the bulls run at Pamplona."

"It is a grand event, Mildred, but hardly on that par, and since you've never even seen those bulls—"

"Oh, shut up, Edythe, just shut up."

Lisa drifted into oblivion, until she heard Mrs. Walburton insisting, "You must never take a sit-down bath, once you get into your house."

"It's okay in the hotel though," Mrs. Sheetz amended.

Lisa opened her mouth to protest, then shut it. She hated showers.

"You'll get a vaginal infection if you do. From the water, of course," Mrs. Walburton went on.

Mrs. Sheetz interrupted again, "You know you must boil it to drink it and …"

"And while we're talking of such things," Mrs. Walburton steamrolled over her, "You can't go into any of their religious places, well, if it's …" She looked at the driver. "… that time of the month," she mouthed silently.

Lisa sat up straight and stiff. "What do you mean I can't go where I want when I want?" She was not big on ceremony, and this obvious rite of passage, their dos and don'ts for new arrivals, was wasted on her. But she would try to squash her feelings for David's sake. She loved him enough to come half way around the world with him, and she wasn't going to spoil it for them now.

The car pulled into a semi-circular driveway. A smartly uniformed doorman, with *Hotel Borobudur* written across a pocket, opened the door. He said something she thought must be words of welcome and ushered them under a canopy and then through great glass doors into the relief of air conditioning.

Lisa had the impression of an immense building with giant crystal chandeliers and blinding light everywhere. She glimpsed smart shops flanking the reception lobby, and then up, up the escalator. She smelled teak oil, and new furniture, and a pleasant fruity odor she couldn't define. Stepping off the escalator, she found herself in a main lobby that could be in any ultra-modern hotel in the world, except that a group of men in bright-colored sarongs and matching head cloths were playing "White Christmas." Their hollow bamboo instruments gave the familiar tune a tinkling and exotic marimba sound.

Then six strange women were shouting into her face. "Welcome to Jakarta!"

"Isn't it nice, dear," Mrs. Walburton said. "Those CAMCO wives greet all the newcomers."

Mrs. Sheetz nudged Lisa. "Don't get too close. They bite."

Lisa looked warily at the women. Jo, Miriam, Lexie—was it? Vonda, Sharon, and Lila. As if from some great distance she heard the oil women say, "And Christmas Eve reservations … shopping at … we will … you must …"

She had forgotten it was almost Christmas. But she'd already taken care of that, thank you very much. A small artificial tree with decorations,

David's filled stocking, and his expensive present would be here by then in their air shipment. And she wasn't going to be sucked up by a bunch of wives. She'd do something important with her time here. Maybe write a book. She was good at research. Perhaps a comparison of the two cultures' fights for freedom?

Then Mrs. Walburton said, "A caftan is what you need. They have some really nice ones upstairs in the shopping arcade."

"The very thing," Mrs. Sheetz said, "to wear to the wedding."

Lisa stumbled against David who, with the other men, had joined them now. They exchanged a guilty look. He squeezed her hand, hard. The sham wedding ring bit her finger, reminding her they were here under false pretenses.

"Get me out of here," she muttered. "Get me to our room."

❀ ✦ ❀ ✦ ❀ ✦ ❀

In the morning, they finally woke, not caring what day or time it was, but the jangling phone interrupted their lovemaking. Caught up in passion, they tried to ignore it, but it insisted. "Ah, shit," David said, rolling over, staring up at the ceiling. Lisa groped for the phone on the bedside table. First, all she heard was a conversation in some foreign language. Then, in spite of buzzes and squawks over an instrument that was a throwback to the Fifties, Mrs. Walburton's voice came through loud and clear.

"I've sent the car. We'll be eating at five sharp, so don't dawdle."

"I don't like command invitations," Lisa told David when she'd hung up.

"Maybe you'll get to see some of the old city along the way," he said. "They called it Batavia, right? Isn't that what you read to me on the plane?"

She hated it when he felt he had to humor her in exchange for her compliance. She didn't remember his being that way before.

"It was the bastion of the Dutch Colonialists, wasn't it?" he went on.

"You were listening," she said, smiling to take the edge off her tone. "I am curious about the kind of house we'll live in."

"It's probably a Christmas party," David said. "I bet we'll get to meet a lot of people."

On their way they passed a whole street of poinsettia trees, shacks nestled beside tall office buildings, and a hanging goat with its throat slit, bleeding onto the ground. When their car almost collided with another, the grinning expat passenger in it called out, "Welcome to Jakarta," giving the words a whole new meaning.

Mrs. Walburton greeted them, joyous she'd finagled her Embassy friends out of a turkey from the commissary. At first, Lisa thought the house, except for terazza floors and more bedrooms than most people needed, could have been any decent tract house back in Texas. When Mrs. Walburton showed her the servants' quarters—small cubicles for sleeping, an open cooking area, a cement block cistern with large dippers for bathing—Lisa saw the house as quite different after all.

Lisa was anxious for the other guests to arrive. She'd try to make a good impression for David's sake. And this was a great opportunity. She could get this mandatory socializing over with before she began her research. But after awhile, she realized they were the only guests. David seemed to be trying not to show his disappointment.

Mr. Sheetz and Mr. Walburton had a mild argument. Mr. Walburton wanted to put on an Andy Williams Christmas carol. Mr. Sheetz wanted his carols with chimes and organ. Mrs. Sheetz peered out at everyone over her martini glass, her nervous sips soon becoming nervous gulps.

"Well, here we all are," Mrs. Walburton said when drinks had been served all around. "These crackers are called *krupuk*." Lisa hesitated, then took one from the barefoot housegirl. When Mrs. Walburton said it was made from shrimp paste, she looked for a place to put it down.

Mrs. Sheetz was torturing the final dregs from the martini shaker.

"You take a few days to get oriented, boy," Mr. Sheetz said to David. "Get over your jetlag."

"I can't wait to see how the Minangkabau tribe does the ceremony," Mrs. Sheetz said. She turned to her husband. "You will bring him in from offshore for the Sumatran wedding, won't you? Plan ahead, I always say. It's going to be here before we know it."

Lisa watched David's face pale.

"Offshore?" he said. Despite the air conditioning, he wiped sweat from his forehead with his cocktail napkin. "I understood I would be working in the office."

"You'll only see a ceremony like this once in a lifetime," Mrs. Sheetz went on. "And we're only getting to go because the bride's brother is one of CAMCO / INDONESIA's executives."

"Women should …" Lisa started, then changed her mind. Why waste her breath? "We aren't really into … weddings." God, how she'd agonized over them saying they were married when they weren't. But It wasn't anybody's business, and David probably wouldn't have gotten this transfer if he hadn't declared marital status. In the interviews, it had been easy to let the personnel people assume they were married.

"Me neither," Mrs. Sheetz said as she teased an olive into her mouth. "Marriage is a lot of bunk."

"Oh, I don't know," Mr. Walburton said. "It's kind of nice to see two young people happy like we are." He smiled at his wife.

Mrs. Walburton chuckled. "You know that old saying, 'Happy the bride the sun shines on.' And here the sun shines every day. Even when it's rainy season."

"And you know what that means," Mrs. Sheetz said, nudging Lisa. Lisa didn't know and put a cream cheese something in her mouth to keep from having to answer.

"The groom is the happy one here," Mr. Sheetz said. "These Muslim men just say 'I divorce thee' three times, and it's all over, baby." He made a Groucho Marx leer at his wife.

"Or they just take another wife." Mr. Walburton grinned at Mr. Sheetz. "I understand they can have up to four of them."

"Yeaaah," Mr. Sheetz said. He turned to his wife. "You're bruising that martini."

Mrs. Sheetz stopped stirring the gin in the shaker. "In Iran the house-boy made the best martinis I've ever had."

"You mean the *amah* in Singapore. You get every place we've been mixed up," her husband said.

Annoyance tinged Mrs. Walburton's voice. "Horace, I think it's time now—high time—Isn't there something you had to say?"

But the housegirl called them to the large teak table in the dining room. It wasn't until dessert that Mr. Walburton said, "It has come to our attention ..." He cleared his throat. "Your documents, well—there is a marriage license missing, isn't there?"

David squeezed Lisa's hand.

"Mother, maybe you'd be better at this," Mr. Walburton said.

"A brief ceremony at the Embassy is what we had in mind, perfectly painless and over in a few minutes. You don't even have to dress up if you don't want to." Mrs. Walburton's voice was cold and firm.

"Eloping might be more fun," Mrs. Sheetz said. "Somewhere romantic, like Bali. Ed, couldn't you give him some time off?"

"Look, kids, it's not us," Mr. Sheetz said, ignoring his wife. "The Indonesian government will not issue a work permit or residence visa without a wedding certificate if you are a couple. Period."

"Actually that should have been made clear to you stateside," Mr. Walburton said. "I guess somebody goofed."

Mrs. Sheetz spoke in a dramatic voice. "Single women are *verboten*."

"I don't know if it's that bad," Mrs. Walburton said, squashing Mrs. Sheetz with a look.

"Sometimes they can get a three-month visa, like a tourist," Mr. Walburton said.

Lisa looked from one to the other as they spoke, but she couldn't find her voice.

She and David hadn't meant any harm. Exotica had lured them—a wonderful expense-paid vacation. They'd stay a year, only a year. David could skip two steps up the ladder in this office position. He'd convinced her there was plenty of time ahead to get her master's in history.

Strangely, it had been harder to accept she wouldn't be in Fort Worth to celebrate her country's two-hundreth birthday. She had been so full of the details of her proposal to the Bicentennial committee. It had been thrilling when her plan had been accepted, and she'd been welcomed as an integral part of the Fort Worth celebration. Her heartbeat resounded in her ears now at the thought she might see her plans through after all.

David was saying, "We aren't ready for that kind of commitment. We need time to get to know one another, and Lisa may be going back to school."

Lisa straightened in her chair. What was this "may be" business? She tried to look important and intellectual. But the faces staring back at her were stone.

"I came for the money," David went on, "and right now I want to build a nest egg for the future. Then someday, when there's still time for a family—"

Incensed by his apologetic tone, she wanted to scream, "This is my life, my decision!" But what came out was a shrill "We're not big on rituals."

"Bully for you!" Mrs. Sheetz tried, in vain, to get her papaya to her mouth. "Hear a different drummer. Do your own thing. Live and let live, I say."

"Surely, you don't condone this, Edythe. It's living in sin, pure and simple" Mrs. Walburton said.

"How does that go? If you can get milk free from the cow, why pay the farmer?" Mr. Sheetz laughed and slapped his knee.

In the pregnant silence that followed, the pulse in Lisa's neck drummed in her ears as she watched David flush with anger.

"It was just a joke," Mr. Sheetz said.

"That is not the issue here," Mr. Walburton said. He turned to Lisa. "You have no choice, my dear."

Damned if she was going to be dictated to by some company. "Women do have choices today," she said with vehemence. But all her umbrage escaped like sudden steam from a tea kettle at his next words.

"You get married and stay, or you don't and leave. It's as simple as that."

"So it's settled," Mrs. Walburton said, rubbing her hands together. "When would you like it? I'd think the sooner the better. And no one need know, except the six of us. We can have a little party afterward."

"Ah, sub rosa," Mrs. Sheetz said. "Sub rosa in Southeast Asia."

A confused, pale Lisa, and a taciturn, tight-lipped David endured both couples' reminiscences of their own weddings over after-dinner drinks. As soon as possible, they pleaded jetlag and got up to leave.

At the door, Mr. Sheetz said, "You kids will make the right decision."

Mrs. Walburton said, "If you're in love, what's the big deal?"

"Remember, Sheetz with a zheee," the drunken woman slurred.

But the last thing Lisa heard was Mr. Walburton saying to David, "If you want that desk job, boy, you better make your decision pretty damn soon."

❀ ᗡ ❀ ᗡ ❀ ᗡ ❀

All through the dark streets, huddled in a corner of the Walburton's car, Lisa wallowed in homesickness for her classroom and the safe boundaries of their relationship back home, dating mid-week, being together week-ends. Nothing had threatened her independence then, but now she felt all her beliefs and values to be in jeopardy.

David ran his finger back and forth over the token to conformity she wore on her third finger, left hand. Pulling away, she removed the wide band and shoved it deep into her handbag.

"Why did you bring me here?" She whispered her rage and frustration because the Walburtons' driver seemed to understand a lot of English.

"You said you wanted to come."

"I want to do something important with my life!"

"This is my turn. You'll have yours, honey. I promise."

"I want to go home." She sounded like a petulant little girl, but she didn't care. And if the mayor would let her be on the committee again—

"Okay, we'll go home. The hell with my career. The hell with the job promised me, scouting out supplies and equipment, right up my alley, and sure to lead to better things. The hell with me. We'll just do what you want."

"But they're sending you offshore instead."

"They only said that to get us to do what they want."

Lisa sighed. The decision was so much more than stay or go. At home it had been clear-cut. When David worried about his work, his advancement, Lisa knew he was telling her he couldn't marry yet. And she was careful not to tell him just how much she wished to quit her job and be a student again. He might think she meant he should support her. And anyway weren't they happy just the way they were? They both believed marriage had little to do with love.

The driver braked suddenly, throwing them forward. In the glare of the headlights, a visored white hat and white gun belt gleamed against a khaki uniform. The officer growled what must have been an order. The driver turned to them as if to apologize. Then ashen-faced and trembling, he got out of the car.

As harsh foreign words rang through the night, Lisa's neck prickled, her stomach trembled. Unbelieving, she watched more men in white hats and white gun belts lead the driver away. The policeman ordered them to produce documents. Her fumbling fingers dropped her passport, and for eons she groped the black floor.

He looked at their photos and stared into their faces. *"Jalan, jalan,"* he said finally. At their blank look, he said, "You walk now. *Sopir tingal.* We interrogate driver." He made a shooing motion. *"Jalan, jalan."*

"You can't do this!" Lisa flared. "We have to get to the Hotel Borobudur."

He grinned. His white-gloved hand motioned behind her. "Borobudur *disana.*"

Probably further than it looked, a picture postcard with row upon row of balconies etched against white stucco, emblazoned by floodlight, the modernistic edifice beckoned. Lisa thought of the drawn draperies, the turned-down bed with chocolates on the pillow, the carafe of brandy. Her breath came in short gulps as they walked away from the police. David held her arm tightly. She shivered, remembering Mrs.Walburton's warning that robbers here cut off fingers for rings and hands for watches. It really was a terrible place.

The black streets closed in around them, the only sound their own questions to one another. "What do you suppose he did?"

"Will the Walburtons get their car back?"

"The driver was really terrified, wasn't he?"

"What if we had already turned in our passports for the office to process our resident visas?" And then, "Oh, David, what would these Muslims do to us for not being married?"

They stopped short. Looming before them was a cement giant; in joyful liberation, his muscles bulging, he stood breaking the chains of Dutch

Colonial rule that had bound him for 300 years. It thrilled Lisa to recognize one of Jakarta's many freedom statues she'd read about in the *New York Times* travel section.

There in its shadow, harking back to the problem, she said, "It's really a question of autonomy. Loss of personal freedom is bondage, David, and we are being persecuted for independent thinking, besides."

"You sound like you're teaching a class."

"A woman should have her own life," she said. Her, yes, *merdeka*, was important to her, and had been since it was drilled into her as a little girl by her father. "Don't ever be like your mother," he'd said—her passionless mother whose only opinions were echoes of her husband's. Lisa had tried, but he'd left them anyway. She was still trying.

"I want to be in charge of my life as much as the next guy," David said, "but we don't even have jobs to go back to."

She was appalled at the desperation in his voice and backed down. "They call this a *'guided'* democracy. I would like to find out more about that."

"It's my whole future we're talking about," David was saying. "Can't you bend a little?"

He hadn't even heard her.

"The question is," he went on, "now that we're here, do we really want to leave, just to prove a point?"

Lisa gave one last look at the statue as they moved on. She fought the urge to ask, "What about my future?"

David's cornflower blue eyes pleaded with her, plumbed the depth of her love.

She took a deep breath. "Weddings are only ritualistic mumbo-jumbo anyway," she said. "Right?"

❀ ᴗ ❀ ᴗ ❀ ᴗ ❀

The ceremony took place on New Year's Eve day in a stifling, nondescript office at the Embassy. The background music from the open window was Jakarta traffic and Jakarta citizens already blasting the silver paper trumpets sold on every street corner. She wondered why she'd worn the navy suit, why someone didn't see that at least she had a corsage, a goddamn corsage.

The slam-bam-thank-you-mam business neither enhanced nor diminished their relationship. They enjoyed each other's company, made love, discovered the many facets of a new life in a mysterious culture. She didn't ask David what their new status meant to him, nor did she discuss the violation of rights convention had forced upon her. On the other hand, David complained loud and long about not being given the office job anyway. His humdrum assignment to the gas plant platform in the Java Sea didn't interest him at all. It wasn't challenging enough.

In spite of the Sheetz and Walburton avowals that no one would know about the wedding, Lisa noticed that the CAMCO women stopped talking when she approached and that clique of six women who had welcomed her to Jakarta outright snubbed her. She retaliated with long hours in the Lembaga Indonesia / America, poring over the Indonesian Declaration of Independence.

"See, the gossip has stopped now," Mrs. Walburton said a couple of weeks after the wedding. They sat in an alcove of the lobby that was actually part of the reception hallway for the banquet rooms. Away from the comings and goings of arrivals and departures, it seemed a secret place. It was almost enclosed by towering potted hibiscus and furnished with settees covered in brown-and-gold-striped satin.

"You told us no one would know," Lisa said.

Mrs. Walburton's eyes evaded Lisa's. "Well, it's impossible in a small family—You do realize we here at CAMCO are family, don't you, my dear? Anyway, once they realized you had been an officer of the Greater Fort Worth Junior League and are a long-time friend of our Mrs. Hoopes' younger sister—"

Right on cue, Lila Hoopes appeared in the break between plants. "Pardon me," she said, giving them an angry look, then moved away.

"Now for a little talk, dear." Mrs. Walburton squared her shoulders, then gave Lisa's hand a pat. "I would be remiss in my duty as a leader of our little community if I didn't advise you ..."

"Is Jo here?" It was the Dutton woman, Miriam. She hovered for a moment and then was gone.

Mrs. Walburton cleared her throat and continued, "... on proper deportment befitting your husband's status in the company. You have to attend to family business while he's offshore instead of, well, spending time in musty old libraries. And when he's home, you should entertain."

Lexie Rogers peered between blossoms at them, then disappeared, leaving nothing but the remembrance of a frown. Mrs. Walburton beamed, struck by inspiration. "Like her," she said. "Lexie would be a good role model for you." Now there were whispers and mumbles just beyond the screen of flowers.

"Come along," Mrs. Walburton said, standing. "I think we're in their place."

After the smarting lecture that continued as they took the elevator to Lisa and David's room, Lisa truculently began *Bahasa* Indonesia lessons, made inspection of their assigned house still under construction, had coffee at the Ambassador's residence with other newcomers, and went on endless shopping tours for *batik* skirts. But Mrs. Walburton did not appease easily.

❀ ꒰ ❀ ꒰ ❀ ꒰ ❀

"Wonderful, just wonderful, Missy." Mr. Walburton rubbed his hands together, sniffing. "Texmex, just like home," he said, the evening she'd invited the older couple to their room for dinner.

Tired of Asian food, longing for a bit of home, many expatriates were cooking in their rooms although it was not allowed. Back home, Lisa's culinary experience had been limited to omelets, muffins from a mix, and zapping things in the microwave. But she was confident. After all she'd been eating Mexican all her life, and it might be the ploy that would prove her new domesticity and influence them about David.

Looking slightly green, he had just arrived from offshore. Riding in the helicopter made him ill. He gazed longingly at the bed.

Mrs. Walburton beamed at Lisa's makeshift kitchen on the dresser top and patted her shoulder. Lisa's confidence soared as she busied herself with refried beans in the electric egg poacher, empanitas in the electric fry pan, enchiladas in the toaster oven.

When she looked up, her nemesis was studying the collection of photographs Lisa had taped to the mirror over the dresser. She was not sure what she was going to do with them, but she had been systematically snapping the city's freedom monuments and studying what they meant in Indonesian history. She had not thought to take them down before the Walburtons arrived.

"A monstrosity. Absolutely grotesque!" Mrs. Walburton's blunt finger stabbed at Jakarta's dominating landmark. Topped with a pure gold flame, the national monument, Monas, reached 137 meters into the sky.

"You should go to the museum in its base," Mr. Walburton offered.

"For all those gory historical depictions?" Mrs. Walburton's red face reflected her indignation. "One thing sure, those fellows talking garbled English over the bullhorns aren't going to tell you about the blood bath after the aborted coup when neighbors, and even families, denounced one another as Communists to settle old grudges."

Lisa could scarcely believe that the old warhorse had cared to read the same banned book she'd been reading last night.

"Even the nationals secretly call Monas 'Sukarno's Last Hard-on'—er—Erection," Mr. Walburton amended at his wife's look. He tapped each picture, making his own identification. "We call this statue the Pizza Man, and there's the 7-UP Man, and this one here is Thank God Our Furniture Has Come, and—"

Lisa seethed at such irreverence. She had been about to tell them about the famous Indonesian leader's fall from immense power to total disgrace in the Sixties, but decided it would be wasted on them.

"You'll be going to Singapore soon for your brown envelope," Mr. Walburton said. Then seeing their puzzlement, he amended, "That's what we call your mandatory trip to Singapore to visit the Indonesian embassy and pick up the necessary papers for obtaining your resident visa."

"Sounds crazy to me," Lisa said. "Why can't it be done here?"

"That's just the way it is, dear," Mrs. Walburton said. "Don't knock it. You'll get three days in Singapore at the company's expense. You'll love Singapore."

"And be sure and put a 10,000 *rupiah* note in your passport when you hand it to customs. That way they'll look the other way at anything you want to bring back in," Mrs. Sheetz said.

Lisa and David exchanged looks.

"Oh, yes," Mrs. Walburton said. "It's rampant corruption and bribery here. So you just go along with it."

"What kind of democracy is that?" Lisa exploded.

But Mrs. Walburton didn't answer. She had found the pile of books from the British Council Library. "Oh, dear, oh, dear," she sighed at each new title she picked up. When her eyes at last engaged Lisa's, it was quite clear she considered this research blatant defection.

"Now, Mother," Mr. Walburton said, "even you have your little hobbies."

The cooking smells were clearly bothering David. He hadn't even wanted his usual bourbon and soda. He excused himself to go to the bathroom.

"You *have* made a little nest for yourself here," Mrs. Walburton said, looking around the room at the *batik* -covered pillows, the wood carvings, and other artifacts gathered on forays around the city.

"If our air shipment ever arrives, I can make it even homier." Lisa paused a moment, then added "Mildred." She didn't intend to be cowed by these people any longer.

David returned, looking only a shade less green. She felt sorry for him and wondered how soon the Pepto-Bismal would kick in. He kept rearranging his food on his plate. The Walburtons were doing the same. Then her own taste buds told her the beans were insipid goo, the empanitas and enchiladas too spicy even for Texans.

Mr. Walburton gave his wife a meaningful look. "I had a really big lunch," he said, offering up his plate. Mildred said, "We promised to look in on Lexie and Buck, down the hall." When she looked at her watch, Lisa knew the woman was wondering if they could still get a table in one of the restaurants downstairs.

"Keep up the good work out on the platform," Mr. Walburton said to David on leaving. "It's a great place for young men to season."

"So sorry you couldn't stay longer, Horace," Lisa trilled as she slammed the door behind them.

"Damn, damn, damn." David sent the fry pan lid banging across the room. "I was hoping it was just a test period, a sort of probation. And now this—this fiasco. He'll never have me back onshore in the office."

Insurrection rose in her breast. She clattered a load of dishes to the double sink in the bathroom.

"And you're no help!" he called after her.

She left the dishes and returned to the room, ready to defend herself.

"You've always got your nose in a book!" he continued.

She looked at him, bewildered. What else was there to do here?

"What am I doing?" he groaned as he pulled her stiff body toward him. "I'm sorry. You're just you, and I love you."

Lisa relaxed into his embrace. But she had made up her mind not to show up tomorrow for the bridge lesson Mrs. Sheetz had insisted on. Instead, she would go to the Lembaga library, which wasn't a bit musty but all chrome and formica, to study the *Pancasila*, the five-point doctrine of the Indonesian government.

❀ ⌁ ❀ ⌁ ❀ ⌁ ❀

Edythe Sheetz had dropped by and was into her second gin and tonic when the two big boxes arrived, torn, crumpled and open. The contents of the errant air shipment looked like rubble from a bomb, well stirred with a stick. Lisa tossed the mangled little Christmas tree into the waste can. Ornament slivers, mixed with powdered candy canes, were the only evidence of the fat Christmas stocking. No! The tape recorder was smashed. Worst of all, the carriage on her typewriter wouldn't move, and she had all those notes to type up.

Weak knees forced her down on the bed. David's present, the gold-initialed, genuine calf leather briefcase was gone, of course. Edythe's words startled her.

"You don't ever cry, do you?"

No, it's something I pride myself on, she wanted to say, but couldn't.

"I do," the older woman went on. "Every afternoon, I go into my bedroom, pull the drapes, and cry. Then it's cocktail time, and everything is all right."

"My mother was a vacillating Southern belle, clinging and dependent on anyone and everyone. If there's one thing I've learned it's to rely on myself." Lisa said.

"My mother was a shrew, a know-it-all, and a nag. The only thing she taught me was to always wear clean underwear in case I was in an accident," Edythe replied.

"So I've been trashed. It makes me sick and angry. But it's not the end of the world. I can put in a claim down at the office. Things will get fixed or replaced."

"I'd be devastated." Edythe studied the bed's fake brocaded headboard attached to the wall. "I couldn't be like you in a million years—the company, you know. But I admire you. We knew you were different when you didn't want to get married. You're one of those liberated women. Seems funny to find one here."

"You might be surprised. Some time ago an Indonesian heroine, Kartini, preached emancipation for women and Western education for progress. Since then Indonesian women have influenced their society. As a matter of fact, equality of women is rooted in some of their myths and …" She stopped, realizing she sounded like a text book.

"Mmmmmm. Interesting." Mrs. Sheetz leafed through the most recent copy of *Time*. Lisa wondered why David had bought it. All the good parts had been blacked out by Indonesian censors.

"Maybe I'll write an article about Indonesia's patriotic women." She hadn't thought of it till now. It was just too hard comparing her country's democracy to the "guided" one that she'd discovered was really a dictatorship.

"Mmmmm," Edythe said into her glass of straight gin.

Lisa tried again. "I applied for a position at the Joint Embassy School, only to find expatriate wives aren't allowed to work here."

Edythe came back from wherever she'd been and reached for the gin bottle. "You are bored, aren't you? But you're going to be much too busy, my dear, for any of that. I really shouldn't tell you. It's to be a surprise—let's talk about what we're wearing to the Sumatran wedding—no, I just can't wait. Guess what's happened?"

"I wouldn't dare."

"Ed and Horace have pulled some strings, and you're getting the Patterson's lovely old house instead of that crappy new one. Aren't you thrilled?"

Thrilled? At such manipulation? Slowly, she rallied. "We really don't need all this help, Edythe. We're quite happy, bumbling along on our own."

Edythe was carefully filling a silver flask with gin from the bottle. Once it was corked and safely in her handbag for the trip home, she said, "Don't think another thing of it. What are friends for?"

❀ ↝ ❀ ↝ ❀ ↝ ❀

"Friends, indeed," Lisa said to David as they sat on the Walburton's patio drinking their morning coffee. In spite of herself, she was enjoying the swaying banana tree—its great red blossom about to give birth to green fruit, and the brilliant-hued bird trilling from the seven-foot bamboo fence.

She had not wanted to house-sit for the Walburtons while they were in Central Java seeing the Borobudur temple. She had set up some interviews with several prominent Indonesian women, and she feared the move would disrupt her work. Edythe had further confirmed her misgivings. "Stay where you are as long as you can. Handling a household is no day at Samudera Beach."

But David had prevailed. He said living offshore was like living in a hotel and he'd had enough of it. And why was it taking so long for their house to be finished? And now that their furniture, just off the container ship, was sitting in a warehouse down at Tanjung Priok, why couldn't she go to the office and light a fire under someone in Housing? He picked up the little *banka* tin bell from the table and rang for more coffee.

"Why do I have to be the one? You could do it just as easily." Lisa put her hand over her cup to keep the housegirl from pouring coffee into it. "Back home you'd have realized I have important things to do, too."

"You say the Pattersons were supposed to have loved the house," he insisted.

"David, I'm going inside to work on my questions for the general's wife." But it was all beginning to seem too much. Perhaps she would just stash away the information she'd already collected and take up Indonesian Studies when she went home. They said the best place for that was Cornell. But what would David think of her going so far away?

"And Mildred said it had a perfect dining room for entertaining, and we could do a lot with the garden?" David interrupted her musing.

"It's an old house, David. I want a new one."

She could see David was going to insist they take it. Even so, the first day at the Walburtons' continued to be one of peace and order until an impromptu chat with Edythe Sheetz brought on a guilt attack. On the second day, like a good wife, she went shopping for David's favorite foods and presented them to the cook, whose laughing face took on a serious look.

"*Nyonya,*" she addressed Lisa, then paused. "Me good *koki,* but me good Muslim. No cook piggy."

Lisa found Mrs. Walburton's cookbook and roasted the pork while the cook sat tight-lipped, arms folded, at the kitchen table. "Me not wash piggy dishes," she announced. "Get housegirl." Although a Christian, the girl wouldn't do them either.

Lisa requested dinner at eight. It was ready at six "because *Nyonya* 'burton say so." The housegirl insisted on starching and ironing David's shorts "because *Tuan* like."

"No wonder the old fart is such a grouch," David grumbled. He blew his top the morning the housegirl came barreling into the bedroom while they were making love. Giggling, she opened the drapes, then began taking the giant house plants outside to water them—a task Lisa had been trying to get her to do for three days.

Then the transformer for the freezer went out and all the frozen food had to be moved next door to the Sheetz's. Suddenly, the servants no longer understood English or even gestures. Edythe Sheetz laughed and laughed. Lisa wanted to strangle her for being right about getting caught up in domestic demands.

David and Lisa stood in the middle of the dirt road between the Sheetz and Walburton houses, trying to catch their breath after delivering the final load. "I've had enough of this one," David said. "When can we see the Patterson house?"

Hot, disheveled, and angry, Lisa turned him around to face the house across the street and made a grand sweeping gesture.

They stared at the jungle growing up around it, the peeling paint and the holes in the roof that surely meant water damage inside. A goat bleated at them through the open gate. "Yea, though I walk through the valley, Walburtons and Sheetzes are my shepherds," David intoned in a deep voice. They both laughed, but it was mirthless.

❀ ﹏ ❀ ﹏ ❀ ﹏ ❀

Global Movers and the momentous occasion their mentors had been heralding for so long arrived almost on top of one another. After she sat two days in the empty house awaiting the promised truck, it arrived the day before the Sumatran wedding. So far the only damage Lisa had found was mildewed bed linen.

"We really should stay home and finish unpacking," she said as their new car wound its way out of the city and down the road to Bogor.

"What and miss the wedding of the century? We'd never hear the end of it."

She knew he was trying to make her lighten up, but having work done on the house at the same time they were settling in was madness. It all seemed so permanent and difficult. His two-week stints offshore dragged on, while she fantasized how wonderful it would be when he returned for five days. But it was always different from what she'd anticipated. He wanted her by his side at the pool while he talked shop to the other men. She didn't understand what they were talking about, and besides she freckled horribly. Or he spent hours on the tennis court, and it was too damn hot out there for her. And she hadn't found any servants she liked, except the driver, who appeared to be a nice boy. But now on the open road he didn't understand their commands to slow down.

And then he did. They were behind a slow-moving truck. It was filled with soldiers wearing fuchsia berets. At sight of the rifles and cartridge belts slung over their shoulders, the fear, always waiting to burst out since her arrival, attacked. She shivered and moved closer to David.

"Makes one think of Vietnam," he whispered. Then, "What do these people have to be so damn patriotic about anyway?"

She thought of the national spirit and unity professed in the *Pancasila*. It claimed a democracy guided by agreement after deliberation among representatives. Its intent was to create social justice for all Indonesians. But what kind of freedom expelled wire service reporters and put the country's great writers under house arrest?

No, this was not the Indonesia of her expectations. Declaration of Independence or no, it wasn't the home of the free and the brave. Her anger at that disappointment surprised her into speech. "Go around them," she ordered.

"*Tidak, Nyonya*," the driver said, his voice bordering on the hysterical. "No, *permisi!*" Then a tortured "please."

"The US of A it's not, Honey," David said, taking her hand.

Merdeka, merdeka, her heart cried. "I said go around them. Now!" Her voice was shrill in her ears, just like the voices of the silly women here, telling her what she could and couldn't do.

The driver cocked a shaking finger at her. "Maybe bang-bang."

"For Pete's sake, Lisa, leave it alone," David said. "No wonder he's scared. An old Indonesia hand told me in election year these army trucks scour the city, battering dissenters, hauling them off to prison."

The American flag waves before her eyes, and she is back home at the Bicentennial. People clap and cheer as she gives her speech about how important a true democracy is, and that personal freedom ...

The fear squeezed her heart as they were halted by a soldier. But it was because they had arrived, and he was directing parking for the General's daughter's wedding. Then the Walburtons and Sheetzes pounced on them and dragged them off to a vantage point near the entrance of the handsome villa to watch the arrival of the bridegroom. Shielded by a purple umbrella, surrounded by dancers clad in the same royal color, he was escorted to the front door by members of the bride's mother's family.

"That's because the bride's ancestors come from a matriarchal society," Mildred said, looking smug about her knowledge.

Some kind of welcoming formalities were happening at the threshold to the house, but Lisa couldn't see very well through the crowd gathered there. On the porch, accordion music began, soon accompanied by violin and guitar. Then the guests, following on the heels of the groom and his entourage, were pouring into the house.

The first thing Lisa saw were shoes of all shapes and sizes, discarded everywhere just as they'd been stepped out of. How would she ever find her own again? Hibiscus and frangipani and blossoms of the flame tree bloomed in every conceivable spot in the house. The air was sweet with the juices of great mounds of pineapple and mango, starfruit and rose apple, red bananas and other fruits Lisa had never seen before. A traditional tiered wedding cake graced an antique Dutch serving table.

Ed steered them past the children sitting on the steps of the sunken room to a row of folding chairs. Great steaming platters of yellow rice surrounded by delicacies as foreign to Lisa as the fruit had been, were laid out on an L-shaped runner that covered most of the floor of the vast living room. More flowers were strewn among the dishes. The groom's family sat cross-legged before the food. The women in traditional dress, with heads covered, sat at the far end of the room; the men, all wearing squat black hats, sat immediately before the groom and a man of religion standing on a dais.

"The bride stays in the bedroom while the ceremony goes on out here," Mildred whispered. "They read her the dos and don'ts of marriage from a paper, which she then signs."

"They're married by microphone." Edythe giggled until shushed.

The strange rite in the language Lisa couldn't seem to learn went on and on, the groom's family continuing to chew and gulp, carrying on loud conversations. Lisa thought it would seem more like a real wedding if the music on the porch had been brought inside.

She closes her eyes and this is all taking place in a clearing of Sumatran jungle, perhaps in the shadows of a great fire with strange huts nearby, a lion, a rhinoceros, an elephant for witnesses. And the music is definitely tom-toms.

At last the ceremony was over, and the bride, her plain face beaming beneath a towering, gold filigree headdress splayed at the back of her head like a peacock's tail, appeared and was presented to her bridegroom. A member of the wedding party mantled the new husband's business suit with a resplendent robe, placed a puffy turban on his head. The couple, bejeweled and dazzling in gilt and crimson and turquoise, were led by attendents, also in centuries-old attire, to two ornate and garlanded thrones.

Lisa's eyes close again. This time, she and David are in a field of daisies, speaking wedding vows they wrote themselves. A circlet of flowers graces her head, and she wears—not a traditional gown—but probably white lace anyway. No matter the custom, it is still the joining of two lives.

Voices on the loud speaker interrupted her reverie. Blaring static hushed; then Karen Carpenter singing, "We've only just begun ... white lace and promises ... and we're on our way ... ."

The great sob wrenched from her heart was just as unexpected as the song had been. As hard as she tried she couldn't hold back the tears making rivers in her makeup. She turned away, hoping no one had seen her capitulation. The two older couples were in line to pay their respects to the bridal pair. Other guests were occupied with finding a place at the runner of food, which had been reset for them.

But David was there, leading her to a corner, inhabited only by a large white cockatoo chained to a perch. Carefully, he wiped her face with a clean handkerchief.

"It was just, just ..."

"I understand."

"You know I don't blame you."

"It's nobody's fault."

"I've really tried."

"I know." He pulled her closer. "We'll chuck it all."

"But we're half moved in."

"They can send it back."

"Who will tame the Patterson's jungle?" It was an inane thing to say, but she couldn't think of anything else.

He cupped her chin with his hand so she had to look directly into his eyes. "Probably snakes in there anyway."

"I wouldn't doubt it." She snuffled into his handkerchief. "Or else those big lizards."

"We'll never know. I'll make the arrangements tomorrow."

"They're going to be mad," she said.

He said, "I don't care. The main thing is you'll be home for the Bicentennial."

"Certain inalienable rights," she reminded herself, "and among these …"

Then they agreed. After the festivities, the ceremonies, they'd get the divorce.

LESSON IN RUBBER TIME:
Maddy

IRST, LET ME TELL YOU HOW MIXED UP I WAS WHEN I ARRIVED IN Jakarta. I wouldn't even change the time on my wristwatch for three days. It was hard to accept cocktail time here being yesterday morning back on the East coast, but once I did, I felt brave enough to leave the Hotel Borobudur for a walk. I never went farther than the corner where two raggle-taggle girls waited for someone to buy their clove-scented cigarettes. My stomach turned over when one started to pick lice from the other's head as they squatted there in the dirt.

Suddenly, it wasn't 1976 any more. I had been transported to some mysterious dimension, neither here nor there, not now or then—an elastic moment stretching like a rubber band, where I couldn't move or speak. Eventually, I heard the great mosque's scratchy loudspeaker calling the people to prayer. Slowly, I became aware of the bustling, traffic-laden street and the permeating odor of overripe vegetation and stagnant, sultry air smothering me. It was a bad foreign film I'd give no stars at all.

I ran until one of the hotel doormen ushered me back into a world where everything was the way I thought the Far East would be when I was still reading about it in the newspaper travel section. Then I believed a geographic relocation—a place where I'd be recognized as a woman of the world— was all I'd need to change myself from dull provincialism to exotic sophistication.

In the hotel lobby a chef wearing a stiff white hat passed by, wheeling a tray of canapes toward the banquet rooms. I allowed one of the brown leather chairs to devour me and stared at the brown and blue wall hangings reflected in the blue glass of the coffee table. The well-watered palms and other potted tropical foliage around me gave off a pleasant earthy odor.

Across the hall, the piano tinkled in the Pendopo Lounge, punctuated by the clickety-clack of telex machines in a room nearby. An airline hostess escaped the Pan Am flight crew to sniff the speckled Vanda orchid arrangement gracing the information desk. It was a movie set, and I, the star, was on location. Outside, I could be raped, or robbed, or maimed by the traffic, but here I would be Lauren Bacall, or maybe Myrna Loy.

The great mosaic wall of clocks, telling time around the world, mesmerized me as usual until I realized my husband, Pete, would be home from the office now and waiting for me at Happy Hour in the Merak Bar. We were to meet his boss there and go on to dinner with him. I took the escalator to the level above the lobby and soon stood in the opulent doorway, savoring the moment. Expatriates from all over the world crowded the Merak, and I was one of them now. It was thrilling to know I was a guest in one of this hotel's 866 lavish rooms with 23 acres of landscaped gardens protecting me from the city. Butterflies teased my stomach as I stood there waiting to be discovered.

Obviously, my transformation wasn't complete. The group of six oil wives, who went everywhere together when their husbands were offshore, didn't even look up when I passed their table. As usual, they had their heads together like a bunch of cattle in a John Wayne movie. I called them "The Herd." Little thrills tickled my spine as I sensed their eyes following me.

I gave my shoulder a confident tilt, put on a world-weary smile, and swaggered forth. My husband could call me June Allyson all he wanted; I did look a bit like her with my wide-eyed stare and page-boy hair style. But it was really Roz Russell who joined him at the bar.

Pete, who always said he could talk to Jesus Christ Himself if the occasion arose, pulled away from a group of men to take my hand. "My wife, Madelyn," he said. The Swiss United Nations man gave me a cursory nod. Before the Mercedes Benz dealer from Germany could get his greeting out, Pete's other companion interrupted him. "I am Tomas," he said, pushing in between us. He stroked his pencil-thin moustache. "I am from Belgium."

His military bearing commanded my attention. I half expected him to click his heels. Instead, he bent and kissed my hand. My mental movie catalogue activated. Another Belgian, Paul Henreid—*Now Voyager*. Yes, if I were a smoker, he'd be lighting two cigarettes at once now. I studied his square jaw, his thick lips, his steady smile.

He looked at me with serious, bottomless eyes. "How are you liking Jakarta, Mrs. Mad-a-leen?" he asked.

"Just fine," I lied, thinking of the terrifying unknown outside the hotel perimeters. "At least I will be when our papers are cleared and we can get into our house."

Before Pete had a chance to give me his seat, Tomas insisted I take his. As I settled in, I heard myself saying, "… five bedrooms, marble floors, an indoor fish pond, and quarters for the servants, of course." I hoped I sounded as if I'd had people waiting on me all my life.

"I see you like to read," I said, trying to elevate the conversation. The book lying on the bar was Plato.

"I study the philosophy," Tomas said in a rich accent. "It is something to do when I am not collecting the butterfly or listening to Beethoven."

He was absolutely charming, and I wanted to be his friend. I glanced at my husband. He was talking to an Australian we'd met two days ago, who had something to do with drilling equipment. And so—since Pete was a mechanical foreman aspiring to be a supervisor for CAMCO, the world's largest oil company—I didn't feel I was neglecting him, even though he'd soon be spending a lot of time offshore on a drilling platform in the Java Sea.

I'd be left on my own, and I didn't want to think about that. I turned back to Tomas to chatter about books and great thinkers, subjects I hadn't been much interested in till now. But it felt right for my new image.

No one had ever thought me special except Pete, and I guess the most exciting thing that ever happened to me was when we eloped to Atlantic City. As Young Marrieds, it was almost impossible to have a social life. To save for a house, I worked nine-to-five with people as uninteresting as I saw myself. Pete's job revolved in shifts around the clock, and he did management courses by mail. I smothered my loneliness and boredom with old movies, as I had in high school. I'll tell you about that later.

After the orientation CAMCO Personnel put on, Pete said our lives would never be the same. I hoped not. Surely a new me was emerging, and intriguing people here would see me the way the urbane Tomas seemed to. Shivering with anticipation, I half expected to see a white-suited Sydney Greenstreet waving from a peacock chair across the room. I was wondering when the torrential rains would begin, as they had in Pago Pago in the movie *Rain*. It was practically the same part of the world, wasn't it?

"Your hair becomes you that way, Mrs. Mad-a-leen," Tomas said. "You always wear it so, yes?"

My hand strayed to the French twist I'd slaved over, striving to find a look worthy of my new persona. Hoping he wouldn't notice, I tucked in a limp wisp of mousy hair. Tomas' own hairstyle showed refined taste. It was auburn with a defined part, sleek to his head, except for bushy gray side-burns, which made him look distinguished.

He told me his company taught meat packing to the Indonesians, that he had a wife and a sixteen-year-old daughter who hated her English lessons. He himself spoke five languages. "I also collect the butterfly." His eyes searched mine, for what I didn't know, nor did I know why he repeated this. But I did know living in this hotel was going to be better than watching old movies on TV. In spite of myself, I glanced at my watch. Mr. Sheetz, Pete's boss, was late.

"Why do you look at your timepiece, Mrs. Mad-a-leen?" Tomas asked. "No one pays attention to time here. Time accommodates whatever is desired. Its flow advances or stays to suit the person or the circumstance. As a matter of fact, I've heard it compared to Mexico's mañana, but without that degree of urgency." Tomas threw his head back and laughed, a deep baritone sound.

I hoped he thought my answering laugh meant I'd been to Mexico and understood perfectly.

He picked up the book in front of him and began to expound on Plato's theories of thesis and antithesis, finally saying something about the present becoming the past and the future becoming the present. "In this philosophy of time ... " he droned on. It was more than my poor brain could handle.

I turned back just in time to hear him say, "The Indonesian concept of the flow of time is very different from ours. Here, there is no urgency to get something done before a season changes. And, of course, the days vary little, always it is light at five, dark at six, with no dusk or dawn. It just is."

"Fascinating," I said. My heart sang. He'd said "ours," lumping me with Europeans, who I knew were all cosmopolites.

Tomas tapped my watch. "You must remember that time is always speaking." His solemn tone told me this was important.

Just then *The Women* passed by on their way to the hot hors d'oeuvres. For a moment I pondered which one of the self-appointed welcoming committee of CAMCO wives might be Joan Crawford, the one to look out for in that movie. Frankly, I couldn't comprehend their advice or their Texas jokes. Pete said that was because Texas was a foreign country, too. Every time they snubbed me, he said, "They're in a higher echelon, baby. Someone has to get this promotion, and it's going to be me. It'll be different then."

Since Pete wasn't taking my problem seriously, I didn't tell him what they'd said about me when I was alone at lunch in the hotel's Japanese restaurant where I had been separated from them by nothing more than a thin screen. "From Sandusky, Ohio, for gawd's sakes." "A bookkeeper no less," "She'll never make it."

Now, as The Herd, plates full, eyed me, I thought I might tell Tomas my problem, but his bony fingers tilted my chin back until I was facing him again. "Never mind them. We will dine on *nasi goreng,* the national dish, one day. Speak of Tolstoy, yes?" He motioned to the band of wandering *Batak* folk singers who looked the way I imagined Mexican troubadours would look. They came over to us with their stringed instruments, placed a serape over my shoulder, and gave me a personal serenade. And for a while, The Herd forgotten, I was exactly who I thought I should be. Then Pete came and said he was starving and wasn't waiting another minute for Mr. Sheetz.

The next morning I forced myself out of the hotel. I would show those women I could "make it;" then they'd invite me to be one of them. At first I hugged the wall beneath the portico, watching the constant flow of arrivals and departures. I ignored the doorman's "Taxi, *Nyonya?*" and sauntered over to the concrete pond to look at the largest goldfish I'd ever seen. Feeling braver, I crossed the driveway, recognizing giant versions of house plants I'd had back home.

Then I was on the edge of a huge soccer field. A whole crowd of ragged Indonesians were rolling up makeshift beds and stamping out cooking fires. Smoke and the odor of cooked rice clogged the air. It was hard to comprehend that these vagrants, or whoever they were, had spent the night just yards from the swank Borobudur. They were moving toward me. It looked like a mob scene out of Cecil B. Demille. Terror overcame me, and defeated, I ran back inside.

The mirrored and leathered grandeur of the Borobudur's lobby calmed me. Robes flowing, Arab sheiks strode by, ignoring me. The Japanese, clicking their cameras at imitation sculptures of Central Java's famous Borobudur Temple, averted their eyes when mine made contact. Some British ladies fluttered about me, and I hoped for an invitation to tea, but no. I'd boned up on Amy Vanderbilt, too, for just such an occasion. There was nothing to do now but look forward to another evening in the Merak, talking to the sophisticated Belgian. I didn't understand why Pete thought him tiresome and boring.

I liked it most when Tomas talked about rubber time, or *jam karet* as he said the Indonesians called it. "For them, time is recurring, moving in circles, unlike our idea of sequential time," he told me that evening. "So action in time is relatively unimportant to them. They see it as a spiraling progression from one inevitable condition to the next with the present a hardly worthwhile, yet necessary, stop."

He was a wonderful teacher. I could see that even Westerners here had adopted the attitude that nothing was important enough that it couldn't wait. But it was still comforting to look up and see the time back home on the mosaic wall clock.

I struggled to say something of interest to this man who was so impeccable right down to the last hair on his head. But what would he care that I'd seen *Gone with the Wind* seventeen times? "Perhaps we could all go to the movies sometime?" I ventured, testing his interest.

He grimaced. "Here the rats run over your feet in the theater. There are other things to do." As he took my hand, his eyes burned into mine in a strange new way. This look made me say. "We are friends, Tomas, just friends. You do understand?"

"Friends? Of course." Then he sighed. "Oh, Mad-a-leen, don't you want to be a butterfly?"

I was still thinking of Tomas when Pete and I were alone in our luxurious room, the ever-present spice of the teak oil applied daily by the roomboy complimenting the perfume from the basket of exotic fruits management kept supplying. "Tomas tense person," I said, as I took off my earrings.

"Tomas work much hard," Pete said, and we giggled at our unexpected use of the pidgin English we spoke with the Indonesian roomboys. We hugged and kissed and fell together across the bed because we were in love and happy here where our every whim was catered to.

After we made love, Pete came from the shower with a serious look on his face. "Mads? Honey?" he said, sitting on the bed beside me, draped only in a towel.

"Ummm," I mumbled. The sheets, cool from the air conditioning and scented like some tropical flower, pulled me toward sleep, but his bare back aroused me again. After all, he was leaving tomorrow for his first two-week stint offshore.

"Listen to me now. It's about Tomas."

"Uhhhhuhhhh." I tattooed his beautiful back with kisses.

"He's European."

"Soooo?"

"They don't understand American women, Honey. He thinks your open friendliness is something different, something indecent. In other words, Maddy, I'm sure Tomas thinks you're coming on to him."

I sat up. "That's silly!" I punched the pillows in place behind me against the headboard. "What makes you such an authority anyway?"

Pete gave me his "Why don't you know this?" look. "I was an exchange student in Europe, remember?"

After all this time, this was still a sore subject. It had broken up our going steady in high school. After he went overseas, I decided to have a glamorous life, too. I knew I would be popular when I landed a part in the school play. The role required that I bound on stage, screaming. At the audition, the screams were real. In my exuberance to exhibit my talent, I overshot the makeshift platform and broke my leg in two hard-to-heal places.

So I became a heroine, languishing on a couch, wishing for Pete's infrequent letters, watching old movies on TV. With Davis I faced down Hopkins for my man. I was Garson seeing hers off to war, Hepburn sparring with Tracy. I think it was the insouciant Carole Lombard Pete discovered when he came back from France to graduate. Soon after, he took a job in an oil refinery. I went to business school. We married two years later. Our fifth wedding anniversary was just last month."How can you think such a thing?" I lashed out at Pete. "You know I've never loved anyone but you. I'm not flirting!"

"I know that, Honey, but he thinks you are. And I won't be here to protect you. You're in a different world now. Remember what they told us at orientation about culture shock?"

Yes, the personnel man had harped on how we would feel anxious and frustrated in a society so different from ours. I shut all that out and remembered how silly some of the symptoms sounded—excessive washing of hands, fits of anger, even something called the tropical stare.

"That has nothing to do with Tomas," I flared again.

"Yes, it does, Maddy. You're running from one different culture slambang into another."

"No, Tomas is Belgian. That's just like us."

"You're not very experienced, you know." Pete snuggled me to him like a nestling spoon. "You've always had romantic notions about seeing the world, but not everybody is like—" And then he was asleep.

"Not very experienced" rankled, but this time Pete didn't know everything. I had flown halfway around the world, hadn't I? I'd stayed in a Japanese hotel in Tokyo, ridden a ferry in a sea of sampans in Hong Kong, and even been in the Singapore airport. I was a world traveler now, and Tomas' sophistication would rub off on me. Then, instead of sluffing me off, The Herd would beg for my attention.

"Tomas isn't a bit like those inscrutable Indonesians," I insisted to the sleeping Pete. He snuggled closer and mumbled, " … a butcher, a goddamn butcher."

I woke, slept, woke, dreamed I was in a classroom where The Herd took turns drilling me on how to get over culture shock. I walked confidently to the blackboard and wrote, "I am not Norma Shearer" over and over again. When I woke I remembered Norma was the heroine persecuted by the witchy social set in *The Women*.

When Pete left for the oil platform, all my awareness of time passing seemed to leave with him. Today was like tomorrow, and tomorrow like the next day, and the next. I had nothing to do but live in an endless summer of tropical sunshine, perfecting my tan for his pleasure. Now and then I did an Esther Williams backstroke through the pool to cool off, but mostly I read whatever I could find from the list Tomas had given me. Surprisingly, the hotel drug store had a whole rack of classics.

Cocooned in rubber time, I have no idea when it actually was that Tomas came looking for me. Feeling a brooding presence one afternoon, I looked up from Somerset Maugham's *Rain* to see Tomas across the pool, hands clasped behind his back, pacing the hot concrete and staring into every face. Then his gaze locked with mine.

"Mad-a-leen! I am so 'appy to see you," he called. Then he sprinted around the pool to be at my side. In lounge chairs circled like a wagon train awaiting attack, The Herd was staring. I squirmed in my chair and felt my first annoyance with him. I told myself it was only because my reading was interrupted. It had never occurred to me the movie had first been a story in a book, and now that Tomas had pointed that out, I was anxious to compare them. By the way, that was Joan Crawford, too.

He preened before me, smoothing his flawless hair, as I squinted up at him, the sun blinding in spite of my sunglasses.

"Why do you not come to the Merak? I wait for you."

It was too gauche to say going to the Merak wasn't much fun without Pete, even if we didn't talk to the same people. Out of the corner of my eye, I saw The Herd approaching and wondered how to head them off at the pass.

In my mind, I stood up slowly, stretched sensuously, eased into a chiffon Betty Grable cover-up that covered nothing. No, I would dazzle them with Norma Shearer simple charm. After all, she did triumph at the end of *The Women*.

"Please, please," I heard them beg, "come with us where you will be safe from the Indians." Now how had Norma gotten into that covered wagon scenario? Before I could figure it out, Jo, the feisty one, rudely changed the script. "Aren't you going to introduce us to your boyfriend?"

He beamed. They smirked. I offered a weak June Allyson smile, then surprised even myself by rising to the occasion. "No, ladies, he's mine, all mine," I cooed, entwining my arm with his. "Let's get that gin and tonic," I said to Tomas.

Much as I tried to ignore it, Pete's warning caused me disquieting thoughts. I really did treasure Tomas as a cosmopolitan peer, and the compliments, the attention to my every word, were certainly flattering. But I'd begun to feel him even when he wasn't there. It was as if a strong will and a powerful mind were reaching out to control mine. I thought about this every night just before drifting into sleep.

It seemed much longer than a week that Pete had been gone. I couldn't envision him ever being back again. And it was silly to coop myself up like I'd been doing, so I planned a trip to a wood carving shop and the handicraft center, then lunch in another hotel. "I can do this, really I can," I told myself as I stood uncertainly at the Borobudur's entrance, waiting for the English-speaking doorman to be free to direct the driver of the car I'd rented. Suddenly, Tomas took my elbow and ordered the car away. "I teach you tennis today, then maybe we have big wine lunch," he insisted.

How could I even think of being angry with him? He was only trying to help me adjust. But as the days without Pete dragged by I came to realize Tomas was following me everywhere. He even pulled up a chair, uninvited, to my dinner table as I waited for Noreen, a new arrival, to join me. I still thought I liked him, although he ordered food I didn't want and was abusive to the waiter. I told myself everyone had idiosyncrasies. I saw Noreen enter, make a face when she saw Tomas, and head straight for The Herd's table. Yes, he *was* my only friend, but I was no longer so sure that through him I could get The Herd to like me.

Pete came home unexpectedly, and it was as if I'd been given a gift of time. But it was only for a few hours; he was on his way to Singapore to pick up machinery parts. It was Happy Hour at the Merak, but Pete insisted on going to the hotel's other cocktail lounge, the Pendopo.

"It will hurt Tomas' feelings if we don't go to the Merak," I said.

"You couldn't hurt that guy's feelings with a ball-peen hammer," Pete said. "You know there isn't anything I wouldn't let you do if you wanted, Mads, but people are talking."

"What people?"

"Company people. I heard it offshore."

I didn't ask what he'd heard. I could well imagine what The Herd was saying. But I hadn't done anything wrong. "What do I care about them? They don't care about me."

"If you get involved with them, Mads, it might help me get that promotion."

I just looked at him. Didn't he realize how much I wanted to be one of them?

Lord knows I'm no good at this company politics stuff, but I'd try anything for my husband's sake. Somehow I got up the nerve to approach Miriam, who seemed the least intimidating member of the bunch. Over a revolting avocado drink she made me try, she talked me into volunteer work; practicing English conversation with Indonesian social workers. It was obvious she wanted me to be her replacement. "It's only two blocks away at the Cathedral. Meet me at two sharp by the fish pond out front. And don't be late, you hear?"

But I was late because Tomas waylaid me in the lobby, insisting I write down more books he wanted me to read. She was nowhere out front when I finally got there. Sure she'd left without me, I started for the Cathedral on my own.

A purple haze hovered above the street I had to cross. It came from the exhaust of hundreds of cars, trucks, motorcycles, and strange two-passenger scooters called *helicaks* that thundered by. There wasn't a traffic light in sight. I don't know how long I stood there, hypnotized by the incessant horn blowing, the cries of food vendors, the diesel wheeze and gasp of lumbering buses with brown people hanging from windows and doors. There was no way I could walk out into that mindless sprint of wheels and hold up my hand like the Indonesians did. Hot, thirsty, and unnerved, I returned to the hotel, knowing I'd muffed my chances with The Herd.

Pete came home on his five-day break, then was gone back offshore all too soon. Tomas went to Solo on business. I spent moments, hours, days—I don't know—in the third-level arcade peering at pictures of exotic destinations in the travel offices and shopping for *banka* tin goblets—a cross between silver and pewter—I wasn't even sure I wanted. I don't know what I'd have done if Nelia, the pianist Pete and I chatted with in the Pendopo, hadn't taken me in hand. I was in the middle of buying a blue-and-white porcelain vase that was much too expensive for us, even with the great money Pete was making now.

"You never pay what anybody asks, and certainly not without bargaining." Nelia put it back on the shelf, much to the proprietor's annoyance. The next thing I knew she had spirited me away to the Jalan Surabaya flea market.

It was a whole street of open-air stalls crammed with the most wonderful junk I'd ever seen. Nelia said there were real treasures here if you looked. I fell in love with an old brass teapot, and she taught me how to negotiate a good price.

I felt a surge of triumph when I looked up and saw Lexie, The Herd's most poised member, staring at us from the next stall. I even heard Vonda say, "Well, I never." Most everyone I'd talked to thought the Indian pianist intriguing, even mysterious, so I felt quite smug at her befriending me.

Nelia made me admit the outing hadn't been so bad, and we were giggling and gloating over our purchases when we got on the hotel elevator. The Herd piled in behind us, and I stopped laughing, completely unable to think of what leading lady to be in this circumstance.

Miriam, who always looked as if she'd just come from the beauty shop, actually beamed at me. Jo said, "I've been thinking. You could probably use a language teacher, and my Mrs. Lydia is the best." The austere Lila's eyes locked with mine. Perhaps she was the conniving Joan Crawford. "We brought your mail from the office," she said. Sharon gave me a shy smile. She was the chunky one with all the children. I felt compelled to say something, then stopped because poker-faced Vonda unnerved me.

I turned to Nelia. "I'll be glad to get back to the 'womb.'" I don't remember when I started thinking of my hotel room that way, but everybody began to laugh, Vonda the hardest, wiping tears from her eyes. Then it was my floor and I stumbled out, wondering what had come over them.

Once in my room, I went to the window. The sight of tiny red clay roofs and dottings of palms so far below and the traffic sounds, muted and unreal, soothed me.

Flipping through the mail, I found an interoffice memo announcing Pete Chulach's promotion to Maintenance Supervisor and a note saying he'd be staying offshore through his normal break.

I thought things might change because Nelia had befriended me and because Pete had an important new job, but it seemed forever before The Herd invited me to sit in the Merak with them one night after the dance band started. It was my triumph, but I still didn't feel genuinely included.

"I don't know what you mean." Lexie shouted to be heard over the full-piece orchestra. "I've never experienced culture shock." Then Lila nudged me. "There's your boyfriend."

It didn't seem possible that days had passed, and I hadn't even missed the absent Tomas. In fact, relaxed and happier every day, seeing Jakarta with Nelia as my guide, I'd almost forgotten he existed.

But, ignoring my protests, he pulled me onto the dance floor. I was not amused. The Herd was. Then his tone changed. "A woman of your experience must be a great dancer, yes?" he said, and my resistance shattered. But I regretted it when I felt his hard penis pressing against me. My face flamed, and I looked to see if any of the other women had seen the bulge in his pants. I told Tomas I had a headache and fled the room, too chagrined to even make excuses to The Herd.

I started having breakfast in my room, tried to get out of the hotel while he was still in the telex room, didn't sit in the lobby to do my letter writing, but he would call late at night. "Mad-a-leen, you will come to my room now. I must see you, talk to you." Once he said, "Don't you know time is always speaking? Today is not the last day of the present, but first day of future." I usually hung up then. His clichés in fractured English didn't charm me anymore.

Now there was always one of The Herd watching my every move, and I understood why Nelia told me there was a story going around that I had been seen coming out of his room. I had a serious problem. What if Pete heard this lie? Somehow I must handle this.

"Friends only," I reminded Tomas when I next saw him. As usual, he was hanging around the coffee shop waiting for me to come to breakfast. "Just friends," I said, edging in behind the potted palm that guarded the door, peering through the leaves. "Remember?"

"Men and women cannot be friends, Mad-a-leen. Only lovers. But I can speak with you, eh? About myself, my passion. You not get mad? All my life I 'ave waited for a woman like you. I cannot live if you do not go to bed with me."

Wow! A woman like me.

He bent and kissed each of my fingertips. I looked to see if anyone was watching.

"You are woman of the world," he said.

Suddenly, I was sleek and brunette, statuesque instead of petite. I was, yes, I was Roz Russell, filled with confidence and savoir-faire. I ran away to think things over, choosing a lounge chair at the pool for my rumination. My sun hat positioned over my face, I tried to imagine how a woman of the world should handle this. Maybe to get the "grand and glorious" experience out of his system, she would go to bed with him to prove him wrong. She would lie there, passive, letting him do all his strange European techniques. Perhaps Europeans did it standing up. I looked at the still and empty pool. Or maybe under water.

I rolled over on my stomach, thinking how disappointed he'd be, for he'd probably been wondering what it would be like with an American. Perhaps he'd ask why I was here if I wasn't going to participate. Then I'd explain that even if time was always speaking, you couldn't force it to give up what wasn't there. He'd smoke a cigarette, and we'd talk about how friendship was better for us. No one would be hurt. Then I remembered

Pete, saw his great body, cool and wet from a swim, felt it graze mine as he sat on the edge of my chair, giving my bottom a proprietary pat. God, I missed him.

Sharon and Miriam caught me looking in my compact mirror for June Allyson. Then they actually asked me to go somewhere. I knew it was only because they wanted to know more about Nelia, but I went anyway. Although I had fantasized outings with them, now that it was happening, it seemed a dream.

Out the car window, I glimpsed a *satay* vendor cooking on the street. At a traffic light, a one-legged man ran up and washed the windshield, drying it with newspaper. Someone gave him some change. As we drove along the canal that ran through Jakarta, the usual was going on—clothes washing, bathing, defecating.

Then we were on a broad street, shaded by tall trees, that lead to Merdeka Palace, the official residence of the Indonesian president. Comfortably attached to their rifles, military police at the stately gates nodded us on toward our destination, an art gallery at the palace compound.

Once again, I saw a little girl picking lice from her sister's head, but this time— as a beautiful oil painting—it affected my sensibilities in a different way. This world was beginning to be real to me, thanks to Nelia. I looked at my companions. One-to-one, they weren't so bad, but I wondered now what had made their acceptance so important to me.

Returning to the hotel, feeling in perfect rhythm with *jam karet*, I didn't look once at the mosaic wall clocks. Then I became abruptly aware that time was speaking after all. A frenzied Tomas paced at the top of the escalator.

"Where 'ave you been?" he demanded. "I look for you all day. Mad-a-leen, you make me crazy for you!"

I had no intention of explaining my whereabouts to this man who hadn't shaved, whose clothes appeared slept in. The only debonair thing about him now was his perfect coiffure.

"I have no grand passion for you. I love my husband."

He pulled to his full, imposing height. "I will leave as I entered." He stalked away. "There will be no problem," he called across the lobby. "Do you think I am kid?"

I went to my room, relieved I had done the right thing. It was over. Unlike Scarlett, I might not even think about it tomorrow. I walked to the window and peered down at the glittering emerald pool. A rain shower had passed; pool boys were wiping the chairs and tables; people were returning to the bar. I thought I saw Nelia there. Maybe I'd join her.

But I lingered, watching the boys sweep away the puddles on a tennis court. Then from behind the bushes, the familiar figure appeared, hands clasped behind his back. He patrolled the pool area again; he even looked up at my window. I lay down with a serious headache, a prisoner staring at the ceiling.

Surely there was a ladylike way to handle this. Maybe I could convert him from roué—I'd heard Vonda call him that—to nice guy again. Jean Arthur had done that once to Cary Grant, or was it Joel McCrea?

At cocktail time, feeling all would right itself, I floated into the Pendopo in my new caftan with the long, flowing sleeves. Nelia began to sing the butterfly song. I followed her nod and saw my tarnished man of the world peering in from the doorway. I hoped Gwen, someone I was trying to make friends with, would meet me soon for dinner. I had no idea what time it was supposed to be since I'd stopped wearing my watch.

"You were not in the Merak," his angry voice said in my ear.

"I have another engagement," I whispered, trying to tame his loudness. I walked to the end of the horseshoe piano bar closest to Nelia. We started planning lunch together at an Indian restaurant she'd been wanting to take me to, but Tomas kept interrupting. When I ignored him, he prowled up and down behind me, finally returning to hover over me, grazing my neck and shoulders with his fingertips.

If only Pete were here. In my head, I heard him say, "Listen, Bozo... ." I stood and faced Tomas. "Sit!" I ordered. "Now."

He went to one of the semi-circular booths and sulked. Victory was sweet, but I kept an eye on him. It was not like him to give up so easily. Soon he moved to an empty seat at the other end of the bar. Then the Turk, who was with the International Money Fund, left and Tomas moved over two seats. When the Dutchman, who was here showing his daughter where he once lived, moved to a table, Tomas moved over three more places. He kept doing this musical chairs act all around the bar until he was beside me.

Nelia played "Ring Around the Rosy," and I started for the door. Tomas grabbed my arm. He pinned me to him with his gaze. "Mad-a-leen, you have stolen my heart and I have to go sit down. In my language there is a name for you which is not nice."

Even my earlobes burned. I would miss the Lobster Pescador and the string quartet in the Toba, but all I really wanted was for my husband to come home. I thought of going to the office in the morning and calling him on the radio-phone.

I ran for sanctuary. Once in my room, I fell into a deep sleep. In its fog, I answered the phone.

"I am not a toy you can put down, Mad-a-leeen. I know you want me," Tomas crooned.

"Leave me alone," I tried, but it came out in a little girl squeak rather than the chilling tone I'd meant.

"If you do not sleep with me, Mad-a-leen, I will tell Pete that you did."

I groped for my robe in a fury that propelled me to the elevator and down a hall, where I pounded on his door. "You lunatic!" I shouted. "I want you out of my life."

He stood in the open door, a smug look on his face. Knobby knees and spindly, chalk-white legs showed beneath the hem of his blue terrycloth robe. He wore a heavy gold cross on his hairy chest. Before I could get my wits together, he yanked me into the room and slammed the door.

"You really must listen this time," I started. His usual smile was now a sneer. I tried another tack. "You must listen to time speaking."

"The train is in ze station, Mad-a-leen. Time of talk is passed." He pushed me back on the bed and started to unzip my robe. I pushed his hand away; it returned to reach for a breast.

"This can't go on," I struggled to a sitting position.

"No," he said, misinterpreting. "I 'ave been called home."

I jumped up and grasped the door knob. He moved quickly to lean against the door, pinning me to it.

"Tomas good lover," he growled. "You stay."

I racked my brain for some scathing thing Joan Crawford said to Walter Houston in *Rain*, but to no avail. I called to my patron saint, Roz Russell, but she had deserted me. I was alone in a foreign country with this kind of man and my husband away. And who was I? What kind of woman had I been playing?

I tried a disdainful look. Instead of wilting under it, he peppered my cleavage with loud, smacking kisses.

"And I thought European men were gentlemen," I heard myself croak as I fell to the floor with him crashing on top of me. I grabbed for the heavy gold cross that was gouging me and twisted hard. Tomas reared back, bumping his head on the door knob. A hairpiece went sailing through the air, landing on the plush carpet. It lay there like a small dead animal.

His tormented eyes pleaded with mine. I burst into laughter. In that instant, I wanted to be pure Maddy, to do what she and no one else would do.

"The train is not in ze station," I said, plunking the thing on my own head and stalking around the room, hands clasped behind my back. "The train, she is gone."

He cringed before me, his arms protecting his nude head. Still wearing his crowning glory, I peeled my robe over one shoulder, sucked in my cheeks, and vamped out the door.

❀ ↷ ❀ ↷ ❀ ↷ ❀

I am sitting here in the lobby, waiting. Pete's helicopter should be landing about now. If Tomas walks by, I may torture him by saying I'd love to meet his wife when we go to Europe on home leave. If I could, I'd move the hands on the wall clock myself. Merak Happy Hour starts at five, and I can't wait to go back there. You meet such interesting people. And surely Pete won't object. Not now—not when I know how to handle European men.

LADIES OF THE BOROBUDUR:
Sharon

AFTERWARDS I NEEDED COMFORT, SOLACE. SOMETHING. BUT I never could find it, not even in my Daddy's old Bible. It fell open to the underlined words that should have stayed with me, words my Daddy preached in his itinerant church back in a dot on the Louisiana map no oil people ever heard of, words I doubt I'll ever forget now: "He who is without sin among you, let him cast the first stone."

The morning it started was like all the others of the three months and two days I'd spent in the Hotel Borobudur, trying to create some kind of normal life for my two boys, three girls, and their father when he's home from drilling oil offshore in the Java Sea. Being a pampered, long-staying guest in a sophisticated hotel in Jakarta, at CAMCO's expense, was not all bad. But sometimes, outside its doors, I felt like a time traveler who'd left 1976 and wound up somewhere in the far past of this third-world country, where both women and men wore sarongs, chattered a musical language with neither articles or the verb "to be," and thought me angry if I had my hands on my hips.

I don't want to make excuses for any of us, but I can't help wallowing in my guilt. If it hadn't been for me, they'd never have given Celeste another thought.

As usual our rooms were in utter chaos with my kids getting ready for school, so I escaped to the coffee shop for a pre-breakfast of papaya and yogurt, before the one I shared with the others. You can see I wear my disappointments on my hips, stomach, chin—pounds and pounds of them for all the world to see. To get myself away from the breakfast buffet, I always took a doggie bag out to Rocky, our Irish setter. He had to live in the kennel behind the tennis courts and was not doing well because he'd spent most of his life on kids' beds in air-conditioned rooms.

After Rocky and I polished off the doughnuts, I walked around the pool a couple of times, savoring the waking flowers and the sparkling water colored by the pool's emerald bottom. At this hour, Jakarta's insane traffic noise was muted, and even the air seemed clean again. This place and this time had become my oasis before heat, humidity, and coping took over. It's the way I prepare myself for being school bus mother, a chore I'm trapped into more often than other mothers because of the size of my brood.

When I felt put together, I went to meet the others in our special alcove in the lobby near the banquet rooms, a place well away from the bustling front desk and practically hidden by tall palms and a trellis covered with climbing hibiscus. It's where us girls make all our decisions, plan how we will fill the long hours of the day ahead.

Six of us had gravitated to one another. We were irreverently called "The Herd" by others in the hotel. Lila Hoopes hated the designation passionately. Jo Moody said "consider the source." Lexie Rogers thought it funny. Obstinate as usual, Vonda Hutchison said she sort of liked it. We rarely knew what Miriam Dutton thought about anything serious. Me? I've been called worse. You know, because of this weight problem.

We all arrived in Jakarta about the same time and had been in the hotel together longer than any other CAMCO people because we'd buffaloed that little Indonesian man who runs housing. We demanded we all get homes in the same complex, or we'd make our husbands go home. We got our way and soon were insisting on extra ceiling fans and air conditioners and specific colors of paint for houses we hadn't agreed to yet. Oh, yes, together we had power, and we knew it.

What we really wanted was to be in Vonda's neighborhood, a quiet street, lined with tall flame trees, burdened with blossoms of orange and red, and walled-in houses near the American Embassy in Menteng. Her husband's position demanded they do a lot of entertaining. He got the job David Anderson wanted, and everybody says that's why David and Lisa left. Vonda picked her house almost right away. And what a house! No compound living for her. It was a remodeled Dutch Colonial, and her neighbors were Indonesian generals and high-ups from other countries. We assumed she paid under the table to get it.

Even with all her money, Vonda is regular people. She spends every day with us just like she was still in the hotel. Maybe that's because she and Lexie were so tight back in Houston before the fellas were transferred. I've digressed again, but I think you need to know all this. You understand, I'm not asking you to judge, just listen.

Lila, the *doyenne* of the group (I learned that word from Vonda) was the first one to the alcove as usual. Soon the others greeted me, grumbling about the coffee in the coffee shop. The *kopi* Indonesia serves reminds me of liquid tar. We always ask for a pot of hot water to dilute it.

Vonda, always late, rushed in. "What's the plan today?" she managed as she caught her breath.

"I don't know why we have to go through this every morning," Miriam said. "Why can't we just let the day happen?"

Lila began folding her paper, making sure all the edges met. She never pays any attention to us until she finishes reading the *International Herald Tribune*. "Franny Ward has been here seven years, and she's still finding a place to go every day. She says it's very important to your mental health."

Miriam sighed. "Sometimes it's not worth the bother." We had been wondering what to do about her. She'd been lethargic and depressed recently. We figured she'd be on her way again soon. You might call her our jet setter.

Although Darrell Dutton had been assigned to Jakarta a long time now, Miriam was always leaving for the States or arriving from some exotic country. She had a million reasons for staying away, but we knew none of them were the real lowdown. Some said she got lonely for her two kids, who were back home in private schools. Some said she just liked to travel. Well, we all coped in a different way so we never questioned her. Now the Duttons were back in the hotel because the lease had run out on their house. Just like us, she was waiting for one to be available.

"You give in to things too easily, Miriam," Jo snapped. She was irritated about everything these days.

"I've had the flu or something for a week, and I still make it down here. God knows what I've picked up in this place," Lila said.

Vonda nodded sagely. "Culture shock, that's what we've all got."

"Bite your tongue. You know we never admit to that," Jo said.

"Amen," Lexie said.

Miriam said, "Look at this rash, Sharon, and tell me what to do about it. Do you think I got it because I forgot and brushed my teeth with tap water the other day?"

Since I used to be a nurse, they considered me the final authority on their medical problems, real or imagined. I'm not a *nurse* nurse, the kind that does that administrative stuff. Mama said I wasn't smart enough for that, so I stopped at LPN. But I like to diagnose, and it makes them feel better. Just like

I felt better when they took an interest in my weight problem. I remember Vonda said, "It'll be our cause celebré." Then she answered my dumb look. "It sort of means we're going to be giving you a lot of attention."

I opened my mouth to give my medical opinion, but they had all turned to Lexie, our voice of reason. She was saying, "We owe it to the company to immerse ourselves in this culture and to find things to volunteer for. You-all don't want to be 'Ugly Americans,' do you?" While they contemplated that in the heavy silence that followed, I took the opportunity to make my pitch about Celeste.

Wayne and Celeste Morrison and her son, Denís, had arrived the night before. As usual, the six of us lined up at the top of the escalator to welcome them, as we did all newcomers. Actually, it was a chance to look them over and see if there was anybody we wanted to shepherd along—and that's all. We were a closed corporation. "Celeste is married to my husband's old college buddy," I began, "and I think we should ..." I took a deep breath. "... you know, show her around."

"But she's French, Sharon," Miriam said. "Probably doesn't even speak English. No offense, Vonda."

One half of Vonda is French, the other is Japanese. She mimed "inscrutable" by pulling on her eyes to make them more slanted than they were. Then she made like she had buck teeth on top of a silly grin. It cracked us up every time.

"Vince and I were in Montreal on our honeymoon. Lots of people speak English there." Jo's dared us to dispute her.

Always our final authority in things foreign, Vonda said, "Actually, French Montrealers have been trying for years to get English outlawed completely. Street names are in French, and if you own a shop its name has to be French." Vonda often told us more than we wanted to hear about anything, but never what we were dying to know—how did a Eurasian snag a Texan?

Lila gave us a sour look. "French Canadians sound complicated, not down home folks at all."

"I heard this Celeste was a barmaid," Miriam said.

"I'm glad I never had to resort to that," Jo said.

"There are worse occupations, I suppose," Vonda said, "but I can't imagine what."

I decided then and there I'd never tell them I worked my way through nursing school as a waitress, eating everything in sight. Mama never did think I could do anything right, and taking food away was her favorite punishment up until she got so sick and all. But I was still hungry a lot because Daddy was traveling his preaching circuit then, and he never left enough money for both food and Mama's medicine.

"I told you we'd have nothing in common with her," Miriam said.

I didn't like the way the conversation was going. I had to be friendly to Celeste because my husband, Cory, had said us Matheneys were going to see the Morrisons settled no matter what.

I turned to Lexie because, in the end, we always did what Lexie thought best. "She's really very nice," I started, wondering what might appeal to Lexie.

"We better study long and hard on this," Lila said.

"*You* think it's all right, don't you, Lexie?" I persisted. If they'd agree to take up Celeste, I wouldn't have to give up any of my time with them. Encouraged by Lexie's smile, I said, "She's anxious to go out and see things. And she's … well, sophisticated."

"A barmaid?" Lila shuddered. "Really, Sharon."

"She married a Texan, Lila. That's good enough for me," Jo said.

Even Lila couldn't argue with Wayne's hometown credentials and graduation from the "good ole boys" school, Texas A&M. Jo and Lila were both Texans, and Miriam not too far off—originally a Californian. Lexie was born in New Orleans and never lets you forget it. Of course Vonda is universal. Besides, you might say she'd bought us.

"It's settled then," I said. I needed to celebrate, so I rooted through my handbag till I found the half-eaten Baby Ruth I'd forgotten about. I had to pick fuzzies from a tissue off it.

"Disgusting," they chorused.

The chocolate had melted several times, and it was hard and brittle, but I didn't care. I grinned and stuffed it all in my mouth at once.

"Sharon!"

"I'm ordering your lunch," Miriam, slim as a string bean, said.

"It's my treat today," Vonda said.

"Let's take a vote on Celeste," Lexie said. "Yea's?" Everyone put up their hand because Lexie had. I relaxed and told them I was sure Celeste would be most appreciative.

It didn't take long for us to see how different Celeste really was and that she had every intention of staying that way. She wasn't really a barmaid, but had managed a popular wine bar in Montreal where Wayne met her when he was on a business trip two years ago. Twelve-year old Denís was her son from a previous marriage.

Celeste was petite and dark-haired, with luminous eyes that lit up her otherwise plain face. Even the humidity didn't stop her from looking like an ad from *Mademoiselle*. Because she wore spike heels and black stockings, Lila said she was "cheap." But Jo said that was the way women in Montreal dressed. Whatever—Celeste was everything I longed to be.

"A goddamn harlequin! That's what she looks like," Jo snorted the day we took Celeste to lunch at Art & Curio.

Celeste had a thing about wearing all-black or all-white, or a combination of both. Our group wore sandals, simple sleeveless blouses, and long *batik* skirts that Indonesia didn't make in my size. I was stuck with the polyester pants and baggy tops I'd brought with me.

At Art & Curio we had a view of railroad tracks and a pond, most certainly contaminated. Out another window we saw the parking lot of one of the expat supermarkets where we shopped. But the restaurant had always charmed us with its wizened waiters, who seemed like they'd been here forever, wearing those little black hats they call *peji*, a contrast to their white aprons. *Batik* tablecloths, *banka* tin tumblers, a huge brass gong, background *anglung* music, and cedar fragrance lulled us with Indonesia's timelessness.

Celeste was disappointed the menu was European instead of Indonesian, and she didn't seem to enjoy the house specialty, prawn steak. When we browsed through the adjoining antique shop, she was full of surprises. She didn't think the marriage bed, big as a room, one bit vulgar, as we did. She actually liked the wooden *Wayang* puppets with garish expressions on their faces on heads too big for their stick bodies.

Looking at other things, she said, "I don't buy tourist junk." I put back the little frog the man had said was real Kalimantan jade.

Next we took her to the American Women's Association meeting. Technically, she can belong since Wayne is American. She fidgeted through announcements about the book club, bowling, bridge lessons, and square dancing. She got up and left halfway through the fashion show. "I want to know the real Indonesia," she told us when we found her waiting in the car later.

"You mean Unrealesia." Vonda never cracked a smile, and we all nodded in agreement.

After that, no matter how nice we were to her or what juicy tidbit we had to share, she declined our company. She spent most of her days at the pool, writing in a big ledger book. At first we thought she was doing Wayne's expense account, but she said it was for journal writing and that John Steinbeck had written his novels in ledgers. It surprised us a French Canadian would even know who he was.

❀ ᤛ ❀ ᤛ ❀ ᤛ ❀

One morning, in our alcove as usual, Lila barely glanced at the headlines. She couldn't wait to tell us what she'd seen. "I couldn't sleep last night and went to sit in the lobby." We all nodded.

Lila pursed her lips, unpursed them, then went on. "I just happened to look into the Pendopo, and there was Celeste, chattering like a magpie, like she never does with us, to that Nelia, the piano player. And that Uganda fellow—you know the one always picking up women—he was ogling her bosom for all he was worth. Serves her right, I'd say. Gallivanting at that hour of the morning in a bar."

I thought of the nights I'd been driven from my bed to pace the hotel room, thinking of Cory and why wasn't he there beside me, and how it was still five days until he'd be home again. I don't drink alone, but I often poured myself a half a glass of vodka, hoping it would make me sleep and stop catastrophizing what might happen out there to keep him from coming home at all. On those nights, I wanted to go wake up every one of our group and say, "Talk to me." I almost said, "Maybe she just missed Wayne."

"All she does is write in that damn diary," Jo said.

"I'd love to get my hands on it," Miriam said.

A week or two went by—I'm not sure. You don't have to be here long before you're thinking of time in the way Indonesians do—something elastic that no one pays any attention to. No wonder they call it rubber time. It was one evening when Miriam and I were in the coffee shop. I took a swig of that awful coffee, but it didn't take away my desire for something really *good*. I was half out of my chair and on my way to the pastry table when Miriam pulled me back.

"No, you don't," she said.

I really should have been grateful for her interest. The others seemed to have forgotten they were going to work on my weight problem. But I had to test her. "I need a neopolitan," I said.

"You mean a napoleon, and willpower is what you need. You're the one who says she wants to lose thirty pounds."

In that moment, I felt totally worthless. That's what drove me.

"I'm going on a 'nothing but ice cream' diet this week anyway," I said, trying to get a rise out of her.

Instead, she said in her best stage whisper, "Get a load of that." We hadn't noticed Celeste with Wayne and Denis. They were eating *nasi goring*, a nasty mess of fried rice, flecked with bits of fish and real chilis, and topped with slivers of fried egg. With them was a handsome young Indonesian chattering in English.

"I've had some university," we heard him say. "As your driver I'd have the chance to learn French."

Lila joined us. "She's giving French lessons now?"

Jo slipped in beside me. "Sounds like T-R-O-U-B-L-E to me."

I stared out the wall of plate glass overlooking the tennis courts, but I saw only the reflection of someone I didn't know, someone who felt compelled to say, "Inviting servants to dinner for an interview is a bit ridiculous, don't you think? What next?" I rolled my eyes, not sure myself what I was suggesting.

We made a big thing of saying *"selamat tidur"*—the Indonesian version of good night—to each other, hovering close to the Morrisons' table until Wayne said, "This is our new driver, Rudi."

I couldn't look at Celeste, and I didn't want to postmortem this with the others. I hurried away, telling myself I needed a lot of rest. Starting the next morning I had school bus duty for a whole week.

❋ ᴣ❋ ❋ ᴣ❋ ❋ ᴣ❋ ❋

"There's a whole world of expat parents out there who will never know I stopped their little darlings from getting them deported this week," I said, when Friday finally rolled around. The six of us were sitting in the pavilion at the pool, drinking beer and tomato juice. It had been five days of hell, keeping the brats from throwing food and soft drink cans out the windows and making rude gestures and remarks to passing Indonesians. Yes, after sweating out Jakarta's dodge-em traffic and two hours in a tin can in my polyester, I needed it. I was starting the "drinking man's diet" here and now.

We stared out through the brown slats at Celeste sunning herself. A group of kids at one end of the pool were screaming "Marco" to another group at the other end who answered "Polo." It was some kind of universal water game of tag my own kids played. A toddler ran screaming, nude and unattended, among the lounge chairs.

"They let them pee right there on the cement." Lexie wrinkled her nose.

"That kid's mother is either French of Dutch," Jo said. We nodded agreement.

"Do you think that's business or pleasure?" Vonda asked. Her face was a mask, but the corners of her mouth twitched. We followed her gaze to two Japanese men in stiff business suits chattering with a bikini-clad young Caucasian woman.

"Now that's bizarre," Miriam said.

Then, right before our eyes, Rudi, jaunty in an unbuttoned sports shirt, his neck gleaming with a gold medallion and chain that looked much too expensive for a driver, pulled out a chair and sat down next to Celeste, just like he belonged there. Even from the pavilion we could see they were poring over the *Guide to Java*. Rudi seemed to be explaining something. His hands waved everywhere, and once in a while they grazed Celeste by accident. Or was it?

Last night I was up at three o'clock in the morning with Paula, who had diarrhea. She'd eaten salad again although I'd told her and told her you can't eat it here. But, of course, teenagers think they know it all. Anyway, I'm only on the third floor, and my room looks out over the pool. In that glaring spotlight they keep on all night, it's bright as day. I was surprised to see someone in the water, since the pool closes at eleven. Looking closer, I saw the woman getting out of the pool was Celeste.

She chatters on with Indonesians all the time, so I supposed she'd conned the security guard into unlocking the gate. She was talking to someone, but even with my face pressed tight against the window, there was a blind spot. I saw a walky-talky glint in the moonlight, or was it? Maybe she wasn't talking to the guard. Maybe it was someone else. Maybe it was Rudi with that tape recorder he was always fooling with.

I felt obligated to tell the others—just to see what they thought—or was it to get their attention? They had become so preoccupied with Celeste they never mentioned my weight problem anymore. I felt shut out. Empty as those times Mama locked me in my room when she caught me overeating. Empty as when Cory was caught up in his job, and the kids preferred their new school friends to me.

I felt forced, you understand, to blurt out what I'd seen. The more I thought about it, the surer I was it had been Rudi. I didn't tell them how Celeste had sat down under those bright lights and began to write in the book that had replaced us. And I didn't tell them I'd decided to get my hands on it somehow.

Understand, we're not bad people. Vonda is generous with her money. Jo comes across tough, but she's a big softy. Most people don't notice how smart Miriam really is. In spite of her caustic remarks, Lila always tells the truth, and Lexie is chock-full of common sense.

Anyway, that day in the pavilion with the sun glinting on the water and a slight breeze ruffling the cocktail napkins on the glass-top table, Jo nodded toward Celeste's table and said, "They're hatching up something, sure as shooting. Probably another one of those midnight—whatchacallit, Vonda?"

"Assignation," Vonda answered. "At least she could have gotten him a uniform." As usual, we had followed Lexie's lead and supplied our drivers with blue safari suits.

"Servants have to know their place," Miriam said.

Jo said, "It gives me the creepy-crawlies just thinking of them—you know."

"Right there in the water like you saw, Sharon?" someone said. I can't remember who. They were all gazing fondly at me.

"Hey, I didn't exactly say ..." But I was the center of attention again, and it felt so good I shut up.

"There's absolutely no privacy in Indonesia, what with servants or hotel personnel," Vonda said. "And the expat community knows everything about everybody. I've always wondered how people can carry on an affair here."

"So you can try it for yourself?" Lexie waggled a finger at her best friend, and we had to laugh.

"You'd be in real trouble with the Indonesian *polisi* if you were caught making out in a parked car I bet." Miriam's laugh was dirty.

"Speaking from experience?" Jo's eyes glittered with anticipation, but Miriam didn't take the bait.

"No, really," Miriam said, "where do you suppose they do it?"

"In Celeste's empty house," we chorused.

"How could we find out?" Lila asked.

"We could go over there to Pondak Indah and pretend we're house shopping. The way we go around to all the complexes," I said. They looked at me like I'd invented ice cream.

"We'll check it out tomorrow," Lexie said.

"Thank God," Jo made a prayer tent of her hands. "Something to do."

"Amen," we said in unison.

❀ ⌇ ❀ ⌇ ❀ ⌇ ❀

"Too bad it's locked," I said in a loud voice as we crowded together on the front patio of an unoccupied house next door to the one Celeste and her family would live in when their furniture arrived. Somehow she'd already finagled this fancy house in one of the better complexes. But there was no reason for envy; we'd become quite comfortable with life in our luxurious hotel.

"Pretend you're really looking," Miriam hissed as she peered into the wide expanse of glass of the patio door.

"The office said someone would be out with a key," Jo's foghorn voice said.

But it was obvious there was no real need to pretend one of us had been assigned this house. Celeste's car was in the drive, but there was no sign of Celeste and her driver.

"Do you suppose they're doing it right now? Right on the floor?" Vonda's jaw was slack, her bottom lip trembling.

"And how long *has* Hutch been away, dear?" Lexie's grin was absolutely obscene.

"I bet they are," Miriam said.

Lila shuddered. "Animals."

"What will we do if … if we catch them?" I asked.

Five pairs of eyes stared back at me for a long moment. Then Vonda said, "We'll know. That's all. We'll just know." Somehow that made me feel better, as if nothing bad was going to happen to Celeste.

After consultation, we trooped around back to try to see something through the slats of the seven-foot bamboo fence separating the yards of the two houses. Everything next door was silent with no sign of anyone. The women started back toward the house, but I was reluctant to give up.

Then I yelped "Bingo" before I could stop myself, and they all but climbed on top of me to get back to their own vantage points. Miriam giggled, and Lexie pinched her. Vonda shushed Jo's gravelly voice. But Celeste had her hands too full to hear.

Wielding a broom, red-faced with rage, and screaming in French, she chased unconcerned goats from her house and out the back gate. Rudi, a serious look for once on that ever-smiling face, spoke quietly to two Indonesians, a young boy and an old man. He went inside and came out with their belongings bundled together. They looked reluctant to leave, but soon departed out the back gate, too.

Celeste's anger turned to throaty laughter, and Rudi's tenor voice joined with hers. They reminded me of children having a really good time. Finally they disappeared into the house.

"Too, too domestic," Vonda said.

We didn't have to wait long before they returned. Celeste wore a revealing halter and short shorts, not black and white but hot pink and chartreuse. She began to sweep the patio where the goats had overturned great pots of glossy red anthurium. Rudi, now in a bathing suit, washed the car.

"It gets homier and homier," Lexie said.

After Celeste had put the dirt back in the pots, after Rudi had put the hose away, she offered him a sandwich and a Coke from a small cooler. We watched as these objects of their immediate desire passed over sensuous lips, becoming little love bites for two pairs of gleaming teeth until their appetites were satiated.

Then in unison they swigged down the rest of the brown liquid from the green bottles that were collectors' items back home. They spoke now and then, but so softly we didn't even know what language. In the background a tape player crooned a French love song. Their twin *cafe au lait* bodies, one natural and one sun induced, glistened with dewy perspiration. Their combined animal magnetism made me expect to see them mate before our very eyes.

"Look at that torso!"

"I can't."

"Indonesian men are too feminine looking for my taste, but …"

"Tell me you wouldn't!"

"This is disgusting. I'm leaving," Lila spoke too loudly, and Rudi and Celeste looked up, startled.

Celeste said something to him we couldn't hear, and he began unloading young trees and flowering bushes from the back of Celeste's car. She showed him where they were to go; he dug, inserted, and tamped the earth down around them, and then went on to the next one.

Disappointed, we went to wake Vonda's driver, then crowded into her big car. We were almost downtown before anyone spoke. "It's quite obvious what's going on there," Lila said.

"They're really shameless," I said.

"Everyone knows how racy the French are," Miriam said. "No reflection on your French half, Vonda."

Jo said, "They're guilty as hell."

Lexie sighed. "I intended to give her the benefit of a doubt, but she doesn't even treat him like a servant."

"I'm not prejudiced, you understand," Miriam said, "but I do think a line has to be drawn."

"The thing is, it reflects on all of us," I said.

"Sharon's absolutely right." Lexie pressed my hand.

I suggested we go to George and the Dragon for lunch to talk it over. I suddenly wanted lots and lots of pizza—even if it was the lousiest pizza I'd ever eaten. When we were finally sitting there, pretending it was Pizza Hut, I couldn't help myself. I had to confess.

I closed my eyes and said quickly, before I could change my mind, "I got a peek in Celeste's journal when she went to the little girls' room. It was just there, lying open on her pool chair."

"You didn't!" Miriam squealed.

When I opened my eyes, my friends were waiting with bated breath for my revelations. I savored "Sharon in the Limelight" for a moment before I said, "It's in English because she's practicing."

"And?" Jo prodded.

"She said life in the hotel was phony, and most of the expats she'd met were narrow-minded, and Rudi was going to show her the real Indonesia."

"I never!" Lila said. "When we went out of our way to—"

On a roll now, I said, "She called us The Herd, and there was a lot about her son's problems at school."

"Just think how this must be affecting the poor kid," Jo said.

There was more. I could have told them she'd written how homesick she was for snow, ice storms, cross-country skiing, and the feel of the silk lining of her fur coat caressing her skin. Instead, I told them Celeste liked the Pendopo piano bar because she could pretend she was at the Ritz Carleton, where she'd loved to go, back in Montreal.

I took a deep breath. No, I'd tell them everything. "She and Wayne have talked about having an open marriage. Many of her married friends have lovers."

Vonda nodded in agreement. "It seems to be the lifestyle in Quebec. They're all Catholic and don't believe in divorce."

"There's your proof," Lila said.

I took the following silence for assent. Celeste must be guilty or everyone wouldn't think so. I took a deep breath. "I couldn't agree with you more."

❋ ⵎ ❋ ⵎ ❋ ⵎ ❋

I was sneaking across the lobby with three cheese Danish, hoping somebody would catch me, when I heard the loudspeaker. The bell captain was calling, "Rudi to the front. Rudi to the front."

We had decided to spy on them every chance we had, but it had been over a week and there was nothing to report. No one knew what we were going to do with all our evidence, but we had come too far to stop now. Their disappointment in me for not getting my hands on the journal again was obvious. Maybe I could redeem myself.

I went down the escalator to be near the entrance and hid just inside the shop that sold handcrafted silver jewelry. Celeste ran down the escalator, calling behind her to Denís, "Hurry up, *cher*, Rudi waits."

I sauntered out of the shop just in time to collide with her, hoping she'd drop the ledger book she was carrying under her arm, and in her haste to get away, not notice.

"*Cherié,* I cannot speak now," she said breathlessly. "Rudi is going to show us the Punchak."

I followed her outside. Denís had run ahead to the car, and now was inspecting a pile of comic books Rudi had handed him. The bellman put the bags in the trunk. The doormen hovered, but a grinning Rudi held the car door open. Right there, in front of us all, Rudi said something to her in French that sounded much too intimate to me.

The day they returned, I pumped Denís. I had convinced my twins, Andy and Andrea, to invite him to the hotel bowling alley. With just a little prodding, he told us all about the trip.

"*Viva la Punchak,*" he said to my children, running his fingers through his thick curly hair, an annoying habit he had. "You should get your mother to take you up there. Along the way are these—what you say—neat? Yes, neat tea plantations and rice growing on terraces. You stay in a little yellow house like the one where we stayed in Switzerland once. From the porch you see many flowers and the mountains look all purple and ..."

"But what did you do up there so far from home?" I interrupted.

"Maman bought Rudi and me these coolie hats with a gold Garuda on them. Rudi says that's a mythical bird, and it's the national emblem, and we hiked and saw a lake and it's cool there, not like here. We went to a place called Bandung, and Rudi helped Maman pick out some pottery."

My, my, I thought, Celeste buying tourist junk after all.

"Maman says we couldn't exist without Rudi," Denís offered on his own.

❀ ৵ ❀ ৵ ❀ ৵ ❀

"And then I asked where Rudi stayed," I told the others the minute I got to the hotel beauty shop for our Friday appointments. An old *ibu* was pounding my flesh, shaking her head and muttering, "*Banyak gemuk.*" I endured this every week, hoping the "*gemuk*" would melt away beneath her magic, massaging hands.

"You didn't !" Miriam got so excited she smeared her fresh polish and had to call the manicurist back.

I didn't think it important to tell them that Denís had said they were talking about Muslim stuff and something called *malu.*

"Scandalous," Lila said, twisting away from her Suzie Wong, which is what we called all the Chinese beauticians. Determined, the girl brushed out the fat sausages the rollers had made of Lila's hair. We'd tried to talk her out of the blue rinse, but she wouldn't listen.

"They really went away together?" Vonda was having her turn with the manicurist now. "Wow."

Using a hand mirror, Lexie looked at the back of her new short hairstyle. Everyone would be doing their hair that way now. "I wouldn't have the nerve to go off with *anyone* for a weekend let alone ..."

"Do you suppose they're circumcised?" Jo only came along to kibitz. She didn't like anyone messing with her hair and had even brought a supply of home permanent kits with her.

"Yes, indeed, *cherié*," Celeste said. Hair dripping, she peered out at us from curtains around the shampoo bowls. "They definitely are circumcised." Her Suzie Wong was tugging at her, trying to get her to her station, but Celeste, water streaming down her flaming face and soaking her white silk blouse, shook her off. Her words struck us like bullets.

"As-a-matter-of-fact-I-can-tell-you-it-is-a-big-happening-when-a-boy-is-eleven-or-twelve-with-a-big-party-afterward-and-they-even-have-a-special-bench-for-the-ceremony-which-most-of-you-probably-bought-a-copy-of-to-take-home-and-don't-even-know-it." She paused for breath, her eyes turning us to cinders.

I couldn't speak. Lexie managed a "But, Celeste, we didn't ...." The rest of them looked down at the floor, up at the ceiling—anywhere they couldn't see the raging accusation on her contorted face. Even we knew the words she screamed must be French swear words. She slammed her journal down hard on the vanity next to Lila. A curling iron clattered to the floor and several pink hair rollers bounced along behind it. "Any thing else you ... you ..." It seemed like she couldn't think of words bad enough to call us. "... want to know, just ask." Black eyes blazing, she stood there forever.

I can tell you we were glad to get away from that look and glad when Vonda took us all to her house, where she had her houseboy, Iwan, make a double pitcher of stiff daiquiris. Even Lila had one. For a long time we didn't speak or even look at one another.

I hadn't told them Celeste had been careless with her journal again, and I'd had another chance to read it. Actually, Rudi wasn't even mentioned. And she didn't write the way she looked on the outside. Mostly it was about how she thought learning everything she could about the culture and the people would help her adjust to life in Jakarta more quickly.

I was beginning to think maybe this had all gotten out of hand, and

I should say something, but then Lexie took over. "We might have this all wrong. It might not be Celeste's fault at all." She took her sandals off, and so we all did. Vonda's oriental rug felt good beneath my toes.

"You're probably right," Vonda said. "You know how crafty and full of guile these Indonesians are."

"Look at all the children. These people must think about sex all the time." Lila said.

"It's the tropics," Miriam said. We nodded.

Jo yelped, "Why didn't we see it? Rudi is the seducer!" This brought Iwan running into the room. When it was obvious we didn't want anything, he made a great show of trying to fill our full glasses. We sat in mutual silence until he left the room.

"Sorry, but I'm not sure I buy Celeste as Little Miss Innocent," Lila said.

"No, Lila, we've done her wrong," Vonda said. "Now it's up to us to save her."

Lexie agreed. "It's the least we can do."

Miriam said, "I don't know. Maybe we should just forget it."

"You don't think … We haven't gone too far?" Jo had a puzzled look on her face.

Miriam looked like she was going to cry. "Maybe we've made too much of this."

"Yes," Lila said. "What would other people think?"

"We owe it to Wayne," I said quickly, never realizing how I would wish I'd never said that later. "After all, he was my husband's roommate in college."

"But what can we do?" Vonda asked.

"It's simple," Lexie said, and we all calmed down because this was Lexie, and she'd tell us what to do. "We get rid of him somehow. Celeste will thank us one day."

That made everything all right. So we hatched a plan. Each of us would speak to our drivers about Rudi's unnatural and unwelcome attentions to *Nyonya* Morrison.

I remembered that Miriam was an avid reader of *Psychology Today* when she said, "Peer pressure can do a lot." She didn't have to tell us how much time our drivers spent together, waiting in the car park for our call.

I felt a kind of uplifting, like we were really righting a wrong, so I suggested we intimate to the chauffeurs they might be "finish," as they called being let go, for associating with such a person as Rudi.

Then somebody—I guess it was me—said in such a situation back home they'd go straight to the offender's minister. Everyone clapped. When

Iwan came running in again, we let him stay because Vonda said bribery was the way Hutch did business with the Indonesians.

Iwan was to find what mosque Rudi attended, and then, for even more money, Iwan would go to that mosque and speak to the person who should know about Rudi's unclean heart.

❀ ᷜ ❀ ᷜ ❀ ᷜ ❀

It's hard to tell the rest, but you see how I need to get it out. I wasn't sleeping well and got up at five. I was starving, but it was too early for breakfast, and I decided to take a walk on the grounds. It was just after first light, and the lush greenery shimmered with emeralds of dew. Early mist hovered over the distant swimming pool, making it ethereal and mysterious. I freed Rocky from the kennel to join me, hoping it was too early for security to catch us. He followed me to a lounge chair near the pavilion, but began to bark and run back and forth between me and the pool. I tried to shush him, but he was beside himself. Finally, I walked over to see what he was carrying on about.

Rudi floated in the pool. Rudi with a plastic bag tied over his head for good measure. Rudi past help. Rudi dead. I don't know when I started to scream. Before or after I tripped over his tape recorder that had the message on it that he had taken his own life.

I have no recollection of time passing until Lila insisted I lie down on the settee in our alcove. Miriam found a cold cloth for my head. Vonda went all the way back home to get tranquilizers for me. It was Jo who found Rocky on the grounds and put him back in his cage. By midafternoon the shock had worn off, but we still couldn't imagine why Rudi had done such a thing.

Then Lexie asked her driver, Bazuki, and he said it was because of *malu* that Rudi had chosen to cast aside his physical body, hoping for redemption in another life. Jo looked it up in her Bahasa Indonesia dictionary. *Malu* meant Rudi had lost face.

"I think these people make too much of that," Lila said.

"It *is* their culture," Vonda said. For once she sounded defensive about the Asian part of herself.

"Well, it *is* a scandal for the hotel," Lexie said.

Miriam's voice trembled as she spoke, "You just never know how long you have, do you?"

"But to do it to yourself is just … is …" I didn't know where to look.

Jo said, "Imagine how his mother must feel."

"We should do *something*," Miriam said.

I could see the others were having second thoughts about the part we'd played in this. I couldn't stand the thought they might blame me, so I said the first thing that came into my head. "We should pay our respects, that's what, go to the viewing or whatever they call it here." Everyone began to talk at once.

"Should we take something?" "Like what?" "Food? Flowers?" "There'll be lots of praying I suppose." "We should go NOW." "Yes, they bury right away." "What do you wear?" "Does my hair look all right?"

"Maybe we should ask Celeste if she wants to go," I said.

"Let her conscience be her guide," Vonda said.

"Yes, it's no affair of ours," Lexie said.

"She wouldn't dare show her face," Lila said.

Looking around at everyone, I saw it was all Celeste's fault again.

❀ ❧ ❀ ❧ ❀ ❧ ❀

Miriam, the only one who ever paid attention to my eating problem now, was in the other car. Halfheartedly, I stuffed down two bananas, three Dutch chocolate bars, and two Danish. At last Jo said, "For gawd's sakes, Sharon."

Bazuki knew the way and said, if I understood correctly, that everyone connected with the deceased was not only welcome but expected to appear. Soon we were deep in the bowels of a Jakarta we'd never known existed, with narrow roads hardly more than a path, each sisal and card-board house oozing more people than it could possibly hold, men and women relieving themselves before our very eyes. We came to a street that couldn't possibly hold another person. The *polisi* had closed the road to vehicles, and were directing traffic around it. There was no other choice but to get out and walk. We seemed charmed, the crowd making way for us as we now passed shacks with red-tiled roofs we'd seen from the windows of our cars or looked down on from our rooms. Everyone else followed yellow paper flags tied to trees and poles, and so we did, too.

I glanced at our group as we walked. Their steps were eager, their eyes inquisitive, unclouded by any doubt. We were doing the right thing.

They were still preparing the body when we squeezed into the stucco house in a better neighborhood than the one we'd passed through. I didn't want to see what the water had done to Rudi. I looked around the room and saw a picture frame lying face down on a table. I turned it over, and Rudi's soft brown eyes questioned me. His tape recorder beside it mocked me. Finally, I made myself look where he was lying on a woven mat. I guess he hadn't been in the water that long.

A woman dressed in the traditional *kain* and *kebaya,* her head covered, was washing the body with flower petals. Her eyes were swollen and red. Now and then a dry sob passed through her. She wore no makeup, no jewelry, but it was Celeste.

An old *ibu* placed cotton with a strong spicy odor under the boy's armpits, between the buttocks, and on top of the body. Other women wrapped him in white cloth and then packed the cloth with cotton, mothballs, and crushed flowers. They sprinkled it all with cologne. Someone crossed Rudi's hands, right over left. Then the others tied three more layers of cloth around him. They all stepped back, except Celeste. She put her hand over his clasped ones, and I heard her say, "Sleep, little brother."

The Indonesians began to pray, and I wanted to—God, I wanted to—but the words stuck in my throat. I looked at my friends, but couldn't read their solemn faces. I couldn't bring myself to look at Celeste whose eyes I felt all over me. When I finally looked up, everyone in the room was denouncing us with cold accusatory eyes.

The room was hot and close. I wanted out but didn't know how to get out. People sitting cross-legged crowded the floor space. Mourners gathered at the door and looked in through windows. The men began to chant. We were the only ones standing now, not knowing where to move arms and legs, or whether we were expected to sit or pray. We had no idea of the protocol, and I hoped for some sign from Celeste, but her eyes were downcast until one terrible moment when she gave us a fierce look that sent us stumbling and pushing through the sitting bodies—even though their heads were bowed.

At the door, I took one last look at the real Rudi. And then at the real Celeste. We fished out *rupiah* notes and presented them to the father, as we'd seen others do, although we had no white envelopes to put them in. He didn't smile; he didn't say *"terima kasi."* He let the bills fall to the floor and kicked them aside. The look on his face was as contemptuous as Celeste's had been.

Outside, angry women shouted what could only be obscenities. They pushed against us and shook their fists, their eyes dark with frenzy, their mouths twisted and distorted, setting up a terrible trembling in my gut. We could scarcely stay on our feet and were quickly swept into the middle of the street where the mob of shouting women herded us together, then encircled us, making us humiliated prisoners of their rage.

Then came an unsettling silence, much worse than the loud, mean voices shouting epithets. Faces were thrust in mine, their eyes condemning. I tried not to look, but they pulled my head up by the hair to see them. I could no longer tell one from the other, but I was looking into the eyes of hell.

Then one of them spit on me. Then another and another came forward and did the same. My friends shrieked as they were spit on. I envied their attempts, although in vain, to break through the circle of women. The sight of Celeste, framed in the doorway, her face an emotionless mask, had paralyzed me.

One of the women picked up a rock from a pile of rubble, handed it to Celeste, and spoke to her in an impassioned way. Celeste stared at the stone as if wondering how it happened to be in her hand. Others put a pile of stones at her feet. The women all had rocks now and were chanting our death knell.

A terrible fury was in Celeste's eyes as she searched our faces, settling on mine. I had to close my eyes. A woman with evil breath poked at them until I opened them. I watched Celeste slowly raise her arm. Pee trickled down my leg. She was aiming at me. My knees buckled and I fell. I tried to crawl away, but seemed frozen. The women forced me to my feet again to face that mesmerizing gaze. Suddenly, as if released by some force beyond herself, Celeste's arm fell. She sagged against the doorway and, released, I slumped to the ground again. She threw the stone down hard. I watched it roll across the dirt and onto the dusty road; then fall into a ditch. I sat in the road, looking up at everyone's legs, my ears deaf to the bedlam.

Nothing is really clear after that. I think it was the drivers who got help. I especially don't remember anything about the police station.

❀ ᨘ ❀ ᨘ ❀ ᨘ ❀

Next morning there was no one in the coffee shop to stop me from making as many trips to the buffet table as I wanted. But I doubted anything could ever fill the void in me now. Vonda sent word that she was too busy to come today. She was replacing Iwan and had interviews. Lexie's maid, Ohney, reported, "*Nyonya* have bad head. Sleep much." But late in the afternoon I saw Lexie leaving the hotel, and I knew she was going to Vonda's to talk things over.

I saw Jo in the hotel drug store. She didn't speak to me, but kept pawing through the book rack like her life depended on it. Finally, she brushed by with five paperbacks. On top of her usual romance novels was something called, "*Wayang and the Indonesian Character.*"

Lila sat in the lobby, well away from our alcove, lighting cigarette after cigarette, a habit we thought we'd broken. All day she hid behind the *Hari Sirapan*, the Indonesian newspaper I knew she couldn't read.

Miriam fidgeted around the lobby for hours, finally pleading "a lot of errands."

No one hates to be alone more than Miriam, but she never asked me to go along. Next day I heard she'd accepted a house the rest of us had turned down, and then without a word she was gone out of the country without a goodbye or anything.

Somehow our plans to hold out until we were given homes together fell apart. Maybe I started it when I went into the office and said I'd take anything, as long as it was right away. Now we meet sometimes over chicken thighs or frozen dog food at Kem Chick's, or at a farewell party or a retirement dinner, but we have little or nothing to say to one another.

Celeste? Despite company disapproval, she drives her own car now. And all her friends are Indonesians—upper class and rich.

PERFECT:
Lexie

WHEN K. D. CADWALDER WANTED TO PROVE A POINT TO WIVES OF men being considered for assignment to Jakarta, he spoke of Lexie Rogers, his rising star in the Far East.

As Vice President of Employee Relations at CAMCO'S offshore operations in the Java Sea, K. D. made sure he attended as many stateside interviews and their subsequent new-hire orientations as possible. Women were why men didn't stay in overseas jobs, and he prided himself on being able to size up which ones were potential trouble and which ones could take to the behavior patterns expected of them.

Mr. and Mrs. Expatriate should be between the ages of thirty-five and forty-five, both with high educational qualifications. Mr. Expat could be a skilled manager, an engineer, a refinery technician, or a refinery construction expert. All K. D. required was that he know his business.

Mrs. Expat was another matter. She should be the kind of woman who wouldn't fall apart because she couldn't find a hairdresser or the brand of canned tomatoes she always used for making spaghetti sauce. He wanted her eager to deal with servants, neither spoiling nor abusing them. He saw her cheerfully converting Fahrenheit to centigrade, boiling drinking water, and ministering to fuse boxes and transformers that adjusted their stateside appliances from 110 to 220 volts. She would love the Indonesian seasons—the one that was slightly hotter and not so wet, and the other that was slightly wetter and not as hot. She should adore all Indonesians and things Indonesian, while obeying company edicts and keeping suitably occupied in her husband's absences. In short, she should roll with all the culture-shock punches.

Yes, K. D. hand-picked his people, but sometimes he had to sell

Indonesia to those he most wanted. That hadn't been the case with Lexie Rogers. In the second and decisive interview, she spoke eloquently about responsibilities to her two children in a foreign culture, and what it would mean to her entire family to learn about a new world. She exuded Southern-lady charm, and with her husband's last assignment to Houston, she was practically a Texan, just like K. D.

Lexie Rogers had scored high on the written test for flexibility and communication skills. In the role-playing exercises, she'd shown superior abilities for tolerance, empathy, respect, and persistence. Her husband, Buck, hadn't fared as well, but his expertise and experience in his work were beyond question. There was no doubt about it: The Rogers family was overseas material.

In Jakarta, Lexie didn't disappoint K. D. When the CAMCO women started wearing long *batik* skirts instead of short ones and sporting gold ankle bracelets, it was Lexie's doing. When a new shop or a new restaurant was discovered, it was because Lexie had already been there. Her two children were the best adjusted in the Joint Embassy School. Six months of the Indonesian language had made her comfortable, if not fluent. She had already purchased rattan pieces to supplement her furniture shipment and yards and yards of *batik* to cover the windows of the house she didn't have yet. Old K. D. raved about "the most adjusted couple we've ever had in Jakarta." And everybody knew who Mrs. CAMCO was, even if none dared call her that to her face, not even her best friend, Vonda Hutchison.

❀ ⤳ ❀ ⤳ ❀ ⤳ ❀

Lexie ran down the sixth-floor hall of the Hotel Borobudur, desperate to get to her room. She'd heard K. D. was on the premises and heading her way, but she couldn't resist—she stooped and grabbed a bottle of ketchup and a bottle of Worcestershire sauce from the room service tray on the floor outside a door, then shoved them inside her huge carryall where they clinked against two others already there.

Once inside room 629, Lexie breathlessly pushed through the clothes to the back of the closet. She added the bottles to the others in a nearly full box. In Buck's side of the closet, behind the safari suits she'd had made for him for five dollars each, were 62 cakes of soap and 57 rolls of toilet paper. Once in their house, she wouldn't have to buy any of these things for maybe a year. Every little bit of money she could save brought her closer to home. Buck had said, "Quit bellyaching. Come up with fifty or sixty thou, and we can go back to New Orleans."

"Finish," Ohney's lilting voice rang out. "Go now." Lexie's maid stood in the doorway of the bathroom where she'd been washing out Lexie's undies. The warmth between them was genuine; they had been comfortable with each other from the beginning.

Ohney waited to be dismissed, but she seemed in no hurry now that Lexie was back. But Lexie had no time for one of their chats. She looked quickly around the room; everything was perfect. The knock at the door came. Lexie tied her apron, took a quick look at her hair in the dresser mirror, and grabbed a measuring cup and a spoon. She motioned to Ohney. The maid opened the door, then sank to her feet in a half-bow, half-curtsy.

With K. D.'s towering presence, the room seemed smaller but just as cozy. Lexie watched him take in the pork tenderloin, fresh from the toaster oven, already sliced by Ohney and ready to pack in tomorrow's lunches. He noticed that Lexie was mixing up a batch of cookies for the after-school arrival of her children. His eyes wandered to the crock of cheese spread next to the full ice bucket, the candles waiting to be lit. He would assume Buck's arrival to be imminent, that he was home from offshore and working his four required days in the office before returning to the platform in the Java Sea.

Ohney's eyes pleaded with Lexie's.

Lexie smiled and patted her shoulder. *"Besok—jam sepuluh. Ohney menawar untuk Nyonya."*

Ohney smiled back and melted out the door.

Lexie answered K. D.'s raised eyebrows. "I had a chance to hire an older woman, well recommended by the Pattersons. Since I have to pay her to keep her till we move, I put her to work here." Lexie dropped spoonfuls of cookie batter onto a small baking pan. "The roomboys aren't thorough, and she more than makes up her salary by sewing and doing my bargaining."

What she wasn't telling him was this was another way to fudge on their hotel expense account. Ohney did all their laundry, but Lexie put down charges from the hotel for it. But what would he think of her cooking in the room? Everybody was doing it now to save expense money, and Lexie was the one who had started it. The room had a refrigerator, and the company did expect them to buy lunch things, but Lexie was cooking gumbo or beans and rice six nights a week now and charging the company for eating out.

K. D. took in everything in the room, right down to a pair of Buck's boots Ohney had polished until they were a mirror. Lexie's stomach muscles tensed, waiting for his appraisal to end. She noticed he was combing his hair in the opposite direction now, trying to get a few sparse hairs to cover a balding area that had grown larger since the last time he'd checked up on her.

He spoke finally. "Little lady, you're the best damn cope-er I ever did see."

Lexie relaxed. In his eyes, she was still perfect.

K. D. put his arm around Lexie's shoulders and she tensed, awaiting the pass Buck insisted K. D. would make one day. Terrified, she stared up into his beefy, red face and forced a smile. Would she always be able to keep one step ahead of K. D.?

Topping herself every time he showed up was getting harder and harder, but they wouldn't dare fire her husband as long as she kept dazzling old K. D. with her footwork. Buck had a long history of losing jobs in the oil business, but living hand-to-mouth was all over now, with Buck's overseas salary. If they could stick it out for eighteen months, they wouldn't even have to pay US taxes. If Lexie could be frugal, they should be able to buy another house and start a nest egg for the children's college. She racked her brain trying to think up something she could impress K. D. with, and then he came up with it himself.

"Little lady," he said, "I'm going to get some photograph fellas up here next week, and we're going to make us a show so those women thinks they want to come here can see what it's really like. You won't mind someone following you around for about a week making a movie, will ya? We'll do hotel living now, and then when you move into your house, we'll show them that kind of living here, too. The good Lord must of sent ya to me. Yes, he must've."

"I've got a lot of ideas for that, K. D.," Lexie said, making her voice and face enthusiastic. Just then, Buck unlocked the door and walked in. His eyes didn't smile when he saw K. D.'s arm still around her, but his mouth did, and he stuck out his hand.

"You're a lucky man, Rogers," K. D. said. "A very lucky man." He turned to Lexie. "I didn't get my grape juice this time, but I'll be going now anyway."

How could she have forgotten? She'd always had it on hand for him since the first time he'd said, "I don't suppose you have any grape juice around." It was not something she normally bought, but she'd made a lot of points that day when she happened to have a bottle the departing Lisa Anderson had given her.

"Do stay and have some," Lexie invited, sweetly brazen. There wasn't a drop in the room. She evaded Buck's glare.

"Got to run, little lady, another time." K. D. opened the door. "Remember our picture show." Then he was gone.

Buck stormed over to the king-size bed, ripped back the covers, and snorted. "I suppose you did it right on the spread. Maybe that animal took you on the floor? Or did I walk in too soon?"

"I've told you and told you," Lexie said. "You have nothing to be jealous about—over K. D. or anyone else." She shuddered a great sigh at the suspicion still in his eyes. "This has got to stop, Buck. I can't even be pleasant to an Indonesian desk clerk without you thinking I want to sleep with him."

"What about last Wednesday night? You didn't call me offshore. I been pondering which of those single guys were onshore, and I'll figure it out, don't you worry."

"I can't go down to the office every evening to call you on that radio-telephone. I have children to tend to—and I get tired."

He eyed the ice bucket, the two old-fashioned glasses beside it. "A little tête-à-tête with old K. D. With me onshore? You losing your marbles?"

"It's for you and me. I thought it would be nice. The kids will go to the pool. Maybe we could relax and try to enjoy each other for a change."

"Vonda was probably here. You two drinking in the middle of the day, weren't you?"

"Buck! Stop it!"

Next would come—"I don't like your hair that way" or "How much of my money did you spend this week?" or—

Right on cue, Buck said, "Change your blouse. There's a spot on it."

In spite of herself, she looked for a spot, knowing she would find nothing. It tore her up inside. Every time she felt good about herself, Buck took it away from her. All she really had anymore was Vonda, who had been closer than ever since the Rudi affair. Of course there was K. D.'s high regard for her. Yes, she had a picture all right for old K. D.

TAKE ONE: CAMCO WIFE'S CONTRIBUTION RECOGNIZED BY COMPANY
LEXIE ALONE AT DESK IN BEST HOUSE IN JAKARTA, HARD AT WORK IN PAID POSITION AS COMPANY AMBASSADOR TO INDONESIA. CHILDREN ENTER. LEXIE LOOKS AT PHOTO ON DESK OF BUCK, WHO IS ON ASSIGNMENT IN THE FIJI ISLANDS.
LEXIE:
I'M SO SORRY, DARLINGS, BUT WE'RE ALL ALONE NOW. YOUR FATHER HAS GONE NATIVE.

Sixteen-year-old Sister and fourteen-year-old Sherman burst into the hotel room, throwing their books down, grabbing for the cookies Lexie had managed to keep from burning.

The dark, brooding pout on Buck's face was replaced by a look of affectionate affability. "Hi, shitheads," he said. "Give Daddy a kiss."

Tomorrow, he might claim that he had fathered neither child and Lexie was a whore, a cheat, and a liar besides. What would K. D. think of the real-life pictures she could stage for him?

TAKE TWO: CAMCO WIFE PREPARES FOR OVERSEAS ASSIGNMENT
LEXIE PLEADS WITH BUCK TO GO TO A MARRIAGE COUN-SELOR, TO LET HER GET A JOB TO PAY THE BILLS, NOT TO TAKE THEM SO FAR AWAY. BUCK SAYS THEY HAVE NO MAR-ITAL PROBLEMS, THAT WORKING OVERSEAS WILL SOLVE EVERYTHING. LEXIE SELLS HOUSE AND MOST OF FURNI-TURE TO PAY OFF DEBTS.
LEXIE:
(CRYING ON PLANE TO JAKARTA) I WILL NEVER SEE NEW ORLEANS AGAIN.

"Mama? Sally Anne to Mama. Where are you?"

"Beam that woman back to earth!" Sherman's giggles stopped only when he'd shoved a cookie into his mouth.

"What is it?" Lexie began piling cookies onto a plate, trying to look preoccupied. "I'm busy, Sister."

"They made Sally Anne have the test today," Sister said.

Her daughter had started referring to herself in that inane way because she didn't want to be called Sister anymore. Lexie had been call-ing her that ever since Sherman was born, and couldn't seem to break the habit. Lexie was still called Sister by some of her own family.

Lexie racked her brain. She didn't remember Sister studying for any test.

"Get an A as usual?" Buck asked. "Lexie, did you get my beer?"

"If you'd look in the cooler in the tub—"

Sister made a silly face. "They made me have the urine test for drugs."

Lexie and Buck exchanged a look. He threw his head back and drew deeply from the bottle of Bintang beer. "Did you pass?" he asked.

"Daddy," she squealed. "Of course I passed."

Lexie let out the breath she'd been holding. "Of course she did, Buck."

Sherman threw himself across the bed. "I'm going to refuse it when they get around to me. Bobby Ford says they can't make you. People have rights. And it's invasion of privacy or something like that."

"Damn right!" Buck said. "We shouldn't let them put our kids through all that. If we stood together on this and all the other bullshit the company piles on. Like how they don't want us driving here and how we have to give Indonesians jobs as servants. It's all horseshit."

Lexie thought carefully about what she would say. Her kids' lives might depend on it. Somehow she mustered the courage to contradict Buck, making her voice calm and rational as she spoke of the school being a responsible one, concerned for the welfare of its students and the expatriate community at large. "And I think it would be a good idea if our schools in the United States had mandatory testing for drugs on the same random basis."

"Bobbie Ford said his mother—"

"Shut up, Sherman," Buck said. "That's a bunch of do-gooder bull you're giving us, Alexandra."

Lexie steeled herself for the tirade that always followed his calling her "Alexandra."

"The company should step in and say they can't do that to our people. I've worked for other companies better than CAMCO. They let these Indonesians pull all kinds of stuff on us, let them work side by side with us when they don't know shit from Shinola. I tell you—"

"That's what you're here for, Buck, to nationalize Pertamina Oil, to train these people to take over." Lexie felt a great relief. For a moment she'd thought he'd be down at the office complaining about school, but as usual he'd twisted the subject around to how rotten CAMCO was.

Sister said, "Sally Anne thought it was no big deal really, except for being pulled out of class and the catcalls and smart remarks."

"Bobby Ford said his mother—" Sherman paused and looked at his father, but Buck was too busy spreading cheese on a cracker to tell him to shut up again.

"Yes," Lexie said. "I'd be very interested to hear about Bobbie Ford's mother."

"She went to school and made a scene about the testing."

"And he wasn't in school today, was he?" She turned to Buck. "The Fords are being sent home."

Buck set his beer bottle heavily on the dresser. "You're shitting me."

"No, it's true. She refused to sign the paper allowing the test, and big Bob was called in and told to be ready to leave in one week."

"It's not right! Just not right. What we put up with from this company, and then they can turn around and do a thing like that over nothing, absolutely nothing—peeing in a bottle, well damned if—"

TAKE THREE: CAMCO WIFE'S FIRST IMPRESSION OF
JAKARTA
LEXIE SITS AT BOROBUDUR HOTEL POOL WITH SHERMAN
ON THIRD DAY IN INDONESIA, DELIGHTING IN TROPICAL
CLIMATE. TEENAGE WAITER OFFERS SHERMAN A PACKET
OF WHITE POWDER. LEXIE HURRIES SON BACK TO ROOM,
LECTURES ON PERILS OF LIVING THIS CLOSE TO THE
GOLDEN TRIANGLE.
LEXIE:
(TO BATHROOM MIRROR) SOMETHING AWFUL IS GOING
TO HAPPEN HERE.

Suddenly, she wanted to be in the deep South. Telling anecdotes about her family to anyone who would listen didn't come close to being there. "Buck, could we go home, too? Just get out of here," she heard herself say.

"You know I'm done in Houston. Blew it. There's nothing to go back to."

"I mean back to New Orleans. We were happy there, and you could get a job on one of the platforms in the Gulf and—"

"Sure, baby, sure," he said.

"Daddy, no! I've just made some friends," Sister said.

"And I finally got on the golfing team!" Sherman wailed.

Buck hadn't taken his eyes from Lexie's. "You can go anywhere you want, my little money manager, as soon as you save—"

"I can't—" A loud banging on the door interrupted them, and she was glad.

Sherman opened the door, and Vonda, in *batik* evening pajamas and ivory jewelry, entered clanging giant cymbals. A string of waiters followed, carrying caviar and salmon mousse, paté, breads and crackers, and great carriers of champagne packed in ice. Vonda directed the placement of everything, then began hanging up Valentine decorations, including a large cardboard Cupid she plastered to the dresser mirror right over Lexie's pictures of her aunts and uncles, cousins and second cousins.

The *Ramayana* dancers, appearing this week in a special show at the hotel, glided in, undulated their arms, arched their toes, swept and swayed around the crowded room, then melted away. The *Batak* singers from the Merak bar strolled around the room, instruments strumming. They stopped abruptly, placed a serape around Lexie and Buck, and began singing, "Happy Anniversary to you…"

Vonda's husband, Hutch, pushed in a cart holding a huge cake ablaze with sparklers. The *Bataks* began playing again, alternating between the room and the hall where the overflow of guests congregated.

"I hope you don't mind. The decorations are recycled from another party, but everything else is just for your anniversary," Vonda said. "I couldn't resist."

"Auntie Vonda shooting the money gun at us again," Sherman said in such a loud whisper that Lexie gave him a fierce look. Then, remembering herself, she put her arms around her husband. He pulled her tight against him and gave her a long, passionate kiss. Everyone clapped. Champagne was poured, and shrimp on tiny daggers passed. Lexie smiled at Vonda.

TAKE FOUR: CAMCO WIFE FORGES LIFE-LONG FRIEND-SHIP

LEXIE AND VONDA SHOP IN HOUSTON'S GALLERIA FOR COTTON DRESSES TO WEAR IN JAKARTA. LEXIE AND VONDA HAVE HIGH TEA AT RAFFLES HOTEL IN SINGAPORE. LEXIE AND VONDA EXPLORE JAKARTA WOODCARVER'S SHOP AND *BATIK* FACTORY. LEXIE PUZZLES OVER HOMEMADE VALENTINE, SHOVED UNDER DOOR. ADDRESSED TO MRS. CAMCO IN VONDA'S HANDWRITING.

LEXIE:

(READS ALOUD) ROSES ARE RED, VIOLETS ARE BLUE, NO ONE COULD BE AS PERFECT AS YOU.

"I was just going downstairs to buy Lexie's favorite flowers," Lexie heard Buck lie to Hutch as he groped in a drawer and came up with the loathsome necktie he loved so much.

The demands for her attention scarcely got through her flash of fury at him wearing it again, and after they'd talked about it, too. He never considered her feelings, and never …

"Lexie, do you think I should order more champagne?"

"And where did you say you found this pottery, Lexie?"

"This is Noreen and Skip, Lexie. They were in Libya when a friend of mine was there, and I didn't think you'd mind if—"

But Lexie couldn't focus on anything or anyone except the cartoon hero's face on her husband's tie—spaceman Buck Rogers.

"Mama, we want to go to Blok M to the bowling alley with the Peterson boys, okay?" Sister's words, and the realities of Jakarta, brought Lexie back to herself.

"What's wrong with the bowling alley right here in the hotel?" No, she didn't want them in Blok M, especially after dark, especially the bowling alley. She understood prostitutes and God knows who else hung out there at night.

Sherman said, "Franz is going. We'll be all right."

Lexie had to weigh that. It was true they were in good hands with the Petersons' driver, who had been to university, spoke English well, and was the most reliable of any of the drivers.

"Let 'em go, Lexie. Don't be such an old party pooper," Buck slurred. "I'm having a wonderful time at our party. The kids don't want to be here with us. And what the hell's wrong with Blok M anyway?"

TAKE FIVE: CAMCO WIFE'S FIRST OUTING IN JAKARTA
LEXIE SKIRTS LITTER AND MUD IN THE LABYRINTH KNOWN AS BLOK M, BORDERED BY BOUTIQUES, PHOTO, AND HANDICRAFT SHOPS. ITS CENTER, A SPRAWLING BUILDING OF SHOPS AND STALLS; ITS HEART, A FOOD MARKET—DIRT FLOORS, REVOLTING STENCH OF THE FRUIT CALLED *DURIAN*. BROWN BODIES JOSTLE, BROWN FACES STARE, TATTERED BEGGARS CLAW.
LEXIE:
(IN SHOWER SCALDING PANIC) I CAN'T DO THIS. I CAN'T. I CAN'T.

"If Franz is going …but get him over here so I can talk to him," Lexie said, the responsible and well-adjusted mother, "and be back by eight-thirty."

The party, getting bigger and drunker, overflowed all the way down the hall to the elevators. Lexie worried they were annoying the manager, who had a suite at the end of the corridor. Everyone else who lived on the floor had joined the party. She looked up, aghast to see Buck and Hutch and Cory Matheney dragging the fire hose out of its glass case and down the hall, giggling like little boys playing a prank. Everyone was laughing and cheering them on, so Lexie laughed too, and then quickly downed two glasses of champagne.

Buck and his cohorts didn't come back to the room, and Lexie smiled and chatted and passed the paté, all the while vacillating between worry and suppressed anger, trying to shut out the remarks:

"Hey, where's old Buck Rogers?"

"Probably blasting off to the twenty-fifth century. You get a load of that tie?"

"Where do you suppose he got it? Remember those old movie serials?"

"Buster Crabbe, wasn't it? Or was he Flash Gordon?"

"Buck's more like Roy Rogers if you ask me. Ha, ha, ha."

Lexie tried to keep her Southern-lady composure in spite of her chagrin. Why did he do this to her? Fleetingly, she wondered if the way she had to struggle to see that he kept this job was worth it. Then she squared her sagging shoulders, remembering who she was, who K. D. had made her.

The party missed Buck and the others he'd taken with him and trooped off to look for them. Lexie dragged behind, wondering who was going to wind the fire hose and put it back. They followed a trail of lipstick-stained glasses, plates of dried-up food, and overflowing ashtrays until they found the others at the rail of the arcade floor overlooking the grand lobby. Buck Rogers was studiously running up the down escalator, his infamous necktie flapping. When he got to the top, he'd ride down and do it again. Everyone in the lobby was watching. His embarrassed party guests were not sure how to react.

Someone gave a rebel yell, then, "Attaboy, Buck!"

Lexie stood at the top of the escalator while her husband, the jackass, grinned up at her. Everybody watched to see what she would do. She stepped onto the escalator. When she got to the bottom, she waved to the crowd above. Then, quite sick to her stomach, knowing there was nothing else she could do, Lexie grabbed Buck's hand and together they raced up the down escalator.

A great cheer went up from the assembled party. They began singing, "For she's a jolly good fellow." Lexie smiled and basked in her perfection.

TAKE SIX: CAMCO WIFE STALWART IN ANY SITUATION
LEXIE IN MODEST BLACK DRESS ACCEPTS CONDOLENCES WITH DOWNCAST EYES, DABBING THEM WITH HANDKERCHIEF. A CONVENIENT CORONARY? THE HORRIBLE TRAFFIC? PERHAPS AN EXPLOSION OFFSHORE? LEXIE AND CHILDREN ON PLANE. LEXIE PUTS BOX OF ASHES IN OVERHEAD COMPARTMENT, SMILES BRAVELY. LEXIE CLUTCHES PURSE WITH INSURANCE CHECK INSIDE.
LEXIE:
WE WILL BE HOME SOON. EVERYTHING HAS TURNED OUT FOR THE BEST.

❀ ↝ ❀ ↝ ❀ ↝ ❀

"*Untuk lumpia, kita pakai tepung terigu, telur, air, vetsin,*" Mrs. Sumardi began the cooking lesson.

"Did you get that?" Vonda whispered to Lexie. They were sitting in the doctor's wife's kitchen with six other women. Before them was a large table filled with ingredients and measuring utensils. Out the window was a pathetic garden obviously untended except for what looked like herbs. An immense banyan tree was its only beauty.

"To make egg roll skins we need flour, eggs, water, and salt," Lexie translated.

"I don't know why I let you talk me into this. I am not the language teacher's best pupil."

"We've been through this, Vonda. It's a good way to learn the names of Indonesian foods. You can instruct your *koki* better. And you might want to cook these things yourself."

"Me cook? Never."

"Anyway she always switches to English after she gets rolling."

Right on cue, Mrs. Sumardi said, "Today's menu is *Soto Ayam* Chicken Soup, the *Lumpia,* and *Tempe Manis,* which is a fried sweet soybean cake." She passed out pages of recipes written partially in English and partially in Bahasa Indonesia.

Vonda squirmed in her chair. Lexie glanced around at the other cooking students. There were four expat women who had been here last week and two new Indonesian women. Lexie smiled broadly at them. It was her duty to make as many friends of Indonesians of her own class as possible. Lexie had joined the Women's International Club, which was run by Indonesian women whose husbands were in high places. "You should join WIC," she whispered to Vonda. "It's a fantastic experience."

TAKE SEVEN: CAMCO WIFE SOCIALIZES WITH INDONE- SIAN PEERS
LEXIE SIPS LUKEWARM TEA AT WIC MEETING AT MIEN DARYANO'S HOME. LEXIE DOES NOT OFFER LEFT HAND, TALK TOO LOUD, OR DO ANYTHING ELSE THAT COULD BE MISINTERPRETED. LEXIE TELLS COMMITTEE ABOUT COUSIN HAROLD'S ALLIGATOR. THEY MURMUR IN DUTCH. LEXIE BREAKS OUT OF PRISON OF SMILES, POLITENESS, AND LITTLE IRRITANTS TO RUSH TO HOTEL TO FIND OHNEY.
LEXIE:
(COMFORTABLE AGAIN) HOW CHEAP ORANGES ARE NOW THAT THE CHINESE NEW YEAR HAS PASSED.

"To make the sauce we use five chilis, garlics, two glasses of water, and if you do not want this *sambal* so hot, you can—" Lexie tuned back into the lesson.

They measured in grams, liters, and kilos. They chopped and minced, mixed and rolled. Then, high on the smell of coconut oil, they were banished from the kitchen while the doctor's wife and her servant finished cooking the food, which they wrapped or put into plastic containers for the students to take home and try out on their families.

Lexie and Vonda chose a bench beneath the banyan tree. "It's hard to believe this tree has been here hundreds of years," Lexie said.

"Lexie, there's something you need to know—" Vonda hesitated. "It's Buck."

"All these gnarled roots. Isn't it magnificent?" Lexie looked into her friend's eyes, waiting. Maybe he'd made a pass at Vonda. No, he was a lot of things, but not unfaithful.

"He's—well—gone off the deep end, and management—Hutch says…"

"What has he done?" Lexie undid the bow of her wraparound skirt, then tied it again. But it wasn't perfect. She tried again.

"Offshore, he puts down any good work that's done. He rides his men unmercifully. You know you can't make these people lose face, and well, Hutch thinks some of them might even arrange an 'accident' if Buck's not careful."

"I'll speak to him." Lexie smiled at an Indonesian woman, one of the other cooking students, who looked out at them from the kitchen.

"That's not all." Vonda took a deep breath.

Lexie steepled and unsteepled her fingers, finally putting them firmly in her lap to keep them from trembling.

"When he's onshore, he sets up camp by the mail room and buttonholes everyone who comes for their mail. He downgrades the company, even some supervisors by name. Hutch says—"

Lexie got up and motioned the woman watching them to join them. She would tell K. D. all about Mrs. Sumardi, the doctor's wife who taught Indonesian cooking. She'd already played up the woman who ran an art gallery and the general's wife she met at Iwan Tirta's *batik* shop. And now there was this woman.

"You're Jono's wife, aren't you? How wonderful to have a husband who is both a golf pro and a captain at the military base. Vonda, have you met my pro's wife? He's the one who told me about these cooking lessons. Jenni, may I call you Jenni? Let's get together for golf soon?" Lexie pulled out her pocket calendar. "What day is good for you?"

❀ ჴ ❀ ჴ ❀ ჴ ❀

For most of the long ride back to the hotel Lexie and Vonda didn't speak. Finally, Vonda said, "Are you going to do something about Buck or what?" Lexie couldn't deal with it right now. It was too fresh, and she was afraid Vonda would suggest something that Lexie didn't want to do. Vonda had a way of making Lexie see things her way. Like the time they sat in the Nirvana Room at Hotel Indonesia, looking down on a nighttime, light-bejeweled Jakarta that camouflaged the shacks and slums, side by side the tall office buildings and modern hotels.

TAKE EIGHT: CAMCO WIFE RELAXES IN ELEGANT SUR-ROUNDINGS

LEXIE:
DOESN'T IT BOTHER YOU? HOW CAN YOU BEAR TO THINK WE WERE IN ANY WAY RESPONSIBLE FOR RUDI'S DEATH?

VONDA:
YOU SAID WE COULDN'T TALK ABOUT THIS ANYMORE. THAT'S WHY I TOOK YOU TO ANYER BEACH, RIGHT? TO GET OVER IT.

LEXIE:
I DON'T UNDERSTAND THIS LOSING FACE STUFF. DO YOU?

VONDA:
YOU THINK I KNOW EVERYTHING ABOUT ORIENTALS. YOU KNOW I TRAVELED EVERYWHERE WITH MY FATHER. I BARELY KNEW MY JAPANESE MOTHER.

LEXIE:
I JUST CAN'T GET A HANDLE ON IT.

VONDA:
YOU SHOULD BE ASKING SHARON, NOT ME.

LEXIE:
I FEEL SORRY FOR HER. ALL THAT WEIGHT, AND SHE'S SO DOWN ON HERSELF. I SHOULD HAVE TAKEN MORE RESPONSIBILITY, RECOGNIZED—"

VONDA:
OH, STOP! CELESTE, RUDI, SHARON—THEY'RE THE ONES TO BLAME. I CAN'T SEE IT ANY OTHER WAY.

LEXIE:
BUT WE SHOULD HAVE BEEN NICER TO SHARON. SHE'S ONE OF US. WE SHOULDN'T—

VONDA:
YOU JUST DON'T GET IT, DO YOU? THERE ISN'T ANY "US."
INDONESIA FIXED THAT. WE'LL NEVER BE THE HERD
AGAIN.
LEXIE:
VONDA?
VONDA:
YES.
LEXIE:
I'M STILL ...MRS. CAMCO?
VONDA:
YOU'RE STILL MRS. CAMCO.

Vonda broke the silence. "And they say I'm inscrutable. Don't you ever
have a bad day now and then?"

"Buck's just misunderstood, that's all. I'm sure these circumstances are
exaggerated."

"By me?" Vonda sounded outraged, and Lexie didn't know what to say
to soothe her. Not when she had to be loyal to Buck.

"By me, Mrs. Perfect?" Vonda asked again.

"At least I don't buy my friendships. I don't desert my one true friend
every whipstitch for someone else. I don't take over people's lives with
money. And I don't go around telling people my mother is coming for a
visit any day now. Do you really have a mother, Vonda?"

Lexie stopped. Where had all that venom come from? And for what?
Because her friend had told her truth she wouldn't face. Now Lexie had
gone too far. She knew all too well that Vonda's mother, who always promised to come but never did, was the heartbreak of Vonda's life.

Lexie hated herself in bruised silence the rest of the way to the
Borobudur. She started to walk away from the car, but then couldn't bear
for Vonda to be mad at her. She walked back and tapped on the window.
Vonda rolled it down, the look in her eyes noncommittal.

"Mrs. Sumardi—" Lexie said. "Did she say Pasar Majestic was where we
could get that mortar and pestle we need to mash those chilis?"

"What you need, Lexie," Vonda said, "well, I don't know where you're
going to get it."

❀ ᨒ ❀ ᨒ ❀ ᨒ ❀

Grand Marnier trickled down a spiral of orange peel and was deftly set aflame by the waiter, engendering ooohs and aaahs from other diners in the Toba. It cast just the right light on Lexie's smiling face, the damask table-cloth, the sterling silver.

The waiter transferred the liqueur to the waiting goblet of coffee, topped it with whipped cream, and presented it to Lexie with a flourish. The camera rolled on. The other diners clapped, and the string quartet began to play. Lexie brought the house specialty to her nose, breathed its fragrance, took a sip. The photographer waved and disappeared out the door.

"I'm glad I trusted you to come up with the right moving pictures, lit-tle lady." Across the table, K. D. saluted her with his snifter of brandy. "What else did you get today?"

"Me, having a hotel breakfast in bed. Me, directing the driver. Me, inspecting my empty house. Me, surveying the garden. Me, shopping for *batik* at Iwan Tirta's. Me, buying *banka* tin mugs. Me, studying with Mrs. Lydia, the Chinese language teacher. And oh, yes, grocery shopping at Hero's. I thought the ladies back home would be particularly interested in a modern grocery store with its large selection of gourmet foods and toilet articles."

"I have to hand it to you, Lexie. You are Mrs. CAMCO." K. D. smiled a benevolent blessing.

When he called her that, it didn't raise her hackles. Instead, she basked in the validation.

"Buck due back in Friday?" he asked.

"I can hardly wait. These separations are difficult."

"Oh, but think of the reunions, my dear."

Lexie batted her long eyelashes and returned his gaze with what she hoped was a demure expression.

"You should be done with our project by then and able to give your complete attention to your husband," he said. "Our men need that after a tour offshore. And there's something—I mean I heard that—now I'm sure it doesn't amount to anything. But if you could speak to Buck about being a little less aggressive with the nationals, even a little less outspoken. After all, you have the perfect marriage. He'll listen to you."

He saw the consternation on her face before she could mask it. "Now, now, dear, it's really nothing. I know the best damn company wife we've ever had can handle a few of Buck's peccadilloes, can't she?" He looked at his watch. "I have an appointment at the Petroleum Club. Gotta run. I'm depending on ya," he called over his shoulder.

Lexie drained her goblet, an overwhelming sense of inadequacy telling her to have more; no, a good oil wife, a real Southern lady, shouldn't sit alone drinking in a public place. She reached for her purse, but then Vonda was pulling out the chair K. D. had vacated, her usually serious face wreathed in smiles. "My mother is coming. In two weeks. Don't look at me that way, Lexie. She really is this time, and I'm taking her to the Long-Staying-Guest-Party just to show everybody she exists. You'll love her. She's tiny and has this doll-like face and…"

"Tell me the truth, Vonda. Was she a geisha?"

Vonda busied herself ordering them another *Kopi* Borobudur, not meeting Lexie's eyes. Finally, she said, "Six years since I've seen her. I can't wait for you to meet her."

Lexie was glad Vonda wasn't holding a grudge against her even though there had been reports that she had taken up with Justine Cassidy. Lexie had learned to ignore these temporary alliances.

The liqueured coffee warmed Lexie's stomach and oiled her tongue. "Things don't stay the same, Vonda. I mean, sometimes people aren't what we think they are, or even what we want in our life anymore."

Vonda's eyes narrowed. "Have you thought of divorce?"

For a minute Lexie couldn't breathe, but she had to talk to someone, and surely she was safe with Vonda.

"Some lives just won't disentangle," she said. "Divorce wouldn't work for us." This restrained admission was the best she could do toward confessing her marriage wasn't perfect. She'd always thought she could make it so by being perfect herself.

The ache deep inside Lexie seeped out before she could stop it. "You don't know how lucky you are, do you? I wish someone would look at me the way Hutch looks at you. Then I wonder, what would I do if someone did?"

"Buck told Hutch that he's going to bag this job, that he has offers from Libya and Iran."

"You know Buck. It's all talk. He likes the money he's making here fine. The kids are doing well in school. Everything's perfect. I'm just tired tonight. Forget whatever it was you thought I said. Now, let's find that carpet factory tomorrow. Sisal rugs will be fine for us, but I can get you orientals there to add to your collection just as beautiful as any made in Taiwan."

❀ ↝ ❀ ↝ ❀ ↝ ❀

The red brocaded walls of the Crystal Room screamed at Lexie. The glare of the glittering chandeliers made her temples pound. She looked around at the same people, at the same affair she'd been to every month for the past six months. It annoyed her. It smothered her. But she would do her Mrs. CAMCO duty at this Long-Staying-Guest-Party. Ready to do battle, she approached a grinning chef. These cooks were here to answer complaints, or so management said. "Can you tell me?" she asked, smiling broadly, making her voice as sweet as possible. "I was wondering how the food can be so wonderful in the Toba and so horrible in the coffee shop. It is the same staff, right?"

He whipped out a paper and pencil. "You name, Madame? I will have the head chef get back to you personally on this."

Her eyes were drawn to the exhibition another chef was performing. He had a series of sharp knives in the air, juggling them, dodging them. The flashing, spinning steel set up an aurora borealis behind her eyeballs. Where was Buck? He'd said he had to meet someone. She was always on edge when she didn't know where he was when he was onshore.

Mr. Jedtandi, the hotel manager, who pretended he didn't notice the food odors coming from her room, pulled Lexie toward a young Indonesian woman. "Miss Indonesia, Nani Daryano," he said. "Meet our most special long-staying guest, Mrs. Buck Rogers."

Lexie cringed as the reigning beauty queen looked her up and down, amazement in her eyes.

Miss Indonesia laughed. "But it's a joke, no? Mr. Jedtandi makes fun. You are surely not married to a comic book character?"

"If your real name is Algernon—" Lexie said, trying to appear amused as well.

Mr. Jedtandi, embarrassed over not knowing what was so funny, began apologizing, as did Miss Indonesia.

"I must find Mr. Cadwalder," Lexie mumbled as she made her escape. Pinpoints of light, signaling the approach of a migraine, exploded before her. Oh, God, don't let Buck show up in that awful tie, or worse, that helmet he'd conjured up somewhere. The vise holding her head tightened. "Have you seen K. D.?" she kept asking as she pushed by familiar faces looming a her like surreal movie characters. Everything about the elegant room seemed bizarre now. She turned away from the sickening sight of food and put her hands over her ears to mute the piano someone must have forgotten to tune.

When she finally found K. D., he had Justine Cassidy in tow. "You know this little lady, Lexie? She has a brilliant husband, a regular geological whiz kid, really going places with the company."

Meaning my husband's a stupid oaf and a jerk besides, about to lose his job if he doesn't watch out. K. D., I'll straighten him out. Really I will.

"She kind of reminds me of you," K. D. went on. "Lots of moxie, you know?"

Meaning you've got her in mind for my replacement? Right on. I hear you,

K. D., but Mrs. CAMCO is all I got. Please!

"Get her out there golfing with the executives' wives like you do, Lexie. Give her a break."

Over my dead body. Besides, we've all made up our minds about Justine Cassidy. I couldn't do a thing to make her acceptance more than the superficial thing it is.

"I'm getting a headache," Lexie said, making a big show of digging in her evening bag for Excedrin. "If you'll excuse me—"

She snaked through the boisterous crowd and stopped to wash down the tablets at a fountain gushing champagne. Suddenly, Jo Moody and Lila Hoopes backed her into a corner.

"I'm so sorry," Lila said, "but maybe it's for the best."

"Why didn't you tell us?" Jo whooped.

"What we'll ever do without you, I don't know," Lila said.

"I don't know what you're talking about." But the feeling in the pit of her stomach told Lexie she knew very well.

"The divorce, of course," Lila said.

"Ooops." Vonda started to back away.

Lexie made her voice as quiet and calm as she could. "There's some mistake. I'm not going anywhere. Divorce is the last thing on my mind. Tell them, Vonda."

"Has anyone seen that new kid, Noreen? Hutch and I promised to take them to that Woody Allen movie at the Petroleum Club." Vonda didn't respond to Lexie's searching gaze.

Lexie dragged her away from the others. "You know I never said DIVORCE. What are you doing to me?"

"Well, you should say DIVORCE," Vonda said, mimicking Lexie's tone. "There's something else I didn't tell you—well, Hutch thinks we shouldn't see so much of you and Buck right now. You know, we'll be tarred with the same brush." Lexie's betrayer disappeared into the crush of bodies, calling, "Mama, I want you to meet—" Lexie searched the crowd again for Buck. She tried to will him beside her, but instead it was K. D. who materialized. "Lexie, I'm so sorry. I just heard. This is most disappointing. I had no idea you had marital problems. On the other hand—" His eyes seared hers, his hand on her back scalded.

In shock, she staggered away. It had been strictly a business relationship. How could he make it ugly and not special anymore?

Over by the door, there was some commotion. Lexie tried to see. A fight perhaps—Buck wouldn't?—but there was too much noise to hear, too many people she couldn't see through, and everything was such an effort.

It was more important than ever that she find Buck.

She started to push her way to the door, but rowdy revelers propelled her near the table where a great roast was being carved. She watched the blade cut through a huge hunk of meat, watched the blood run out, watched a chef wipe it clean with a cloth before he started slicing for the next person. She couldn't seem to take her eyes from the knife, the blood. But there was Buck at the cake table, laughing and gesturing and flaunting that damn tie. It mesmerized her, drew her toward him.

"Buck," she said, in a voice she'd never heard before. All she really wanted to do was lay her dizzy head on a cool pillow. "Buck," she repeated, finally getting his attention. "I have to tell you. about K. D." What was she doing? Buck was so hazy.

"Hey, baby, you don't have to worry about that old fart anymore."

Ripples of nausea forced her to turn from the cake, a perfect replica of the Hotel Borobudur.

"I've quit this fucking company," he said, "as of this afternoon, and you know what, kiddo? You don't have to worry. I got another job. We're on our way to the Alaska pipeline within the week."

Lexie looked at the cake. Suddenly, the knife beside it was in her hand, and she was stabbing the flour-and-sugar Hotel Borobudur, stabbing it until it toppled and crumpled, just as her life had.

"Baby, baby, what's the matter with you?" He was trying to take the knife from her but she wouldn't let him. "You can be Mrs. ARCO now."

Lexie plunged the knife where it belonged—right through the necktie face of spaceman Buck Rogers and into the heart of her husband.

TAKE NINE: CAMCO WIFE'S ASSIGNMENT COMPLETED
LEXIE ON PLANE. MALE PSYCHIATRIC NURSE PUTS ASHES IN OVERHEAD COMPARTMENT, THEN SITS BESIDE HER IN EMPTY FIRST-CLASS CABIN CAMCO HAD TO BUY UP TO GET HER BACK TO STATES. EMPTY, EXCEPT FOR PSYCHI-ATRIST WHO SITS BEHIND HER. EMPTY, EXCEPT FOR K. D. CADWALDER WHO SITS AS FAR AWAY AS POSSIBLE. K. D. CADWALDER, WHO HAS RESIGNED FROM INTERNATION-AL SERVICE. LEXIE ROOTS THROUGH PURSE, THEN CLUTCHES PASSPORT, KNOWING WHEN THEY SEE SHE'S "MRS. CAMCO," EVERYTHING WILL BE ALL RIGHT.

HOUSE SITTING:
Srikandi

KANDI HOWARD GOT THE IDEA WHEN SHE WAS PAINTING HER TOEnails Hot Tomato Red. They could house sit! It would be financially easier as well as getting them into something that felt more like home. She mulled over the idea between bites of a pizza she'd made herself, upsetting her sister's servants. Returning to her native Indonesia with her Caucasian husband, a professor on sabbatical from a small Indiana college, had not been what she'd expected. Affluent foreigners from all over the world had come to Jakarta to form joint venture companies to exploit Indonesia's resources. And this had driven up the rental rates for suitable housing beyond the Howards' small budget.

She loved being with Fawn and Leo and their children, and Leo's partly Dutch parents. Tante and Uncle were as kind as if the Howards had been their own children. It had been eleven years since she'd seen any of them, but their house, with Leo's furniture factory attached, was hectic, crowded with workers and a steady stream of customers. Fawn and Leo's life was busy with friends, visiting relatives, and their children's activities. Kandi yearned for the kind of privacy she'd learned to enjoy in America. She'd quite forgotten that Indonesians, who hate being alone, did everything together. And she really missed having a Western bathroom.

Yes, house-sitting for Americans, who didn't want to leave their homes and servants unattended for two months while on holiday, was the perfect solution. She had found out over Danish pastry and coffee at the American Women's Association meeting that the Walburtons were looking for someone. She was a little worried about dealing with the formidable AWA president, Mildred Walburton, but it had all worked out, and Kandi and Jack Howard had slipped into this house as if they'd known no other.

Now she sat at a desk in the study, writing down her menu for their first dinner party. She had no doubt it would go well. The Walburtons' servants were most cooperative, especially Sukami, the old *ibu* who went around giving Kandi a thumbs-up gesture, saying, "*Bagus sekali.*" And Sukami was right. Everything was "very good."

Kandi's gaze strayed out the window to the courtyard where Sukami was greeting one of the medicinal herb-drink vendors who worked their foot-traveled routes from early morning till late afternoon. The *Jamu* Lady carried a basket of potions on her back, held by a scarf, the *selendang.* In a graceful motion, she swung her wares down onto the driveway. Sukami talked excitedly, gesturing toward her stomach. It was a scene Kandi remembered from her childhood—after her Javanese mother had brought her here from Ambon in the Moluccas, the Spice Islands, where she'd been born. It was after her Ambonese father died.

The *Jamu* Lady was so young—thirteen, fourteen? Her youth suddenly brought a picture to Kandi's mind—herself, even younger than that at the ceremony for her first menstruation, an initiation into the mysteries of womanhood by her women relatives and close friends.

Her mother had prayed: "You little girl, blood of my blood, soul of my soul, may you grow into a woman as fertile, as strong, as resilient, as eternal as Mother Earth."

Kandi had listened in awe, feeling the magic forces of Mother Earth flow through her, transmitted by the power of her mother's soft-spoken words. Even very young Indonesians knew how powerful words were.

The elder women gave their blessing by showering Kandi, who was wearing a sarong with a special design, with water scented with fresh, sweet-smelling flowers and fragrant leaves. In memory, she drank her first *jamu,* smelled its intriguing odor as though the intervening years had never happened. "This dirt has a special meaning," she heard them say. The bit of earth they'd bade her pick up with three fingers of the right hand from the hole that had been especially dug in the garden was warm to her remembered touch.

Absently, Kandi doodled on the menu list, still smelling the jamu and the earth steamed together. She sat in a daze, back in that long-forgotten world where magic was real, where people were close to the universal, where the unexplainable was normal. She had felt those forces again since her return here, but she had no intention of giving in to them. Remembering that the words hadn't been able to make her fertile after all, she passed on to other memories.

Once, in the same traditional dress the *Jamu* Lady wore–a *kain*, the wraparound ankle-length skirt made of hand-blocked *batik* in the island of Java's national brown-and-yellow design, and the *kebaya*, a tight, three-quarter length jacket of lavender organdy embroidered with green and yellow mythical birds—Kandi, then Srikandi, had been a secretary at the US Embassy. Then, too, her jet-black hair was smoothed back from her face and into the traditional chignon at the back of the head, held by an ornamental comb.

She saw herself running into the street at lunch hour to drink the medicines of leaves and plants, roots and barks, and fruits that were said to cure anything or to be the key to the Javanese husband's eternal devotion. But she had wanted a brash, blond foreign correspondent from America instead. Their grand love affair had taken her away from Sukarno's strife-ridden reign in Indonesia to a land where her beauty treatments would be Estee Lauder, her medicine Midol and One-A-Day vitamins—with Geritol not too far off, she thought wryly.

Outside, the girl knelt in the dirt, cleaning the used glasses in water from her basket. Then she slipped out the gate as Musti, the yard boy, opened it for the Walburtons' car, bringing Jack home from his tennis match at the Hotel Borobudur. Kandi rushed out to meet him, determined not to allow these insistent memories of life before her husband to disturb her idea of who she was now.

Jack looked like a triumphant Greek god in his white shirt, shorts, shoes, and socks. "We skunked them!" He rubbed sweat from his face with the towel Sukami handed him.

The driver, Wijoro, said, "I watch. *Tuan bagus sekali.*"

Young Musti reached into the car for the racquets, finding the chewing gum Jack always brought for him. "*Terima kasi, Tuan,*" he said, grinning at his gift. "*Bagus sekali.*" Sukami came out the kitchen door. "*Makan ikan untuk makan malam, Tuan. Bagus!*"

It's not good they speak Bahasa Indonesia to us all the time, Kandi thought. It *was* her native language, of course, and Jack spoke it fluently, but it wouldn't help the Walburtons if their servants got into the habit of not using the little English they knew. Another good idea came to her. She would teach them more English. She was so grateful to be in this house, it was the least she could do.

Once inside, Jack grabbed Kandi, giving her a very satisfactory kiss and a quick pat on the tush. She answered with a swift hug, then drew back, her nose quivering at the state of his sweaty shirt. "The showers for you, mister."

Later, they sat comfortably sipping iced tea. Jack wore a sarong, short-sleeved white shirt, and sandals—clothes most older Indonesian men wore. The only thing missing was the little black overseas cap. While she tried to hang on to America, he totally embraced Indonesia again in a way she didn't know whether to resent or envy. He rode the careening Jakarta buses, without fear, though everyone said they were rife with thieves. He interviewed everyone in sight as he had in the old days, winning over all who first said "no."

He often went to mosque with Muslim friends, or brought them—as well as Hindus, Buddhists, and Christians—home to dinner to discuss how their religion was practiced in Indonesia. The consensus of these conversations was that most Indonesians were tolerant of the variety of religions in their country. And whatever their faith might be, they also embraced centuries-old animistic beliefs that even a volcano had a spirit and the universe itself a soul.

"Are you happy?" Jack asked.

"Why wouldn't I be happy? We're alone, and after this there's the Moodys and the Cassidys to sit for." She squeezed lemon into a new glass of tea. "But I never dreamed Jakarta would be so expensive." She picked up the stuffed Balinese monster, the *Barong*, sitting on the end table near her, put it down again.

"Bali would be nice, wouldn't it?" As usual, he'd read her thoughts.

What would be nice would be a bedroom look, she thought, but difficult to manage in the middle of the afternoon with servants lurking about. They hadn't had much love life lately. Their room at Fawn's had been next to that of Tante and Uncle. With such thin walls, they'd lain there just holding each other. Jack had been too tired since they moved into the Walburtons'. He spent a lot of time out on the streets or at the embassy, drumming up free-lance stories to send back to the USA, and he had started teaching at the University of Indonesia. Perhaps Indonesia was her rival.

Or perhaps her beauty was fading, her womanly wiles on the wane. But sexuality wasn't the secret of success in a marriage, was it? Kandi had learned to allow their relationship to change and develop, but she often wondered if there was something she was not giving Jack. Perhaps he was being put off by her take-charge manner now that she was back in her own country.

"I'm sure glad USIS supported me in getting the Fulbright," Jack was saying. "The check will come soon. We can go anywhere you want when I'm not lecturing."

She thought of home, the social life at Clifton Arnold College in Richmond, Indiana, the attention she received as wife of the respected journalism professor. Jack hadn't wanted her to work, but to stay home and wait for the family that would come. Still childless at thirty-eight, she'd blended into his college world with a part-time job in Admissions.

"You mean what *you* want. You were the one who really wanted to come back."

Why had she said that? She'd been more excited than he when they were planning the trip. She had felt like she did in their early married years in Seattle, when her exotic beauty had charmed his newspaper cronies and she'd enjoyed being the window dressing for an important man. But he'd given up editing the leading daily paper for peace and quiet, he said, and moved them to the sleepy Midwest.

"Just tell me what you want, Babe," Jack said. "I'll get it all for you. I've just given you Indonesia for another year. Don't you want it?"

Yes, she did, she knew in that instant. She yearned for its beauty, its mystery, the arts, her relatives, the slower pace, the new way of seeing things—familiar again, yet foreign. But having it terrified her. She didn't know why.

Jack bent his head over his glass, rattling his ice cubes. Straight hair fell into his eyes. "It's just like it was when I found you—only without the fear of some Indonesian Communist bashing my head in with a rifle butt because I'm American."

For no good reason, she felt tears in her eyes. "Nothing's changed, but everything's different." She didn't expect him to understand. She wiped her wet cheeks before he looked up.

"We're going to miss the Indy 500 time trials next month for the first time in seven years," she said, and he smiled.

❀ ᔧ ❀ ᔧ ❀ ᔧ ❀

Sukami, Wijoro, and Musti sat with pencils and pieces of paper around the Walburtons' magnificent old oak table, faces eager, anxious for their English lesson.

First, Kandi had to re-enforce her position as the one in charge here. Because they were the same nationality was no reason for them not to give her the full respect she deserved. When she went out back Musti had not even stopped chewing his lunch while answering her questions. Wijoro had told her a faintly blue joke. When she wanted Sukami, she was often off, shrouded in white, on her knees facing East, saying prayers. These were not big things, but irritating.

"Before we begin, I have made changes in your work schedule. I do not believe *Nyonya* Walburton will mind. They are for the better." Her tone was imperious, with just the right amount of determination to show she would brook no infractions. The list was long.

"Wijoro, I see you taking chances in traffic. If you are stopped for violations, the fine will come out of your salary."

"I want the patios scrubbed *every* day, Musti."

"*Ibu*," she directed the term of respect meaning "mother" to Sukami to show she appreciated the respect the older woman showed her. "I cannot stand germs. I cannot be sick here. Wash down everything in the kitchen with Milton. And in the bathroom—"

That hadn't been on her list, but she realized she'd feel better if it were done. When she lived here before, she'd never noticed how filthy and disease-ridden this country was.

She smiled to take the edge from her orders and began the English lesson. She had thought of a novel way to do it. It would be something familiar to them. All Javanese knew the *Wayang* stories.

"This is just a short paragraph about the Battle of Karna," she told them. "You write down what I dictate." They scrabbled for their pencils. "Turn it into English this week, using these books." She handed them brand new Bahasa Indonesia/ English dictionaries. "Ready?"

They looked at her expectantly. She began to read from the paper in her hand: "*Dewi Wara Srikandi, daughter of King Drupada, the noble, proud, and haughty wife of Arjuna, bitterly told her husband how Karna humiliated her by shooting off her dress, forgetting to explain she forced Karna to fight her, rousing her husband to fight him.*"

Wijoro and Musti had the glazed, mesmerized looks on their faces of any *Wayang* audience wanting more.

Sukami's eyes turned suspicious. "What kind of name is Kandi? I worked for a foreigner once who called her dog that. Kandi? Sweet to eat?" She laughed and laughed, clapping at her own wit.

"My real name is Srikandi," Kandi said. "*Tuan* shortened it when we met." She stood straight and tall, proud as she'd always been to be named for such an aggressive character, rueful that like that mythical princess, she didn't always act like a dignified lady.

Wijoro stood, head bowed. "Noble Srikandi," he said. Musti covered his mouth to suppress giggles of delight.

Sukami said, "I am *santri*, devout Muslim. We forbid *Wayang*. I despise it and everything connected with it." She walked to the sliding door and spat across the yard, a betelnut splash as red as fresh blood.

If Kandi could have seen herself, she would have realized she tossed her head arrogantly, as haughty as the *dalangs* made their Srikandi puppet appear on the *Wayang* screen. Wijoro stared at her, struck dumb, as if she really were the character.

"It is only a little paragraph to get you started writing English, *Ibu*," Kandi said.

"Nothing to offend your religious beliefs." They stared deep into each other's eyes, and Kandi turned away first. Her throat felt sore, and she couldn't seem to clear it.

She was getting a headache, too.

❀ ↝ ❀ ↝ ❀ ↝ ❀

Mornings, Sukami served Kandi's yogurt, papaya, and wheat germ in the sunny breakfast room, which was furnished in white rattan splashed with navy blue upholstery, accented with lime and butter pillows on the settee. Assorted Indonesian knickknacks cluttered a coffee table. One such morning, Sukami leaned an elbow on the glass-topped breakfast table and said, "I see in Wijoro's newspaper a married woman was raped by a monkey in the jungle in Sumatra." Kandi buried herself in the *International Herald Tribune*.

The next morning it was "*Nyonya*, did you know a bag of snakes was lost on the way to the zoo?" Another day, "I see in the paper this morning, *Nyonya*, a girl in Central Java says a *dukun* she hired as a matchmaker raped her on the river bank. Can you imagine a man of healing and supernatural powers doing that?"

"Really, Sukami, I don't believe in witch doctors and mystical healers any more."

"Do not say that, *Nyonya*! Something or someone might hear you. Better say your prayers to Mecca so nothing bad happens."

"I'm not Muslim, *Ibu*, I'm Christian."

The next morning Sukami didn't stop to chat and laugh, but hurried away, murmuring she had work to do. The day after that, Kandi said, "*Ibu*, tell me your plans for the Hajj." She felt sure that would get the woman talking because she'd told Kandi how she saved her *rupiah* for the trip every Muslim was expected to take—the trip to Mecca. "If only I make enough money before I die," she'd said once.

"Much too serious to talk to you about," Sukami said, and Kandi thought it her imagination that the woman's tone was insolent.

One day Sukami stopped cleaning a mirror to turn to Kandi and say, "Why do you wear short pants like Western women?"

"I like them. They're cooler."

Sukami rubbed hard at a spot on the glass. "Your hair, it is too curly and unbound for a married woman."

In spite of her annoyance, Kandi excused her servant because of her age. "It suits me now. It's who I am."

Sukami's crafty eyes commanded Kandi's attention. "Tell me other *Wayang* story about Srikandi." Kandi remembered something amusing and took up the challenge:

"Princess Srikandi liked manly arts such as archery, and at one point spent a part of her married life as a man after she'd persuaded the hermit, Mintuna, to exchange his sex for hers. As the man, Kandihawa, she helped King Dike drive away his enemies, but eventually reunited with Arjuna as a woman again."

Puzzlement etched the housemaid's face. "I never hear of her being a man before." Sukami picked up her pail of water.

"It is not in the Javanese *Wayang*, but in a version of the original Mahabharata. My Indian friend, Nelia, told me about it."

Sukami lugged the pail toward the kitchen. At the door, she stopped. "Maybe you think like man. Maybe you want to be man, like Princess Srikandi." She looked back over her shoulder. "Maybe you want to fight like a man. Ehhhh?"

Suddenly Kandi felt dizzy and disoriented. She stumbled to her room. She wasn't American. She wasn't Indonesian. And the servants didn't know who she was either.

❀ ꒰ ❀ ꒰ ❀ ꒰ ❀

When Kandi woke in the bed she'd fled to with her confusion, the curtains were drawn. The ceiling fan stirred the manufactured cold air. She didn't remember seeing the Jamu Lady, but she must have. She felt the green paste from out of her past daubed on her forehead. No, Sukami had done this. Kandi went looking for her.

The old woman sat over a glass of tea, winding her long gray hair into a knot at the nape of her neck, her eyes still heavy from her late afternoon nap.

Kandi didn't know why she had to make a point of it, but she did. "I told you I don't believe in any of this anymore."

Sukami peered up at her, fastening a comb to hold her hair. "You feel better now?"

Kandi was surprised to realize she did.

With narrowed eyes, Sukami drained her tea glass, then stood up. "You are not so smart, Princess Srikandi. Or should I say Prince Kandihawa?" War had been declared.

Musti opened the gate. Motioned by Sukami, the *Jamu* Lady entered and set out her potions on the patio. As if in a dream, Kandi sat down on a peacock chair across from her. "The headache paste," she said.

"I can have for you tomorrow. It's late in the day now. All gone," the *Jamu* Lady said.

"*Nyonya* wants something for to make baby," Sukami said, leering at Kandi.

"I do not! I'm much too old for babies."

Sukami rolled her eyes and made a comic face. "She needs something for the husband."

This was too much. "Sukami, I want to see you inside. Now!" Kandi stood up.

"Something for beauty then, *Nyonya*," the *Jamu* Lady said, and began her sales pitch. "*Jamu galian singset* to keep the body firm and strong, *Jamu padmosari* for a clear skin and radiant complexion?" She lowered her voice, "Perhaps *jamu galian sepit wangi* to keep the vagina clean and supple?"

A picture of her mother's great beauty at the menstrual ceremony came back to Kandi, and she ordered it all—and rice powder to absorb perspiration, and the jelly of the *ilyat baya* to make the hair grow as well.

"Drink this now, *Nyonya*, I bring the rest tomorrow." The *Jamu* Lady offered her a glass.

"When you prepare it, *Nona*," Sukami said to the *Jamu* Lady, "make only half dose. This *Nyonya* has a foreigner's constitution now."

Kandi was furious, but she didn't want Sukami to see she'd gotten to her. She had no doubt the woman was demented. If she fired her, she'd be doing Mildred Walburton a favor.

❋ ᛔ ❋ ᛔ ❋ ᛔ ❋

Two weeks later, Jack was late coming home for dinner. "Sorry, I went to the Borobudur for a drink. The UPI chief, Karen Webster, is in from Singapore."

In the kitchen, Sukami banged pots and pans around. Jack raised his voice. "Nelia wanted to know when I was going to bring you by." Kandi went to the kitchen door. "Stop that noise, please," she said. "We're trying to talk in here."

"I work for *Nyonya* Walburton, not you," Sukami called out. Jack raised his eyebrows. Kandi gave a "what's the use?" shrug and closed the kitchen door.

"You're not playing tennis tomorrow, are you? I don't know how you can do it in this heat." She bit her lip. Why was she taking her anger out on him?

"You felt the same way about winter in the USA. You didn't want to do anything because you were too cold."

"I don't remember that." She picked up a deck of cards and began to shuffle them.

He said, "You should have heard them at USIS this morning. Another reporter's been expelled. Chin from Hong Kong's *Far Eastern Economic Review*."

"And one from the French press last week," she said.

"*Far Eastern* wants me to string for them, sub rosa," he said. The unnecessary clatter began again in the kitchen. "Of course, I could wind up getting thrown out, too." They looked at one another. She knew he was going to do it.

"Let's go out," she said, looking at the kitchen door. "I've lost my appetite for eating here. Let's go listen to Nelia sing and not be serious about anything."

"Not serious, huh?" You know that story about the rapist monkey?" Jack grinned. "The story now is that the woman really had a human lover, but she was afraid her husband could tell, so she lied. But my money's on the monkey."

"Yes, the ones we saw at the zoo were quite lustful, weren't they?"

"Actually," he said, "when I was doing an interview at ARCO's training school, I saw a poster on the wall of that very monkey. He wore a stethoscope and a lab coat and was grinning from ear to ear. He was on the phone, too, telling all the guys how good it was."

"Just wanted to play doctor, no doubt," she said.

"You catch on fast. You wanta play doctor?" He grabbed for her, but she ducked him, laughing. She loved him like this, and she did want him terribly—always and forever.

But they were going out, something they hadn't done for a while, and she wanted to tease him a little. "No, I want to hear Nelia sing 'I'd like to run away from you, but if you never found me I would die.'" He pulled her close. "I'd always find you, but you're not going anywhere. As the song says, 'Never, never, never.'"

Kandi knew tonight was going to be different. "I couldn't live without you," she whispered. Reluctantly, she pulled away. "I won't take long."

She did take long, but it was worth it when she saw the old look in his eye. She wore an elegant matching *kebaya* and *kain* of turquoise, embroidered in pink and gold thread, an expensive *ikat* Vonda Hutchison had wooed her with. Matching slippers she'd found at Sarinah's Department Store complemented her outfit. She'd brushed out her usual curls, and her hair flowed around her face, a frangipani blossom behind one ear.

"You take my breath away," he said. "You're the picture of when I met you." He caressed her shoulder, her arm, whispering his love, his devotion, his enslavement.

All the *jamu* was working. It seemed even her hair had grown quickly. She forgot everything but him and the night ahead. He had made brandy alexanders, her favorite, and they carried them out to the car. It was a bit much, but both Wijoro and Musti often bowed before her since they'd found out her name was Srikandi. Wijoro did now as he opened the car door. Musti puffed his chest, pounded on it, pointed to Jack, and said, "Arjuna!"—his changing voice breaking into giggles. She decided to take it all in stride. Unlike Sukami, they seemed to be having fun with it.

Sukami appeared at the car window, tapping on it. A middle-aged woman Kandi had never seen before stood behind her, watching. Kandi rolled down the window.

"This sister, Ohney," Sukami said. "She worked for *Nyonya* Rogers. Ohney's husband very sick, die maybe. I have to go. Need salary. Be back soon."

Kandi looked at Jack. He pulled some *rupiah* notes from his wallet. She handed them through the window. Sukami grabbed them, and without a thank you she and her sister were out the gate.

Wijoro backed the car down the driveway. "I'm going to fire that woman," Kandi said. "I've had enough of her audacity, and heaven knows what she's up to. Dying brother-in-law indeed."

"She's not your servant to fire," Jack said. He pulled her closer to him and put his hand over one of hers.

"She calls me Princess Srikandi all the time now. Am I Srikandi or am I Kandi? I don't know any more."

"You're my wife, that's all you need to be," he said, nuzzling her ear. "And tonight you are very sexy."

Jack spoiled her terribly all evening. They had champagne and the most expensive things on the Toba Rotisserie's menu. He made a generous

donation to Nelia's tip glass when they stopped in the Pendopo after dinner. Kandi didn't object. Last week, he'd sold several free-lance articles, and
they could afford this big night out. There were several people in the
lounge he could have talked shop with, but he concentrated on pleasing
her, making her laugh, making her want him urgently.

Later, they descended valleys of passion, ascended mountains of rap-
ture they'd never known possible. Desire overcame them again and again,
and they saw in this renewal of banked fires that their love could only grow
and grow. But Kandi lay awake long after Jack fell asleep, pondering his
words, "This is who I married."

❀ ᛣ ❀ ᛣ ❀ ᛣ ❀

Evenings now they spent doing and saying romantic things, their ten-
derness a loving foreplay for the nights of deep satiation. Days, Kandi
indulged in herbal sitz baths and the vaginal exercises she'd been taught as
a virgin to keep muscles tight and supple. She went for *lular* treatments,
wanting the yellow cream to remove all the impurities of her skin so it
would be smooth, fragrant, and glowing with youth for Jack.

Sukami had returned quickly with no talk of funerals or continued ill-
ness. She was quiet and withdrawn, giving no trouble. Musti mumbled
something about her going to a *dukun*, and Kandi decided the brother-in-
law really had been sick. But now Wijoro and Musti were getting on Kandi's
nerves.

Every morning Musti would say, "You feel good today, *Nyonya*?" When
she assured him she felt fine, Wijoro would ask, "No sore throat, no
chills?" Sukami was never anywhere around during these interrogations.

Then one morning, Kandi couldn't get out of bed. Her entire body
ached. She burned with fever. Her throat was parched, her lips dry and
cracked. Nausea overwhelmed her. Her bowels rumbled ominously. She
must call around for Jack. She tried to get up, but sank back, defeated. She
fell into restless sleep, waking, sleeping, waking. She didn't know what
time it was, what day it was, where she was.

Someone stared down at her, eyes sharp and inquisitive. "Speak,"
Sukami ordered. Kandi opened her mouth, but nothing came out.

"No, you cannot speak," the housemaid said. "You cannot order me
around any more. You cannot take my work away so I have no means to
save money for Mecca. It is not easy for old women to get work. The foreign Nyonyas want strong young girls."

To Kandi's fevered mind, it was at best a bad dream, probably an hallucination.

"Your power is gone. Your words." The old woman's face loomed closer. "No English or Indonesian to help you now." Sukami grinned a mirthless grin, showing her crimson-stained teeth. "Now you stay in bed. I run house. Because they are afraid of me—Wijoro will wash windows, Musti will do dishes. I have the power now. My *dukun* said so. He gave me a *rapal*."

A mystical numerical formula from a witch doctor had made her sick? "No! No!" Kandi shouted, but no sound came from her mouth. Sukami sat on the bed. Cringing away from her betel-nut breath, Kandi began to shake and shiver.

Sukami cupped Kandi's chin, forcing her to look into her eyes. "You have to learn a lesson, Dewi Warsa Srikandi. You are one of us. You cannot turn your back on our ways."

Mustering all the strength of will and body she could, Kandi managed to crawl to the other side of the king-sized bed and slip over the edge, putting the bed between them.

"Desire for your husband made you distracted and empty, easily entered by spirits." Sukami walked around the bed. "Yes, thinking of your cunt, you let a spirit get in. Perhaps you know the one. Your soul is weak now. Nothing will make you well unless I say you are well."

Kandi decided either she *was* hallucinating or the woman was truly mad. No, these things happened here where minds were not cluttered with the material, the technological. How could she have pushed that out of her mind? She should have known, should have been more careful. Knowledge came to her of the very spirit who would have been waiting for the opportunity. Then she knew nothing.

When consciousness returned, Kandi found she was back in bed in her best nightgown, Sukami sponging her wrists and temples with tepid water.

"Darling," Jack said. "You're awake! It must be dengue fever. I know you have no faith in that British clinic. I can get the embassy doctor to come. He owes me a favor." He smoothed her tangled hair from her forehead. "Sukami, brush *Nyonya's* hair."

"No!" Still she had no voice. She shook her head.

"Does it hurt too much then? Okay, we won't do it. Just rest. I'll go call Dr. Clark."

Kandi nodded again, making lights go off in her head, making her as dizzy as a mad carousel ride. With utter determination, she forced out whispers, "I am Indonesian. Get Indonesian doctor."

Sukami gave her a malevolent smile, gaping and blood-red. Kandi's shivers now were uncontrollable. Jack brought another blanket and snuggled it around her.

"You are serious?" He studied her.

"Get Fawn here," she mouthed. "She knows doctor I want."

"Come on now, Darling, You don't believe—"

"Send away," she managed.

Jack nodded at Sukami, who didn't budge. "*Pergi,*" he ordered, giving her a stern look. She smirked at him, then sauntered to the door.

Kandi motioned her husband closer. "Tell Fawn. No *dukun*. White magic doctor, a *kebathinan*."

"You're raving now, Baby. I'm sure Clark will come immediately."

Kandi had to make him understand, but couldn't make her voice work again. Finally, "Spell on me. Fight evil with good."

"This is nonsense, Honey, the fever in you talking."

"Spirit of miscarried child we left behind … you took me away … entered me … now." The last came out in a croak. "Wishes harm … didn't get to come into the world."

Jack looked at her in disbelief. Weakly, she pulled his head closer. With lips tight to his ear, she managed to rasp, "The unseen is here, all around us." She laughed mad, uncontrollable laughter that had no sound. Jack ran for the door. Kandi sank into the darkness so greedily devouring her.

❋ ᨆ ❋ ᨆ ❋ ᨆ ❋

When Kandi was aware again, there were many faces around her bed. Fawn was crying. Leo was ashen. Tante and Uncle wore serious expressions.

Jack looked from one to the other. "Are we doing the right thing? It's dengue fever. Don't you think so, Leo?"

There was a disturbance at the door. A man appeared, followed by an enraged Sukami. "It won't work. Nothing you do will work. My *dukun* has more power than yours. Just last year, he stopped the rain for three weeks of the Jakarta Fair."

Jack ran his hands through his hair and looked to the others for direction. They were staring at the stranger in the doorway. Finally, Jack said, "Come in, come in. Let's do it."

The middle-aged *kebathinan* was tall and had a bulbous nose with large pores. He wore Western trousers, a white dress shirt open halfway down his chest where a heavy gold chain nestled. Rolling up his sleeves, he approached the bed.

Sukami didn't take her eyes from him. No one thought to ask her to leave.

He went to all four corners of the bedroom, briskly returning to the bed in between each trip. He said Kandi's head must be at the bottom of the bed. She cried out in pain when Jack moved her.

"My magic is omnipotent." The *kebathinan* addressed the assembly. "I am adept at exorcising evil spirits. My power is superior because it can only be used for good, because it is in the name of Jesus Christ."

Sukami spat her red poison in his direction.

Leo whispered to Jack, "Give him some money, or he'll go on like this forever. Jack put *rupiah* notes on the bedside table, weighing them down with a brass ashtray. The *kebathinan* smiled thinly.

"Get out of here, Sukami," Jack said. She didn't budge, but stood with her eyes squeezed shut, mumbling an Arabic incantation.

"She may stay," the holy man said. "Her black magic words have no potency. The fight is between me and her *dukun*."

"Your magic won't work," Sukami screamed. "My *dukun* wrote the spell in Arabic, chewed it up, and swallowed it."

The *kebathinan* counted the *rupiah*, nodded to Jack, and shoved it into his shirt pocket. His whole demeanor changed. From a canvas bag he took out bark and a dried plant. He dumped candy from a dish, placed the items on it, and set them aflame with his cigarette lighter. He placed the dish on the bed next to Kandi and began chanting. Nimble fingers fluttered around Kandi's neck faster than the eye could follow, while a wreath of pungent smoke encircled her head.

"You must all leave," he said softly, never taking his eyes from his patient. No one protested but Jack. The others drew him into the living room.

"In the name of Jesus, the Merciful, the Compassionate," the man wailed, "where are you going, Spirit-child?" On the other side of the bedroom door, Sukami screamed Arabic words, drowning out the *kebathinan's* faint chant. Kandi struggled to hear his "*OOOOeeee, OOOOOahhhhhh*." It became louder, then louder. Finally, it was all she heard.

❀ ꙮ ❀ ꙮ ❀ ꙮ ❀

Kandi found herself hovering over a desolate plain. She levitated midway between thick clouds above and a misty sea of nothing below. Her white-magic doctor was still with her, whispering words of comfort. They were old Ambonese words she remembered now.

She became aware of another man standing on the other side of her, leaning on a cane. He wore one sarong knotted at his waist, another as a cape. He used the cane to draw a line from her forehead to her stomach to her feet. Was he there to help her? All *dukuns* were not necessarily evil. Then he began spewing curses and ugly, unnatural words. Sukami's witch doctor had paralyzed her. With his cane, he drew a figure eight above her head. It became a large bubble. Inside, she saw a tiny baby, curled in the fetal position. She felt the most excruciating pain she'd ever known.

"Breathe, deeply, deeply," she heard her own man of magic say, but she had forgotten how. "Innnnnn, ouuuuut," he said over and over. Finally, a great breath shuddered through her, and she was gulping air. The bubble above her burst and shattered into myriad rainbow shards. They re-formed, becoming her other selves.

There was the mixed-up person she'd been on her return to Jakarta after so many years away … the docile American wife … the feisty young Indonesian girl … the happy Ambonese child. It was this child, determined and real, waving the *cendrawasi*, who approached Kandi. She had forgotten how profusely bird-of-paradise grew in Ambon.

When she took the flower in her hand, she became the soul of the slender stalk carried by the child through Ambon's wide tree-lined streets, past the Dutch stone houses and imposing public buildings where the smell of cloves permeated the air. Then Kandi became the child, who turned onto a footpath that led through luxuriant vegetation to the mangrove swamps, then to the water. Perhaps she would find a turtle shell. But the volcanoes rumbled and spoke, the earth shook—and she was frozen to the terror of the moment. The real adult Kandi began to run, but her child-self was reaching, trying to hold her, wailing, "Stay, stay, staaaay … "

In suspension again, back in that vast unnamed place, yellow mist blanketed Srikandi. Far away the chanting continued. *"OOOOeeee, OOOOOahhhhh."* The sorcerers, giants now, towered on either side of her. *Wayang* warriors Arjuna and Karna, dressed for battle, appeared. Vast armies of foot soldiers, valiant steeds, and splendid standards stretched behind each of them. She knew Arjuna would fight Karna for Srikandi, who had been insulted.

Cymbals clashed. Drums reverberated. Conch shells sounded as battle trumpets. With leonine roars and clamorous shouting, the warriors threw themselves upon one another, fighting as if possessed by demons. The air was thick with neighs of chargers, groans of combatants. It was a spectacle, both beautiful and furious. The sorcerers' towering presences alternately diminished and surged, as one and then the other army prevailed.

Horses and elephants fell. Great chariots were crushed. Golden banners were torn to pieces. Arrows flew in all directions. Swords flashed. Then Arjuna and Karna took to wrestling, their *krises* at the ready. Death crept nearer and nearer to Srikandi with each defeat of Arjuna's army.

"OOOOeeee, OOOOOahhhh," came from far away now, but it was enough to give her hope. "Kandihawa, Kandihawa," she heard her male name called again and again. There was something she must do, but she didn't know what it was.

As raining arrows darkened the sky with the clouds of war, Arjuna and Karna jumped from their chariots for one-to-one combat. Wound upon wound they dealt one another, and Kandi grew weaker and weaker, but she clung to the fact that Jack—her Arjuna—was fighting for her somewhere, as was her *kebathinan*. Now Arjuna shot a dart of fire. Karna shot one of water. Arjuna shot arrows like razors piercing the limbs and standard of Karna. Cheers and shouts went up from Arjuna's soldiers. But Karna rallied and shot five golden arrows at Arjuna, pinning him to the ground. The white magic man whispered encouragement. It was up to her now. Desperate purpose and a terrible fury turned Srikandi into the warrior Kandihawa, who put his lips to a conch shell and, calling forth every power he'd ever had, bellowed a tumultuous sound.

The earth trembled, the rivers stood still, the sun set in pallor. "OOOOeeeee, OOOOOahhhhh" resounded again, the great vibrations shattering the hearts of all the enemy. The two *Wayang* heroes and their battle vanished. Kandihawa's triumph had strengthened her, but the confrontation was not over.

In that desolate, eerie place again, her *kebathinan* and Sukami's *dukun* cast long shadows as they faced one another, shouting out magic words—words that alternately healed and destroyed, words that smothered and set her free, words that gave pain and joy. The feelings grew stronger, unbearable, as the witch doctors strained their powers. When she couldn't bear it another minute, their spirits entered her, good and evil each claiming her. In the rending of her being, she ceased fighting them. Down, down went her deeply wounded spirit, dark, dark, darker, dying ... until she found Ambon again, this time filled with the darkest forces, forces that would ... but no, now she is about to know the answers to everything, to ... but instead, the *kebathinan* is smiling down on her gently. And she is looking up at him from Mildred Walburton's bed.

The bedroom door burst open, and Sukami staggered into the room, her eyes wild with fever. She clutched her throat, and moaned low guttur-

al sounds while tears rolled down her leathery cheeks. She knelt at the
kebathinan's feet, her forehead touching the floor. The others stood in the
doorway, staring. Jack pushed by, rushing to the bedside. He drew Kandi's
hand into his and looked deep into her clear eyes.

"Take away. Please. Help me," the old woman's voice rasped. "Meant no
harm. Teach arrogant Srikandi a lesson." She plucked at the hem of the
kebathinan's trousers.

"What the hell's wrong with Sukami now?" Jack asked.

The *kebathinan* said, "I have won the battle of good over evil. Srikandi
Howard's soul has returned to her. Her spirit is clean. I have turned the bad
magic back on her enemy, who is now under a powerful spell." He took
Kandi's hand and helped her to stand. She felt wonderful.

Sukami beat on the wall with her fists, then fell to the ground, rolling
and writhing across the floor, spouting gibberish.

"No!" Kandi stood proud and tall, noble and imperious. "I do not want
this."

"Darling," Jack said, "Please sit down. You've been through so much."

"I want this curse taken from this woman immediately," Princess
Srikandi demanded. "I will not be responsible for doing this to another
human being."

The man of white magic bowed. "As you wish, *Nyonya*."

Sukami dragged herself to Kandi and tugged at the bottom of her nightgown. The *kebathinan* laid one hand on Sukami's head and said words to
unlock the charm. With the other, he took a flower from a vase on the
dresser; with this bird-of-paradise, he touched Sukami's shoulders, her
forehead, her throat, and her chest. He ordered tea, which Fawn ran to
make. When it arrived, he spat in it, rubbed some on Sukami's navel, then
bade her drink it. When she had, a violent shudder convulsed her. Then
she was still, her limbs stiff and contorted.

"My God! My God!" Uncle cried out.

"*Mati! Mati!*" Tante shrieked.

But Sukami was not dead. She sat up smiling, free of the curse. She
turned to Kandi. "I'd have called it off if you'd only begged my pardon."

"Out," Srikandi ordered. "Out of this house right now."

Sukami scurried away, but not before she gave a blistering look of
hatred to all in the room.

Kandi's legs were about to give way. She sank to the edge of the bed. "I
do not feel as well as I thought." Jack helped her under the covers.

"It is best to take things slowly," the *kebathinan* said, starting for the
door. "You will be weak and vulnerable for some time. Maybe even a year.

Yes, you must take care."

Kandi thought of her Ambonese child-self who had visited her in the mystic realm where she'd fought for her life. "I will go home," she said.

"Oh, Darling, no!" Jack was wounded deeply.

"Not to Indiana," she said. "I doubt that will ever be my home again. No, I will visit Ambon."

"It's not the same," Leo told her. "It's full of greedy pearl divers and pirates, and the very primitive so close by."

"Ambon is no longer the jewel of the spice islands, Srikandi," Tante said. "I hear the trees have all been cut."

"Enormous freighters to carry away the timber crowd the harbor," Uncle said. "Their oil has destroyed the famous coral gardens below."

"Fire walkers and grave robbers and worse, little sister," Fawn said, shivering.

The Princess shut her ears to their warnings. Out of her ordeal on the plain, only one thing was certain. The Ambonese child within had told her the way to find her true self. "I will go to Ambon," she repeated, tossing her head haughtily, the noble and headstrong Dewi Warsa Srikandi no one dared argue with. "It is my destiny."

❀ ꒦ ❀ ꒦ ❀ ꒦ ❀

When word came that Kandi Howard had disappeared somewhere in the Moluccas, there was renewed talk of the missing young Rockefeller, as well as of cannibals, and uncharted islands where tribes of peoples didn't even know they were part of a country … the unknown … the unexplained … the unspeakable… .

ON THE ROAD TO THE VILLA:
Ohney

WHEN THE COCK CROWED, SHE WOKE SLOWLY. HE CROWED AGAIN, and she couldn't place where she was. In the distance, the amplified *muezzin* called the people to prayer. The turtle dove in the cage suspended high over the house yard cooed. Someone hawked and spit. A muffled laugh. Snapping twigs for the cooking fire. The crackle of it. Odors of coffee and rice. Ohney was cold. It must be down to eighty degrees. She threw a sarong over her shoulders and went to greet the new day.

It was still gray and misty. She remembered then. They were living in her half sister's neighborhood now, and so grateful this *kampung* had accepted them. The best part had been that it was on the road to the villa where Mrs. Lexie Rogers lived.

A breeze stirred a *rambuton* tree, and she shivered, feeling old—thirty eight, two years younger than her husband, Agus; twenty years younger than her sister, Sukami. So much had happened this year. Her son had taken a wife and given Ohney a grandchild. He had gone out on his own, working for foreigners, too.

But Ohney had lost Mrs. Lexie Rogers, and nothing seemed right now. She needed to tell her son: Be careful. Don't get to like the *Nyonya* or the *Tuan* too much. It can break your heart.

She drew in the odor of the dewy earth and exhaled it gratefully. Living in this *kampung* on the edge of the city made her feel as if she were back in her home village in Bandung. She missed it even after all these years, but no one could make much of a living in the country. The city was the place to be. And there had been the trouble. Even the headman had thought it wise they leave under the circumstances. She had been happy to hear that Jakarta *kampungs* operated in the old way. Members of these neighborhoods were considered one big family, bringing harmony to all by mutually assisting one another and voluntarily sharing each other's burdens in the custom called *gotong royang*.

She had been miserable in their old *kampung* in West Jakarta, its worn-out houses huddled along a canal sluggish with garbage. The people there had begun to think themselves more important than harmony. They claimed it was impossible to maintain *gotong royang* in these days of social unrest.

In the heavy rains, the canal had overflowed, making the neighborhood a morass of mud and undermining the houses. Cholera had come and wiped out most of the residents. Ohney's drawn, sallow cheeks and hollowed body were a testament to her own bout with the deadly disease. With no one left in that *kampung*, they had no choice but to leave. And so they had come to this place where *gotong royang* was strong, a comfort in these times when the government forced modern ideas on everyone.

She and Agus had been truly lucky, just as the numbers conjured by the leader of Ohney's mystical group had foretold. So far her studies with them on the inner life seemed vague and unreal, and she was considering not going to meetings any longer. She had only been to a few, and then only at Agus's insistence she do something to become happy again.

"With your Mrs. Lexie, you became too attached to everyday life," he had said. And so knowing her son and his family were secure and would not fall into poverty or neglect because of any spiritual ambitions she might have, she was making an effort. But nothing she did now seemed to matter much.

She looked around at the sisal houses with cardboard roofs. The glistening grass had grown overnight. She should take a machete to it today. She needed to show her new neighbors that she was eager and willing to assist them. She would also take that job selling fruit in the Blok M *pasar*. She would use the money to share the expense of the circumcision ceremony for the boy who lived next door, just as others had contributed to her own son's circumcision years ago.

There was much to do today. She had promised to take Sukami, who seemed very weak now, to a new *dukun* who had come to the neighborhood recently. Since Sukami had lost her job, she imagined all sorts of things, but it wouldn't hurt to take her to a white magic doctor. She heard her sister praying inside the house. Through the door she saw the prayer rug spread on the dirt floor and Sukami bent over, dressed completely in white, a privilege reserved for those who had made the pilgrimage to Mecca. Sukami was not yet Hajji, but since her misfortune, she acted like she was. Taking time this morning to dress as one had made her late starting her prayers.

Ohney was not *santri* like her sister but *abangan,* She believed in Islam by confession, but actually practiced the old Javanese traditions and beliefs that existed long before Islam came to her country. But lately, she'd been questioning everything she'd ever put faith in.

Just as the sun appeared, burning off the fog, Ohney's husband rode his *becak* into the *kampung.* With its hooded seat for two passengers and him riding behind, the pedicab was a handsome sight. He'd named the tricycle "Java," printing the letters on the side himself. In brilliant colors, he'd also painted a smoking volcano, a placid lake, and a rice field. His muscular legs were bare in short pants, but he wore a jacket to protect him from the cold of his night shift.

"Are you a lay-a-bed? Where's my breakfast? I've work to do before I can get some sleep," he grumbled.

Paying no attention to his bad mood, Ohney followed him inside and gave him a plate of cold rice. He came home every morning this way. She waited for him to get it out of his system.

"Oh, for the days when I was a teacher back in the home village," he moaned.

"Teaching is noble, but we couldn't live on the little pay for it. You know you make more money letting the whores at the cemetery use your *becak* to solicit customers." She knew he was old for a *becak* driver now, his physical powers diminishing. The other drivers in their twenties and thirties were probably jibing him, a grandfather, to quit. She couldn't imagine what he would do if that day came. He'd never go back to teaching.

He'd been so bitter when the other teachers had expected him to charge students for admission, examinations, and passing. It was accepted as *gotong royang* in the home village, and Agus had upset the harmony by refusing. It was an agonizing time for the village and for them, and they had left so there would once again be peace in the place where they were born.

Ohney looked at her sister, sitting in a corner, holding the Ku'ran, looking off into space, mumbling, "There is no god but Allah, and Mohammed is his prophet." Where would they have been when fate turned bad if it weren't for Sukami, who had spoken eloquently for them to her neighbors? But Sukami could not, would not, accept her humiliation at the hands of the American's Ambonese wife, whose magic had been stronger than Sukami's.

"You'll have to change those clothes," Ohney told her sister gently. "Remember, we're going to the *dukun* this morning, and you can't wear that white in public."

"I fixed her. I fixed her good. Right?" Sukami smeared lime on a bright green betel leaf, then folded it around a red betel nut. "And *Nyonya* Walburton wouldn't give me my job back, but she said, 'What a fuss over nothing.'" Sukami popped the betel nut bundle into her mouth and began chewing happily.

Ohney sighed. That old stuff again. There was a lot Ohney could bring up about working for foreigners, too. It didn't have to be the way Sukami saw it. Mrs. Lexie had been kind and considerate, but also firm. She always knew exactly what she wanted. Mrs. Lexie had picked up Ohney's language quickly, and they'd had long talks about being a woman, politics, the history of Indonesia—things Ohney always had an interest in, but she had no one to talk with about them. Mrs. Lexie had a wonderful laugh she used often, but she wasn't happy. No, it was in her eyes, her voice, the tight way she held her body—as if something dangerous might get out.

When Ohney went to the *pasar*, Mrs. Lexie would say, "Buy a little extra for yourself." Ohney always bought oranges. And Mrs. Lexie always wrinkled her little nose; she thought Indonesian oranges too bitter. She didn't have to put Ohney to work at the hotel so she could start earning a salary right away and not have to wait until their fine house came through, but she did. And there'd been new sarongs from Mrs. Lexie's own hoard of *batiks*. That time Agus had the bad toothache from three rotten teeth, Mrs. Lexie had given her extra money. She'd said it was for sewing a party dress for Mrs. Lexie's daughter, but Ohney would have done that anyway, as part of her job.

Agus lit a cigarette, filling the house with the odor of cloves. She couldn't imagine sticking him with a knife. Perhaps *Tuan* Rogers had deserved it, but she would not judge him or anyone else. It was just his unfortunate fate. He had only spoken to Ohney through his wife—"Tell her to do this. Ask her to do that"—so she had never really known him, except to observe that he was mean to all his family. A wave of great fondness for her own husband washed over her as she remembered when their life together had been new and sweet.

Rice had been a year-round occupation for her home village, its ageless pattern of flooded rice fields spreading across the valley in a patchwork of multi-hued greens and ascending the hills in stepped terraces. She'd never forget the joy of transplanting the spring-green rice seedlings, with the rich greenness of a maturing crop in adjacent fields. There had been the dry fields, too, golden and heavy with bursting kernels. She'd cut their stalks swiftly with a crescent-shaped knife, then carried them to the rice cooperative. But what she most remembered was that their only son, Taji, had been conceived as part of the fertility rites when they lay in the rice field just as the rice was about to germinate.

Now she reached out to pat her husband's shoulder, then held out her hand for the money instead. He fished in his shirt pocket and gave her some coins and a few grubby notes.

"If the government hadn't banned *becaks* on the main streets, I wouldn't have to work with the prostitutes." Agus continued his grousing. "*Waduh!* It is better not to hope for anything, be content with little, suffer." He lit another cigarette. "At least the transvestites aren't in my territory."

"You should sleep now," she said. "This work is too hard on you."

"I can't sleep. How can I sleep when there are whispers of that Chinese, who owns my *becak*, raising the license fee again? I tell you, hard work is not rewarded. And there is loss of good manners." He looked at Sukami, who was folding her white clothes. "People do not know shame any longer."

"But here there is *rukun,* the harmony we can share in, my husband," Ohney said.

He smiled. "Yes, and we must contribute to that. I will sleep later. Today, I have promised to go on the other side of the wall to the foreigners' *kampung* with the other men. They say two families are moving in today. There will be many large boxes. We can make new roofs for all the houses from them." She nodded approvingly, and he went to the *mandi* to bathe.

In a while, Ohney left Agus dozing in a chair and led Sukami down the path toward the *dukun's* house, her sister protesting all the way that local *dukuns* were no good, she never used them. She had heard of one in Bogor, and why couldn't they go there? "Hush," Ohney said as they stood in front of the best house in the *kampung*, better even than the headman's. "This is a good woman. I know her from my *kabatinan* group."

"That nonsense," Sukami scoffed. "The only true religion is Allah's. You will come to no good."

Ohney said, "You should talk about anyone's beliefs after the trouble your black magic got you into." Without another word, Sukami led the way inside.

They followed the routine of "*Apa kabar?*" and the expected response, "*Baik, baik saja,*" with the *dukun,* a middle-aged woman with wise and piercing eyes. Sukami placed two hundred *rupiah* under the *dukun's* unopened pack of cigarettes. Ohney went to the kitchen with a small gift of food for the witch doctor's daughter. When she returned, there was more small talk. Finally, Ohney nudged Sukami.

"An Ambonese she-devil has taken my potency," Sukami said. "I need strong magic to return my power."

Ohney said to the *dukun*, "It's true my sister is not herself, but the Ambonese woman has gone away now, they say."

The *dukun* placed her hands on Sukami's shoulders, then entered a meditative trance. When she finally came back to them, she said, "I see rheumatism, old age."

Sukami said, "But I have her hoarse throat. It is the evil eye upon me."

The *dukun* began to chant, "In the name of God, the Merciful, the Compassionate! May the prophet Adam repair Sukami. May Eve order Sukami. Untangle the tangled veins, make the body fluids feel pleasant, make everything well again."

The woman of magic pounded some iron filings into a dust. "For strength," she said. She handed Sukami a ginger paste for her throat.

Placing her hands on Sukami's shoulders again, her eyes shut, the *dukun* concentrated deeply. Finally, she returned to them. "It is done. The spell has reached your twin guardian spirits."

Sukami's effusive thanks were interrupted by shouting outside, and the thud of running feet. "A taxi, a taxi!" someone screamed. "Who would come here in a taxi?"

Ohney ran to see, pushing through the murmuring crowd. She couldn't believe her eyes. It was her son, Taji, proudly paying the driver. His wife, Titin, wore a Western dress and cradled their sleeping baby against her in a *selendang*. Taji wore denim pants and high boots like Mrs. Lexie's husband. There were new gold earrings in the ears of both the baby and Titin. They had not yet visited their mother and father's new home, and Ohney had not expected to see them until their holiday next month. Delighted, she reached for her granddaughter.

The driver pulled children from his taxi doors, but they only clambered onto the hood. One got inside and pretended to steer the big wheel. The driver spoke with anger to Taji, who handed him another *rupiah* note. Mumbling to himself, the man leaned into the car and brought out a large laundry basket of bedding. The crowd stood quietly now, waiting. He opened the trunk and Taji helped him lift out a television set. Oohs and aahs, giggling, and pleased looks rippled through the onlookers. Even more amazing, Titin leaned into the back seat and brought out a black, short-haired dog on a leash. It was so black that seeing the whites of its eyes and the red panting tongue was a shock. The dog barked loudly, and the murmurs of Ohney's neighbors became nervous twitters.

"A feast! A feast!" someone shouted. "The boy has brought us a feast."

Yes, Ohney thought, black dog is delicious. Agus came forward to welcome his son. He insisted on carrying the portable TV inside all by himself.

Ohney watched her excited husband turning the buttons and knobs of the television set. Sukami pawed through the basket of linens. Ohney hugged her blessed grandchild to her, crooning a song her mother had sung to her. The dog began to lick the baby's head. The child had reached the age when it was the tradition to shave and grease her head. Ohney wanted to kick the dog away, but was afraid of it. Her children grinned broadly, not a bit perturbed at the dog's actions. Outside, the voices of Ohney's neighbors, still abuzz with excitement, rose and fell.

Agus inspected the back of the television. "It has no batteries. Did you expect it to run on kerosene? You could sell it maybe. Is it worth anything?"

Titin said proudly. "Mrs. Sharon Matheney brought it all the way from Singapore in a canvas bag on wheels. She hid it under a pile of dirty underwear and didn't have to pay a tax on it."

Sukami suddenly screamed and sat down hard on her bed. She held up a fistful of *rupiah* notes of large denominations she had found secreted between the sheets and blankets. "We are rich! I can go to Mecca! Allah be praised. The spell is working. Already, I feel strong and recovered."

"No, no," Taji said. "It is ours."

"Yes," said Titin, "Mrs. Sharon says she will not be back from her home leave. She wanted us to have money for our future. The television will not work in America, and she said she couldn't bear to look at the dog anymore because he reminded her of something sad."

"I am going to learn to be a driver for foreigners," Taji said.

"I will not have to work while I wait for the new baby," Titin said. "And there should be money left for me to study to be a secretary."

"Yes, we are going to have a fine house someday," Taji said. "You can all live there with us."

"Many children, much happiness," Ohney said, pleased. As modern as her son's wife seemed, evidently she was not interested in the pills they gave away free now to stop babies from coming. Having many grandchildren quickly would make up for her old sorrow at having only one child.

Agus eyed the money. "I would like to be a driver of cars instead of *becaks.*"

"You are too old to learn new things, *Bapak*," Taji said.

"Son, have you forgotten respect?" Ohney's tone was sharp.

"It's just that we've had this good fortune, *Ibu*," Titin said quickly.

Taji changed the subject. "We have come to stay. We can buy our own food."

Agus's face was dark and gloomy. Ohney knew he was trying to hide his anger at being told he was old. As Sukami found more and more money in the basket, Titin kept taking it away from her before she could count it. Ohney gave her wet and fretful granddaughter back to Titin. After the child was changed, Titin set her on the floor, and she began to crawl toward the dog, who had dragged a sheet from the basket to curl up on, and now defied anyone to take it away.

"*Waduh!*" Sukami cried. "What is this? Our babies do not crawl like lowly and dirty animals." She swept up the child, who clutched the dog's fur. The child began to cry. The dog jumped up on Sukami, licking her hands. She recoiled in horror, and would have dropped the baby, except for Titin's intervention.

"Unclean! Unclean!" the old woman wailed, and began to pray in Arabic.

Titin quickly put the child to her breast to still her cries.

"You mean that child had not been weaned yet?" Ohney was shocked.

Taji and Titin looked uncomfortable. They knew they weren't to have sexual relations before the weaning. His semen would mix with her milk and cause the new baby to be sickly. Ohney held her hand on her granddaughter's head, looking for fever. The child stopped suckling and smiled up at her.

Sukami started counting the money again. "Ours, all ours."

"No, *Bibi*, it is not," Titin said. "It is a year's salary, and we earned it."

"We should give a *selamatan* for your good fortune," Ohney said. "Yes, let's," Agus said, "and we will serve roast dog."

The dog ran to Titin and tried to get on her lap.

"*Selamatans*," Sukami said, derision in her voice. "Devout Muslims do not have *selamatans*. I will not come." She spat a red glob neatly out the door. "I will use some of this money to go to the right *dukun* in Bogor."

Taji's fists pounded the table, and his face turned red. "It is our money, and we will do with it what we want. Maybe we'll even take a trip to Bali like the foreigners do."

There was no harmony in the house, and everyone, including Titin, stared at the floor, embarrassed for him.

❀ ↬ ❀ ↬ ❀ ↬ ❀

When Sukami began her midday prayer, Ohney realized Agus had not slept, and she hadn't been to the *pasar* yet. "I'll just run out on the street and get some vegetables for the rice from a *tukang*," she said. She glimpsed a walking restaurant with a glowing charcoal brazier jiggling from a pole on the shoulders of a food vendor, and her mouth watered. Agus sniffed the aroma of roasting meat. "I want *satay* with my rice." His eyes dared Taji to dispute him. "Our son is buying."

Taji nodded sheepishly to Titin, and she pulled a *rupiah* note out of Sukami's hand and offered it to Ohney. Sukami's eyes glittered. "And papaya and some chicken and lots of vegetables for soup."

"And salt and chilies to spice up the dog," Agus said.

Titin hugged the animal to her, and Ohney thought about the different ways of her Christian daughter-in-law. Ohney was not intolerant of other religions. Nice Christians came to her mystical group, along with Muslims and Buddhists. Sukami ran out the door, shouting to all who would hear, "I'm going to Mecca. I will be Hajji."

After their meal, no one napped as usual. Taji managed to get the television set hooked up to the foreigners' electricity. He had found an electric box that was used for the big security lights on the wall between the *kampung* and the American compound.

Mesmerized, they watched "Popeye, the Sailor," a half-hour of commercials, and "Know your country—Jambi Province." Little by little, the men, women, and children of the *kampung* sidled into the house until their packed bodies bulged out its sisal walls. Disagreements broke out as to viewing positions and who was crowding whom, and there were bickering political assessments of "The Home News." It was when "The Quiz" came on that they became really rowdy. No one, not even Sukami, heard the *muezzin* call the late afternoon prayer.

When the arguing drowned out the sound of the program, Ohney turned off the set in an effort to get them out of her house. Agus made a speech about establishing order before they could watch again, but the people were angry and would not listen. Someone turned it back on. Taji went outside and pulled the connection wire from its source. Several women gave him a tongue-lashing when he returned. An old man kicked the television set. A young boy knocked it over on its side. Someone tried to make off with the dog, but Taji grabbed it. Then the jostling neighbors spilled their anger out of the house and into the clearing in front of the *kampung*.

Only the headman remained. "It should be on a pole outside, like some of the villages have," he told Taji. "You have money for such a pole."

"*Lurah*, it is my money, my televisions set," Taji told the headman.

"You should use it for the good of our community," the *lurah* said. "Sharing is the age-old tradition of *rukun* among the people, sharing both the good and the bad." He stalked out the door before he heard Agus's apology for his son.

"One should be willing to sacrifice for the common good," Ohney told her son softly. "Have you forgotten what it is to be Javanese?"

"Yes, he has," Agus answered for him. "Today, young people think only of the material. Too much contact with the Westerners. But they have trained you well as a houseboy. Forget this money. Get a job with a fine Indonesian family. They do not pay as much, but they do not leave either."

"You know how our rich countrymen treat servants, *Bapak*," Taji said. He righted the television set.

"That's only talk," Ohney said. "Just because they are more fortunate than we are doesn't make them bad people."

"Plug it in again, Taji," Titin said. "The baby always watches the story for children at this time."

"You don't understand," Taji said. "We have goals now. Mr. Cory Matheney explained how important that is. We are going to learn things to get us jobs that will make more money so we can have a better home than this someday. Mr. Cory said we could be middle class." Taji's eyes pleaded with his mother and father to understand.

Agus shook his head. Ohney threw up her hands. Sukami had entered, going right to her stash of betel nuts. "Goals? That's some Western nonsense. You can live only one day at a time."

"You have a goal, *Bibi*," Titin said. "You have a goal to go to Mecca." Sukami's answer was a contemptuous red splat out the door.

Ohney slipped outside, but returned quickly, the sound of raised voices following her. "They are calling for a discussion," she said, "for all voices to be heard to decide this matter."

Sukami, dressed in white again, beat her breasts and wailed. "I will never visit the Great Mosque or greet the black sanctuary where I direct my daily prayers to make seven circuits around the surrounding courtyard. I will never—" Coming to herself, she turned toward Mecca and began the sunset prayer, then stopped and sat up abruptly. "It is all your fault because you are stingy," she told the young people.

Ohney buried her face in her hands for a moment, then looked up at her son. "The meeting is about you. It is a grave crime you have committed." She nodded her head to include Titin, too. "You have upset the harmony of this *kampung.*"

"Yes, they should be *jotakan,*" Sukami cried. Ohney was appalled at her sister. It was unthinkable, but possible, that her children would be punished by declaring them socially dead for a certain length of time. This sentence, *jotakan,* would require all, even Ohney and Agus, to act as if they didn't exist.

"I'll fix you," Sukami called, running out the door. "I'll tell them my wealthy relatives won't share with their impoverished aunt." Ohney ran out to stop her, but soon returned with only Sukami's white prayer scarf.

Agus's face was ashen. "This is very serious," he said. "These are crazy times, an age in which the wise suffer for their wisdom." He looked pointedly at Taji. "And fools profit from their folly."

Taji studied his Texas boots, but Titin spoke spiritedly. "People should adapt themselves to modern times, prosperity, our president's five-year plan, university diplomas. And build more big hotels." She looked at Ohney. "I'd be so happy to go to work every day at the busy Hotel Borobudur, like you did, *Ibu.* I want to be a secretary there and meet lots of foreigners."

Mention of the hotel brought back the ache for Mrs. Lexie. Where was she now? In prison? She couldn't imagine how such a fine lady could endure that. Perhaps they'd acknowledged her dementia, and she was getting better in a hospital. Or better yet, now recovered, she might be living happily with her children. But would there be money? Would she have to scrabble for every *rupiah* to survive, as Ohney and Agus did? But Ohney hadn't been doing her part since the shock of Mrs. Lexie. She'd had an odd job here and there, but she had not been able to bring herself to apply for work in any of the other foreigners' villas.

Ohney pushed her sorrow away and got down to the matter at hand. It was the time to speak to these young people quietly, lead them along as one walks beside an ox or a bicycle, make them conscious of what they'd done and arouse in them the proper feelings of shame. It was better they have conflict with her, if necessary, than cause their father to feel shame or anger, which would disrupt his spiritual power. Although Ohney was one of the minority of women who had some interest in developing her own spirituality, she well knew it was the man's potency that determined the family's fortune and status.

"Son and daughter," she began, "you should know your place, not be ambitious or competitive, and accept your station in life and make the best of it." Outside, there was an angry roar from the crowd now assembled in front of the *lurah's* house.

She raised her voice to be heard. "You should be obedient to those in charge and willing to sacrifice for the common good. Material gain and power are only sources of disruption and disharmony that should be avoided."

Outside, they heard Sukami's high screeching voice, punctuated by the *lurah's* low rumbles. Ohney saw that fear made Agus give his son an ultimatum.

"You must do as the *lurah* says. Buy a pole to put the television on for everyone to see. You must give the headman a large share of the money for improvements to the *kampung*. And the dog must go, one way or another."

"No!" Titin cried. "Not Rocky!" The baby was curled up with the dog, both sleeping now. "But it's up to Taji—except the dog."

Outside, people beat on the light poles on the wall of the foreigners' compound. Angry buzzing that had been murmurs grew louder. Ohney ran out, but was quickly back to report. "There may be violence. I think you should go. Our home is here with these people now."

"Isn't your home our home, too?" Taji asked.

Ohney started to speak, hesitated—

"Only if they agree," Agus said. "But go now. We do not want you to be hurt."

"See our side of it," Ohney said. "We owe these people more than we can ever repay. They took us in when they didn't have to."

Titin was grim-faced. "Where would we go?"

The crowd screamed, *"Polisi, polisi, polisi."*

"You must *go.* Now!" Ohney said.

"Go to the home village at Bandung," Agus said. "They will not turn you away. But you cannot take the television. I will make a gift of it to the *lurah.*"

Agus eyed the dog, and Titin began to cry. "In the home village, they would eat this Rocky, too." Titin cried louder. Agus sighed. "All right. I'll tie the dog to one of the American's gates. They will take care of it."

Through her sobs, Titin handed him the leash. The dog followed him readily, as if glad to be away, Ohney thought.

Agus was scarcely gone when a jeep roared up outside, blaring its horn to disperse the people, its raking spotlights entering the little home. Authoritative voices, barking loud questions, rang out—followed by low, polite murmurs. Then two officers burst into the room.

Ohney listened sorrowfully as her children were charged with causing social unrest and stir. Taji trembled, his eyes wide with fear, as the police took him away. Titin was stalwart, insisting on keeping the child with her, despite Ohney's protests.

Agus ran in, exchanging troubled looks with his wife. They didn't know what to do. If they followed their children to the police station, they might be arrested, too. "If only there had been *rukun*," Ohney moaned. Yes, there should have been harmony, the differences smoothed over with cooperation and quietness of heart.

"It's the headman's fault," Agus insisted. "He should have handled the people."

"I did what was best for the *kampung*," the *lurah* defended himself. He stood in the doorway, holding Sukami by the arm, her face a mask of disbelief, her white clothes soiled and disarranged, her eyeglasses askew.

"There was no unity in the deliberations," the *lurah* said, "and this one—" he pushed Sukami forward into the room "—she made it worse and worse, inciting our people to riot, giving me no choice but to call the police. She has been declared *jotakan*."

From the moment the *lurah* spoke those words, Ohney and Agus, knowing solidarity and conformity were the essence of harmony, turned away from her. "It is a just punishment that everyone act as if she doesn't exist," Agus said.

Ohney agreed. "*Jotakan* is the only way to control slander, backbiting, and jealousy."

"And you," the *lurah* pointed at Agus and Ohney before he stalked to the door, "I fine one thousand *rupiah*."

Ohney and Agus sat in silence for a long time. Agus smoked furiously. Ohney's stomach rumbled, and she realized they'd not had the evening meal. She pretended not to be aware of Sukami, who was in a corner rocking to and fro. Outside, the *kampung* was quiet, justice having been administered.

"I will not go to work tonight," Agus said finally. "My stomach is upset, and my nerves are bad."

"But there is the fine now. I will take that job in the market tomorrow," Ohney said, "even though it doesn't pay much."

He sighed. "Yes, there is the thousand *rupiah*."

"Perhaps Mrs. Lexie's friend, *Nyonya* Jo Moody, could find someone for me to work for," Ohney said reluctantly.

Agus said, "Haven't we had enough of Americans interfering in our ways?" He stood up and reached for his jacket. "If I work tonight, we will be that much closer to paying the fine."

When Ohney heard the sound of the *becak* rattling down the street, she realized it was time for the before-sleep prayer, but Sukami only continued to rock, moaning now and then. The kind of religion Ohney practiced didn't believe God was to be met in Mecca or that prayers had to be at stipulated times. Working, eating, sleeping, meditating—her life was a continuous prayer to Him. The one she'd been saying all evening was answered when a subdued Taji and Titin returned, the baby peacefully asleep in the *selendang*.

Concern and sorrow for her son made Ohney's voice rougher than she intended. "Have you forgotten Javanese etiquette? You do not make bother for others."

"It's all her fault. She did it!" Taji shouted, nodding toward Sukami, who was rocking with her eyes rolled back now.

Ohney said, "She's *jotakan*."

Taji immediately turned his back on his aunt.

"Serves her right after what we've been through," Titin said.

Taji explained, "They let us go because we gave the *kampung* the television and got rid of the dog."

"But they took all our money." Titin began to weep. Her shaking body woke the baby, who began to suck on her fingers.

Sukami walked up to Taji and Titin in turn. "I don't understand," she said over and over, as they turned away.

"You've learned a lesson," Ohney told her son. "Now you will settle down and do right. Perhaps work for your own people."

He turned a defiant face to her. "I want to work for Americans. They have much money. I will go house to house in this complex beyond the wall tomorrow and see if anyone will hire us."

"We must not tell them I am pregnant," Titin said. "They will find out soon enough."

The baby, screaming now, reached for Titin's breast. Sukami grasped Ohney's chin, forcing her to look into her eyes. Ohney could not stand any more and stepped outside, mumbling something about getting a breath of air. After all, she'd been trapped in the house all day. The little patch of earth outside her doorway was really where she lived her life.

She stood there for a long time, comfortable with the dark, lit only by the stars and occasional pools of kerosene lamplight. Above her on its pole, the turtle dove cooed peace. But Ohney was not at peace with herself. She stood there, peering down the road to the villa, fighting her feelings of powerlessness, hoping they would pass. And there was a strong new emotion—frustration. She wondered if that was what had driven Mrs. Lexie to do what she did.

Ohney had wanted desperately to see her, to comfort her in some way. She had made the woman's favorite Indonesian soup, *soto ayam*, and talked the guard into letting her bring clean underwear from the villa, but they would not let her into their embassy, where they kept Mrs. Lexie. The American soldiers were polite, even smiled, but wouldn't take her offerings to the *Nyonya*. Ohney went every day, wishing it had been some terrible mistake, hoping they would release Mrs. Lexie. One day, she saw Mrs. Vonda Hutchison come out, crying "Wait," she told Ohney. "Wait just a bit longer. They're taking her to the airport."

In a while, Ohney's vigil was rewarded. Heart knocking her ribs, she glimpsed Mrs. Lexie moving toward an official car. There were so many men surrounding her that Ohney lost sight of her. The male sea parted just as Mrs. Lexie reached the limousine's open back door. Her eyes, raking the street beyond the big iron gates, were clouded and distant. Suddenly, they locked with Ohney's. The anguish in them stabbed Ohney, who waved madly and gave a thumb's up gesture.

Mrs. Lexie stared back at her as if Ohney were a blur in the crowd, as if she were just another Indonesian, as if she'd never seen her before in her life. Ohney took that hurt out now from where she'd buried it. Within its sting, she looked for answers, finally finding something she'd heard at a *kebatinan* meeting: "If one accepts unhappiness, it will totally disappear."

She started off into the darkness toward the home of her mystical leader. There was no meeting tonight, but he would use some secret words to free her—if only temporarily—of the burdens of being a wife, a mother, a member of the kampung: to free her of this added burden—a broken heart.

Behind her the turtle dove in its cage was silent. Ahead of her the night empty and questioning. She looked longingly down the road to the villa. Then she took a deep breath and turned her mind away from the imperceptible forces at play in the world. Ohney trudged on, determined to find harmony.

MY GURU:
Lila

SHADOWS OF THE DEEPENING DAY PLAYED ON THE WALL, SHADOWS SHE couldn't recall seeing in this private alcove of the Hotel Borobudur's lobby when she had met here daily with her friends—one gone home, another leaving soon, the rest involved with others now. Lila Hoopes sighed and put on the glasses she wore on a chain around her neck. Staring, she tried to define shadow as part of her life.

The vague outlines faded, and then the images became stark silhouettes—one dainty with an elongated nose, the other pudgy and bulge-eyed. That Indian woman she had been trying to ignore was playing with two flat leather *Wayang* puppets. Ugly things. And they called that culture here.

Unfortunately their eyes met. "Good morning, Mrs. Hoopes, back again I see," the musical voice of the Pendopo Lounge entertainer said. "You like my puppets? I am getting in the mood for the performance I will see at Museum Pusat tonight. You would like to come?"

Dressed like a hussy, stomach bare, men, like that Singapore Sam person, always hanging over her at the piano—she probably stayed out all night. Why then wasn't she sleeping until noon like others of her ilk? Lila slapped open the English edition of the Indonesian newspaper. Perhaps if she ignored her—

"The shadow play is the game of life, Mrs. Hoopes, where our visible deeds are reflections of a world outside time, no past or future, no distance between the living and the dead." The melodic voice went on, unaware how the word "dead" scratched at Lila's heart like sandpaper on a knothole.

The reopened wound forced out the rude words. "I'm not the least interested." She was here to read the local news, after all, and she escaped

117

behind her paper. Lila couldn't remember when she'd stopped reading the *International Herald Tribune*. To read about the United States from here was unreal, and she had no interest in other foreign countries. But local newswriting like this amused her: FLOODS HIT THE CAPITAL CITY OF JAKARTA FOR SEVERAL DAYS TILL NOW.

Lila read on past the headlines: "The people greatly suffers from floods as this natural disaster does not care who victims are." A smile twitched her thin lips. She read this paper as much to gloat over the fractured English as anything, but she especially liked it when the news confirmed her own convictions of Jakarta as a place of doom and gloom.

She glanced over a corner of the paper, but no, the woman known as Nelia, black as the devil himself, was paying her no attention, was busy scribbling with a red pen. Occasionally, slender fingers worried a strand of neatly-bound ebony hair as she bent over a schoolchild's composition book.

Suddenly Nelia's almond-shaped eyes met Lila's. "Are you sure you won't come to the shadow play? If you would understand Java, you need to know *Wayang*."

Lila made her voice as frosty as possible. "Perfectly sure." Why should this woman think she wanted to know anything more about Indonesia than what irritated her every day? Attend such heathen nonsense? Her husband, Homer, would laugh his fool head off. No, Lila wasn't interested. She couldn't even fathom the tragedies of her own reality, or the awful things people did within it.

"Celeste is going," Nelia said. "You could meet us here at—"

"Celeste?" Lila's cranky tone carried farther than she'd intended. A tall man with a monocle stared at her over the broad green leaves of the plant divider.

"You remember Celeste, Mrs. Hoopes."

"No, I don't. I don't at all." Why did this annoying woman have to be here in Lila's private place? There were lots of her nationality in Jakarta. Why didn't she mix with them?

"Her driver, Rudi—"

"She must have been the one who left soon after she arrived," Lila said quickly. "Yes, I recall. Anxious to be home for the Bicentennial celebration. Yes, that's her."

"No, no, Mrs. Hoopes. She is Canadian, and here, and—"

Lila folded her paper carefully so all the edges met and tucked it under her arm. Fuming, she brushed by the common piano player. How dare she! How dare she indeed!

❀ ৵ ❀ ৵ ❀ ৵ ❀

Lila hoarded indignation as conscientiously as she'd once collected rain water in a barrel to wash her hair. She found her best specimens at home. "I've got my pride," she'd lash out. "Then that's all you got," Homer would yell back, "because love has no pride." But she could become aggravated over things that happened years ago as well. She'd sort through memories of past hurts, slights, disappointments, recounting them to Homer as excitedly as if she were sharing a photograph album full of adventures and trips. And of course this God forsaken place always—Where was that taxi?

Her occasional escapes back to the Borobudur Hotel to observe the new people flounder around were all that kept her sane. Unlike the servants she'd been saddled with, she, herself, had found a taxi driver she could hire by the day. It was one thing in her life that was working out. Nanarmo seemed to understand her mixture of English and the occasional Indonesian word she'd picked up from her friends. Her foot began to tattoo out a dance of ire. Where was he? He knew better than to keep her waiting.

She ticked off all the things at home she could be furious about when she got there. The latest housegirl would not have boiled the water or cleaned out the refrigerator. They were all lazy or played dumb. The mail would have come and as usual there would be nothing from their daughter. The power would be out again and the house would be stifling, or the fuses would need changing and she couldn't even trust the yardboy to do that. Homer was underfoot every day now, interrupting her chores and housework. He'd flaunted a new motorcycle after she'd refused to let him buy a car. After all, they had to cut corners somewhere while they were here. Then when they went home, they'd be safe if there was ever another depression. Just as she'd anticipated, he'd gotten hurt on the fool thing, breaking his leg.

It was right after he walked out on one of their biggest arguments about Serena. "Your Hindu fiddle-faddle," he'd yelled. They called it hatha yoga she tried to tell him. It was just doing exercises—like going to the YMCA back in Austin. Nothing more. But he wouldn't listen. She had to wait on him all the time now. Like the others before her, the housegirl would quit any day now, and Lila would have to struggle with another. She hated dealing with any of these people. Men even peed on the street here, and worse. Nanarmo, grinning, eased his taxi up beside her. Getting in, she gave him a steely glance and slammed the car door hard so he would know she was not to be fooled with.

❀ ᵔ ❀ ᵔ ❀ ᵔ ❀

"Lila-bird," Homer called the minute she walked into the house. "I need you."

Lila felt her stomach rebel and went to the kitchen for the Pepto Bismol. She looked at other bottles on the counter. Had she taken the Lomatil earlier? No matter, today she was constipated instead of loose. Always one or the other. She'd learned one or two Bintang beers could open her bowels right up. She took a bottle from the refrigerator.

"Lila-bird," the plaintive call, a bit more forceful, came again.

Lila opened a cupboard and began counting the jars of vegetables she'd put up, just like she would have if she were home. It passed the time, and doing what she would be doing back there in the hot weather comforted her. She'd tried growing her own vegetables, but the green bean vines, strong and unproducing, reached to high heaven like the beanstalk Jack climbed to find the goose that laid the golden eggs. The tomatoes became trees without blossoms. Only okra flourished, but if she waited a day too long to harvest, it turned huge and tough.

She'd settled for vegetables from the Bandung man who stopped by the expat houses with his refrigerated truck every day or so. His meat was good, and the vegetables and fruits, straight from Bandung in the mountains, lovely. The experience was reminiscent of the days of her past when milk and bread and yes, tea and coffee, were delivered. The expat supermarkets were way too high, but it beat going to open-air markets with dirt floors and strange smells.

Occasionally, there was something she couldn't get from the trucker, and she had to go to one of those *pasars* anyway. She always bathed immediately on returning home, pouring a generous gush from the aqua bottle of Milton into the bath water. She knew all about not taking baths here unless you were in a hotel, but Lila had decided that if the disinfectant was good enough to kill the germs of human fertilizer on the lettuce, it must be good enough to kill the germs on her body. Of course there was now a rash on her legs she suspected came from the Milton, but she could live with that as long as she knew she was *clean*.

"LIIIIIIIILAAAAA!" Homer roared.

She walked into the living room and set her beer on the card table they used for eating. The only other pieces of furniture in the large room were plastic webbed beach chairs. Homer's great body sagged in one of these, his leg, encased in plaster, cocked on a pile of towels. She pulled up a chair.

"Look at this." He shoved a letter at her.

She rescued her reading glasses from their perch on top of her white pompadour. "Where'd you get that?"

"Jo Moody dropped our mail by while you were out enjoying yourself."

"Of course—it was a real pleasure riding in this idiotic traffic in such a downpour the driver couldn't even see out the windshield, listening to him babble about gruesome floods and predict cholera. It's pure joy watching people in the low areas washing their muddy clothes, putting the bedding out to dry, cleaning caked red mud from their houses, knowing they will be doing it over and over throughout the rainy season." She closed her lips tightly to keep the harangue from continuing and snatched the letter from his hand.

Young Lila Mae wanted money as usual. Her husband had left her. She couldn't take a job and watch the children, too. They wouldn't want her to be on welfare, would they?

"Dad, why do those kids always think we have money?" She took a swig of Bintang. "Remember how we had to convince Jeremy we couldn't help him with that deep-sea diving school he'd set his heart on?"

"Sure as shit, I don't know, Lila-bird. He got there anyway, didn't he? They're young. We're old." Making a face, Homer moved his leg a tad. "Put a cushion under there, would you?"

Lila didn't move. Homer didn't seem to notice, his mind on their discussion. "The money we've saved working over here wouldn't be more than a fart in the wind if one of us really got sick, would it?"

Lila went to the kitchen for another Bintang. "No, and we can't touch our stocks and bonds," she called.

"You're going to get drunk," Homer said when she returned, now in her bare feet. "It doesn't take much for a little bit of a thing like you."

"Leave me be, Dad. It's medicinal, strictly medicinal."

"What's she want, skulking around the room?" Homer nodded toward the new girl, Kami or Noni, or whatever this one—grinning at them like an idiot—said her name was. Lila went and found a bucket, sponge, and bottle of detergent with Chinese hieroglyphics on it. She pulled the girl along to one of the bathrooms. "Scrub," she said, waving the sponge above the floor. "Scrub," she repeated in a loud voice as she set the alarm clock for twenty minutes and pointed to it.

Much as she would have liked to have told the company to go pound salt—"I'm not having those people in my house no matter if you did promise Indonesia a certain amount of employment"—she had to admit she couldn't do all the work in this big house herself. Cleaning you could do once a month back home had to be done every day here. Dust and grit sifted through walls not near as tight as Western houses.

Although her friends envied it, she hated the house they were assigned—a roomy old Dutch Colonial with an odd peaked roof. They said it cried out for lace curtains, but she'd sewn sheets together to keep folks on the street from looking in at them. The house was in fancy Menteng near Vonda. But not living in a company compound had meant she had to pay a boy to guard the gate and take care of the pool neither she or Homer would ever use. It lurked behind the house, a waiting enemy, stagnant and covered with leaves most of the time. Neither she nor the boy could make out what to do with it, and she'd come not to care.

"Hand me my crutches." Homer struggled to get up. "I'm going to walk around a bit."

Lila picked up young Lila Mae's letter again. "She says she doesn't have any place to live."

Homer hobbled back and forth across the barren room. "You don't want to tell her she can live in our house, do ya?"

"I do not! Just knowing everything is there the way I left it is the only consolation I have, living in this godforsaken place. And when we go on home leave, papering and painting and fixing it up for the day we return is my great joy."

"I reckon Lila Mae's two young ones are a handful. There'd be dirty fingerprints on everything, and that dog'd tear up the yard," Homer said.

Finished with her beer, Lila was feeling relaxed, much as she often felt at Serena's. "I'll send her a hundred dollars tomorrow."

"Mother, do you think—?" Homer stopped and rubbed a hand over his crew cut. "I bet Brian would have really been somebody. He had a quick head and was so smart with his hands. Maybe a doctor—"

"We'll never know, will we?" Lila said sharply. Then kinder, "Don't dwell on it now, you hear?" Homer engineered himself to a window, pulled aside a sheet and stared into the passing traffic.

Lila peeled strips of the beer bottle label away, crumbling them into tiny balls. "Maybe two hundred, I'll send her. That wouldn't break us come another depression."

"Hmmph."

"She'll get on her feet. You'll see. She's tough stuff, like you and me." Lila helped him ease back into his chair. "Maybe she wouldn't tear up the house none." Homer's eyes were closed. "I'm going to think about it," she yelled in his ear. Homer snored in reply.

Lila looked for a spot on the wide expanse of marble floor to lay out her three green and white scrolled prayer rugs, one on top of the other. Lying on her back, she pushed her palms against the floor and slowly raised her legs. "Knees straight," Serena had said. Lila concentrated on swinging her legs over her head in the Plough position. She did manage to get them past her rump this time, but it wasn't the same without Serena's graceful body before her, showing her the way.

She allowed her butt to slump against the rugs, then slowly slid her legs down. She had promised not to go back to Serena's. Dad had said the books Serena gave her to read were just as spooky as Indonesian Muslim stuff.

Who'd asked for his two cents anyway? Although he'd always asked for hers. When there was trouble on the job, he'd come to her, whining about no one else but him knowing their ass from their elbow, including assorted bosses.

She'd come to know just what to say to him. "You'll just have to take it, Homer, if you want to make more money for us. That is what you want, isn't it? You don't want your family in the poor house, do you?" And all the time she was thinking, yes, take that and that and that, and I hope you hurt as much as you hurt me.

Lila sighed. How had she wound up being the one "taking it" in this bizarre part of the world? Those hours with Serena had come to be the only thing making her life endurable. She didn't believe in all her rigamarole of course. No, Homer didn't have to know where she was every minute, and next week he'd start back to work, cast and all. She'd have her days back, and wouldn't have to feel guilty anymore about doing what she damn well felt like.

❀ ৵ ❀ ৵ ❀ ৵ ❀

Lila forced herself to concentrate on the flame, to shut out all but its inner glow, to imprint it on her consciousness. "Ommm," she repeated, as instructed, letting it resonate through her. She began to enter the flame. No, this was silly. She wasn't here for this. She was here for an exercise class. She needed to get rid of the flab she'd built living the good hotel life all those months.

"Ommmm." Serena's soft voice stilled Lila's thoughts.

Once more Lila put her mind to the flame, willing herself to be part of it. She had made her thumbs and forefingers meet in an "O" as instructed, but she hadn't been able to sit in the Lotus position. Serena had said it would be okay to sit cross-legged until her body got used to doing it the right way, but even that felt uncomfortable and unseemly for her fifty-seven-year-old body.

She wished she had a leotard and tights like Serena's instead of her ill-fitting shorts and Homer's "Texas A&M Forever" T-shirt shrouding her menopausal body. Serena might have mediocre brown hair and a face like a mature elf, but her stomach was taut and flat. Lila was gratified to see Serena did have a problem with her thighs.

Muted sounds of water flowing over rocks in Serena's indoor spring that wound around the combined living, dining, and library areas lulled her. Then a giant rumble of thunder shook the room, and Lila squeezed her eyes tight, shutting out the zig-zag of lightning outside the window. Hard splats of rain bit the clay tiles of the roof.

Two servants tiptoed around them, silently placing buckets and basins under leaks splattering the marble floors, and turning on table lamps. Slowly, Serena returned from wherever she had been in the flame.

"And so, Lila, when you looked away from it, did you still see the flame with your third eye?"

"I did not."

"It will come with practice."

"This isn't what I come here for." Lila stretched her cramped legs.

"These meditation exercises I've given you are truly beneficial. Be sure to practice them at home. You do want to relax the grasp the personality has on the consciousness, opening an awareness to inner realms of experience, don't you?"

Serena was doing some exercise now she'd never taught Lila. Her constant movements, though graceful, were getting on Lila's nerves, and she wasn't about to leave herself open to losing her consciousness to anything—even though she didn't much like what was in it sometimes.

"You have a fascinating inner life to be discovered, Lila. I can tell by your beautiful lavender aura. You might even have an out-of-body experience."

Lila felt she could stand up now. "Not me. Not in your lifetime."

Serena's smile was one she might give to a recalcitrant child. "You do feel more at peace since coming here, don't you?" She didn't wait for an answer. "The mantra you say in the car does help get you through the traffic, the errands? You don't have that apprehension anymore of being attacked by those terrorists you read about in the paper? The ones caught just as they were setting fire to the shops at Pasar Senin?"

Something was making Lila feel better. Perhaps it *was* the mantra. Perhaps it was having someone she could tell her fears to—well, not all of them. She looked at her arm, trying to see a lavender light coming from it.

That was rather interesting. She looked longingly at the two mats waiting for them near the whispering stream.

Serena followed her gaze. "We will get to that in a minute, but first you must dwell on the thought that yoga is more than just doing the asanas. The positions we do in hatha yoga are the key to inner beauty of the body and mind. But I like you, Lila, and I want more for you than that. I want to take you down the highway of meditation to divine communion. I want to liberate you from mental disharmonies and spiritual ignorance."

"I've always been a good Methodist," Lila said. "But at this interdenominational church here, they don't even say the Lord's Prayer right."

"You don't need that, Lila, for a direct personal relationship with our Creator. No middleman but me. You do trust me, don't you?"

Lila thought about that. Her inner life was something she'd learned to share sparingly. She had let Homer see deep inside her when they'd lost the boy, and look what that got her. He'd betrayed her when she needed him most. He'd been sorry, penitent really, and they'd moved on. But even now, there were days when the old wound itched, burned, festered. Trust? She wasn't sure what she'd found here with Serena these past six weeks, but it was something she wouldn't know how to replace. She found herself nodding vigorously. Serena led the way to the mats.

The yoga master closed her eyes, breathing deeply. Lila had the feeling Serena had gone somewhere she couldn't follow. Finally, "We begin, as always, with the Salvasana, the deep relaxation posture."

Lila followed Serena's directions to go limp, to get her arms and legs comfortable. The guru led Lila in relaxing. She tried to relax each part of her body one at a time as she listened to rain slamming the house, the ping-ping of water dripping into pots, a kind of sacred music here in Serena's sanctum.

"Keep your attention on what you're doing," Serena breathed softly. Lila heard whispering over near the floor-to-ceiling bookcases that were free-standing like shelves in the library.

"If your mind wanders, bring it back gently to that part of the body from where it was distracted. Remember—"

It would be late when Lila got home, but she'd made a big pot of Four Alarm Chili and could heat it up for their dinner. Maybe some papaya? It was one thing they liked here.

"Yoga is the holistic approach to…"

Lila's mind finally responded, and she became aware of the total relaxation of her body, became aware of… nothing—until the annoying whispers became murmurs. Until Serena, coming as close to annoyance as Lila had ever seen her, said, "You're disturbing us. Can't you see I have a pupil?"

A college-age boy and girl came out of the recesses of the large room. "Stop it now, Mother." The boy pulled Serena to a chair.

"You've been doing this stuff since dawn," the girl said.

"Yes, and without your father to stop me, I will do it till bedtime," Serena said, but she looked confused as to where she was, who she was talking to.

"She hasn't had a bite of anything today," the boy said. As if Serena were hard of hearing, the girl shouted, "I'll have the cook make you something nice to eat."

"Some nuts maybe," Serena said, "a few berries. And grains, of course." She turned to Lila. "I didn't see you come in. Welcome. Have you been eating yogurt every day as I instructed? We will begin now." She started to get up, but her children pushed her back down.

The girl shoved Lila's pocketbook at her. "You have to go. She's really not well."

The boy opened the door and pushed Lila through it. The storm had passed, and she stood, blinking and puzzled, in the bright sunshine. Then she woke Nanarmo who was napping in her hired car.

❀ ⤳ ❀ ⤳ ❀ ⤳ ❀

When the message came that Serena couldn't see her the following Wednesday, Lila decided to go out anyway. With her newspaper, she settled into an opulent chair near the Borobudur's front desk. She was taking no chances on running into that Nelia person, who was sure to look for her in the private alcove. 4 DIE IN JAKARTA'S RECENT FLOODS. She read about citizens drowning in various rivers, children losing their lives in a drainage ditch, and one couple who touched an electric cable.

Lila shook her head. "Terrible, terrible," she muttered, instantly depressed. But depression, a close relative to the rage that kept her alive, was what she knew best, and she settled into it. She *had* come here to read about the horrible things that happened in this godforsaken country.

Then the Indian woman, or whatever she was, was bending over Lila, pointing to a photo. It showed a nature-made "lake," trees sticking up here and there, a vehicle on its side. CITY BUS SKID AND GET LAME IN STREET IN FRONT OF TRISAKTI UNIVERSITY. Nelia laughed, and in spite of herself, Lila did, too. She was instantly sorry. Encouraged, Nelia made herself at home on the leather couch next to Lila.

Her hair, tightly pinned to her head, made Nelia appear older. She wore something that looked a lot like a dress Lila had in her closet, one of the cottons she'd bought through the Sears catalog. Last time, the woman had worn slacks and a tailored blouse. The daytime Nelia looked far different from the nighttime one in the Pendopo. Lila preferred to think of her that way—in exotic caftans or traditional Indian dress, a lot of makeup, ink-black hair, first caught up high on top of her head with elegant combs, then flowing to the middle of her back. It made it much easier not to want to know her.

Lila looked at the menagerie tromping by them. She always thought of it that way, though she'd heard some liken the mix of nationalities in this lobby to a meeting of the United Nations. They were all foreigners to her, strangers she'd never understand, so she ignored them. Seemingly unaware of all that was going on around her, Nelia's glossy head was bent over that damn composition book. "What are you writing?" A vague suspicion that it might be about her had put voice to the irritation Lila felt every time she came in contact with this woman.

The Indian person looked up, smiling an enigmatic smile. For the first time, Lila noticed a scar, shaped like the new moon, on Nelia's chin.

"No," Nelia said. "I am not writing about you. It is a journal. I write only to explore myself. I am not yet the storyteller, only a devout listener. Someday when I have studied the *Wayang* more, perhaps? Perhaps not. Not many women here are *dalangs*."

"That is your name for storyteller?"

"Yes, but it is not as simple as that. A *dalang* is also a person of magic, a mystic, a healer sometimes, and even—yes, the shadow play goes back to the time when shadows were believed to be the souls of the dead and the *dalang* the medium between souls and the living."

"Your mumbo jumbo is worse than that of someone else I know," Lila said. Still suspicious, she asked, "You think I have a story, don't you? And that you could tell it."

Nelia stared long at the open pages before her. "We all invent our own stories, Mrs. Hoopes," she said. "I do sense, however, that yours has not been revealed to you. I had hoped that If you saw a performance—"

Lila felt the old comfortable anger flush her face, a tic beating a crescendo at her temple.

Softly, persuasively, Nelia continued. "Seeing our shadow play could help you understand yourself as well as our culture. It is from *Wayang* we derive our sense of values, the feelings of what is right or wrong."

"Don't tell me about right and wrong," Lila blurted, fists clenching and unclenching. "I could write a book on that."

Nelia's satin voice rolled on, "—concepts of relationships with our fellow man—"

Trembling with outrage at being forced to hear such twaddle, Lila folded her paper, making sure all the edges met, closing the conversation.

Ignoring that, Nelia said, "Have you ever thought of a mystical approach with the deity? I would be glad to guide you in the ways of—"

This was too much. "I'll have you know I may not go to church here, but I'm a true-blue Methodist!"

"Ahhh, we do have something in common. I was raised in a Methodist orphanage in Sumatra. I, too, am Methodist at times."

Nelia closed her book and attached her red pen to it. "Are you happy here, Mrs. Hoopes? Is your spirit at ease?"

Lila bit off the words. "The condition of my soul is no one's business but my own." I must be strong, Lila told herself; the devil is in disguise and testing me. She reached for her pocketbook. "I have an appointment for my yoga lesson." She wished she did. She longed for tranquility.

"Are you learning about chakras then, the points of the body where—"

"Nothing like that. I go for the exercises, for God's sakes. Serena is not one of those people in a loincloth, sleeping on a bed of nails, always saying 'Omm.'" Realizing what she'd just said, Lila clamped her mouth shut.

"Ahhh. You go to the seeress, Serena Thompson. The Australian woman whose husband works over on Kalimantan and leaves her to fend for herself in Jakarta."

Lila mulled over the word "seeress," then rejected it. Her friend, Serena, had never prophesied a thing.

"I have puzzled you. You do not think of her as your guru?"

Lila studied a moment. "Perhaps," she said. "Yes, Serena helps me through the days. I suppose she is my—goo-ru." It made her feel better not to pronounce it goor-u, the way Nelia had.

"Ahhh, you are wise," Nelia said. "Treading the mystic path alone, one can become possessed by evil, or even go mad."

❀ ⸙ ❀ ⸙ ❀ ⸙ ❀

To make sure she did understand the words "seeress" and "guru," Lila went right to one of Homer's dictionaries when she got home. He was a crossword fanatic. When they'd been on home leave, he'd bought near fifty of those puzzle books. She allowed him this extravagance since he never said a word about the money she spent on a year's supply of Jean Nate talcum powder, deodorant, and splash-on.

She picked up the phone. Yes, there was a dial tone. They'd gone through a period of the phone not working. A general had moved into the neighborhood, and the Formalities Department at the CAMCO office had implied he might have "borrowed" the line. Now that the general was on a tour around the world, miraculously she'd regained use of the phone. It rang and rang. No one was answering at Serena's. She might have a student, but where were her servants? Just as she gave up, she heard Serena say hello in a faint voice. No, she thought she'd made it clear it was *not* convenient for Lila to come today. Not tomorrow either. Two weeks, and she *was* sorry. Yes, Serena looked forward to it, too.

Then Serena said, "You must learn the great truths now, Lila. It is time we explore your deepest feelings." Lila put the receiver in its cradle. In that moment, she felt unanticipated hope. With Serena, it might be all right.

❀ ❧ ❀ ❧ ❀ ❧ ❀

Lila stood waiting her turn at the Kemang hotel desk because she couldn't stomach running into that pushy piano player at the Borobudur. She'd come to this smaller hotel to mail her letters, and stood now watching the clerk put the stamps on the envelopes. You had to do that here. Everyone knew these Indonesians would take your money and throw the letters away if you didn't stand over them. And if you could find a post office, you couldn't even trust the people there.

She walked slowly toward the door, the paper she'd bought open before her.

10 KM CANAL TO PROTECT JAKARTA FROM FLOOD COST RP 11 BILLION. Thank goodness. These poor victims. She read on. CITY FLOOD CONTROL PROJECT WARNS CITIZENS THROUGH TV ANNOUNCE-MENT. That was really dumb. How many Indonesians had televisions or even access to one? Despite the satellite the USA had put into orbit for them, the masses were lucky if they had electric, if—

She looked up to see a beaming Nelia striding toward her. "How is the news today, Mrs. Hoopes?"

"Not good," Lila said and made to pass, then stopped. "You're kind of out of your territory, aren't you? You aren't following me?"

Nelia laughed. "The Kemang Hotel is buying a piano. They asked my advice."

"Mmmm," Lila said, her head back in the paper.

"There is an interesting story here," Nelia said.

Lila watched warily as brown fingers turned a 'page and tapped at a spot on it. "I have no time now," Lila said. She tried to put the paper together again, but getting all the pages to meet was hard to do standing up.

"It says a whole *kampung* rose up in anger against a man who tended a reservoir, because they wanted him to divert the flooding water from their neighborhood. Frightened, he tried to do what they asked but drowned in the reservoir. The Mayor maintains opening those gates would only have made a worse condition."

Lila shuddered. "Untimely deaths…"

"It is all choice, Mrs. Hoopes. The man had a choice to make. He could have said no. He could have run away. He could have learned to swim better a long time ago. We design our lives through the power of our choices, Mrs. Hoopes. That is what the *Wayang* teaches."

"Poppycock!" Lila flared. "No one chooses to die."

"I think we do," Nelia said. "Not making a choice is a choice, too, you know. Worse, we can give our right to choose to others."

"My boy didn't choose to die on a goddamn motorcycle after he'd made it through Viet Nam." Lila shouted. People were looking at her, but she didn't care. Nelia tried to lead her to a chair, but Lila shrugged her off. "He didn't choose that drunk driver to come out of nowhere.

"On a goddamn motorcycle, and now that old fool has one. I don't have enough to worry about here. And why should I worry about him anyway after what he—"

"Ahh, I see," Nelia said. "The anger you collect is fear, of course. You dread some loss then of your husband, of—"

"I lost him when I lost Brian. The only one I can lose now is myself." Lila was surprised at her own insight. Anger at that, and at this impossible woman, propelled her out the revolving door.

❀ ✄ ❀ ✄ ❀ ✄ ❀

Where was that housegirl? Why didn't she answer the door? Lila wiped her face with the towel hanging around her neck. She was breathless from trying to do The Plough again. That's what she didn't understand about these exercises yet—how and when to breathe. But she had managed to hold her rump up in the air for a satisfactory amount of time, and the way she'd come down out of it would have won compliments from Serena. Lila opened the front door. "You!"

Nelia's bright face peered into the room behind Lila. "You have no furniture, Mrs. Hoopes?"

Lila closed the door a little. "We have no need, Miss Nelia. I don't spend a dime in this country I don't have to. I have a real home back in Texas. My furniture is there where it belongs."

"Can you really see yourself, Mrs. Hoopes? May I call you Lila? The best way to see ourselves is by the shadows we create. You could learn much from *Wayang*. It teaches aspects of character."

"What do you want?" Lila closed the door farther.

Nelia waved a newspaper at her. "You weren't there today. I brought this." The long brown fingers with the white half-moons tapped the front page. 8 DIE OF CHOLERA IN CENTRAL JAKARTA.

"I'd expect nothing else in this damn place," Lila said. The door was a slit now. "Why did you really come?"

"I'd like to take over your spiritual advancement, Lila. You have great potential."

"Serena told me it is dangerous to dabble with Indonesian mysticism. And why aren't you into Hindu poppycock instead of shadow nonsense?"

"Hinduism may be my genetic heritage, but make no mistake—I am Indonesian and proud of it. The only things Indian about me are my physical characteristics and my love for that food. What you see in the Pendopo is not who I am."

Lila wished she'd go away. She wanted a cigarette. She allowed herself only three a day, and it was time for one.

"Serena Thompson is not the answer to everything, you know," Nelia said. "I, myself, am not without power. I could tell you—"

"Please don't." Lila shut the door, grabbed up a cigarette, and began smoking furiously.

Nelia read from the other side of the door. WOMAN RAPED BY MONKEY. *"Never mind, her husband said, it is just a monkey."*

Lila opened the door enough to let the paper through. "Let me see that."

"The monkey failed to rape the woman after it took off her underwear, and she woke from under a tree on her farm land where she had been working," Lila read aloud. *"However, the unlucky woman was later raped after she failed to avoid the monkey."* They both began to laugh.

Lila opened the door wide. "Come in. I'll make some tea."

Much later, Lila said, "You people have no compunctions about asking personal questions, do you?"

"I'm only trying to get to know you better. I wish to understand Western thinking."

"I don't want you to know me better. I share myself sparingly. After what Homer did, when I needed him the most... " Lila stopped. Nelia's eyes were soft with interest. Lila couldn't seem to help herself.

"It was a vulgar girl who sang with a country Western band at the

Triple A Roadhouse. He took to going there right after… Brian had a purple heart, you know. He was so handsome, so glad to be home, so eager to start a new phase of his life. That cheap singer—"

"Ahhh, and I, too, am an entertainer, Lila? Nothing in common? Couldn't possibly guide you out of where you've gotten yourself?"

"I didn't mean—" but Lila's habit of denial had deserted her.

Nelia said, "It does not occur to you that it was how he handled his grief, your husband, losing himself in a stranger who had not the same memories, the same love, the same sadness."

"I'll never forgive him, never," Lila said, feeling the weight of stone in her heart.

"I have forgiven," Nelia said, "but never can I forget. I am married to a Caucasian, an Italian."

Lila leaned forward, interest piqued. "How in the world—?"

"I met him when I played a hotel in Bali. Now he is chef on a cruise ship. Once in a while he writes he is coming to see me, then he doesn't. But I will wait. He will return."

"You forgive this?"

"Oh, yes. I intend to get him back. Already I have a plan. Like you, I save all the money I can. But it is for a restaurant I will buy here in Jakarta. He will not be able to resist his own restaurant. But I do not forget what Mario's friends, who do not like me, say and do. There was much trouble. This will be my vengeance, giving him something they cannot."

"I should forgive Homer, I suppose," Lila said, pursing her lips and unpursing them. "Sometimes I go weeks forgetting what he did. Then it's back badgering me."

Nelia smiled gently. "Don't listen to that voice that says, 'You *should* do this, you *should* do that.' If you say I *could* do this or that, it makes it a choice instead of an inner rebuke. The best way to see ourselves is through our choices." Her black eyes pierced all Lila's shams. "You really *choose* to be angry at your husband, do you not?"

Lila's rage returned. "Men, even sons, trap you with love," she snapped, "then they abandon you."

Nelia seemed far away for a moment. "In a *Wayang* story, one of Arjuna's wives, the noble Srikandi, chose to become a man for a while. She learned many new things."

In a moment they both laughed. "You and your choices," Lila said.

❀ ꤮ ❀ ꤮ ❀ ꤮ ❀

Lila was ecstatic to be in the taxi on her way to what she considered her only haven from both the squalor of Jakarta and the turmoil of her own soul. Then they passed a bend in the road, and suddenly were in a flooded area with water lapping at the door handle. The car died. Nanarmo said something, probably a swear word. They sat there in the oppressive heat and humidity, the gun metal sky pressing the car into the dark earth of the road bed. Lila felt claustrophobic, felt some impending and worse disaster was on its way.

Watching the water seep in, she repeated her mantra, but the thought that her shoes were going to mildew kept interfering. A crowd had formed. Nanarmo called something to some boys who were rescuing cases of orange pop from a streetside *warung* that was also inundated with water. They stopped, grinned, then waded in up to their waists. With heaving and grunting and good-natured calls to one another, they moved the car out of the flooded dip in the road onto higher ground.

Nanarmo turned to her and said, "Yes, *Nyonya?*" She didn't understand. The crowd began to chant, and an unwanted picture of the mob of women at Rudi's funeral clouded her mind. "Get us out of here, Nanarmo," she said. "Quickly."

Nanarmo made a motion with his hand, rubbing three fingers against his thumb. The chanting grew louder, the boys stretching out their hands. Of course. She must pay them something. She was glad to do so and grateful the taxi started after a few sputters.

"Solar," Nanarmo said, patting the cab's console. Later, Homer would explain it had been a diesel car, and there were no spark plugs to get wet.

In midst of a full-blown hot flash, Lila imagined headlines as they pulled up in front of Serena's. FOREIGN WOMAN DROWNS GETTING OUT OF TAXI THAT GOES LAME IN FLOODING. No, perhaps: ANGRY JAKARTA CITIZENS TEAR AMERICAN WOMAN APART. Or even: FOREIGN WOMAN STONED FOR... Unreasonable anger swept over her. She didn't know whether it was at herself or—yes, that was it. Trembling with rage at Celeste, Lila knocked on the door.

❀ ꥁ ❀ ꥁ ❀ ꥁ ❀

Inside, soft sitar music prevailed over the trickling spring water. In the middle of the large living area, Serena Thompson sat in the Lotus position, concentrating a portrait of her hero, the guru Paramhansa Yogananda. The two youngsters Lila had met previously zig-zagged about the room, picking things up and putting them down. Clothes were strewn everywhere. A hair dryer sat on the table beside a half-eaten apple. More clothes straggled from an open suitcase on a sofa. Papers spewed from a wastebasket. No one greeted her. No one accounted for this chaos. She didn't know what to do. She went into the bathroom and came out in her shorts and T-shirt. She started to sit on the couch.

"Don't sit there," the girl said, pulling a skirt and blouse out from under her. Lila went to the bookcase to replace her borrowed book.

"Don't mess them up," the boy yelped. "I've just sorted out the ones she can take." He looked at his sister. "Most of this is no good for her, no good at all. Really off-the-wall shit."

Not knowing what else to do, Lila went and sat beside Serena. Serena was far away, and Lila didn't want to disturb her, but she did need their session to begin. Lila looked at the portrait, trying to see what her guru saw.

Eyes closed, face expressionless, Serena spoke, "This pose is called the Lotus because in this traditional asana the yogi views the varicolored lotuses—the chakras—the wheels of the cerebrospinal centers." Lila tried to do some deep breaths and choked on her own saliva.

"The Lotus pose holds the spine upright, locking the body securely against the danger of falling backward or forward during the trance state."

Lila checked herself. No. As usual, her mind had the good sense not to slip away to God knows where.

"Yogic science was taught to John and other disciples of Jesus. According to Revelations—"

"Mother, for Pete's sake," the boy said, shaking Serena.

The girl intervened. "Leave her go. It's her last pupil."

Serena stood, her arms reaching to heaven in supplication. "Objects around me are vibrrrrating. Now they're violently agitated. See! See! That brass pot moves. The picture speaks to me. Now, now, they've all melted. Everything. Into a luminescent sea. I feel endless blisssss. Glorrrrry swells in me. The entire cosmos is—"

"Good God!" The boy crossed himself.

"I'll get one of those pills the doctor prescribed," the girl said.

"If you're not well—" Lila looked to the others for some kind of explanation. They looked back with stony eyes.

Serena continued her oratory. "—glimmering within the infinitude of my being, dazzling light, all dazzzzling light—" Finally aware of Lila, she smiled benevolently.

"Come, we will do the asanas together." Lila stumbled to her feet. Instead of going to the area set aside for the lessons, Serena began doing standing asanas right in front of Lila, who started to follow suit, but Serena was doing them erratically, like the fast-forward on a tape machine or a jerky silent movie. Lila tried to keep up. The—was part of the—and then it turned into the—Lord, Lila didn't even know the names for such mixed-up jumble.

Seeping raindrops from the roof pattered into the gurgling spring. The house was eerily silent without the hum of air conditioning. The boy piled books helter-skelter into a box. Making ironing motions at her, the girl shoved a dress at a servant.

"Pay attention now, Lila," Serena said. She described the movements of the Plough, but was demonstrating something else by standing on one foot. In confusion, Lila froze.

"Come on, Lila, come on. We have to do this. NOW. You and I." Serena moved closer, putting her mouth to Lila's ear. "You're my friend, aren't you?" She glared at her children and the servants. "My only friend." Then proudly, "I am *samhedi*. All night I watched a rock in the stream. I became the rock. In spite of THEM." She ran to the drawn draperies and peeked out. "Do you understand?" She ran down the hall toward the bedroom.

Bewildered, Lila looked to the boy and girl.

"You should not be part of this," the boy said.

The girl said, "Our mother has flipped, as you can see."

"She's perfectly fine," Lila said. "Staying awake all night makes anyone a little whifty. We're going to do the Plough when she comes back. I've really got it down now. She'll be so pleased."

"I doubt she'll even notice," the girl said.

The boy shook his head. "The old girl is round the bend."

Lila was incensed. "That isn't very respectful."

Serena appeared, wearing a flowing white robe, her head and face mostly covered by its hood.

Her children took a place on either side of her. "Our father has instructed us," the girl said. "She has to get away from all this."

"Yeah," her brother nodded. "Ma's taking a little vacation back to reality."

Serena broke from their grasp and climbed onto a dining chair, then the table.

"The Western day is nearing when the inner science of self-control will be found as necessary as the outer conquests of space," she intoned. "The Atomic Age will see men's minds sobered and broadened by the now indisputable truth that matter is a concentration of energy. Yoga is a bombproof shelter—"

She isn't mad at all, Lila thought. She's just reciting something from one of her books. Lila hadn't gotten much sense out of the books Serena had given her to read, but she did remember that "bombproof" sentence. She went to Serena, offering her hand to help her down. Serena reached out for Lila, then drew back. "Do I know you?"

Serena got down from the table without help, and with a tender look in her eye, she placed her hands on Lila's shoulders.

Lila turned to the young people. "See, she knows me. She's not crazy. She's going to tell me some great truth now. That's really why I've been coming here. I didn't see it before, but she *is* my guru. She will teach me how to have some reason for living."

A look of terror came over Serena's face. "You must flee. NOW, Lila. These people are our enemies." Serena crawled behind a chair, pulled another to it to barricade herself in, then curled into a fetal position.

For no good reason, Nelia's pleasant face careened back and forth before Lila's eyes. She strained for the sound of the tinkling wind chimes on Serena's front door, hoping for the highly unlikely.

"Go now." Serena's voice was a whisper. "But be very careful. They are trying to stop us. The CIA is watching the house. They are working with the Mafia. Your car might explode. I know for a fact that—"

Devastated, Lila went, not even retrieving her sodden skirt and shoes from Serena's bathroom. Who would help her cope now? Not Homer. He did try, but didn't really understand her need for something beyond their glued-together relationship. Once there had been The Herd—yes, that awful name—but it had been a solidarity against a strangeness none of them had ever really comprehended when they'd agreed to come here. Then this confusing world had changed everything.

❀ ↝ ❀ ↝ ❀ ↝ ❀

The brilliantly lit nighttime Hotel Borobudur, in its glittering chandelier splendor, teemed with women in long dresses and men in long-sleeved *batik* shirts, Jakarta's formal dress for men. Lila waited patiently as a Pan Am stewardess ahead of her maneuvered her portable luggage cart off the escalator. There were clumps of people everywhere, standing, sitting, waiting for cocktails, for dinner, for some performance.

She saw the Australian couple she'd met in the hotel drug store when she was buying hemorrhoid medicine. Somehow it hadn't seemed out of place when the robust husband had said, "So American Sheilas have the same problem as the Missus." She caught a glimpse of Miss Indonesia, remembering her from that disastrous Long-Staying-Guest party. A few other faces seemed familiar,but she couldn't place them. She passed the chatter of the open coffee shop and finally reached her alcove. She was shameless. Tonight she didn't even have the excuse of reading the news-paper.

Lila concentrated on a beautiful folding screen, intricately carved with *Wayang* figures, passing by on broad shoulders. A cart followed with stacks of folding chairs. Lila cleared her throat. Nelia did not look up from the book she was reading. Lila craned her neck to see the cover. Another one of those *Wayang* things was splashed across it. Now and then Nelia wrote something in her composition book.

Lila studied her fingers. In a while a group of Indonesians passed in exotic costumes from the time of the princely courts, the great Sultanates. They carried a variety of instruments: some stringed, some of bamboo, a zither, and drums in a variety of sizes. A swelling crowd tromped in their wake. The atmosphere was charged with the excitement of a special event about to happen.

Lila looked hopefully at Nelia's bent head. She cleared her throat again. "Ahhh, Mrs. Hoopes."

"Please—Lila," she said shyly. Then, "I looked for you, but a man in a tuxedo was playing your piano."

"My day of rest, you see. Do you remember I invited you to go to *Wayang Suluh* with me tonight?"

Lila did not want to acknowledge that. "Suluh?" she asked instead.

"It is an invention of the twentieth century. It relates contemporary his-tory and educates the public on matters the government would have them know and understand. As a developing country, my people need to have stories of the present to learn from as well as the *lakons* of the past." Nelia wiped her fountain pen with a tissue, capped it, and dropped it into her large bag where the notebook had gone.

"There are many problems of my country to get interested in besides flooding." Nelia engaged Lila's eyes. "That is all my power is, Lila, showing you that you can choose to help others choose or you can wallow in your own reflection."

Lila stood. "Homer will be wondering where I am."

"You *should* see this performance," Nelia said. "It's just down the hall in one of the party rooms."

A voice in Lila's head shouted, "I *could* see this performance," but her lips said nothing. She picked up her purse, put it back down, picked it up again.

They looked at one another sadly. "Lila, you have to stop this," Nelia said. "This being neither here nor there is no good." She turned away and entered the foot traffic.

Lila watched until she disappeared, then started for the lower lobby. But something stopped her, a new feeling, a need. She turned around. Taking a deep breath, she walked toward the doorway where Nelia had disappeared.

She stared at the hushed audience. A smiling boy handed her a program, assuring her it would explain everything. Still she hugged the wall. He turned away to seat someone else.

The traditional orchestra was making strange tune-up percussion sounds. A man wearing a turban, a Nehru jacket, and a sarong entered. A dagger was stuck in the back of his cummerbund. He checked his intricately carved and multi-colored puppets that were stuck in a banana tree log, then sat cross-legged before them. The room darkened, only the screen illuminated. The *gamelan* made exotic music. Phantoms fluttered across the screen. The *dalang* began to speak in the distinctive voices of the narrator and his characters.

Still hesitant, Lila searched the audience for Nelia, but she was someone vague and nebulous now. The boy appeared again, and with trembling legs, Lila followed him down the aisle, seeking salvation in the projections at the front of the room, finding herself a shadow cast on the wall of Ballroom A.

SATU LAGI:
Edythe

EATRICE HAD WORKED FOR MRS. SHEETZ FOR ALL OF THE SIX YEARS THE Sheetzes had been in Indonesia, performing miracles at the exact moment Mrs. Sheetz couldn't possibly cope. Mrs. Sheetz often told herself she would give up anything to keep Beatrice, except that one beer she allowed herself at 11 a.m. and the martinis at cocktail time, which was whatever hour she declared it.

Beatrice got her up in the morning with a Virgin Mary and pads of witch hazel for her eyes and helped her to bed at night with gentle understanding. Beatrice was a renowned cook in the expat community, so no one ever turned down a dinner invitation from Edythe and Ed Sheetz. Beatrice managed the household accounts and supervised the old man who was the houseboy and the young girl who did the bathrooms and laundry.

Beatrice was what other Indonesians called an Indo, offspring of an Indonesian and a European. When Mrs. Sheetz first heard the expression, she thought it a Western abbreviation for all Indonesians, but was quickly put straight by Beatrice, who told her they would be insulted if referred to that way. It didn't matter one whit to Mrs. Sheetz who or where Beatrice came from, just that she was here, a friend and confidant who calmed her fears and never disagreed with her. Nor did it seem to bother the other servants in the neighborhood. Everyone had great respect for Beatrice's capabilities.

Beatrice was of a heavy girth, which set her apart from the small, delicate Indonesians. She was taller, too—statuesque, Mrs. Sheetz often said. Her eyes were a piercing blue, set in a beige face that was always serene. Unlike Mr. Sheetz, Beatrice never got excited when Mrs. Sheetz made mistakes. In fact, she never seemed to disapprove of anything Mrs. Sheetz did. Without her, Mrs. Sheetz would never have been complimented constantly for her ability to take everything in stride and to orient the green arrivals to their new world. Beatrice dosed her daily with cups of confidence, tablespoons of ingenuity, and soupcons of gentle humor that helped her laugh at herself at just the right moment.

It was her precious hours with Beatrice that Mrs. Sheetz treasured most in an otherwise dreary and lonely existence. They were truly the times when she was just plain Edith, or even Edie, the name of her youth, and not the blithe, caustic Edythe Sheetz— with a "z"—at all. That was the armor she used to face a world where she was thought a fool by many, merely tolerated by others.

Best of all, Beatrice helped Mrs. Sheetz keep her dream alive—the dream that one day she would go back to Philadelphia's Main Line and live happily ever after on the estate she'd inherited from her father. Beatrice let her ramble on about that wonderful house she'd grown up in, with its wainscoted library and music room, the chandeliered ballroom, and great French doors opening out onto terraced grounds.

Her father, a famous cartoonist, had many friends in the arts. Stokowski had played their piano. Most inspiring to Edythe—a fledgling ballet student at the time— Pavlova, in her last days, had danced, with the oriental rugs rolled back, in the grand parlor. Beatrice was to see it all, of course, for she had promised Edythe she would go with her when the time came. And Ed? Edythe's husband was only a shadow in her picture of how it would be for her and Beatrice.

❀ ⤳ ❀ ⤳ ❀ ⤳ ❀

The day that turned Edythe's life upside down started out like any other. She arose late, as usual, when most of the housecleaning had been done. The *babu cuci* was just tucking in the clean sheets in Mr. Sheetz's bedroom. Edythe sat in the cozy sunroom, lingering over her coffee—a bright bird in red satin robe—resting temporarily in a sea of white rattan and tall green philodendron as Beatrice spread marmalade over her croissant. Beatrice baked them herself every day even though Edythe kept telling her, "I really shouldn't." Then, in a conspiratorial whisper, "I have to keep my figure."

Beatrice grinned broadly, not a bit self-conscious about her missing eyetooth, and moved the powdered milk and coarse brown sugar closer for Edythe's second cup. She stood companionably beside Edythe until the other servants scurried away to have their mid-morning tea. It was then that Edythe would ask Beatrice to bring a cup and sit with her.

As usual, Beatrice brought the appointment book from its place where she kept it on the cookbook shelf in the kitchen. On Fridays, Beatrice always insisted on going over the next week despite Edythe's protests at planning so far ahead. Absentmindedly, Edythe began spreading a second croissant with marmalade. What the hell! She never ate lunch, and she hadn't gained an ounce in years, She thought with glee how this irritated the hell out or her neighbor and tormentor, Mildred Walburton.

"We need a plan for August 17, Madame," Beatrice began.

Edythe sighed happily. She'd been a sucker for Beatrice since the first time that lyrical voice had called her "Madame." It always made her spine tingle. It was so European.

"Ah, yes, Independence Day for Indonesia, but not for me. I have to babysit the wives of those damn bigwigs coming over for the management seminar." She heaved a great sigh. "But it's our ticket out of here, Beatrice."

Beatrice was staring out the window. Edythe couldn't see anything out there to look at. It was always the same, no leaves changing color, no snow, just tropical beauty that had been getting on her nerves lately. "Beatrice," she reminded.

Beatrice came back to herself. "Yes, Madame." She consulted the appointment book. "You can put off showing the new women at the hotel where the duty-free store is. You'll have to send your regrets for all your usual activities that week, including, I suppose, the Petroleum Club Indoor Picnic. Instead, you'll be having a dinner here for those important people—" Beatrice paused, her eyebrows arched.

Thinking how imperative it was she please these visitors, something she could never do without Beatrice to guide her, she suddenly felt a great thirst. "My beer, Beatrice? It's almost eleven."

Beatrice did not jump up immediately as she normally would. She sat there playing with her pencil, a pensive look on her face that Edythe had never seen before. "Madame," she began. Then heaving a great sigh, she got up to get the beer.

They went over the revised schedule. There was to be a cocktail party at the Walburtons on the two visiting couples' arrival. The next day, the Walburtons and Sheetzes would take them offshore to visit the new gas platform. Then Beatrice thought Mrs. Sheetz might take the women to Mini-Indonesia, where they could see costumes, handicrafts, and housing of the other islands. Beatrice knew a place the women not only could buy batik, they could also watch the complex process involved in waxing and dyeing the cloth in intricate patterns.

Edythe got into the spirit. "And Ancol Dreamland. There's supposed to be something for everyone in that entertainment complex, and they'll be staying at the hotel out there anyway."

"I'd have thought you'd have them at the Borobudur."

"Normally, of course. But the men insisted on staying where the seminar is being held. How about that casino next door to the hotel?" Beatrice made a face. "Do you really think Mrs. Walburton would let you take those women to a casino? Can you see her sitting next to what she calls the 'lower element' playing card games?"

They both laughed. "Old warthog," Edythe said. "Warhorse," Beatrice said. Edythe said, "Battleaxe." They laughed until tears came, playing their favorite game. Edythe went a step further. "Knock her on her keister someday."

"I wish I could see that." Beatrice wiped her eyes.

"If I couldn't cut loose like this once in a while, I'd never be able to face that hippo's malarkey," Edythe said.

Beatrice suddenly became professional, wanting to plan the menu for the farewell dinner party.

Edythe waved her hand airily. "Just do it. Whatever it is. I know it will be wonderful."

"But, Madame, you should know that I am not—" Her eyes met Edythe's, and she looked away.

"I'll write it down and put it on the kitchen table so anyone can see," Beatrice said, gathering the dirty dishes. She looked reflective for a moment, then said, "You know, that old houseboy is quite a good cook. You might let him do it sometime."

Edythe patted Beatrice's shoulder. "Whatever for? You're my *koki*." It was time to bathe and dress. Edythe looked at the empty beer glass. "*Satu lagi?*" she asked. "One again?" She passed the glass to Beatrice, who giggled and waggled a no-no finger. It was a game they played every morning, and always, in spite of her desire for alcohol, Edythe went off to the shower where she stood under the hot water, visualizing Beatrice tending Edythe's mansion back home.

❀ ↜ ❀ ↜ ❀ ↜ ❀

When Edythe came home from mah jong, she was thirsty because she'd won a thousand *rupiah*. Happiness always made her want to declare cocktail hour, as did sadness, loneliness, and anger. She couldn't find Beatrice anywhere. Perhaps she was next door gossiping with the Walburtons' housegirl. Through Beatrice, Edythe always knew what the neighborhood servants' problems were, what expat couple wasn't speaking, and who had bought what on their last trip to Singapore. Just this morning Beatrice had told her that the new couple, three doors down, were trying to have a baby. Miriam didn't know much about them, except Hans Wilhelm was a Dutchman who smoked big black cigars while walking his dog and his wife Katherine, who was not Dutch, kept to herself.

Carrying the gin bottle, she went to her room to change her clothes for cocktail hour at the Walburtons.' It was their turn. She took a couple of swigs from the bottle. She needed a little glow on before the official cocktail hour. On Mildred's turf, they were prone to gang up on her.

All her shoes had been polished. Everything in her closet was freshly pressed. Even her dresser drawers had been straightened. Sharply creased white pants and a crisp white blouse with crocheted puffed sleeves and no back lay on the bed beside fresh wispy underwear. Next to them were her favorite gold earrings and all her gold bracelets. White sandals with a nice heel sat at attention on the floor nearby.

❋ ⤳ ❋ ⤳ ❋ ⤳ ❋

The pre-cocktail glow carried her through Ed's arrival home from the office and through fitting several pieces into the jigsaw puzzle spread out on a card table in the dining room while he showered and changed. Then she was trying not to appear greedy as she was presented her first martini by Horace Walburton. Once again, she'd lived up to their unspoken demand not to have any martinis until the first one with them.

"The Perkins and Auslanders will want to see a lot of cultural things, I expect," Horace was saying.

"I've got that covered, old boy," Edythe said.

Ed said, "The big day is really the one offshore. That's when we're going to make points."

"I would wear something—" Mildred looked Edythe up and down "— a little less youthful."

Edythe reached for the cocktail shaker, but it was empty. "If you've got it, flaunt it, I always say." Edythe might be menopausal, but she prided herself on a slim figure that looked good in clothes. She let her glance run over Mildred's pudgy body in a pointed way that didn't seem to register.

"They're both vice-presidents," Ed said proudly.

"Hopefully, they both stand up to pee," Edythe said, noting that Horace was mixing more martinis. She sat on her hands to keep from peeling off fingernail polish while she waited.

"What do you think the women will be like?" Mildred asked.

"Typical tourists." Edythe gulped down her martini, then poured another. Everyone looked the other way as usual.

"We'll have to tell them not to eat salad in the hotel while they're here. I have extra Lomotil in case they do get the Jakarta jets, and—" Mildred chattered on. Edythe canceled her out, making another martini disappear.

"Look, Ed, Mildred and I are going to do everything we can to help those guys see you're the man for that Philly job. They've really got the clout to get you in. If we just work on them, it's in the bag."

"Personally, I don't know why anybody would want to go back to state-side living," Mildred said. "I'm perfectly happy right here."

Edythe was trying to pin an olive down with a tiny spear when Mildred's hand closed down over the top of the glass. Mildred looked at her with what Edythe had always thought of as slitted pig eyes. "You know you'll have to behave, don't you?"

"Moi?" Edythe shook her head coquettishly.

"Yeah, Edythe, you," Horace said. "You'll have to lay off the sauce."

"I beg your pardon," she said.

Damn them! It had started on their first assignment overseas. London was parties, pub lunches, after-theatre nightcaps—three years of champagne, lager, and brandy, always at a decreed place and time. She carried the British civilized way of doing things to Iran, where she lost the baby because of poor medical care. But she found a houseboy who for two years made good mixed drinks that rocked her depression to sleep early in the evenings.

During seven years in India, she made it a ritual—telling Ed about her long days as they sipped icy manhattans carried in on a brass tray by the Indian bearer; spicy snacks prepared by the cook; the glow after the second cocktail arriving simultaneously with the lighting of the candles on the dinner table. Part of that ritual involved discussing truly important things—which never happened now with Warthog and her toad husband. Four years into Saudi Arabia, she'd discovered her true drink was gin.

Then Ed got a cushy job in Singapore, but he sent her to the States to dry out, and when she returned it was only a few months until he was assigned to Indonesia. She was frustrated at leaving Singapore, a place she'd loved at first sight. She became overwhelmed with packing up and moving again, and felt uncertain if she could handle another culture or sort out the company pecking order in yet another place. Ed came home one day to find her waiting with martinis and cheese sticks the *amah* had made. This time Edythe added some Mozart to the ritual. Once in Jakarta, Ed had added the Walburtons.

"Whatever happened to Mozart?" she asked them.

They looked at her as if she'd lost her mind. Ed ground his cigar into a stuffed mushroom on his hors d'oeuvre plate. "I don't know why I'm even bothering. She's sure to ruin it for us."

He was right, of course, and the panic she'd been trying to bury was suddenly in full bloom. She stood, a bit unsteady, the martinis now ashes in her mouth.

Mildred's housegirl edged into the room. "For you, *Nyonya*," she said, handing Edythe a folded piece of paper. The girl's eyes studied the floor.

"Yes, of course, my lover. An immediate assignation, no doubt," she told the others, who exchanged glances of long suffering.

She opened the note and began to read aloud: *"Dear Madame, I am sorry to leave you but I must."* Edythe's voice faltered. She forced herself to read on. *"I am not a young girl any longer. You know how that is. Forgive me. I will always remember your kindness. Your friend, Beatrice."*

Edythe sat down abruptly. "I don't understand."

The housegirl began to giggle. "Beatrice go away big Sumatran."

Edythe's hand caressed her throat as if to smooth away the lump thickening there. Ed and Horace began to laugh.

"This must be a joke. Yes, somebody's idea of a joke. Beatrice wouldn't—" Edythe couldn't finish the sentence.

"Don't be so dense, Edythe," Mildred said. "Your precious Beatrice has eloped."

❀ ✁ ❀ ✁ ❀ ✁ ❀

Edythe took to sleeping later and later in the mornings, having no reason to get up. When she could no longer stretch out her pointless dreams, she headed for the refrigerator and the beer. Now that there was no one to waggle a finger at her when she asked *"Satu lagi?"* she had one again and one again and one again, but she spaced them out over the afternoon while she waited for the ritual cocktails to begin.

Grief and loss were her companions even when she had to stare down Mildred or make excuses to Ed for something, anything—existing even. She couldn't bear to answer the phone. She had always mouthed to Beatrice what to say, then Beatrice would say what she wanted, which was always better. All day she paced between the bedroom and kitchen, alternately sniffing the sachet Beatrice had placed in her lingerie drawers, picking up and putting down Beatrice's treasured wok or her favorite vegetable-dicing knife.

Looking at the gold and blue and green dazzle outside only made her pain worse, for Beatrice had always wakened her with, "Another beautiful day, Madame." She began to wear an odd assortment of clothes to cocktail hour because Beatrice wasn't there to pick them out. Every evening, they harangued her about pulling herself together, about how much was riding on "appearances" to the Perkins and Auslanders. But Edythe only slid further into the "martunis" as she began to call them.

Then one day, she woke up angry. How dare Beatrice do this to her! She was only a servant, after all. Edythe would show her, show them all, she could get along very well without her. The first thing she did was have a tomato juice instead of a beer. Then she dressed carefully, complimenting herself for her excellent taste. Since it was another fucking beautiful day, she might as well go somewhere.

She thought of the Hotel Borobudur, but there was always the chance she'd run into someone she knew there, so she went to the cozy Hotel Kemang instead. "Iced tea and satay and salad, *mas*," she told the waiter as she took a place on the patio by the pool. She'd show Beatrice she could eat a decent meal if she put her mind to it.

At the next table, she heard an unmistakable male Australian accent ask a Eurasian girl if she wanted company. Edythe sighed and sipped her iced tea; then irritated—by what she didn't know—pushed the glass away. In the pool, an expatriate woman clung to the edge, thrashing her legs, wedding ring obvious. Crouched on the concrete above her, a grinning Englishman made his pitch by calling her a Yankee and teasing her about the American Revolution. Edythe shuddered at the reminder. Indonesia's Revolution celebration was only three days away, the day the Perkins and Auslanders would arrive.

The waiter placed the satay before her, still sizzling, encircled by spicy condiments and rice. Her stomach turned over, and she pushed the food away. "A martini," she said, "very dry and very quick." The first long draw was sheer heaven. She finished it quickly. "*Satu lagi, mas*," she called to the waiter. She listened to the outrageous things the Australian was saying. The Englishman had entered the pool, continuing his banter with the married woman. For some reason Edythe had a lump in her throat. "*Satu lagi, mas*," she called, "one again."

She clanked her bracelets against the table in annoyance. Yes, there had been another man once. Actually, she had met him here. She hadn't wanted it at first, then she'd thought how nice the newness would be. She hadn't felt like stone then, prisoner in some isolated wasteland. But she had waited too long and he'd found someone else. Anger invaded her, then was gone, leaving cold, gnawing emptiness. *"Satu lagi, mas."*

❀ ⤳ ❀ ⤳ ❀ ⤳ ❀

Edythe woke at first light and didn't know where she was. All she remembered was that she had two days to get herself together or she'd never get out of Indonesia. It *was* a beautiful country with a beautiful culture and beautiful people, but she'd lived overseas twenty years, and that was quite enough, thank you.

Now she remembered coming home from the Kemang, determined to find Beatrice and bring her home. The Walburton's housegirl said Beatrice had gone to Anyer Beach to cook in the motel her boyfriend managed. The romance could already have run its course, and then, too, face to face, Beatrice would not say no to Edythe.

She stretched her cramped legs and bumped—no, the gear shift. My God, she had taken the car, and yes, there were brown faces looking in the windows at her. They tapped and knocked and wanted cigarettes or a ride or chocolates. Through the windshield, she saw she was parked in a kind of meadow at the dead-end of a deeply rutted road almost covered with grass. Thank God, she hadn't killed anyone—but how would she know?

When she'd made them understand she didn't want to buy duck eggs, when she thought she understood the directions for getting back on the road to Anyer, she inched out of the field, concentrating on not hitting any of the crowd she'd drawn. Edythe sipped courage from the silver flask she found on the seat beside her. If she'd come this far, there was no use turning back. On a slightly better road, she forged on, side by side bicycles and jeeps, ox carts and *becaks*, people thronging to early morning market. Many times she thought to turn back or better yet to find a phone and have someone come and get her, but then she'd remember her quest—rescue Beatrice. She gritted her teeth, raised the flask, and kept going.

Finally, she came to a bumpy gravelled road in such bad repair it couldn't possibly lead to a resort like Anyer Beach. She was exhausted and hopelessly lost, but she couldn't return to Jakarta without Beatrice. Stately trees arched over the road, reminding her of Bryn Mawr Avenue back in Philadelphia. She clung to the safe, closed-in feeling, trying not to give in to her rising panic. There was not a soul in sight, the way ahead blessed with silent peace and comfortable tranquility where Edythe became one with the timelessness of deep Java.

Around a bend, and finally, through bleary eyes, Edythe read "Anyer Beach Motel" painted on a low-slung building. Across from it was a row of Western-style cottages with driveways amidst dense foliage and brilliant flowers. A manicured lawn, dotted with tables covered by hut-like roofs in place of umbrellas, sloped to the sparkling white sand edging the Sunda Straits. She hunched over the wheel, pulling herself together for Beatrice.

If her housekeeper was surprised to see her, she gave no indication of it. She went behind the bar and came back with Edythe's morning Virgin Mary. Edythe stared out over her glass at bowling alleys, incongruous in this remote place, that took up most of the large room that was also the bar and restaurant. Now that she was finally facing Beatrice, she didn't know what to say. She tried to think of one of her caustic quips that always made Beatrice laugh, but her mind was sluggish and unresponsive. "I—I want—" she began.

Beatrice took over. "We will talk later. Come." She took her across the street and unlocked a cottage that looked, inside, like any shoddy American motel. Edythe showered and slept instantly. It was late afternoon when she woke refreshed and put on the clothes Beatrice had washed and ironed. She walked out on the lawn and sat at one of the hut-roofed tables. Down the beach, naked boys ran from the surf. One scaled a tall palm and began throwing coconuts down to the others.

Edythe felt serene and purposeful when Beatrice joined her. "There's no one else here?"

"Weekends mostly, *Nyonya*. Big buses come."

"But outside of that boy in the office, I didn't see anyone even running the place," she prodded.

"They appear when needed," Beatrice said.

Edythe had seen no one who fit the description of Beatrice's alleged lover. Perhaps it was only servant gossip. Why then had Beatrice left her? But if there was no man Beatrice would be more likely to come back.

"You like it here?" she started tentatively. She made a big show of looking at her watch.

Beatrice looked at her with wary eyes, then looked away. When their eyes met again, Beatrice was her old self. "Sometimes, *Nyonya*, sometimes."

Edythe looked at her watch again. "Goodness, it's five o'clock already." Their eyes locked, but Beatrice did not offer to get her a martini.

"I never ask before, *Nyonya*—it was not my business. How did you ever let the gin bottle get between you and life?"

Shocked, Edythe looked out at the famous volcano, Krakatau, etched against a pale pink sky on the distant horizon.

"There is a group of people in the city who help people with your problem, *Nyonya*. You have to go to meetings and confess that—"

"And you think that I'm... " Edythe laughed and laughed. It was so funny. "Alcoholics Anonymous? In Jakarta?" That was even funnier.

A look came over Beatrice's face that Edythe had never seen before. It made her say, "I'll stop having my little pick-me-ups. Really. I will. But my nerves are so bad after the ride. Just this once." There were only a few drops left in the silver flask to dribble down her throat. As she swallowed, she watched the deepening rose of the sky rouge Beatrice's noncommittal face. She searched for some quick-witted drollery or a sarcastic gibe at herself, but her audience had turned away to pick dead leaves from a pineapple bush.

"Look, *Nyonya*, look!" Beatrice pointed to Krakatau, bathed now in deep coral, a magnificent sunset such as Edythe had never seen before. But all this cloying beauty stood between her and what she wanted. She threw herself into Beatrice's arms, no longer able to keep the sobs back. "I can't do it without you. You must come home with me. And when *Tuan* gets the reassignment, we'll go back to Philadelphia, and everything will be as I promised."

Beatrice smoothed away the strands of hair plastered by tears to Edythe's face. "Listen to me, *Nyonya*. Some things are not meant to be." Beatrice's hand and face flamed in the crimson light. "Some things should remain a beautiful dream."

"You must not say that! Not my dream." Edythe was on her knees now, the scarlet sky outlining her silhouette. "I have to have you, Beatrice—at least this once, while I help Ed get this transfer."

"Every year you said he was going to get it, and he never did."

"This time it will happen. Just like I said, we'll go to the gazebo every morning to plan our day, and I'll have deer put on the grounds and—and we'll travel sometimes. I'll show you my country. Only you have to help me now."

Beatrice's face in the salmon light exhibited the first real emotion Edythe had seen there since she arrived, and there was pain in her voice. "Things are not always what you think they will be. Sometimes promises are not kept."

With sudden insight, Edythe said, "I am not like him, Beatrice. I will keep my promise to you."

"He has gone away, without a word, with much money taken." There was no emotion in Beatrice's voice now, her face impassive once more.

Edythe threw her arms around Beatrice again, this time with unbridled joy. "Then there is no reason you can't come home with me."

"I must stay and pay off the money he stole. I have promised."

"Money, shmoney, I have lots. Whatever you need."

"You are very generous, *Nyonya*. Thank you." She counted the bills handed her. "This is quite enough. You understand it is very bad he ran away. I must give notice and work until they find another cook."

"Okay. I understand that." Edythe could agree to anything. Beatrice was coming home.

"So you must take care of the visitors on your own," Beatrice said. "You must 'lay off the sauce,' as Mr. Walburton would say. Then I will come when I can." In the darkness that had quickly come as the fiery orange sun was swallowed by the sea, Edythe could barely see Beatrice's expression. No, it couldn't be pity.

"You *are* coming home?"

"Yes, yes, *Nyonya,* but first you must do exactly what I say."

"Anything."

"You will leave in the morning. I have called Mr. Sheetz so he would not worry. I have someone who will drive you. If you were to hurt one of the children who play on the road, the people would attack you—with stones probably."

Edythe shuddered, remembering, and then hard as she tried, she could read nothing in Beatrice's moonlit face that hadn't always been there.

❀ ᷇᷇ ❀ ᷇᷇ ❀ ᷇᷇ ❀

It was eleven o'clock in the morning, and Edythe wanted her beer. Instead, she went into Beatrice's room. Preparing to move Beatrice into the house had been the first thing she'd done when she arrived from Anyer Beach. Beatrice was really her housekeeper, and not just a cook. The best guest room would be a surprise when she returned. Edythe had put a brand-new comforter on the bed; Beatrice would not be accustomed to air conditioning. She'd hung her own dressing gown that Beatrice loved on the back of the door and put an elaborate sewing basket she'd been given as a Christmas present on the dresser.

Visiting the room she had prepared for Beatrice became Edythe's new eleven o'clock fix. She could almost feel Beatrice there with her, talking about everything as they had every morning. On Monday, she told Beatrice how she'd drank only tonic water at cocktail hour and saw how inane the Three Cocktail Mouseketeers really were. She'd called Horace a pompous windbag and actually told Mildred she was going to knock her on her keister if she didn't stop putting her down, then went off to bed early to be fresh to meet the plane.

On Tuesday, Edythe went to Beatrice's room and sat at the dainty desk, flipping pristine pages of the new account book she'd placed there. The VIPs had arrived on schedule, amazed to find Indonesia having an Independence Day just like the USA.

There were more guns on parade than usual, and firecrackers all day and night were unnerving, but they had marveled at Jaya Ancol's Dreamland where they were staying.

Edythe took everything out of the sewing box, looking at each item. "I doubt they'll swim in any of the pools with their artificial waves and slides," she told Beatrice, "or play golf at night under lights." Edythe couldn't make everything fit back into the sewing box, so she lined up spools of thread, a packet of needles, a measuring tape, a darning egg on the top of the dresser. "Do you think they'll go to the oceanarium or the bird park?" Her friend and confidante didn't answer. So Edythe told Beatrice what she really wanted to know. "I drank gallons of iced tea and impressed even Ed with my knowledge of Indonesian history."

Edythe had no chance to have elevenses with Beatrice on Wednesday because they left early to go offshore to see the new gas platform. But she would have told Beatrice that the helicopter ride out there over shoreline, rice paddies, and villages was a big hit. As was the sumptuous lunch in the platform's mess hall. Except Pam Perkins said she couldn't see how such a gorgeous cake could taste like cardboard. Edythe promised one from her own kitchen and basked in the look of gratitude from the plump Sally Auslander, who had a Mamie Eisenhower hairdo. Pam Perkins, who wore ribbons in her hair and looked at you like a wounded animal, said, "I like chocolate." But then the illusion that Beatrice was home, awaiting Edythe's bidding, faded, and she realized she didn't know a damn thing about baking a cake.

On Thursday night, late, Edythe danced into Beatrice's room, drunk with success. She hugged the dressing gown to her breast as she swayed around the room. "Ed said that Perky Pam and Silly Sally were raving about me. Can you believe it, Beatrice?" She threw herself across the bed, her head indenting a pillow, knowing she had knocked herself out—explaining Wayang performances, identifying fruits at the pasar, bargaining for silver jewelry, showing them what real Chinese food was like.

"Then I took them to the Balinese craft shop—you know the one, Beatrice—where the doorway is guarded by a mythical wooden character sporting a huge red penis!" Edythe laughed and laughed at the memory of the look on their faces. Mildred's had been the best. It had not been until she took them to the Ramayana ballet and showed them the night view of the city from Hotel Indonesia's roof that they finally started speaking to her again.

❀ ꜱ ❀ ꜱ ❀ ꜱ ❀

The insistent phone interrupted Edythe's wonderful dream—she and Beatrice were waving goodbye to Perky Pam and Silly Sally. She looked at the illuminated clock on the bedside table—2 a.m. Sally Auslander was beside herself. Her husband's deep sleep had been broken by a woman calling to ask if he needed company in bed.

Edythe laughed and laughed. "It's only the 'night butterflies.'"

Pam Perkins grabbed the phone. "We won't put up with this sort of thing. You've got to get us out of this hotel."

"It's no big deal, Pam, unless your husband says yes."

Sally was back on the phone. "Now. Tonight. We'll be packed and waiting."

Eventually, Edythe had them settled in the Hotel Borobudur and went home to spend a sleepless daybreak, apprehensive something was still wrong. An outraged Paul Perkins called at 8 a.m. They'd not slept at all. After she left, a desk clerk kept calling their rooms saying, "Very bad, two people in a one-people room. Very bad."

Trying not to laugh again, she explained that it was common for the desk to get registrations mixed up, that the clerk thought one person had booked their rooms, trying to evade the double rate. "I suppose it was because I made the arrangements."

Paul's frosty voice said, "The women do not want you to come for them today. They are sleeping late, and then they want to explore the Borobudur. They've fallen in love with it."

There were mumbles in the background, the sound of the phone being dropped. Keith Auslander said then, "Call off the dinner party, too. We've decided to get in an extra session before we leave tomorrow."

She slammed down the receiver and went next door to tell Mildred, who said, "I'm glad not to deal with them today. I have the Jakarta jets."

Edythe said, "We have to do *something*. You know. The transfer. We can't let them leave with a bad taste in their mouth."

"Maybe *you* can't, but I can," Mildred said.

"Eat more salad in hotels, why don't you, Mildred." Edythe slammed out the back door.

She passed Ed and Horace getting into the Walburtons' car, but didn't acknowledge them. In the kitchen, she rummaged in the back of the refrigerator for tomato juice, her hand hesitating over a bottle of beer. She closed the door firmly. It was eleven o'clock and time to go to Beatrice's room. Reality caught up with her. Beatrice was not here. She took a beer out. What the hell. One couldn't hurt, not watered down with tomato juice.

She carried the glass to the phone, and after some delay was speaking brisk Indonesian to the Anyer Beach Motel. No, Beatrice could not come to the phone. Beatrice was out, or unavailable, or busy. Edythe could not make out the end of the sentence over the static and buzzing on the line before it died.

She stared at the glass, reached for it. A vision of Beatrice came, waggling her finger, taking the glass away. Yes, of course, Beatrice was on her way. Edythe felt it. That's why she couldn't get her on the phone. Everything would still be perfect. The Perkins and Auslanders would take back glowing reports. In Bryn Mawr, she'd be a patron of the arts. With Beatrice, she could do anything. She ran out the gate. A mirage of heat shimmers wavered over the dusty road as far as she could see, but her housekeeper—her friend—wasn't anywhere in sight.

❋ ꒜ ❋ ꒜ ❋ ꒜ ❋

Edythe arrived at Hotel Borobudur in late afternoon, determined to get back on the good side of Pam and Sally. They'd stayed in the sun too long at the pool, worn out their legs riding exercise bicycles in the gym, forgotten lunch, and sat, lost and bored, amidst a sea of shopping bags from the arcade. "It'll be fun," she told them. "An evening in Jakarta few tourists ever see."

They were hesitant. The boys might be home soon. "The 'boys' aren't worrying about you," Edythe told them. They were easily convinced of that, and soon the little group passed the Pendopo Lounge on their way to the car. Nelia motioned to Edythe, and she hesitated. No, all would be lost if she went in there—even for a moment. It was all up to her now, and she didn't intend to lose this transfer. "No, it's a surprise," she said blithely in answer to Pam's question. "You'll long remember this night."

Jakarta, out the car windows, bejeweled with lights, seemed as inviting as any other great city, and she began pointing out places of interest: the famous statue in front of Hotel Indonesia—slight interest; the bank where she changed her money—bored looks; the travel agency where she bought holiday tickets—polite coughs. She shrank back against the upholstery, racking her brain what to do to knock their socks off. Undefeated, she ordered the driver to Glodok, the Chinese enclave.

"Isn't that temple there interesting? The word for temple here is *c-a-n-*

d-i, pronounced with a *ch* sound. Beautiful word, isn't it?" Her voice raced on, but she still had no idea where to take them until she saw the strings of lights, the oil-cloth covered tables. "Here. Stop here," she ordered the driver of the car she'd hired at the last minute when her own driver didn't show up. He kept going. "*Disana! Disana!*" she shouted. He braked suddenly, almost sending them into the front seat. Then, in reverse, he backed up so carelessly that people at the tables jumped up in alarm.

Often in Singapore, Edythe had "eaten on the street" as they called it, but never here, although she'd heard such places came alive at night in Jakarta's Chinatown, empty lots instantly turning into eating stalls. Now she crowded the three of them in at the only available table.

"I'm glad you thought of this," Sally said, "I'm starved."

"Me, too," Pam said.

"Just bring us your best dishes," Edythe, drunk with new confidence, said gaily to the attendant.

"Really, Edythe," Sally said, looking with disdain at her neighbor's plate, "don't you think we should ask—?"

"Just leave everything to me," Edythe trilled. "This *is* my town. Relax. Enjoy a new experience."

Two Indonesian women approached the table, looking for a place to sit. Their dress was the last word in Western fashion, their hairdos impeccable, although they might have been wearing a bit too much makeup.

"General's wives, I bet," Pam said.

"More like models or actresses," Sally said. "Squeeze over." She banged her hips against Edythe's, motioning to the women to come sit with them.

Edythe took a closer look and was appalled. "No, you don't want to do this."

But Sally and Pam were grinning broadly at their new table companions.

"You dummies," Edythe whispered. "They're *banci* boys."

She answered their uncomprehending look. "You've just invited transvestites to sit with us."

Pam immediately turned her back on the *banci* boys and faced toward Sally and Edythe, which was not easy, considering they were all sitting on the same low bench.

Sally glared at Edythe. "You have brought us to a place we shouldn't be without our husbands."

"Where's your spirit of adventure?" Edythe asked. "You can dine out on this story for months in the States."

"An adventure?" Pam shuddered.

"Anyway the food's here," Edythe said. "Enjoy."

Edythe wasn't hungry, only thirsty. She watched the women pushing palm leaf-wrapped bundles around their plates as if afraid to see what was inside. Pam took a tiny bite of the gray square of *tahu*. At least Edythe could tell her that was soybean curd; she wasn't sure about the brown-looking noodles or the even darker sauced meat dish. It was probably goat, but she kept that information to herself.

The *banci* next to Pam reached over and, with a brilliant smile, spread a deep red paste over her food. "*Makan,*" he said. "*Baik sekali.*"

"He says it's very good," Edythe said weakly.

"Why not?" Sally held her plate up, and the gorgeous creature slathered the same goo on her food. Then both Sally and Pam toasted him with a fork and took a large bite.

Sally began to cough and spit, her face crimson. Pam grabbed for someone's bottle of beer, tears streaming down her face. The *bancis* laughed and laughed as both women jumped to their feet and ran from the table, clutching their throats. Her VIPs had been given *sambal,* a fiery paste of shrimp and chilies that made any other chili in the world appear mild. A chagrined Edythe followed them to the car where they waited for the driver, who didn't show up for twenty minutes.

❀ ⤳ ❀ ⤳ ❀ ⤳ ❀

Sally's voice croaked, "Can you imagine that? An amusement park right in the heart of downtown?" She pointed out the car window at the ferris wheel and roller coasters lighting up the night sky.

"There are many interesting things at Jakarta Fairgrounds," Edythe said, testing the waters.

Pam blew her nose loudly. "I don't like amusement rides. I want to go back to the hotel."

"I know," Edythe said, suddenly exultant. "Bingo. I bet you like to play bingo."

Sally looked like a kid at Christmas. "I play all the time at the Catholic Church at home. As a matter of fact, I'm quite lucky."

"No!" Pam said.

"C'mon, Perky, ah, Pam," Edythe wheedled. "It'll be fun." She couldn't think of anything more boring than bingo, but maybe—

"Okay, I'll go," Pam said. "if I can get a soda there to put out this fire," but her face was pulled into a pout.

The driver knew the way, and soon they were approaching rows of green benches and tables facing a stage under the stars where a raucous rock and roll band played. There were plenty of seats available. Sally insisted on four bingo cards, while Pam took one. Edythe thought she'd watch. If it had been the old days, she'd have declared cocktail hour immediately.

The leader of the band stepped up to a cage filled with small wooden coins with numbers on them and gave it a whirl. When it stopped, he took one out and began to sing. And then another and another, and he kept on singing while the band backed him up. Players were eagerly placing little paper dots on numbers on their cards. One woman leaned over Pam and pointed to several numbers. *"Disini, disini."* Her index finger stabbed a card.

"Oh, my God, he's *singing* the numbers," Edythe said.

"But I don't know Indonesian," Sally wailed.

"He's going too fast even if I did know what he's saying," Pam said, an I-was-right-not-to-want-to-come-here look on her face.

"I'll translate," Edythe offered, but she hardly got the number out before he'd sung two more. Pam pushed her card away. Sally doggedly tried to cover the numbers. A man came and sat beside Pam, indicating he would do it for her, and she let him without any fuss. The woman in front of Sally turned halfway in her seat and watched both her cards and Sally's. Edythe felt a sudden rush of affection for these Indonesians and all their countrymen.

Pam was trying to get a Coke from a *Kincamani* man, but he kept telling her, "Finish, *Nyonya*, finish."

"Give it up, Pamela," Edythe said. "He's out of soft drinks."

People were winning, games were starting over. Sally kept paying for more games, buying extra cards, a flushed, excited look on her face. Pam had given up and was morosely studying the players.

Edythe woke up when the man helping Pam kept asking her to play again, when the woman being so kind to Sally started winning, when the attendant hovered near, constantly waiting to collect more money.

Edythe made herself yawn. "It's getting late. We should go."

"No, no," Sally said feverishly. "I'm going to win soon."

"I'm going to play again," Pam said, after listening to the gentle voice of the man next to her. "I might be lucky after all."

The blaring music, the strain to catch the numbers, and the fact they were being cheated gave Edythe a headache. She wanted her bed. She'd done the best she could. "We really must go." Pam and Sally ignored her, caught up with watching the busy fingers of their bingo friends.

Edythe stood up, all patience gone. "They're shills for Christ's sake. You're being played for suckers."

Both woman looked toward their helpers, who were now melting into the crowd. A fat Chinese moved in. "I help." Edythe steered them away in the direction of the car. But after a fifteen-minute search, she had them totally lost out near some storage buildings in a deserted area.

"Are you sure this is where the car was?" Sally stood like a stork, rubbing one foot against her leg.

"Maybe we got turned around. That's it. This is a big place," Pam said. Then, "Oooh, my stomach's upset."

"Look, the driver has gone on a jaunt on his own. He'll find us when he gets back." Edythe hoped this was true.

"I need something to drink," Sally said, "those damn chilies."

"A soda would settle my stomach." Pam looked pointedly at Edythe.

"It's very late," Edythe said. "Most of the vendors have packed up and gone home. Besides, if we stray too far, the driver will never find us." She led her little party nearer to where she thought she'd last seen the car. A pile of cement blocks bloomed nearby amidst weeds and broken glass. Edythe was glad to sit down on one of them. Sally limped over and joined her. Pam reluctantly spread a handkerchief on a block before she sat. Voices and sounds of the closing fair reached them less often now.

"Really, Edythe, you should know enough to get a driver you can depend on."

"He might never come back," Pam wailed. "Then what will we do?"

From nowhere, a group of young men sauntered toward them. They laughed and pointed fingers. Sally glared. Pam began a low keening sound that sent the young toughs across the road to confer. Edythe picked up a large rock and held it in her lap beneath her handbag, telling herself Indonesians were not violent unless riled.

"There must be a phone somewhere," Pam shrieked.

"Don't guards patrol this place?" Sally asked.

The men approached them again, this time encircling them.

"Oh, my gawd," Pam cried. "I've wet myself."

Sally became a wary animal. "It's some ritual they do before attacking. For god's sake, Edythe, do something."

Suddenly, the men were singing in sweet, clear voices, and Edythe couldn't stop laughing. She wanted to tell the women they were merely being paid homage with a love song serenade, but it only made her laugh more to see Perky Pam and Silly Sally huddled together, looking at her as if she were a madwoman. Finally, with exuberant waves and shy smiles, the youths wandered off toward the Jakarta streets.

Edythe hesitated. But then extreme situations did call for extreme measures, and the women were on the verge of hysteria. She reached into her bag and pulled out the flask she'd been carrying—for reassurance only, of course. She looked at it longingly, made a decision, and offered it instead to the women.

"Really, Edythe," Sally's lips curled in a supercilious sneer, "at a time like this."

Pam glared at the flask. "You actually have been carrying that thing with you all evening?"

Something that had been holding Edythe together shattered into a million pieces. She was fed up with hand holding and babysitting. She was fed up with the Jakarta Fairgrounds and undependable drivers and another fucking beautiful night.

Shutting out the looks Pam and Sally gave her, she uncorked the flask and brought it to her lips where, just for a moment, she sniffed the inimitable perfume of gin, her tongue just grazing its razor sharpness. Then she re-corked the flask and put it back in her handbag. It wasn't what she wanted at all.

Edythe wanted Beatrice, and by now she'd be at home waiting for her. With that certainty in mind, she began to run without a backward glance. Soon she was out on busy Merdeka Square, looking for a taxi.

❀ ✧ ❀ ✧ ❀ ✧ ❀

Every morning Edythe Sheetz went out the gate and looked down the hot, dusty road. Every afternoon she went in Beatrice's room and talked to her about how she'd done the best she could. It was only a matter of time until the transfer came through.

Every evening she refused cocktails because she wanted to live up to her promise, wanted Beatrice to see she'd kept her word. Beatrice, who had been detained. Perhaps she still waited for the Anyer Beach Motel people to replace her. Perhaps she'd taken a slight detour to visit her family. Or some misfortune had befallen her on her way. But Beatrice would triumph and be here any minute.

One day, Edythe's husband came home with the letter. Horace Walburton had been assigned the Philadelphia position. Ed Sheetz would take his place here in the Jakarta office. It was then she remembered. At Anyer Beach, Beatrice had never once called her "Madame," only "Nyonya." Mrs. Sheetz went to her room, pulled the drapes, and cried. Then it was cocktail time and everything was all right.

FROM A SULTAN'S COURTYARD:
Katherine

S HE HAD LOOKED ALL OVER JAKARTA FOR JUST THE RIGHT DESK FOR HER husband, but came home, instead, with an intricately carved teak chest for herself—a place to keep her most precious things. Katherine Wilhelm's long fingers traced the *Wayang* puppet figures deeply etched into the varnished wood. Her husband would revere the craftsmanship of the famous Jepara woodcarvers as much as she did. Memories of his youth in Indonesia, and his love of things Indonesian, came naturally to him. As the son of a Dutch Colonialist, he had been invited to watch Javanese shadow plays, the *Wayang,* in the royal *kraton* with the Sultan's son, now the Sultan himself.

She opened the brass clasp and lifted the lid. A wonderful aroma filled her bedroom: part teakwood, part the waxy smell of a double stack of folded *batiks,* some in the 2½ meter dress lengths, some in yardage. The stockpiling had begun when she realized she couldn't stay here forever, but could take a piece of Indonesia back to Canada with her to have always.

From the bed she picked up a stack of even more precious things. For a brief moment she held their softness against her cheek. While Hans had ben offshore on the oil platform, she'd sewn three tiny undershirts and three gowns with drawstrings to cover little feet, hemstitched four receiving blankets, and crocheted a pale blue shawl. Tenderly, she arranged the baby clothes in the teak chest.

She heard the car and had time only to pat light brown bangs into place and survey her makeup with calm green eyes before Hans was in the room, throwing his bag on the bed, calling, "I'm home." He nuzzled her ear, then placed his tongue in it as his hands roamed her flat stomach and long waist.

159

She pulled away, unable to keep the secret another moment. Her heart sang, and her voice was a trumpet of triumph. "I'm pregnant!" Now they were both living their dream—his to return to this country where he had been born; hers, after a year of hellish anxiety, to be finally with child.

His eyes narrowed, and she couldn't read them. He was off somewhere she couldn't reach again. He clapped his hands loudly, and the old servant woman who did the housework and cooking appeared in the doorway, out of breath. "Yes, master," she said in Dutch.

Hans had wanted only older servants who knew the language, even though he spoke perfect Bahasa Indonesia, which Katherine had become better at, lately, under his tutelage. He insisted the driver, Jumah, a man of fifty, could also care for the yard and the heavier housework "because you don't need to gad about so much, my Katrinka, and because servants should never have too much free time."

"Heineken *bier*," he barked. He always asked for it, and this week she'd been able to get it at the duty-free store. Now he stroked the bald spot at the crown of his head, then smoothed his moustache with the thumb and forefinger of one hand—his habit when something bothered him.

Hans chug-a-lugged from the green bottle and replaced it on the tray Ibu held before him. "*Satu lagi*," he ordered, and the servant woman went off to get another.

He put his arm around Katherine, and together they walked into what she called the Rattan Room in the rear of the house. It overlooked a beautiful tropical garden that Katherine sometimes tended herself, much to her husband's dismay. It was not Menteng where they lived, or one of the fine old Dutch houses her husband had wanted so much. No amount of arguing swayed the Indonesian in charge of CAMCO's housing assignments. Hans was not important enough to be given anything but an ordinary expat house in the Cipete compound.

Hans bent and rubbed a finger over the terrazzo floor. "Ibu, you scrub the floor today?"

She looked at Katherine, then said, "Yes, master."

Knowing there hadn't been time, knowing Ibu had extra kitchen work to do with his coming home, Katherine said nothing.

"Isn't it on Jumah's schedule to be watering plants and flowers at this time of day?" he asked Katherine.

She said airily, "He did that before he went to pick you up."

"I hope you're keeping a tight rope on them. They'll take advantage if you don't. My father's servants knew their place, and they did everything without being told. They lived to serve us."

Katherine sat with downcast eyes, trying not to cry. After a long silence, when she thought he was never going to say anything about her big news, he finally took her hand in his. "There have been false alarms before."

"This isn't. I know it."

"I suppose it's about time something worked after the money I've foolishly spent."

She thought of the trips to Singapore they'd made for tests. Then the fertility drug, the charting of the right time of the month and trying to coordinate that with his schedule home from the rig. In desperation, she'd bought a medicine for his potency in the *jamu* shop at Sarinah's Department Store because she couldn't believe anyone who wanted a baby so much could possibly be infertile. He'd never known she put it in his coffee regularly.

He barked for *Ibu* to bring his pipe and for Jumah to check the propane tanks. Then he wanted *kopi* that would bend a spoon. Ibu didn't laugh. Jumah must stop polishing the car and go for cigars, then someone must shine every pair of his shoes. He wasn't sure which ones he wanted to wear. Katherine felt sick inside for the servants. It wasn't so much what he asked of them as how he did it. To make it worse he tried to joke with them afterwards.

Once he had everyone scurrying around, he pulled Katherine onto his lap. "If you have this baby, I might call him Hendrick, a name from my family's past, but good for the Seventies, too. I would tell him of life on Java before the Revolution changed everything, back when there was still an Indonesian aristocracy, and we permitted them to pursue their cultural traditions and court ceremonies."

Katherine snuggled against him, his five o'clock shadow rough against her cheek, his pipe smell strong in her nose.

"My father was an important man, a resident of the court of Solo, with a sugar cane plantation besides. Court life was dazzling. I still see the Sultan's *kraton*. We are going there, I promise you. We are going to the prince's palace."

Now he was coming to the part he always told best, but she was having trouble staying awake.

"Yes, in the courtyard of the Sultan, at the palace in Solo, known as Surakarta then, I played with his son, just my age. I can see the great pillars we hid behind. I came to know many of the *Mahabbharata* and *Ramayana* stories by heart from the royal *Wayang* performances. And one of the *Gamelan* players taught me to play his instrument. Before the Japanese came—"

Katherine was half dreaming, but she knew the story. She saw the Dutch families, allowed one suitcase each, herded together, then shoved onto a train ...

Hans is twelve years old, and has to go to an internment camp with the rest of the Dutch during the Japanese occupation of Indonesia ...

When she woke it was dark. She wondered why Ibu had not turned on some lights. Her husband sagged against her, asleep, too, she thought, until he spoke.

"I do not want a child. I've tried to tell you that. I am already a father with two grown daughters, but it is hard for me to deny you anything, my little Katrinka. I thought perhaps nothing would come of your obsession for a baby. I thought you must be barren or you would have become pregnant our first year together when we were so careless."

A sob almost escaped her as she pulled herself from his arms and stood, bereft, alone in the darkness.

"What are you really saying?" she asked through tight lips.

"There are *jamus* to take care of it."

How had she been blind to the fact he was merely humoring her? How had he not seen she desperately wanted a baby to validate their love? Knowing he wanted to erase their baby with some herbal brew, she felt the death of all that had been dear to her, all that had been reason for living.

"Ibu, lights! Now!" Hans shouted, but it was Jumah who appeared behind two candles. He placed one on the table and carried the other with him. When Jumah spoke Dutch you could hardly hear him. Katherine believed it was because he hated the language and what it stood for: three hundred years of oppression for his people.

"No electric," Jumah said, using simple Dutch words he had taught her himself. "Something wrong with generator."

Ibu came and knelt before Katherine. "*Tidak memekan,*" she said. "No see, no cook." In candlelight, Katherine watched her tremble. It embarrassed her to see Ibu press her forehead against the floor.

"Please, Ibu," Katherine said, "get up." She pulled her frail servant to a standing position. She loved this gentle couple who were so kind to her, loved calling the woman by the respectful name that meant mother.

Hans clapped his hands, and the servants melted away. In a low growl, he said, "Haven't I taught you anything about handling these people? You must keep them subservient."

Abruptly, his mood changed. "Since there is no electric, we will go to the Borobudur Hotel for a festive dinner and the night. I'll charge the company." He grinned. "It's CAMCO's responsibility to keep my house in working order."

The room at the Borobudur brought back pleasant memories of their four-month stay here when they first arrived. It had been a time of discovery for her and rediscovery for Hans. She had fallen in love with his Indonesia, and soon she joined him in dread of the day the oil company would be nationalized and they'd be sent home. There was so much to see and do before that happened. And the highlight of their time here would be the trip to Solo to see the Sultan.

Hans reached for the long-sleeved *batik* shirt she was hanging in the closet. "We will talk this baby business out," he said, "in the Toba over a good red wine and a rare steak."

"I'm not hungry," she said, knowing she could not talk about this now, maybe never. "I'm getting right into bed."

He did not coax her to come to dinner, but only shrugged his shoulders like he did when he didn't care for something the servants did, but was not angry enough to berate them. The look on his face told her he would have his own way as usual.

When he had gone downstairs, she unwrapped the foiled chocolate left, earlier, on her pillow by the roomboy when he turned down the bed. It reminded her of Hans' story about his father's servants traveling, with no money, what was a far, far journey for them, just to bring the Wilhelms a gift of chocolate in the internment camp because they knew how much the Dutch family loved it.

Her stomach convulsed in a cramp. She put down the candy. Something was not right. She felt a gush and looked down to see a growing circle of rich, dark blood staining the beautiful satin sheets.

❀ ⋟ ❀ ⋟ ❀ ⋟ ❀

The next day, Hans said, "Let us forget your false alarm and go on a little tour. You are pale and wan, and it will cheer you. I have heard of a Dutch nun up in the Puncak who makes real Dutch cheeses. The cooler air of the mountains will do you good, and a change of scene will make you forget this other business. In fact, I want you to put it behind you and concentrate on learning my language. I will find you a suitable teacher. Then you can make friends with upper class Indonesians, the ones who still know the value of a good Dutch education and send their sons and daughters to college in the Netherlands."

She knew what was coming next. He always said she spent too much time with the inferior servant class. But she loved them, and all the servants in the neighborhood knew they were always welcome in her home.

She wanted to tell him she was already learning Dutch from Jumah, but thought she'd better not. Poor Jumah might be reprimanded for it.

Jumah swung by Hero's to pick up the cigars Hans wanted to smoke on the way to the mountains. Jumah started to get out of the car, but Hans insisted on getting them himself. Jumah did not always bring fresh ones, he said. Jumah kept the motor running for the air conditioning, but Hans reached over and turned off the key before he went in the supermarket. It was quickly steaming inside the car, and Katherine rolled down a window.

Suddenly, a dirty upturned palm was shoved into her face. "*Baksheesh, baksheesh*" came the plaintive cry. The beggar woman had dirty fingernails and dirty bare feet. Her dress was rags barely held together. At her breast a skinny baby fretfully searched for food. "*Baksheesh, baksheesh.*"

Jumah, sounding a lot like Hans, barked something at the woman.

"No, Jumah, no," Katherine said. She fumbled in her pocketbook and came up with a five-hundred *rupiah* note.

"*Terima kasi, terima kasi, Nyonya,*" the woman said, backing away. The baby was howling now. Katherine's arms ached to hold the child to her body, feel the warmth, do the calming.

From nowhere came a mob of beggar women, all in rags, all with babies at their breasts. They surrounded the car, beating on its radiator, its trunk, the roof. "Me, me, Nyonya," they wailed. "*Baksheesh, baksheesh.*" Katherine passed out all the money in her purse, but they wouldn't leave. Even when she showed them her purse was empty, they kept tapping on the windows, pounding on the fenders and doors, chanting, "*baksheesh, baksheesh.*"

When she realized they'd been joined by men beggars, many of them with disabilities, she couldn't stand it; she wanted Hans to come back so she could give to them all. She knew she should be scared of them, but she wasn't until they began to rock the car.

Jumah, mesmerized by the onslaught of the beggars, too, now gunned the motor. Hans ran from the store, red-faced and screaming at the motley crowd. They didn't budge. Somehow, he managed to tear a body or two away from the door and get inside. Jumah gingerly backed the car out of the parking spot. The beggars fell away just in time. Katherine looked out the rear window. Many of them were still shouting and shaking fists.

"Thank you for not hurting them, Jumah," Katherine said.

"You gave them money, didn't you?" Hans said to her.

"I didn't see any harm in—"

"Why do you think I told you never to do that? This is what happens. One gets money, and they come out in droves." He wiped his perspiring face with a fresh handkerchief.

"But the babies were so sick looking. I'm sure none of those mothers could give milk, and I thought—"

"You're damn right they couldn't give those kids milk," he said, "because they're not their mothers."

She looked at him, disbelieving.

"You can believe it," he said. "It's rent-a-kid. Those women are professional beggars, and they rent those babies by the day from their friends so expatriate suckers like you will feel sorry for them."

"But the babies were still hungry," she said. "The money I gave could be what they pay the real mothers to buy food."

"Do you know what happens when they get in a frenzy like that? They might have easily turned the car over. You could have been hurt. Promise me, Katrinka, you will never give money to beggars again."

Katherine leaned back and closed her eyes to shut him out. Before her was a montage of babies at breasts, babies crying, babies needing love.

❀ ꝫ ❀ ꝫ ❀ ꝫ ❀

Near Bogor, the road ran uphill through a tunnel of huge trees. Then a handsome wrought-iron gate came into view where a sentry box housed a soldier, stern and stiffly at attention, rifle at the ready. Beyond stood an imposing, porticoed palace, one of several residences of the Indonesian president, Suharto. A wide veranda and open windows gave a false invitation. Herds of white-spotted deer looked out from sweeping lawns. Already it was cooler; they were 290 meters above sea level.

Hans reached into the picnic basket and brought out a sandwich and a Heineken. "That's the famous botanical gardens," he said, pointing out the window. "I must take you sometime. They did a lot of research there for cash crops—tea, cassava, cinchona, and, of course my father's prime interest, tobacco. You will love the orchids. Five thousand varieties, they say."

She didn't tell him she'd already been to the gardens with Jumah. Hans would not like that she had gone there with her driver as a guide instead of him. With Jumah's help she had selected several handsome orchid species she hoped to find in Jakarta for her own garden. Nor did she tell her husband that walking through such beauty had convinced her, as certain authorities maintained, that Java had been the site of the biblical Garden of Eden.

They were on the road to the Puncak now, climbing steadily. There was a brief rain, and the people along the road used banana leaves for umbrellas while water buffaloes wallowed in the full ditches. The ascent became steeper as they left the pale green rice fields behind. Then, as far as the eye could see, a manicured landscape of green and glossy tea plants beckoned. Female tea leaf pickers, their faces shrouded by broad flat hats of straw, were almost hidden in the dark, symmetrical rows of tea as they napped at noonday.

"Jumah! Don't go so fast," her husband ordered. It was true the road was full of treacherous curves, but she had every confidence in the man's driving ability, and there was little or no traffic on this weekday. He was obsessed with dominating the servants, dominating her.

He hadn't always been like this. Or had she been too blinded by first love to notice? When Indonesia ousted all the Dutch, his family had settled in Vancouver, Canada. He had grown up there, eventually worked for Royal Dutch Shell, married, divorced.

Katherine had lived in Bellingham, Washington, where she managed a small, but popular book store. She had relished her day off when, with her many girlfriends, she'd gone to the little town of Birch Bay, close to the Canadian border. Every weekend, the small town on a horseshoe curve of the bay was inundated with Canadians. They came to the bars to drink because British Columbia was dry on Sundays. She always sipped slowly— just two Tom Collins—and danced with Canadians and Washingtonians alike.

But once she met the tall, courtly Dutchman with exquisite manners, she had eyes for no one else. He was forty then to her twenty, but it hadn't mattered. They were wildly in love, married quickly, and she moved to Canada. Sometimes, now, she wondered if she ever really knew him, or was it that he'd changed since his return to Indonesia? But she hadn't stopped loving him and probably never could.

They were at the summit, passing Puncak Inn, going through Puncak Pass. In the distance were the volcanic slopes of Mount Gede and Mount Pangrango, peppered with weekend cottages and guest houses with terraced lawns, umbrellaed tables, and deck chairs. They started a descent past pines and conifers on steep hillsides. Then the roadside was crowded with brilliant poinsettia trees and restaurants offering golden freshwater carp.

"The countryside is quite different in Central Java," Hans said. "You will see when we go to visit the Sultan. I'm sure he'll want us to stay with him in the *kraton*."

Katherine opened the window to breathe the cool mountain air. Reading from a piece of paper, Hans told Jumah to make a turn, and then they bumped along a small dirt track until they reached the nunnery.

Eight black-and-white milk cows stared out at them from their cow shed, placidly chewing their cuds, thriving in the cool, invigorating climate. An elderly, raw-boned woman with a ruddy complexion stood in the doorway, explaining something to a French family, occasionally mixing French words with Indonesian. "Come in. Come in," she boomed in English as the other guests departed.

"I am so excited to find real Dutch cheese," Hans said in the woman's own language, and immediately he and the Dutch nun were friends. Great rounds of fresh cheese were everywhere, maturing on shelves, sitting in brine. Some were soft, some firm, some flavored with caraway seeds, and all they sampled—delicious. Preserved fruits and syrups had their own shelves. Brown eggs sat in a basket beside a sign in three languages saying fresh chicken was available.

Katherine tuned out Hans' boasting to Sister Joanna of his friendship with the current, though in name only, Sultan, his boyhood friend. She looked out the open top half of a split door at a nun picking watercress. As far as she could see, fields of flowers and fresh vegetables flourished. Soon Sister Joanna called the other nuns in from their labors and was speaking excitedly about "Mynheer." They went to a large, bare room and sat around a table, all drinking hot tea with real lemon and eating great slices of home-made bread slathered in rich, creamy butter, topped with chocolate jimmies.

Hans licked his lips and reached for his third piece. "As a boy growing up, this was my favorite breakfast. My boyhood friend, now the Sultan, came to my house to eat it with me." He was speaking in English now for the benefit of the other nuns, who were Spanish, Italian, and French. This launched him into his *kraton* stories. As he charmed the Sisters, Katherine squirmed in her seat.

"Would you like a tour?" the Spanish Sister Carmelita whispered shyly. They slipped away, giggling like children once they were in the hall, but they walked no farther than the chapel, a simple room, made beautiful only by the profusion of flowers and candles. In her own niche was a blue-robed Madonna, holding a perfect baby Jesus. The sight of the carved, life-like figures, the hushed tranquility of this sanctuary, the presence of the little nun with compassionate eyes—it was all too much for Katherine.

Tears streamed down her face. "I desperately want my own baby, Sister. All my life I have looked forward to the day I would be a mother." She could not still the avalanche of words. "We've tried so hard. So many tests and procedures. I've even bargained with God."

She answered Sister Carmelita's questions as the nun wiped Katherine's eyes with her own pristine handkerchief. "No, we don't have a regular church. Yes, my husband's Catholic, but I'm not."

"This is a very special Madonna, madame," Sister Carmelita said. "She has granted many wishes. Come, we will pray together." The prayer the little Sister said was in Spanish, but Katherine knew it was fervent, an intercession from Carmelita's heart. As they were leaving the chapel, Sister Carmelita said, "Think on this. God gives us what we need, not necessarily what we want."

Katherine barely heard her. She felt light, as if she'd left a burden behind. She floated down the long hall and back into the cheese room, where reality forced her to face a husband who sometimes did, and sometimes didn't, want a child.

"Come pick out your cheese," he said. "It's time to go."

"Mynheer, will you ask around if there is someone who would like to adopt a baby, a Dutch baby?" Sister Joanna wiped her rough hands on her apron. "I just heard today—"

"Yes, the mother is very special, and the baby will be born soon," the Italian nun, Sister Josephina said.

Katherine and Sister Carmelita exchanged a look.

"The only Dutch I've met here, besides yourself, Sister," Hans said, turning to Sister Joanna, "are former colonialists making pilgrimages to see their old homes now that the Indonesian government lets them return as visitors."

"Yes, there was such a couple here the other day. He had been governor of Bandung, and they were full of nostalgia," Sister Josephina said.

"Dutch babies should have Dutch families," Sister Joanna said.

"Madame would make a wonderful mother," Sister Carmelita said.

The nuns looked at one another and nodded in excited agreement.

Hans stroked his bald spot, then smoothed his mustache with his thumb and forefinger, saying nothing.

❀ ⤳ ❀ ⤳ ❀ ⤳ ❀

"But it's a Dutch baby. They said so. Doesn't that make a difference?" Katherine sat on her husband's lap, wheedling.

"Adoption is a serious matter, Katrinka," he said.

"It looks like the only way for us."

"For you, Katrinka." He gave a big sigh. "People would think I was trying to recapture my youth."

"But it is not fair for you to deny me. I'm a young woman."

"My mind is on a visit to the Sultan now, Katrinka. We will talk about it another time." He sighed and patted her head.

She ducked away from him. "Don't treat me like I'm the child! I'm a grown woman, and I want children."

"Children!" he exclaimed. "Not so fast, young lady, one at a time, please."

"You're grinning. We can do it then. I can tell Sister Joanna yes?"

"It might not be so bad if we got a *babu anak* so you'd be free to spend time with me," he mused. "And she would get up in the middle of the night, and our sleep would not be disturbed. There'd be a lot more laundry, but Ibu could do it. These old Indonesian women have the endurance of oxen."

The phone rang; Hans was needed offshore immediately. He ordered Ibu to re-iron three shirts and pack his bag. Jumah was in considerable trouble because he had polished all of Hans' shoes except the pair he decided to wear. He spewed out more instructions than the three of them could attend to before he returned, then entered the company car sent to take him to the helicopter. No farewell, but "I'll think on this Katherine, but don't—" She couldn't catch the rest.

She went out to her exhausted, rattled servants standing at the gate awaiting her bidding. She took Ibu into the house and from her private hoard in the carved chest gave her a brand-new length of *batik* for a new sarong. Then she gave her nearly half the food from the freezer and sent her off for a three-day holiday with her large family in her home village. She gave Jumah the left-behind cigars he liked as much as Hans did, and a bonus of five thousand *rupiah*. "For safe driving," she said, but they both knew what it was really for.

First thing next morning, while everything was still shrouded in mist, she and Jumah were on the way to the nunnery. Hans had kind of said yes, hadn't he? She must tell them before someone else took her baby, and she needed to know the exact days, weeks, or months until he would be born. But she didn't want any information about the mother and father. They didn't exist. This was the baby of Hans and Katherine Wilhelm, little Hendrick. Yes, it had to be. Hans had never had a boy.

Back, back through her own private Garden of Eden she went, up, up into the Puncak, past the tea plantations again with women dwarfed by their hats, bent over, picking and placing the leaves in bags they'd made of their *selendangs*. Katherine marveled at the way they moved. It was a silent dance, surely as graceful, as classical, as the court dancers her husband spoke of. But he would never see these women as noble and genteel in their own right. Wanting to absorb this beautiful country through every pore, she opened the car window. Yes, she would come here every week until she brought her child home.

"Sister Joanna said to tell you the baby's from fine stock."

"Ummmh." Hans did not look up from the newspaper.

"Sister Carmelita says she's sure it's a boy because the mother is carrying it all in front."

Silence.

"I think the mother is actually staying there, but they won't say, and I wouldn't dare ask."

Hans stayed buried behind the newspaper, great puffs of smoke from his pipe floating out now and then.

"Sister Josephina made a beautiful quilt, all of *batik* scraps, for Hendrick."

A great sigh from behind the paper, some mumbled Dutch words, and then he went for a walk.

The next time he came in from offshore, he said, "That new cheese is very good. The nuns are well?"

"Yes, and they have sent you homemade bread. I found chocolate jimmies at Hero's."

He sat down to make a lunch of it immediately, smiling broadly, talking effusively, making plans for golf and the trip they would take soon to the *kraton* in Solo to see his old friend.

"What do you do up there with the nuns, Katherine?"

She looked him in the eye. "We pray. We pray that all will go well in the birth, and the baby will have all its fingers and toes, and —" Her voice faltered. "—that you will not deny me this."

His piercing gaze almost unnerved her, but she took a deep breath and said, "They told me we should start the paper work now since it takes a while."

"This is very serious. We should not decide rashly."

"Just think, Hans—a son. Your very own son."

He stared at her, then his hand began to stroke his bald spot. He smoothed his mustache with a thumb and forefinger.

She persevered. "The nuns say he·will need a passport right away. Do you want him to have a Canadian or a United States one?"

He said, "Are you really sure you want another woman's baby?"

"But it isn't. It isn't at all. God gave me this baby. It's mine."

"It is a Dutch baby?"

She said quickly, "A social worker is coming this afternoon to talk to us."

"Oh my," he said.

She pushed her edge. "Come and see the cradle I found at an expat sale."

"Jumah," he called, "I'll need some cigars."

❀ ⤳ ❀ ⤳ ❀ ⤳ ❀

"Tien Sumardi," she said, extending her hand to Hans first, then to Katherine.

She was young and pretty with short hair held back on either side with barrettes. She wore a crisp white blouse and a peasant skirt well past her knees. Around her neck were three gold chains, the current fashion for expatriate women, but these were fine and delicate, not thick and ostentatious. She opened her briefcase and removed a notebook.

"You are Dutch, I understand, Mr. Wilhelm?" The social worker didn't wait for an answer. "That is good, very good."

After the tour of the house she'd requested, she began filling out papers, asking them many questions; some personal, some about their background, and some about their finances. Finally, she said. "Now if you'll just sign here."

"That's it?" Katherine had never thought it would be so easy.

"I suppose—" Hans said to Tien Sumardi, ignoring the pen she offered, but more than affable, "you earned your degree in the Netherlands."

She was looking for something in her briefcase. "No," she said. "Right here, at the University of Indonesia."

"Your parents are of the upper-middle-class, the *priyayi*?" he prodded.

"I do not care to be labeled as a cultural type, Mr. Wilhelm, although my father *is* a white collar worker. *Priyayi* has all kinds of past connotations I do not want to be associated with."

"Really," he said, his eyes narrowing. "Like what?"

"That term originally meant only those who belonged by birth to the older aristocracy, the lower nobility of the feudal courts, who let themselves be used as local rulers and go-betweens by the Hollanders during their occupancy of our country." The social worker's dark eyes predicted a storm. "Have you forgotten that, Mr. Wilhelm?"

"That was back in the time of the Javanese kingdoms, right?" Katherine was so scared now she couldn't remember Hans' history lessons.

Hans turned to Katherine. "There was only one empire left, the

Mataram, and it was divided into three sites. I've told you that." His eyes challenged Tien Sumardi. "I have fond memories of the *priyayi* I knew in the *kraton* where I played with the Sultan's son."

"And which *kraton* would that be?"

"Solo," he said. They were openly glaring at one another.

"The man we still allow the worthless title of Sultan is your friend?"

"Yes, as I'm sure I'd find many other friends in that class you don't want to be associated with. We gave them Western education and status."

"They were traitors! The Dutch would never have been able to exploit Java and treat it like a labor camp without the support and treachery of the nobility!"

Hans face was red, his eyes popping. Katherine placed a hand on his arm, her eyes entreating. Unseeing and unknowing, he moved closer to the social worker, his face in hers now.

"We had a mission to perform for the world, which was denied us!"

Ibu walked in with a pitcher of iced tea, and Katherine mentally blessed her for listening and trying to stop a situation that was getting out of hand. Trembling, Katherine poured tea into glasses no one touched.

Tien Sumardi's face was white, her tone sarcastic. "Because of his cooperation, the Prince of Jogyakarta is now one of our vice-presidents. Your great friend in Solo sided with the Dutch during the Revolution. He should have been shot, but he was stripped of his power and eclipsed in the minds of the people instead."

"The Solo court has a history of loyalty to Holland since the 1800s. I must congratulate him."

The sugar, Katherine thought, seeking escape. Ibu forgot sugar. Even in the kitchen she couldn't shut out the shouting that went on interminably.

"We could have made this the greatest nation in Asia!"

"You Belandas are impossible!"

All she could think of was that Hans had ruined their chances for getting the baby. She did not want to go back into that room.

A sudden silence was more frightening than the vicious argument had been, but she had to break it. She knew there was no stopping Hans. Better to plead with the social worker to ignore his prejudices. One look at Tien Sumardi standing in the open doorway, her posture stiff and defiant, and Katherine knew it was too late.

"If you want to label me, Mr. Wilhelm," the social worker said, "then call me a modern woman of Indonesia, one who believes her country will one day outlive its past turmoil, preserve its precious culture, and with its great resources become an economic success." She paused dramatically, holding the door open wide, etched against a cloudless blue sky, her face dark and unreadable against the light behind her.

❋ ﹏ ❋ ﹏ ❋ ﹏ ❋

It seemed the announcement, stating the Sultan would be in residence the last two weeks of July, came one day, and they were on their way to Central Java the next. Hans said, maybe on the way back, they'd stop at the Buddhist Borobudur Temple and the Hindu Prambanan, but they would not bother with the other two palaces at Jogyakarta and Mangkungnegara. *His kraton* was the one worth seeing. It had been the seat of the Javanese culture's greatest flowering, the cultivation and preservation of which would be best enjoyed there. From the front seat, next to Jumah, Hans looked back at her and smiled.

Katherine huddled near a window, miserable and defeated. Three weeks had passed. It was clear; they were never going to hear from Tien Sumardi again. And if they did, it would be some legal-looking document that said, "No baby for the Wilhelms because Mr. Wilhelm is a boor and a bigot so we can't possibly give you a child for your very own."

As beautiful as it was—this glorious patchwork of agricultural endeavor, small villages, tobacco fields with thatched long houses where tobacco dried—the countryside could not soothe Katherine's pain. "Yes, we will probably stay in Solo the whole three days," she heard him say and didn't care. "The Sultan will want to reminisce. Do your realize, through the years, the Sultans of Solo were the only Javanese we paid full respect? Their enclaves were places where we deferred to their ancient laws and traditions. Of course it was political but—"

She wanted to scream, "I don't care! I don't care at all!"

She tried to picture in her mind the baby she had lost, and did not see the city of Solo or anything else until, as if by wizardry, she was transported into another world. She faced a pale blue pavilion sheltered by two royal banyan trees. She floated over an expanse of cool marble tiles and past a glassed-in audience chamber. They mounted a broad flight of steps guarded on each side by iron railings and old cannons that led to another great pavilion, the *pendopo*, or entrance to a temple, Hans told her. Mostly he was silent, in great awe of the surroundings, his dream of reunion with the Sultan and his *kraton* now resplendent reality.

On the fringe of a band of tourists, they wandered a series of sun-washed courtyards and pavilions. Listlessly, she listened as Hans talked about the collections of spears, krises, photographs, personal memorabilia, and other sacred heirlooms of the long reign of the sultans. Proudly he showed her gilded carriages, ornately carved litters and sedan chairs, and remnants from great weddings and funerals.

She had only known *Wayang* puppets to be made of flat leather, but the ones here in Central Java had wooden heads and bodies, and real clothing. Several sets of *Gamelan*, which Hans called percussion instruments, were displayed, but the words he used for them—*saron, rehab, gender, gambong*—only confused her.

Here, where gongs resounded every half hour to tell the time, where the odd-sounding *Gamelan* orchestra was both discordant and exotic to Western ears, Katherine felt a mellow calm. Rubbing elbows with the courtly retainers who acted as guides, and the beautiful female attendants with bare shoulders, she was transported back to a time she'd never known. It was a place she welcomed because neither pain nor emptiness existed for her there.

Excited now, Hans pulled her toward yet another courtyard and through the shade of leafy trees with sweet unpunctuated chirps of little sparrows, then into a large audience hall. Crystal chandeliers hung from intricately carved rafters, and marble statues lined walkways graced with ornately glazed Chinese pottery. He broke from her grasp and ran to one of the richly designed and gilded columns that supported the roof. With a mischievous look and a deep sigh of pleasure, Hans hid behind it, just as he and the young prince had concealed themselves when they didn't want to be found.

"It is some special occasion today," he told her knowingly. "Otherwise these pillars would be hung with protective drapes." The orchestra began to reverberate with the soft tones of the strange instruments. The crowd of tourists thickened. Slowly, nine beautiful maidens advanced in single file toward a stage in the midst of the pillars. Two female attendants followed on their heels to see that their feet did not tread on the wine-red cloths attached to and trailing from their ankles.

The stately dancers with downcast eyes wore dark blue, gold-embossed cloth draped about their hips, and heavy gold armlets and bracelets on their arms. Crescent-shaped medallions hung from slender necks. Their hair was coiled into buns with centerpieces of the mythical *garuda* bird surrounded by quivering butterflies, flowers, and metal spirals. Their slow, languid dance mesmerized Katherine.

Occasionally, the dancers flicked their long sashes and gently kicked their swirling trains. Bell-like sounds and dreamy chanting drugged Katherine with tranquility—somehow everything would be all right. She looked at Hans who was restless, his eyes darting everywhere. A deep gong resounded, and the royal dancing ceased as effortlessly as it had begun. The young women silently filed away to some inner chamber.

"Do you know how lucky you were to see that?" Hans asked. "It is rare and unforgettable to see this dance. 'The Bedaya' was originally ordered to commemorate the queen of the Indonesian Sea, *Laro Kidul*. Today is perhaps a royal birthday or some holiday I've forgotten."

His eyes became brightly expectant. "The Sultan will tell us." With no hesitation, he led her straight to the royal living quarters.

Katherine was surprised to see that only a thin screen, a woven matted wall, separated them from an audience with the Sultan. Beyond it, someone cleared a throat, a rustling page turned. Through a slit she peered in at a man of Hans' age sitting at a desk, poring over a book with a worn binding.

"Don't do that!" Hans hissed, pulling her away. He spoke rapid Dutch to an old man stationed nearby. The court attendant put hands together in prayerful position and bowed low. "This man remembers me. He has gone to tell my friend we are here."

Pen scratching, chair creaking, then whispers behind the screen. Finally, the old man reappeared. He did not look directly at Hans, but kept his gaze to the floor. "*Susannan* is not receiving any visitors today," he said in Javanese.

Hans answered in the same dialect. "But it is I, Hans Wilhelm. Did you tell him that? Once again, go tell him. He did not understand, or you did not tell him properly."

Hans stroked his bald spot.

Reluctantly, the old man went back inside. Whispers again, the steady drone of the old man's voice, almost a pleading tone. Then he was back, looking down at his feet again. "Sorry, *Tuan*," he mumbled, this time in English. "*Susannan* not available."

Hans was stunned with disbelief. "But I wrote a personal letter," he said, smoothing his mustache. "Someone in official capacity notified me he would be in residence. Here. I can show you, you can see it is—"

The man looked at Hans with pity. "*Susannan* say he not receiving Dutchmen—ever."

Hans started toward the screen that separated him from a world only one other person remembered. Katherine grabbed him as he was about to tear it down. He kicked and struggled, and the old man called for help to lead him away. In the car she couldn't look at the stranger he'd become, alternately silent or raving, speaking in Dutch the words she supposed he had been saving up for the Sultan. She felt only coldness toward him now.

❀ ꕥ ❀ ꕥ ❀ ꕥ ❀

The day of the unexpected came on the same day Katherine thought Hans seemed more like his old self. He had already argued with Ibu over the quality of his breakfast and insisted that Jumah rewash the car. Someone was at the gate; Ibu came back at a run Katherine had not thought her capable of, breathless, but smiling broadly. Behind her was Tien Sumardi, holding a swathed bundle.

Katherine's heart quickened. She said a hurried prayer to the Madonna, to her friends—the Sisters of the cheese, to this young woman with a forgiving heart. Tien Sumardi smiled at her. "Your son, Mrs. Wilhelm." Katherine took Hendrick into her arms.

Katherine looked at Hans, who looked back at her with eyes confused and uncertain—but he didn't say no, and even managed a weak smile.

"Oh, Hans, I'll never stop being grateful for this," Katherine breathed.

Eagerly, she peeled back the blankets, leaving the final one. With trembling fingers, smiling broadly now, Hans reached out and revealed tiny fluttering fingers and the top of a dark head of hair.

The social worker turned to Hans, her face a mask of triumph. "Now you will remember the royal court of Solo forever, Mr. Wilhelm. The woman who gave your son life danced there for the tourists, at least one of whom—the father—was Dutch."

Hans stared and stared at small brown eyes in a brown face looking up at him; then turned away. Katherine was surprised to see that he was much older than she'd realized, his step a shuffle, his shoulders burdened. She turned back to her precious son, glad she could soon pick up his passport.

GREAT WHITE HUNTERS:
Miriam

I STILL BELIEVE IT WAS ALL BECAUSE OF RAMADAN. AFTER LIVING FOUR YEARS in Indonesia —more or less— I should have known better than to come back during the Muslim holy month of fasting. But I don't pay much attention to that sort of thing, and anyway, it's at a different time every year. Something about the moon.

I've always had this sixth sense about when I should step back into whichever of my two lives I'm not in at the moment. For Jakarta, it's when a sudden nostalgia comes over me—a yearning for gin and tonics around the pool and a respite from all household duties. It's also the sobering fact that Darrell, my husband, all alone in our villa, is pining away for me, and I have a duty to him as well as our two children and my mother. I admit I was long overdue in returning, and that I needed Darrell. There was something about his longing for derring-do that piqued some secret yearning of my own.

I was drawn to Darrell when we first met because he dreamed of seeing the world, perhaps even going on a real safari one day in the tradition of Robert Ruark or some Hemingway character. I thought he was on his way when he dragged me to the wilds of the Pacific Northwest. He grew a he-man mustache and beard and started collecting rifles for the big trip he was going to take over the border to hunt elk in Canada. The trip never happened, but he did get interested in salmon fishing, pleased as punch to be doing something he'd read about in *Field and Stream*.

"Just think, Babe, a bi-i-i-g salary, travel perks, no taxes," Darrell said when he wanted to switch oil companies so he could work overseas.

"No!" I said, shutting out the thought that if I were the least bit like his first wife— who was too homebound to consider ever going up in an air-plane—I'd lose him.

"You've always wanted me to live my dream," he coaxed. "There's a lot of wild game on some of those islands."

"All right," I said finally. I'd make it work for all of us somehow.

To tell the truth, making changes has always unnerved me. It had taken two long years for me to accept Anacortes, Washington, as home. Much to my surprise, I came to love the misty rain, clear fresh air, pleasant odors of wood smoke and damp evergreens, beaches with interesting rocks and driftwood, the view of a snowcapped mountain from the backyard so real it looked like a painting.

But I've become quite good at being a global person, too. I can shut out the responsibilities of one side of the world while I'm working on those of the other. I can easily go from dealing with a yard boy who used so much fertilizer on the tomato plants I'd brought over that they became trees, to shopping for the children's school clothes or attaching name tags on their camping gear. Or I can shift my attention from a houseboy who thinks there's a demon in the washing machine because it "bit" him to dealing with my mother's latest ailment and her problems of living alone—although it is in a double-wide in an excellent mobile home park in Orange County.

Pay no attention to the stories people have made up about why I'm back and forth so much. Don't get me wrong. There are lots of things I like about living in Jakarta, but one can only be on vacation so long before the real world calls. That's usually about the time I'm getting weary of hearing what Darrell is never going to do in the wilds of nowhere, and when I'm thoroughly tired of being just a wife. It's usually about the time my skin starts erupting, and I'm out of Helena May Cosmetics. Or I begin to imagine I'm coming down with dengue fever, or cholera, or at the very least, sprue. It's then I head for the good old state of Washington.

Of course, there's a valid reason for my spending so much time away from Darrell. Our children are in private schools in the States. I could probably sacrifice my real life if I had to, but I would never force these kinds of adjustment on adolescents. I told them they wouldn't like it, and sure enough they didn't that Christmas they came to Jakarta. Darrell said they were having a wonderful time, but they couldn't fool me. Mother was miserable, too, without a traditional American Christmas. So you see I couldn't abandon them all. Darrell understands.

And now I wanted to be with him again. Maybe I'd even stay this time.

So I'd changed to fresh clothes when the plane stopped over in Singapore, dabbed myself behind the knees with my best perfume, and put on the sheerest stockings I could find. Darrell always was a sucker for my long legs.

As the taxi disappeared, I stood at the gate of our villa, actually savoring the gritty taste of dust in my mouth, enjoying the permeating smell of coconut oil and rice, even titillated by my usual fear of snakes, though I've been told there are none in Jakarta. I put all stateside thoughts out of my mind. Who would get Howard Hughes' estate? Was the Swine Flu virus swimming around in my body? I'd be missing those new miniseries novels on TV. I pushed the bell.

I peered through the slats of the gate, but absolutely nothing stirred beyond it, not even a breeze. I struggled to keep my highest heels from slipping into the grooves and ruts of the dirt road and tried to ignore the stench of the open bin of garbage that hadn't been collected (probably because the collectors were busy strengthening their spiritual and mental powers as ordained by Ramadan). Unladylike as it was, I shook the gate in frustration.

"Supardi," I shouted. "Rasmin. Somebody!" Because they weren't allowed to eat or drink from sunrise to sunset, I imagined the servants must be napping to conserve their strength.

I looked at the stucco wall, its top studded with broken glass. There was no way I could safely climb over it. I put down the heavy shield I'd stopped over in Fiji to buy. (I found it right in the duty-free.) I had planned to hide behind it and race inside to terrorize Darrell, brandishing the spear I'd also acquired. He likes things like that. You should see the pages in my passport of places where, coming and going, I've stopped to pick up surprises for Darrell. Often I can find something right at a hotel and be on my way the next day. It's not that I have to buy my way back. Not at all. It's just—well, our relationship is complex.

So there I was standing at the gate, waiting for someone to let me into my own house. I considered going around to the other gate near the living room and calling to Darrell. He'd be there, wearing his bush shirt over khaki shorts. The white nylon mesh helmet I'd bought him somewhere I can't recall would be shading his eyes as he read about the Tasmanian Devil in his *National Geographic*.

Or he might be practicing golf putts with a device I sent him last Christmas, when I couldn't get over. You may think golf is a game for wimps instead of someone like Darrell, but he's so good that one day he got one of those chickens that wander around the golf course. A chicken-in-one his friends called it. He's hoping for a goat.

Yes, I know exactly what he's doing because I always planned our reunions for when he'd be on his five-day break from offshore duty. I have to admit these surprise appearances do spice up our marital life. To show his gratitude, Darrell makes me strip at gunpoint—really his cocked finger—to my frilly new panties and bra. Then he chases me around the room as I hide behind the sofa, the recliner, under the dining room table. And when we can't stand it another minute, I call him my Great White Hunter and he takes me on the tiger hide with my derriere resting on the head (but not too close to the fangs.)

Yes, he really did bag a tiger when the company sent him up to Sumatra for two weeks. He got to see some Europeans rounding up animals for a circus and was so excited he tripped over a native guide's gun and got that tiger right in the heart. I understand he threw his helmet in the air with a great whoop, just as he does after he climaxes when we are on its hide.

But now the midafternoon sun had my Super-Moisturizing Foundation and Creamy Rouge running down my face, and my long-sleeved satin blouse glued to my back. What breasts I have were bathed in sweat, and above them, my single pearl on a chain felt like a hot coal against my skin. I was dying of thirst, too. I leaned on the bell, not letting up, and then at last, finally—

There was a shuffling on the other side of the gate, the sound of the bar being lifted. Through some slats, I got vertical pictures of a man in a dark folded head scarf, a black shirt, and a bright sarong. He wore no shoes, and when he turned sideways, I saw the Javanese dagger, called a *kris,* tucked in his sarong at the small of his back. A cloud of clove-scented cigarette smoke wreathed his head. The gate creaked open.

"Darrell," I said, feeling as if I'd had the wind knocked out of me. "Is that you?"

❀ ❧ ❀ ❧ ❀ ❧ ❀

My husband, in the costume of a *Wayang* storyteller, led me into my own house with all the aplomb of a puppet master about to begin the show. I was just as lost there as I had been at first sight of him at the gate. Where I walked, I made footprints in yellow dust on the floor. Remnants of meals were stuck to plates scattered around the room, accompanied by overflowing ashtrays and smeary glasses. There were white squares on the walls where the paintings of wild animals, my thoughtful gifts to him, had been. Windows and the sliding glass doors to the patio were open, allowing flies to buzz about my head. The house was darker than I remembered, and the small walled-in court, open to the sky, actually seemed ominous with its brooding giant plants and forbidding stagnant pond.

"Is the air conditioning broken?" I asked, longing for relief.

"Not at all," Darrell said. "I'm trying to build up a tolerance to the heat."

"Where are the servants? Where are my pictures? What the hell is going on here?" I demanded, aghast to hear my voice sounding impatient and impolite. But I wasn't myself. My keen intuition told me something was terribly wrong, and I wanted to get to the bottom of it.

"I like your hair frosted like that," Darrell said. "How long has it been that way? Didn't I notice before?"

I drew a picture in the yellow dust on an end table. "Really, Darrell."

"The place is a little messy. We don't do anything until the sun goes down. Ramadan, you know." He unsheathed his *kris*, then did it again and again, trying to be faster each time.

"Put that thing away. Don't you like what I brought you?" It was then I tripped over the rolled-up prayer rug.

"Sorry, my love," Darrell said. "What time is it? I think I have to pray soon. Are you staying long or just passing through?"

"About those paintings," I said, my foot shoving my carry-on bag in the direction of the master bedroom. The whole house seemed filled with some exotic, fruity-yet-musky aroma. Then through the bedroom door I saw the unmade bed's swirl of tangled sheets, half on the floor.

"We have to have servants, Darrell," I said. "I'm waiting for an explanation."

"Being Ramadan and all, I've given them a holiday. I've studied this fasting thing. In fact, I'm doing it myself to see what it feels like. It's a noble effort, restraining the passions and gratification—"

"No speeches, please," I said, striving in vain again for a polite tone.

"—of the senses," Darrell continued. "This period of self-discipline, of—"

How had I lost control of my homecoming? "Right now, I need a good hot tub."

"You might want to try the servants' *mandi* out back. I've found I prefer it myself." He gave me that probing look he used when he was testing my mood. "Anyway, there isn't any hot water. I've turned off the *listric*, you see. We get along quite well with kerosene lamps and the servants' propane stove to cook our rice."

In spite of myself, I began peeling my Jungle Passion Red nail polish with a thumbnail, as I was prone to do when things weren't going my way, and I was trying to be nice. "Have you lost your mind?" It wasn't what I should have said at all.

He had on his "I'll explain everything to you, little girl" look. "Ramadan is damn hard on these people. Some of them give in and eat anyway, and that's a grievous sin for a Muslim that I didn't want to be responsible for. You remember last year the gardener couldn't stand it outside all day without water, and the driver gave in to his smoking habit?" He stopped and scratched his head. "No, you weren't here then."

Scrape, scrape, scrape. I'd started on the nails on my other hand. I'd have to go for a fresh manicure tomorrow.

"I sent them all back to their home village till Ramadan and Lebaron is over. They can lie around with no demands on them there. I sold the paintings for money for their advance Lebaron gifts." Darrell looked pleased he'd finally gotten it all out. "They didn't really want to stay anyway when—" He stared up at the ceiling.

"When what?"

"I guess you'll find out soon enough."

A horrible thought came to me. "Darrell, you haven't—gone native?"

He gave me a sheepish grin. "I guess you could say I'm trying."

This was the thanks I got for helping him perpetuate his myth all these years. I shuddered at the thought of being married to some new kind of Darrell. I was forced to have a lukewarm double scotch because under this new regime there was no ice. I took it to my bathroom where I had a cold bath that made the bubbles clumpy globs instead of airy clouds.

After I was clean, if not refreshed, I had no heart for cleaning up Darrell's messes or for even talking to him. Anyway, he was busy getting the black and white threads ready. He said if he couldn't tell one from the other when he held them at arm's length outside, then it was truly sunset and he could eat. The recorded *muezzin* up on the hill called evening prayer, and he unrolled his rug and faced Mecca. I wandered out to the servants' quarters. I guess I was just nosy, curious if they'd left anything behind, which would mean they really were coming back. I dreaded going through all that interviewing again.

I used one of Darrell's kerosene lamps to cast light into the first cubicle and came out satisfied Madiun had not taken everything. Good drivers were hard to come by. I knew I should be inside talking sense to Darrell, but I stopped to listen to the laughter and shouting erupting in the neighborhood now. The servants were celebrating the end of the day's fasting. They'd be sluggish tomorrow after eating and drinking far into the night.

A hair-fruit from the tree that towered over the concrete wall fell, startling me, then rolled to my feet. I heard the swish of fruit bats in the night sky. It was eerie here in the shadows cast by the lamp. I heard a noise, a rustling. Fear quivered my insides, but I held my lamp high in bravado. My heart jumped. Yes, there was something—a figure shrouded in white.

Could it be one of the *hantus* the servants talked about? The apparition cowered before me. That wasn't the way ghosts were supposed to act. In my sphere of light I saw brown eyes caught in fascination, like a deer looking into headlights on a Washington country road. Then, in a gesture of defiance I would come to know all too well, the sheet dropped and I glimpsed an Indonesian woman.

"Thank God!" I grabbed her by the arm. Obviously some servant I didn't know had come back. "Come, there's much to do." She allowed me to lead her inside, and I was amazed to hear bells tinkle as she walked.

"Darrell, you didn't tell me—" I began. He had turned the electric back on and the bright ceiling lights blinded me for a moment. Then I saw the most gorgeous, nubile creature I'd ever seen. A Balinese dancer's costume hugged her petite figure. Instead of the usual elaborate headdress worn with it, her hair was pulled back from her face, showing high cheekbones and slightly slanted eyes. A ponytail hung to her waist. The bells on her toes and fingers tinkled imperiously as she moved to Darrell's side, where she only came up to the middle of his chest. The creature looked up at him as if waiting instructions.

"Who is this woman, Darrell?" I asked.

"Miriam, meet Melana. Melana, meet Miriam." He took a long draught of bourbon straight from the bottle.

"Muslims don't drink," Melana said to him.

"That's not a Javanese name," I mused.

"Melly is Balinese," Darrell said. "Can't you tell?"

"It's not Balinese either, "I said, but I really wasn't sure of anything at this point.

"This *bagus!*" The servant girl picked the spear up from where I'd dropped it and lunged playfully at Darrell.

The girl laughed a soft, melodious sound, but I failed to see any joke. "*Nama* Polynesia," she said finally. "Me see in *filem* about Hawaii. Dutt take Melana there."

I was totally disoriented now. "Dutt? You call him Dutt?"

"Dutt. Yes. Big game hunter say him."

She answered my quizzical look with something about the last African safari he'd led. Then she gave me a supercilious look. "You know, Dutt big white hunter." She laughed then, and it wasn't a bit melodious. She quickly clapped her hands over her mouth.

The bemused look on Darrell's face was disconcerting. It was high time I took charge. "Get busy now, Melana. Put the dirty dishes to soak and change the bed and scrub up my bathroom. You can work now? It is past sundown. Or are you Hindu after all?" Everyone knew the Balinese were Hindu, though I had my doubts that's what she was. I had never heard of any Balinese leaving that paradise to work in Jakarta.

"Melana Christian," she said. "Our Father who art in heaven, hallowed be thy name, thy will—"

"Okay, okay," I said. "Just get the basics done. Tomorrow we'll see you give the house a thorough cleaning. Do you cook?"

Melana neither answered nor sped to do my bidding. Instead she stared pointedly at the longest, most beautifully manicured nails I'd ever seen. I'd kill to get mine to grow like that. "How can you scrub floors with those nails?"

"Melana no *cuci* floors. *Tidak*! No!" Her eyes flashed with anger. "Melana dance, right, Dutt?" She tinkled around the room in graceful movements. She bowed at his feet, then looked up at him through long fluttering eyelashes. "Melana sing, too. 'There's a ship lies rigged and ready in the harbor ... Far away from my land of sunshine to yours of wintry gales,'" she trilled in a weak soprano, paraphrasing here and there to suit herself, eventually having the Englishman take the native girl away with him instead of leaving her behind.

I was outraged at her taking liberties with the song I'd come to think of as Darrell's and mine. Every time we heard Roger Whitaker's "The Last Farewell," we always said we felt a twinge of the nostalgia we'd know when we finally and irrevocably left the good things of this country behind.

Melana's and Darrell's eyes were engaged in some kind of combat when I heard her say, "You take Melana when you go. Right, Dutt?"

"Don't talk nonsense," I said. "We have no need for servants in the United States."

Darrell took another swig from the bourbon bottle and wiped his mouth with the back of his hand. "Uhhh, Miriam, I guess there's something you should know. Melana, well she's kind of my—my concubine."

Jet lag had affected my hearing. What I needed was a Valium and a bed.

Melana stamped her foot and shook her fist at Darrell. "Melana, no concubine!"

Of course she wasn't. He was playing some game out of boredom. I could see I'd stayed away too long this time. But I didn't think I could bear being around those women after the Celeste/Rudi business. I wouldn't even talk about my Borobudur acquaintances, except I want to go on record as saying I think they handled the whole thing badly, and that I wasn't their kind of person.

And that story Vonda Hutchison was telling everyone—that I ran away because my self-esteem was shaken—well, it's just not true. The fact is I was planning my trip back home even then, so I was scarcely involved at all. You remember I left just as soon as I could get Darrell settled into the new house. But now I was curious about them. I'd never dreamed how much I'd want my Jakarta life back—all of it.

And now tomorrow everything would go back to normal. He'd go off-shore, and after a good night's sleep, I'd deal with Melana. I'd never been one to look down on Indonesians just because they worked for me. In fact, when I was in Jakarta, I considered them family. The first few weeks I was always interested in their problems.

I headed for one of the guest rooms, hoping to find clean sheets. I was asleep on my feet, surely dreaming that I heard Melana say, "I want a steak, Dutt. Get me one from the freezer."

❀ ৵ ❀ ৵ ❀ ৵ ❀

I woke not knowing where I was. At first, I thought I was napping on the plane, but the tropical day splashing into the room, dappling the sheets in a design made by the bars on the windows, told me I was certainly in Jakarta. Then I remembered everything. Darrell had gone off the deep end, and the only servant we had was so unpredictable I'd probably have to make my own breakfast.

I stumbled into the living room. There were no rusty dust prints on the floor. The glass table tops were devoid of dirty dishes, and they gleamed as well. Melana had been at work after all. Darrell was nowhere in sight. The closed door of the master bedroom told me nothing. I followed the smell of coffee to the breakfast room. I switched on the air conditioning, as much to get rid of the mildew odor as to cool the room.

Wearing what I recognized as a cheap Western-style cotton dress I'd bought for some other housegirl, Melana sat at the breakfast table, reading the English newspaper. Glasses perched at the end of her nose did not hide that incredible face.

At my place sat a bowl of sliced papaya, banana, and pineapple.

"I understand that is what you like for breakfast," Melana said. "Dutt thought maybe you and I could be friends."

I sat down and she poured my piping hot Earl Grey. Her perfect English after the pidgin last night floored me. And what the hell was she doing drinking coffee and reading my paper at my table? I measured sugar and creamer into the tea before I said softly. "There must be something for you to do in the kitchen?" I smiled encouragingly at her, trying to be genteel, a trait that's so worthy, don't you think?

"Dutt did everything this morning." She smiled. "Good man, no?"

I was dumbfounded. I reached for the paper—anything to keep from staring into those guileful eyes—but Melana held on to it firmly. "I am not finished yet."

I searched for what I knew must be said. I was all for equality, but this was ridiculous. "I can see my husband has spoiled you. I doubt it can be corrected, therefore you will have to—"

"You have *Cosmopolitan!*" Melana pounced on the magazine sticking out of the carry-on bag I'd abandoned last night. "I want to be a Cosmo girl. Will you help me?"

I was still asleep, having a nightmare in which I'd walked back into Indonesia with everything becoming less and less as I knew it to be. I pushed my untouched breakfast away. "Do you have references? Who have you worked for?"

A sullen look. "You wouldn't know. They were British."

"They taught you English?" I realized that what was so disconcerting when she spoke English was her British accent.

"Man send Melana to learn." She tossed her head imperiously, her unbound hair swirling around her face.

"They sent me to school," I corrected. "You can speak our language perfectly when you want and you know it."

Melana shrugged. "Expatriate ladies don't like it."

"This one does. I want you to be exactly who you are. Which is—" I prodded.

A pout smudged her face. "You going to airport with Dutt?"

"Stop calling him that!" It was like chalk grating on a blackboard to me.

"I'll go if you don't want to."

Her cheekiness set my teeth on edge. I'd have her out of here by lunch time, then I'd go to the American Women's Association registry and try to get some fill-ins for my sojourning servants. There were groceries to buy, and I did want to find someone to tell me all about The Herd. I had never hated that name as the others had. Actually, I'd thought it quite funny.

Maybe Sharon was the one I should visit for an update, even though she was the one I really blamed for all the doubt and self-reproach I'd endured. Had I felt compelled to return to see how the rest of them had weathered the debacle? Of course not. It was Darrell—all Darrell.

Melana stretched and yawned. "What shall we do today, Miriam?" Over the edge of the paper, I watched her pour herself another coffee. "I could drive you, but we don't have a car until I get all that sorted out."

What kind of housegirl was this? I was still struggling for some kind of response when Darrell sauntered in, wearing my favorite of his safari suits. It was a creamy beige that complemented his sandy hair and hazel eyes. He looked dashing with his offshore bag slung over his shoulder.

"How are my girls?"

"Darr-elll! Really. That's not a bit funny."

His eyes became tight slits, and he sighed deeply.

"What's this about the car?" I asked.

"Dutt thought he could drive like Indonesians," Melana said, and they exchanged a private look that made me uncomfortable.

"I thought driving in LA qualified me for here." He grinned, but I could tell he was really embarrassed.

"Which means—?" I pursued.

"I had a little traffic problem." He paused, gauging my interest level. "Our car wasn't damaged a bit," he said quickly. "That guy turned right in front of me."

"And he was the son of a policeman," prompted Melana, "and they took away Dutt's international driver's license and the papers that make the car legal to drive."

Outside, a car horn summoned him. He switched his bag to the other shoulder. "You didn't understand what I said last night, Miriam, did you? You are always so mannerly, I'm never sure what's really going on underneath."

"You mean you told me about the car then. I was so tired, Darrell, I—"

"You have the right to know before someone else tells you," he rushed on as the car horn blasted again. "I can't say it any plainer. Melana and I are lovers. Take care of her while I'm gone, okay?"

It was out, and I could no longer evade it. I thought I screamed my outrage, but it was drowned out by the insistent horn.

"We'll talk about it when I come back," Darrell said. No one was more amazed than I to see my bowl of breakfast hurtling through the air, but he was gone, and it splattered against the closed door.

"Actually," Melana said, "I expected you to get in more of a tiff than that."

"Clean up that mess," I screamed.

Melana took a nail file from her pocket and began filing her perfect nails, her beautiful face again full of secrets.

❀ ᔓ ❀ ᔓ ❀ ᔓ ❀

I took my shock to bed in the guest room. I existed on pitchers of Tang, now and then a Valium, and frequent Bufferin. Aches and pains told me I was at least coming down with the flu—if nothing worse. Listlessly, I turned page after page of the magazines I'd brought back with me. I tried to read "The Many Faces of Male Infidelity;" "He Cheated on Me;" "How to Keep Your Man;" and even "Is Adultery the End?" But I couldn't focus on anything but the cliché reactions of a scorned woman—me. Meanwhile, outside my door, the TV screamed words I'd never been much interested in learning. Then Melana chose to listen to Linda Rondstadt and Rita Coolidge sing about the hurts of love. I could hardly move. Something terrible had invaded my body. I kept taking my temperature, but it continued to be normal.

I finally cried great, wrenching sobs muffled in my pillow, no longer able to bear the terrible hurt that had been inflicted on me. I cried all day. How would I survive if he left me? Who would ever love me again? That new wrinkle cream—why hadn't I used it? Maybe this. Maybe that. What about me had pushed him into betrayal? Meanwhile, Melana tried on my clothes, my jewelry, and made herself sick eating the box of See's Chocolates I'd brought Darrell from Seattle.

The festering hurt burst into a blister of anger. Who did he think he was? Darrell wasn't so perfect himself. He said what he thought to whomever he wanted even when it wasn't polite. He used the worst swear word there was in front of women. He wouldn't leave the room to pass gas. All he ever wanted to talk about was his work, which I suffered in silence because I'm too polite to tell him I'm not interested. He snored. And when was the last time we'd had a romantic evening at the Borobudur? Maybe I'd have my own affair. There were plenty of single men around. I certainly would never take another woman's husband.

But please, God, don't let him leave, and I'll stay here all year, except for Christmas. Please, God, I won't make fun of him anymore to entertain my friends. I'll play pinochle with him even if I do hate it. I might even pretend to become Muslim. Just, please, God, let him call me Miss Prissy Pants again.

The next day I woke knowing that I was sick of watching the banana tree outside the window grow, tired of counting cracks in the wall, and waiting for the tiny lizards on the ceiling to fall on me. It was time to take control of the situation. She was only a housegirl after all. It was a mere dalliance, and I had to take some blame for staying away too long this time. Nothing serious to worry about. I showered, dressed, made up a perfect face, and rehearsed a firm and terse firing of the little tramp. With her out of our lives, I might even forgive him. Yes, I'd pay her off but I needed her for something first.

❁ ⤳ ❁ ⤳ ❁ ⤳ ❁

There was no getting around it. I had to get the car legal now that Madiun had returned before the holiday with nothing but a shrug when I asked why. But I was certainly glad. If Darrell, who I'd once dubbed "the terror of the California freeway system," couldn't drive here, I certainly couldn't.

I gave Melana my most ingratiating smile. "We will go to the insurance office. You can interpret for me."

"We've already been there, Miriam," she said, a long-suffering look on her face.

"We do things *my* way. I'm the *Nyonya* here."

Melana was right. All I did was get into an argument with the insurance man, who spoke English almost as well as she did. He wanted money from me to give to the police to get the matter straightened out. The amount was exorbitant because, of course, he would take a share for himself.

"No bribes. Not one red cent!" I screamed. "My husband didn't do anything wrong. It was the other guy. Why should we have to pay?"

"It is the way things are done here, Madame," he insisted. "There is no other way."

I stormed out of the office and into our hired car. Melana followed, that secret look on her face again. She did not tell me "I told you so" as I expected. "Dutt not pay either," she said. "I have an idea." She ordered the driver to take us to the Metropolitan Police. At the station, I followed meekly through the warren of offices until she found the right one.

Her Indonesian words had a polite but persuasive tone. Soon we were ushered into a barracks-like room. At one end sat a man in a khaki uniform, of what rank I didn't know. The room smelled like school rooms I'd known—fruit and boiled egg in a desk drawer, books and papers and freshly sharpened pencils. The officer was formal and distant. He had a sparse goatee and gleaming, perfect teeth, visible now and then in his polite grimaces, poor excuses for a smile.

After Melana had finished speaking, he rooted in drawers, rattled through some papers on his desk and called forth someone who brought a file. "*Tidak,*" he said to me finally.

Then he sounded like he was chiding Melana, but she continued to smile. Occasionally, she made a reply in a polite voice. He seemed adamant. She appeared docile. He pounded his desk for emphasis. She turned her gaze to her sandals. When he had wound down, she spoke quietly for a minute, then indicated to me that we should leave.

"What happened? What did he say? Why didn't you get it?" I demanded.

She shrugged. "He says he doesn't have it. We will see. Do exactly as I say, Miriam." She led me to a space on a long bench in the waiting room. Every time the door to the inner office opened, we were staring directly at the official we had just seen. I always made eye contact as Melana had directed me to do. We sat for hours. My back ached. The room was hot and stuffy. I told her I needed a nap before dinner.

"No, Miriam," she said. "Not yet." Eventually, the room was empty of everyone but us, and one more time we were staring stone-faced into the officer's eyes. He conferred with a minor official who handled the office traffic, who eventually called out, "Dutton."

I followed him back into the inner sanctum. Melana was close at my heels, but he barred her from entering. The officer I'd been staring at handed me Darrell's license and the car papers, then dismissed me with a curt nod.

All the way home, she laughed and laughed. I felt a grudging admiration for what she had accomplished. Much as I didn't want to admit it, I now saw her as a formidable opponent. But exhausted from outwaiting the *polisi*, I decided to postpone coping with her until after that rejuvenating nap I'd been longing for.

The cannon they shoot off to signal sundown and the end of the day's fasting woke me. I had slept fitfully with vague thoughts and muddled dreams of how I was going to get rid of her. I hated direct confrontations. We Pritchards seldom allowed ourselves such unrefined behavior. But Melana was nowhere to be found. Hearing the beginning of revelry in the street, I feared she hadn't left at all, but was out visiting.

Then I saw the note on the coffee table addressed to Darrell. "Darling Dutt," it said, "It is too lonely here without you. I do not think Miriam likes me. Perhaps she will go away again soon. I will always love you, and long to be your wife one day. Yours Truly, Melly-Baby."

His wife indeed! What unmitigated gall. I crumpled the note, then set fire to it in the sink. I'd always been able to handle my husband, and I would now.

❁ ↝ ❁ ↝ ❁ ↝ ❁

Far below, I watched the shadow of the helicopter gobble up more and more of the patchwork of green rice paddies, brown fields, small villages encircled by palm trees, and a broad river winding and twisting. Then nothing but green ocean and endless clouds. I amused myself listening to flight commands on the orange headset the Australian pilot, who we'd met while living at the Borobudur, had handed me.

Eventually, he pointed off to the right as we veered in that direction. In the distance I could see the platforms and flares of CAMCO's offshore installation. Shouting over the drone of the motor, he called my attention to the oil rigs, and then we headed where Darrell was—the gas plant.

The pilot left me off on the helipad, and with a thumbs-up gesture he was aloft again. I waved my gratitude. This was strictly an unauthorized visit. Lucky for me the Aussie worked for a private company and wasn't concerned about CAMCO rules. Anyway, once I'd done his wife the favor of bringing her the Bailey's Irish Cream she wanted from Australia.

I knew from Darrell that the helipad topped three floors of living quarters, and the bottom level was a dining hall. Ignoring the amazed looks on the faces of Indonesian workers wearing tan overalls with "CAMCO" stenciled on the back, I made my way down the steep steps, hoping Darrell would be at lunch. In a fluorescent-lit room of chrome, pseudo leather chairs, and Formica tables, I found him filling a paper cup with soft ice cream from a machine. I composed myself for a fresh start.

He scrambled to clean up the mess he'd made when he saw me. I helped him with some paper towels. "What are you doing here? I've got to get you off of here." Men at a nearby table snickered.

"You certainly do." Plant superintendent Ben Moody stepped between us. "Get that chopper back here," he barked into a walkie-talkie. He didn't scare me a bit. I'd seen him wearing the proverbial lamp shade at a party or two.

"I'm sorry about this, Ben. I can't imagine what's gotten into Miriam. She's lost her senses, or—nothing's happened back home? There's no crisis that—"

"None that anyone but you and I need know about," I said. Darrell had the good grace to flush a brick red.

"I'm not that demented," I continued. "The Aussie's coming back for me in an hour. He had a drop to make out on Brava. That's all I want—an hour."

The expat men had stopped all pretense of eating, thoroughly enjoying this diversion from their monotonous tour of duty. Ben said, "Take her to your room, Dutton. I can't have this kind of disruption. And Dutton, keep your family problems at home from now on. The old man will tear me a new asshole if he hears about this. And you too."

Darrell's eyes were tormented as he led me away to his room, where we interrupted a roomboy bundling up laundry. In a fit of giggles, he ran away.

To keep from looking at Darrell I walked around the Spartanly clean room—*batik* curtains at the window, a tightly sheeted bed, a desk, an alarm clock, a fan, a reading light over the bed, a pile of books, and an ashtray. He sat on the bed and stared at me with a hurt look on his face, as if he were the one who had been offended.

I waited for him to apologize and beg forgiveness. I wanted to hear him say he was the bad guy and I was the good guy. I waited for him to say Melana meant nothing to him. He said, "What do you think of the Java Sea Hilton?"

"Don't you know what day this is?" was my reply.

He shrugged. "Sunday? Thursday? They're all the same out here."

When I couldn't stand the silence that followed, I said, " I thought we were happy."

He punched a pillow up against the wall behind his back and leaned into it. "You thought what you wanted to think."

"I want things the way they were." What I meant was I wanted my Great White Hunter back, not this simulated native with a ravishing girlfriend.

"I don't. Melana suits me fine."

I was wounded to the quick. I had magnanimously decided to forgive this adulterer, but I thought he'd at least grovel at my feet first.

"I'm about tenth on your list of important things in your life. I'm that insensitive clod with the mechanical expertise to make it possible for you to be the world traveler you think you are."

"You took a chance on destroying our marriage because you're feeling a little annoyed with me?"

"No, Miriam, I took a chance on destroying our marriage because I feel ignored, undesired, put down, unappreciated, and damn lonely. I've found I want a simpler life with Melana in it."

"You really want to live like your basic everyday Indonesian?" I couldn't believe it.

"Melana could make me a father again. *She* didn't have her tubes tied, and I'd get to see those children." I was horrified, but I tried to look past my anger and pain, past my earnest wish now to punish him, past moral outrage and wounded pride. What gushed out was "Melana this. Melana that. I'm fed up hearing about her. This is about US!"

He sighed and covered his face with his hands, finally looking out at me through his fingers. "Don't think I'm just having a midlife crisis, Miriam. This is about the whole rest of my life."

"Our life, Darrell. It's about *our* life." I took his hand. He pulled it away. As humbly as I could, I said, "I'd like to stay married to you, Darrell." We both heard the approaching chopper.

He picked up a framed picture of Melana I hadn't noticed and stared into it as if to burn it into his memory. Gently, I took it from him and turned it face down. He stood then, looking as proud and manly as I'd ever seen him. "I'm a sportsman after all," he said. "I'll do the right thing."

Meekly, I followed him up to the helipad, where the wind from the blades undid my hair and blew my skirt to my waist. I thought I would be swept away before he put me inside the chopper.

"Let me tell her," he shouted, his face a mask that offered me no surge of triumph, just a hard lump in my throat, a heaviness where my heart should be. The pilot strapped me in. Darrell stood, unsmiling. I wanted more, much more.

"I forgive you," I shouted back over the roaring motor. "We need never talk about this again." Darrell moved out of the way to the first step of the stairs. "She left of her own free will," I called. He didn't seem to hear.

"Please just one moment," I begged the pilot, and the engine noise lowered to a steady hum. I fired the last salvo I had. "Happy Anniversary, Great White Hunter," I yelled.

He gave me a little salute. It still wasn't enough.

❀ ↔ ❀ ↔ ❀ ↔ ❀

We were on our way to Carita Beach and being extremely polite to each other. Neither of us wanted to fight or upset the precarious balance we had somehow established when Darrell came in from offshore. He had moped around the master bedroom for a while, wallowing in that musky, fruity essence of Melana that still lingered. After I'd searched his pants pockets, wallet, and dresser drawers for evidence of other women, and made sure he knew it, and after several silly arguments over nothing, I settled down to forgiving and forgetting.

He wore his navy blue safari suit, the one I'd brought back from Bangkok. Around his neck were three heavy gold chains, one with the medallion I'd picked up in Greece. Curved around his wrist was a snake-looking black bracelet. It was made from a tree root that could be molded in various shapes when wet. It was supposed to have medicinal benefits. Yes, he was trying to please me by looking the old Southeast Asian hand. My aim now was to stop this "going native" nonsense.

I had thought a trip to the Sunda Straits resort—which arranged excursions to a wildlife reserve that included untouched swampland, grassland, forest, and jungle—ideal for picking up where we left off before I knew about Melana. "It's all arranged," I said. "You've always wanted to see the wild cattle at Ujung Kulon."

For a moment his eyes lit up. Then he said, "I don't think so." He played with his snake bracelet. I didn't know then Melana had given it to him.

I was desperate. He had to know I really meant to forgive and forget. "We'll get your picture taken with the one-horned rhinoceros. It's practically extinct you know."

"No, I didn't know."

I let it go for then. Later, I'd convince him. I wanted his picture taken with those beasts so I could get them blown up into posters to cover the spots on the wall where the paintings had been.

"Shall we go tomorrow? I understand we get a very good view of Krakatau volcano on the way—you remember the movie? All those people dying."

"Pull over somewhere, Madiun," he said, "somewhere I can put my prayer rug down. It's time."

"Really, Darrell," I couldn't help saying.

Outside, Darrell was on his knees. Madiun, backslider that he was, didn't join him, just sat grinning as Darrell began chanting.

"This is silly. For a grown man to … " I looked at the passing traffic, glad but surprised, there were no expatriate cars. "Darrell!"

Grudgingly, he got back into the car. "This praying thing is really quite interesting. Their whole life revolves around it."

"You don't say."

"The five a.m. prayer gets them out of bed and early to work. By noon, or one or two o'clock, they say the second prayer because the work is done. At three or four, they've had their big meal of the day and a nap in the midday heat. So then they say a prayer before going back to work or visiting in the cooler afternoon, ending up with the sunset prayer. Then they go home to an evening meal, prayer, and bed."

"And that's how you think you'd like to live your life?"

"I was just saying—"

"How are you supposed to do that working offshore? You'd be the laughingstock of the gas plant."

"It wouldn't be that hard." His face took on a stiff, defiant look I'd rarely seen. "We have a prayer room set aside for the Muslims to slip off to five times a day. For Ramadan, Ben even changed their shift from twelve noon to twelve midnight so they could work and fast, too."

His eyes took on a dreamy look. "What do you suppose it would be like to work a rice paddy, those little green shoots, the sun hot on your back, the ox you're guiding snorting and pawing and—"

"I'd say your feet would be slushing ox doo-doo, that's what I'd say. Just stop it, Darrell. Stop it now!"

Darrell said, "You really don't get 'simple,' do you, Miriam?"

"The bulls are going to be racing at Madura soon," I said. "We could go on your next five-day break."

"Ummm" was the only reply.

There was nothing else I could do. I had to seduce my husband when we got to Carita Beach. "How far?" I asked Madiun. He said we weren't even halfway there, and traffic was bad. Translated, that meant he didn't know. I'd spend the time laying the groundwork. "Keep your eyes on the road," I told Madiun.

He had been our driver almost since we arrived. In the beginning, he'd taken us to see the huge sailing schooners, just the same as they were in the seventeenth century, berthed at Jakarta's Sunda Kelapa, the only surviving sailing port in the world. As we had walked along the long wharf, as far as the eye could see the Bugis ships were a rainbow of giant sails.

"Remember," I said to Darrell now, "you were completely mesmerized."

"Yes, that's part of the real Indonesia, the one I care about." He put on one of those little black caps Indonesian men wore.

"That's when we knew that song was ours." I moved closer, put my lips to his ear. "Tum ta tata tum. Tum ta tata tum," I whispered the opening chords to "The Last Farewell." I hoped it would make him remember our fantasy: one of those magnificent ships slowly leaving the dock, bright sails unfurled, an Englishman on board waving, a native girl crying on the dock as she waves back.

I reached for him. This was the reason I'd returned, wasn't it? "You're on your way to war, Darrell. You'll never see me or these islands again. But we have this one last night together."

His arms went around me. With eyes shut, he repeated lyrics from the song: "For I have loved you dearly, more dearly than spoken words can tell." He kissed me passionately, and I was so glad the ugliness was behind us. But Darrell abruptly pulled away. "I can't," he said. "Don't ask. I just can't."

Stinging from his rejection, I ordered Madiun to take us back to Jakarta.

"You wouldn't have liked Carita anyway," Darrell said, seeming quite happy with a decision I'd made to irritate him. "I heard it's a rustic place—kerosene lamps and Indonesian toilets, bugs." He began smiling and waving to sudden crowds of people surging around our car. I realized then, as they waved back, joyful and happy, that it was finally Lebaron, the holiday at the end of the fasting month of Ramadan. Dressed in new clothes, bearing gifts and food, they thronged the roads. It was indeed a holiday, as well as a holy day, when even markets were closed in the towns we traveled through.

"The visiting begins now," Darrell said. "They'll go to the homes of their superiors or their elders or to some government official's open house, even to the graves of their ancestors. Don't you love it? Let's celebrate, too."

"We aren't Indonesian, Darrell. And we certainly aren't Muslim, and not likely to be. It's an aberration of your mind brought on by cohabiting with native women."

"There was only one woman."

"How do I know that?" I could see him in bed with them, hear their lilting laughter as he probably made fun of my ineptitude at lovemaking.

"Because I'm telling you."

"Why should I believe an adulterer?" Yes, I could see Melana's exultation at winning the prize—The Great White Hunter—saying, unlike his wife, she would stay put. I didn't want to say these things, but some devil had gotten into me.

"See that sign?" He pointed at something painted in red on a building, but we were already past it.

"I don't understand Indonesian," I said in my coolest tone. "You know that."

"*Maaf Batin,*" he said.

"Pardon all mistakes," Madiun translated joyfully from the front seat.

"I told you to keep your attention on the road." He gave me an idiotic grin in the rearview mirror.

"I thought you were over this culture shock stuff," I said to Darrell. He stared at me as if I were a stranger, which really set me off. I gave him my best glare. "Yes, the books say going native is one form of—"

"Fuck the books!" he roared.

"You've been sleeping with her again!" I roared right back.

"When for Chris' sake? Just tell me when."

"You got in early from offshore. Before you came home. Or you sneak her in. You sneak all of them into the servants' quarters when I'm asleep." Who was this shrew?

"Miriam!"

"You're thinking of her then. I know it." I felt sick at the vulnerable look that came over his face.

"I am not. But so help me Allah, I'll go to her if you don't stop this."

Seeing what I'd goaded him into, I couldn't meet his eyes. "You—" I seldom cried. I wasn't going to now. "You hurt me."

"It's Lebaron, Miriam," he said, looking miserable and dejected. "It's the day for begging forgiveness."

I didn't know what to say, but perhaps a truce was in order.

It seemed forever for the car to struggle through the world of inimitable Indonesian smiles. There was nothing defrosted to eat at home. No servants to prepare it, and I didn't want to be there anyway. It still seemed Melana's domain.

"Celebrate, *Nyonya*?" Madiun asked.

"Borobudur Hotel, Madiun."

"Holiday for Madiun."

"Bonus for Madiun."

With *rupiah* signs in his eyes, he said, "Okaaay, *Nyonya*."

❋ ⚘ ❋ ⚘ ❋ ⚘ ❋

After we reached the Borobudur, our ears still ringing with the din of the crowds proclaiming their moral victory, after we found haven in the hotel's opulent Toba Rotisserie, after the tiger prawn cocktail and Chateaubriand from Australia, after the string quartet's Mozart, after the waiter set aflame the liqueur running down a deftly pared orange skin into our fancy coffee, after we'd both passed up the dessert cart—we chattered like old and dear friends.

In a glow, we carried our party to the Pendopo Lounge and were lucky enough to get a seat at the piano bar. I settled into the familiar ambiance.

"The way I see it, the International Money Fund was designed to ..."

"If you ask me, the very best place in Singapore for ..."

"But, my dear, you don't have to go without sausage. I found this recipe that ..."

I closed my eyes to savor it all—Nelia, back from her break, singing Cole Porter, liquid gurgling over clinking ice, bottle caps popping, even the explosion of a champagne cork. I opened my eyes to see my husband obviously enjoying it all. He would forget about going native. Everything would be all right.

In this elegant playroom of visiting multinational businessmen and bored expatriates there were few Indonesians. Now and then one of high status came to meet a foreign colleague, but more often it was someone with a big bankroll obtained from gambling or some nefarious scheme. They seldom had women with them, and the Borobudur was usually successful at keeping "night butterflies"—prostitutes—out. That's why I was surprised to see an Indonesian woman at the bar.

Her bare back was turned to us as she spoke to that Belgian boor, Tomas, who had apparently returned. I saw only her ebony hair piled high upon her head and fastened with a jeweled comb, the flash of an emerald green dress—surely a designer original—and a profile of high cheekbones. Hands with the longest fingernails I'd ever seen reached for her Coke. She turned, and I stared into the coquettish eyes of Melana.

I stole a quick look at Darrell; he appeared to be studying his reflection in the polished bar surface. But when I saw how he was snapping my plastic swizzle stick into pieces, I knew he'd seen her, too.

She was surrounded by several men now; Tomas had been forced out. Darrell stood abruptly, almost knocking his stool over. "I can't stand this," he said. I stared at him until he looked back, his eyes tortured. "No offense, Miriam, but you're not what I need now."

"I can't help it you never do all those things you claim to want to do," I said, mistaking the intent of his words. It wasn't until he left me to go to Melana that I realized he'd meant it as a kind of apology. I watched as he pushed through her admirers and pulled her to her feet, holding her hands tightly in his. They stared into each other's souls, and then finally broke into earnest conversation.

"I see you know Yeti," Nelia said softly as she began playing "The Last Farewell," adding to my anguish.

"Melana," I said through tight lips, not taking my eyes from what was happening across the bar. By keeping a foot in two worlds I'd missed the banana boat through the Congo, which is really called Zaire now anyway, isn't it?

"So she's playing the little girl from Bali again," Nelia said. "Actually, she's just someone from Sukabumi who got lucky as a *babu cuci* for an English family. The husband—let's say he liked her a lot and had her educated. Planned to take her back to England with him, *she* says. They say he took her on a trip to Bali, then paid her off. Now she's a secretary at CAMCO." That solved how Darrell had met her.

"But you must be careful, Miriam," Nelia warned. "She's much more than that. She's what we call a "white hunter.'"

"She takes people on safaris?"

Nelia's fingers rippled into a song from *Camelot*. "A white hunter here is a woman who hangs out in bars in hope of getting an expatriate to marry her."

"Yeti?" was all I could manage at the moment.

"This one is especially determined to get a white husband."

I began to laugh and couldn't stop. Occasionally I'd gasp, "Great White Hunters, all three of us."

❀ ⚘ ❀ ⚘ ❀ ⚘ ❀

An alarmed Nelia said, "Miriam, you okay?"

I nodded. The laughter was gone, all used up. I stared across the room at Darrell and Melana/Yeti, who were still oblivious to anything but each other. I saw it all. They would marry. He would become a man without a country, self-exiled long after CAMCO had nationalized its oil holdings here. He'd probably live with her people, and become an old man with many brown children and grandchildren. Suddenly, I felt something I never expected. I felt an amazing sense of relief.

There was a commotion across the bar as a tall, bronzed man stepped in and pulled Melana from Darrell's grasp. Melana laughed up at the two men as she swayed seductively to the music. I couldn't hear the threesome's heated exchange. The Greek God was that too-handsome American who reminded everyone of the leading man on the TV program "Jason and the Golden Fleece." His booming voice carried over the music and conversation. "Buzz off, little man. This is my woman."

My whole married life passed before my eyes as I waited to see what Darrell would do. In shock, I think, he made the mistake of stepping back. "Jason" took her arm and guided her toward one of the plush booths. Nelia stopped playing. Everyone heard Melana/Yeti call out, "He is single, Dutt. Anyway, you too Indonesian for me."

Then Darrell was sitting at my side again. Neither of us had anything to say. He traded in his seltzer water for a double vodka on the rocks. Finally, he turned to me with an embarrassed grin. "What a fool, huh?"

Now he'd grovel. Now he'd do anything I asked. But I wasn't making it easy for him. I stared into my drink. He took both my hands in his, just as I'd seen him do with Melana minutes, hours, days before.

"You can give me what I need, Miss Prissy Pants. I know you can if you try." I still wouldn't look at him. His voice became an anguished whisper. "The bare essentials is all I want for us. We could be happy with a simpler life, stay here forever. We could take it slow till you get used to the idea."

I looked at this stranger, the father of my children, who was losing his hair and gaining a paunch, who was finally insisting on me making the big decision. The cruelty was that, on my terms, I did love Indonesia. The fragility I was feeling was probably true forgiveness. But a woman was one thing; a whole country another.

Then I saw that giant schooner we'd romanticized, purple sails unfurled. It had been pushed away from the dock, the ropes thrown aboard. But this time I was the one on the ship and Darrell, in a sarong, a flower behind his ear, stood crying on the dock.

HOMECOMING:
Maddy

S HE DANCED ACROSS THE TARMAC, DID A LITTLE SPIN, RAISING HER ARMS in gratitude to heaven, not caring if the rest of the disembarking passengers thought her crazy. Reveling in the velvet drizzle caressing her arms and upturned face, she sang out, "Maddy Chulach's back and Indonesia's got her," mimicking the "Gable's back and Garson's got him" promo for an old movie. But she rarely thought of old movies any more. She was into literary classics now thanks to that oaf, Tomas, for something.

The babble of mixed languages and the usual confusion on arrival in Jakarta blared out the door held open by a soldier. A parody of Tolstoy popped into her head: All Southeast Asian airports resemble one another, but each airport is frustrating, chaotic, and irritating in its own way.

Despite that, she breezed through *Immigrasi* confidently, easily slipping into a world of smiles and references to her as "*Nyonya.*" She placed a 10,000 *rupiah* note inside her passport, knowing that would get her waved through the baggage check. Things might be a bit underhanded here, but nobody got hurt.

Confident in her command of the Indonesian language, she chided the men with illegal taxis, settling finally into the ripped upholstery of one of Bluebird's fleet, the most reliable cab company in Jakarta, a smug fact only a resident would know. Soon Halim Airport was far behind, and she gloried in the lamplit stalls, little pools of light in streets abruptly dim now with the fall of night. Fresh from their third bath of the day, Indonesians streamed forth with gay halloos, eager to chat and watch each other watch each other.

When the horn concerto started, she knew she was truly back in

Jakarta from home leave. "Don't you know?" Pete had teased. "All the horns here are connected to the engines. They have automatic horn blowing instead of automatic gear shifting."

She missed him already. He had stayed in San Francisco to learn the new equipment they were sending over so he could teach it to the others when it arrived. Originally, she had planned to stay, too, lengthening her holiday with her family and friends in Ohio. But she'd become tired of living out of a suitcase, longed for her own things, and, of course, the Sandusky trip couldn't have been more disappointing.

Her family had been polite, but it was apparent no one really cared much for the *banka* tin angel candle holders, *batik* shirts, and root bracelets she'd brought for them. Pete's brother had belittled Pete's statement he'd only paid five dollars for his shantung safari suit by bragging about his own three-hundred-dollar camel's hair sports jacket. Maddy's sister had almost hysterically fixated on her yearly trips to Bermuda as defense anytime Maddy mentioned Indonesia.

Acquaintances said, "Indonesia? That's in the Caribbean, right?" Onetime friends said, "I know, it's near Viet Nam. Aren't you afraid?" Or, like an old schoolmate, they looked blank and said, "I never heard of it till you went there."

No one was the least interested in her photos; they didn't want to see the house she lived in, her servants, or even what the Hotel Borobudur looked like. A glazed look came over their eyes when she told funny stories about "over there." And Uncle Fred actually changed the subject in the middle of one of her sentences when she tried to explain Singapore.

Then, too, their lives had gone on without her, and no one bothered to fill her in, so often she felt tuned out and as ignored as she had been by The Herd when she first arrived in Jakarta.

Trying to resurrect *something*, Maddy went to her old office, but there were a lot of new faces. Her desk had been replaced by a Xerox machine. The other girls had once accused her of being the boss's pet, so she sought out the office manager. "You were a bookkeeper here? Yes, I kind of remember," the woman said. "Sorry, I'm too busy to chat. Some other time."

Now passing the familiar Kemang Hotel and Kem Chicks grocery, Maddy thought perhaps she and Thomas Wolfe were wrong. She could go home again and Jakarta was it now. Happily, she began planning tomorrow. She'd start getting caught up right away on what her Great Books discussion group had been reading. But getting back into Franny Ward's social whirl was tops on her list, too. She'd call her tomorrow, first thing.

Franny had a few rough edges. She never minced words, even if they were less than tactful. She knew everything about everybody and loved to gossip. Her strident voice had told many a wife in no uncertain terms when she was messing up Franny's mandated code of ethics for the expatriate lifestyle. But under her influence—like many others— Maddy had been able to hang on here, cocooned in a bubble of simulated American culture.

The one thing Franny hadn't been able to get her to do was play golf, not after that one embarrassing time when she kept missing the ball. She might take golf up now, but it wouldn't be because it was expected. It would be to see the verdant Cilandak course and the adjacent *kampung* in early morning. Chanting from a schoolhouse where the children learned by rote. Singing from a mosque. White-clothed nurses entering the Fatmawati Hospital across the street. Maybe she'd go alone tomorrow and practice. Chickens and goats and geese wandering the course at will wouldn't criticize her game. Women balancing bundles on their heads, already back from market at 8 a.m., would wave to her. Men carrying babies in the sling they called a *selendang* would call, "*Bagus, Nyonya,*" and make a thumbs-up gesture when she hit the ball, whether it was a good shot or not. Oh, yes, this was *home*.

But they had entered the street "CAMCO Raya" now and her house was in sight. She couldn't wait for the poodle to lick her hand, see the looks on her servants' faces when she gave them their presents, have *Ibu* bring her a red beer—which she had come to like but would never think to order in the States. She'd brought new records to play and anticipated a long hot bath in the oversize tub with her new supply of bubbles and lotions to follow. Yes, she would pull her household around her like a warm, comfortable cloak.

❀ ❧ ❀ ❧ ❀ ❧ ❀

An old man, a stranger, opened the taxi door, grinning toothlessly. The dog raised her head from a nap, then closed her eyes again. Another stranger looked up from under the hood of the Chulach's car, then, with no greeting, went back to checking the oil. The kitchen was a chaos of steam, banging pots and pans, and more unfamiliar faces. Once in the dining room she became aware she was interrupting a dinner party for ten, the standard number that would get you back four invitations. Oh, yes, Franny Ward had drilled Maddy well in the expatriate politics of entertaining, while indoctrinating her into a high life she could never have known back home as the daughter of a supermarket cashier and a car mechanic.

Fred Patterson said, "You should have let us know. We'd have sent the car."

He had retired from the company a year ago, but he and his wife, Ginger, had returned as tourists for an extended stay. Franny had thought they'd be wonderful housesitters for the Chulachs. Maddy had thought she'd leave the house in the hands of her trusted servants. But Franny had said that wouldn't do at all.

"I wish we'd known," Ginger said. "The bedrooms. It's awkward. We weren't expecting you, and I'm afraid that—"

The diners stared at her. The Pattersons introduced the American embassy's First Secretary and his wife, two overnight guests from the oil installation of Ballipapan, an Indonesian couple whose name she didn't catch, and of course she knew Mr. Supardi, but not his wife. He was the head of employee relations at CAMCO and had smoothed out many things for Maddy. The servants had stopped serving and were bringing in her luggage.

"Here, now," Fred Patterson said, "we need this food heated up." Ginger Patterson shooed Zsa-Zsa outside. Maddy had given her pet the run of the house since the day she brought her home.

"You didn't tell me what a pest Edythe Sheetz has become," Ginger said. Her voice dropped to a whisper. "Drunk." She rolled her eyes. "I don't think she'll be back. I took care of that for you."

This saddened Maddy. She rather liked Edythe. Drinking only oiled her tongue for wry and outrageous stories about herself.

Now Maddy had to know. "What happened to Mulyono and Endong and—" She especially wanted to know about young Djaya.

"Finished," Ginger said.

"Not suitable at all. We've got you some good servants now," Fred amended.

Ginger looked at her guests. "Not now. We can discuss it tomorrow."

Swallowing her anger, Maddy stomped into her bedroom and bumped into the vanity. All the furniture had been rearranged. On her heels, Ginger said, "You don't expect us to move out tonight, do you?" Maddy was terribly embarrassed. She wasn't sure what she'd expected. She had just wanted to *be here*.

"No, of course not," Maddy made herself say. "I guess I wasn't thinking."

Then came the ruckus of getting her things moved again to her least favorite bedroom because the couple staying over had the other one, and she had never gotten around to furnishing the other two. Finally—after

saying she'd eaten, thank you, and she would just retire now, thank you—
she sat on the edge of a studio couch, longing for her waterbed, rifling her
handbag for the cheese and crackers, the peanuts from the plane. She was
starving. Outside the door, voices murmured again, plates clattered, *gamelan* music played on the stereo. Maddy abandoned the search, remembering she hadn't saved the snacks after all.

She couldn't be any wider awake if she were on amphetamines. There
wasn't a thing to read in the room except last year's Christmas magazines,
and she wasn't ready for that. In fact, she'd quite forgotten it was the season. She let herself out the bedroom's patio door and slipped around to the
servants' quarters.

The new houseboy said he had work to do for *Nyonya* Patterson and
couldn't get her a sandwich. When he went back inside, she looked in their
rice pot, but it was empty. She went to Zsa-Zsa for comfort, but she was
curled around an Indonesian baby Maddy had never seen before and
growled when petted. Maddy looked at her watch, proud she'd thought to
change the time before getting off the plane. It was only seven. Jo Moody
was usually friendly. She'd walk around the corner and get caught up on
the news.

Her heart sank when she saw all the cars. Another party. She turned to
go, resigned to staring up at the ceiling for the next several hours, but Jo's
driver, whom she recognized as once working for Lexie Rogers, rushed
forward. "*Selamat datang,*" he called, and she was glad, finally, there was
somewhere she was "welcome to come."

❀ ↝ ❀ ↝ ❀ ↝ ❀

"Peace on Earth, Good Will to Men."—the once-gold letters sprawled
across a red foil sign on the Moody's lawn between two papaya trees burdened with rich orange fruit. Lost glitter from the letters powdered the
grass, glinting in the glare of a small light focused on the sagging sign. Twin
electric candles at either end of the scroll-like affair lit Maddy's way
through the Java night with its nocturnal smell of rich frangipani and
loamy earth. Then she was in a crowded room, dominated by women she'd
come to know better, but still not well—the remaining members of The
Herd. Unlike that naive person she'd been in the hotel, she thought she hid
her uneasiness around them well.

"I didn't mean to crash your party." Second thoughts nudged her
toward the door.

"Don't be silly. You'd have been invited If I'd known you were back." Jo hovered over the laden table, fussing with the centerpiece—Santa and Mrs. Santa in a sleigh with eight reindeer. "It's just a little bash for Miriam. She's leaving." Jo rolled her eyes. "She's really leaving Darrell for good this time."

"She'll be back." Maddy reached for a black olive.

"No, I don't think so. Not after the Indonesian mistress."

"You're kidding."

"Not a bit. Be a good girl and mix with the others now. After I see to the horses' ovaries, I have an announcement to make."

Lila and Miriam sat next to one another in companionable silence, each smoking in quick, short puffs. A young woman Maddy had never met ran into the kitchen, a blur of blue denim and Texas-style boots. An emaciated Sharon was a shock; she'd dropped unimaginable pounds and had dark circles under haunted eyes. The taut gauntness of her face made her look like an entirely different person.

She jumped when Sharon addressed her. "You can say it, Maddy. I'm not a fat freak anymore. Now I'm a throw-up freak."

Maddy didn't know where to look. She turned to the goodies on the table, but she'd lost her appetite. She poured herself a cup of punch from the wassail bowl and nervously hummed along with "Jolly King Wenceslas" coming from the record player. Sharon had turned to that strange girl, who now approached her with a plate of cookies. And there was Maddy's rescuer, as always, Franny, beckoning her to join the group surrounding her.

"But we're *not* having the Christmas buffet open house this year," Franny was saying. A chorus of groans met her proclamation.

The Wards had been here longer than anybody in the company, which gave Franny an influence over them even the company manager's wife didn't have. Franny was the one who started the bridge club, taught them mah jong, organized the annual talent show, made whatever office she currently held in the American Women's Association the most important, and discovered the only hotel with an American-style salad bar. In short, she was to the entire oil community what Lexie had been to the women staying in the Borobudur.

But if Franny didn't like you, you'd probably be considered an oddball like Lila or Edythe. Although there were some who considered her the oddity. She picked up offbeat characters like Karen Webster, the Associated Press bureau chief, who wore men's flannel shirts and combat boots to cocktail parties. Franny herself had never given in to the tropical heat by wearing the cooler cotton or *batiks*. In fact, her trademark was Thai silk long-sleeved shirtwaist dresses made for her in Singapore.

"Darling!" Franny hugged Maddy in a distant way. "Kiss, kiss. It's so good to have you back. You must tell me all about—"

Maddy adhered to the group as a magnet to a refrigerator door. These were all ladies, once, of the Borobudur. No one here would let her down. She felt much better now. She belonged again.

"No open house?" they clamored. "What will we all do for Christmas Eve?"

"That's the point," Franny said, her freckled face shining, now red to match her hair, then green, under the blinking Christmas lights framing a doorway. "You all have nowhere else to go on Christmas Eve so you just stay and stay, instead of coming and going like a normal open house. For years, I haven't gotten to bed before 8 a.m. on Christmas Day and still wake to find some of you in my living room."

"You love it, Franny. You know you do," someone said.

"Oh yeah? Last year there was that terrible fight between the Wilcox and Brenner kids and those awful accusations about who did what at the Cassidys' Thanksgiving bash. And drumsticks in the eggnog, someone's panties on my bathroom floor next to Santa's boots. No, it's gotten to be too much. We're going to have a nice, peaceful holiday in Penang this year, thank you very much."

Protestations buzzed like insects around Franny, punctuated by peals of laughter coming from another group across the room. With more shrillness in their voices, the women smoked more cigarettes, made more trips to the spiked punch bowl. Maddy suddenly felt depressed. Perhaps it was the mass-like choir singing in the background, reminding her of late-night Christmas Eves back home. Perhaps it was Noreen saying, "I can't make Christmas here in this god-forsaken place. I just can't do it." Perhaps it was the desperation in all their eyes, a desperation she'd been too new to recognize last year.

Lila Hoopes smiled at Maddy, taking her aback. She wasn't sure she'd ever seen the queen of doom and gloom smile. "You should get into something, Maddy. It helps pass the time, and the Indonesians need our help. I divide my time between the birth control clinic and helping families who get flooded out."

"Franny thinks I should join the Jakarta Players this year," Maddy said. "They're doing *You Can't Take it With You.*"

"That's all well and good." Lila pursed her lips. "And your choice I suppose, but—have you ever considered seeing a *Wayang Suluh* performance? Of course it's used as a link between the urban and rural people but—"

"Better you than me," Miriam interrupted. She took a swallow of punch and held it in her mouth like mouthwash, then swallowed. "I'm heading for civilization where I belong, and I'm never leaving the good old US of A again, so help me God. Not even after I get my divorce."

Miriam had never seriously tried living here, Franny once said. Maddy wondered if it were different if you went back and forth all the time than it had been for her. She still couldn't shake the feeling of being excommunicated from all she'd held near and dear. If it weren't for Franny being here, she wouldn't feel wanted at this party either. Maybe she should go home and rest up for dealing with the Pattersons.

Instead, she took advantage of Lila's good mood and asked, "What in the world is with Sharon?"

Lila whispered, "Doesn't she look awful? And she's so nervous and flighty. She's been back and forth to the States several times. For treatment they say. Left her kids there for a while, but they're all back now."

Jo lowered her voice—as much as was possible. "And the dog, Rocky—she even got rid of him. They say she misses Gwen Smith—they got pretty close, you know. But I think it's much more than that." She checked to make sure Sharon was out of earshot. "I read in *Reader's Digest* about this thing called anorexia, and it said—"

"I heard her children were at the Borobudur last week, running the halls, just wild," Miriam said, "with no one in charge but the driver, and I don't know how her husband—"

Sharon turned and looked directly at them. "*Her* husband is wonderful and worries about her through it all."

Silent night, holy night was all that could be heard in the room. Then some nervous titters. Everyone tried not to look at Sharon.

Franny Ward interceded. "Vonda Hutchison showed me where to get an artificial tree in Singapore. I refuse to deal with Indonesia's idea of a Christmas tree any longer."

"Hero's has some nice gift wrap," Noreen said quickly. "It surprised me."

"Er-ah-they have lights, too, and extra bulbs," Lila said, then proudly. "I bought everything for Christmas right here in Jakarta."

"Who would ever think it in this Muslim world?" someone said.

"Everything was almost back to normal when Miriam said, "Jo saw Celeste today. At Kem Chicks."

Jo looked uncomfortable, but said, "Yes, we both reached for the same package of chicken."

With everyone watching her, Sharon jammed three cookies into her mouth.

"How was she?" Lila asked.

"I invited her to the party," Jo said. "I said it's Christmas. Let's let bygones be bygones."

Sharon choked, downed a cup of punch. "You didn't." She looked toward the door. "She isn't—coming, is she?"

"I think that's a wonderful thing you did, Jo," Lila said.

Franny Ward was amused. "Well, is she coming?"

Jo laughed. "You know what she said? 'Sure I will, *cherie*, just as soon as hell freezes over.'"

In the renewed silence, Maddy watched a variety of emotions play across the women's faces. She felt like a voyeur, just as she had when it was all happening at the hotel. Maddy's dark mood returned. She didn't want to be here, or up the street at her house, or back in Sandusky, Ohio. What was the matter with her?

Jo's booming voice startled everyone. "Listen up, everybody. We're sorry Miriam's leaving us for good, but I've got something to celebrate tonight." She pulled the stranger in their midst into her arms. "My daughter's come back to me!"

Maddy looked at the girl closely for the first time—a middle hair part, braids coiled at each ear, and Sixties granny glasses, which she pushed up the bridge of her nose as she wriggled out of her mother's grasp. Then, as if sorry, she clasped her mother's hand and raised it to the sky in a gesture of victory. "Just for the holidays, folks, that's all."

"She ran away, and all this time I'm thinking of her on the streets, a hippy, getting into trouble. But no, she's a college girl and was in a nice dormitory making something of herself." Jo hugged her daughter, who scrambled from her grasp again.

Jo's audience looked from one to the other. They had never heard of a daughter the whole time they knew Jo.

"Her daddy, my ex, paid for it, and never a word to me about it all this time. He still likes for me to suffer."

The girl grinned. "Mama always liked to make *me* suffer. I just got even."

What a brat, Maddy thought. But Jo's face was full of love. "That's my girl, my baby, my Binky."

The girl scowled. "Bobbie Jo! Please, Mater. My name is Bobbie Jo."

Maddy loved it. Mater? Binky, indeed. "Tell me, *Binky*, what's your major?"

Jo's daughter told them everything they never wanted to know about college, as well as the state of the US government—deplorable; the literary scene—faltering; humanity's ills—many; and why we won't win the space race.

A red-faced Jo urged cake and coffee.

"Butt out, Ma," the voluble Binky told her.

Finally, Franny Ward stood to her full five feet eight inches, and took charge. "Speech! Speech! We need a speech from our departing oil wife." She pulled Miriam to her feet.

"Speeches are so dull, don't you think?" Binky yawned. "Don't you people ever live on the edge a little?"

Considering the past, it seemed to Maddy they'd already been pretty reckless by mentioning Celeste. The reactions of those involved in the Rudi affair proved the wounds were still raw and gaping. Celeste couldn't be more alive in this room if she'd actually shown up. Remembering how posturing she herself had once been, Maddy silently asked everyone to excuse Jo's daughter.

But Lila took her on. "What would you suggest?"

"There's a game we play in the dorm. It can get quite interesting. But I don't suppose any of you have the guts."

"Miriam could tell us her plans now, what she expects to do with the rest of her life," Jo said with downcast eyes, her hands busily pleating the ties of the Christmas apron she wore.

"Why not let the younger generation liven things up?" Miriam was apparently not too anxious to talk about herself.

"What is this game?" Noreen asked.

Binky pushed her glasses back up her nose. "Truth or Dare," she said in a dramatic tone.

Franny laughed loudly. "Christ, are they still doing that in college dorms?"

"I outgrew it in high school," Noreen said.

"Yes, it really is juvenile," Maddy couldn't resist saying.

"As I intimated, it requires brass balls." Binky's eyes assaulted everyone in the room.

Sharon cut another, larger piece of cake. "What do we have to do?"

Smiling malevolently, Binky zeroed in on her. "First, someone spins a bottle."

"Oh, brother," Miriam said, rolling her eyes.

Obviously experienced at taking audiences captive, Binky was unrattled. "Then the spinner can ask whomever the bottle points to, ' Truth or Dare?' If they say Dare, they have to do whatever is dared them. If they say Truth, they must tell the truth about whatever is asked them. Got it?"

Binky unplaited her braids, allowing the kinky hair to fall around her face. In the red and green light, she looked like a garish crone.

"This is stupid."

"No, it's a lark."

"It'll wake me up."

"Here's a Coke bottle," Jo said.

"Tell me I don't really have to get down on the frigging floor," Franny said as they formed a circle, sitting Indian style. She reached for the bottle. Everybody relaxed. After all, if Franny Ward was going to do it—The bottle stopped spinning in front of Miriam. A hiss of communal breath being released, then "Miriam Dutton, Truth or Dare?"

"Oh, what the hell. Dare."

"I dare you to go home after the party and sleep in the same bed with Darrell. And give a full report tomorrow at noon."

Easy laughter. "Sure I will," Miriam said. "You don't get it. The ship is sailing, and I'm on it." When she spun the bottle, it pointed to Lila.

With a sly look on her face, Miriam said, "Truth or Dare?"

"Dare," Lila said, looking pleased with herself.

"I dare you to say 'shit' in three sentences right this minute."

Lila bristled. "Really, Miriam."

"She'll never do it," everyone chorused.

"It's against her religion or something," Jo said.

Stubbornness cloaked Lila's face. "You don't know a thing about my religion, Jo Moody. I'll say 'shit' if I want to, and that's the first sentence. I know you all say 'shit' all the time, and that's sentence number two."

"C'mon, Lila," Binky said, "Cut the bull."

"There's a lot of people in this room who thought I'd never say 'shit.'"

"What a cop-out," Miriam said. "You could have said something really juicy. It might have changed your whole attitude about life."

Amid catcalls and hoots, Lila said, "My whole attitude about life *is* changed. You just haven't noticed."

Binky said, "You're all chicken. Get into some good stuff. You pampered oil wives must have *some* secrets."

Desperation edged Jo's tone. "Wouldn't it be fun to go from house to house caroling the servants?"

"Can it, Mater," Binky said. "Next?"

Lila's spin stopped at Noreen. "Truth or Dare?"

Noreen shrugged. "Why not? Truth."

Lila took a deep breath. "Is it true you dye your hair?"

Glee spread across the women's faces as they waited for the answer.

"It is an unusual shade." Noreen laughed. "But it's natural."

"Sure it is," someone called. The rest booed and hissed. Binky waggled a forefinger at Noreen. "Truth now, *Nyonya.*"

Noreen shammed hurt feelings. "I can't imagine why you don't believe me."

"It's called going back to your roots." Maddy pleased herself with her play on words engendered by the television mini-series even if no one else got it because they hadn't been in the States. She was getting with the program and enjoying it.

"Don't you ever just want to get the hell out of here?" The bottle had stopped at Franny, who opted for Truth.

"Heaven's no," Franny said. Her breathing was heavy and she had a funny look on her face. "But once here, you can never be the same again."

Maddy listened in disbelief at the hysteria in the unflappable Franny's voice. Everyone sat, stunned as Franny's face crumpled, and tears streamed down her face.

Smelling fresh blood, Binky turned on her like a vengeful district attorney. "Remember you have to tell the truth and nothing but the truth." She jabbed Franny's shoulder repeatedly with a forefinger. "Are you sure you didn't just perjure yourself?"

"It's hell everyday, and it never gets any better, but I've made it hell on my own terms," Franny lashed out. "There. Are you satisfied?" She glared at everyone. "And just where would you all be if it weren't for me?"

Maddy felt her words, staccato bullets, had been meant for her.

"Now you're getting into it," Binky cheered them on.

Maddy tried to signal Franny with her eyes to put an end to this right now before it got any further out of hand. But Franny, upper lip bathed in perspiration, wrinkles of concentration corrugating her brow, was staring with narrowed eyes at the bottle stopped in front of Maddy.

Fear scrambled Maddy's stomach. Stop it, she told herself. This is Franny. Albeit a Franny she had a hard time recognizing now, a dead look in her eye, a snarl on her lips. Perhaps Truth was not a good idea. Faraway, she heard her own voice say, "Dare."

But this did not deter Franny, who obviously was out to get as she'd been gotten. "I dare you to tell us if Tomas was a good lover."

No one moved in the room except Sharon, who was throwing cashews in the air and catching them in her mouth. "I never...I never..." was all Maddy could manage. But somehow she had to wipe the smirk off Binky's face. "I thought everybody understood...that..." Maddy stammered. Jo began rattling plates on the table.

Tension blanketed the room as Maddy searched—finding only empty faces, including that of her mentor, Franny. Suddenly furious, she reached for the bottle, dropping it from hands slippery with sweat. She waited until Sharon sat back down. Everyone leaned forward eagerly when the bottle found that target.

Sharon sat up straight and smiled a false smile. "Truth."

Something wild and demanding inside Maddy now wanted to bring down the impervious Herd. Deer hunters, back in Ohio, must feel this way when they saw the animal dead to rights in the sight of their guns, knowing all they had to do was pull the trigger.

In some stranger's voice, unable to stop, Maddy asked, "Did you really believe Celeste slept with her driver?"

"How could you!"

"Sharon, don't answer that."

"Well, I never. This thing has just gotten out of hand."

"Of all people, flaky June Allyson."

Jo said, "Just leave, Maddy. Leave my house right now."

But Maddy was frozen to Sharon, who was wildly spinning the bottle. But it couldn't stop at anyone because they were all on their feet in various stages of anger or distress or puzzlement. A wild-eyed, trembling Sharon looked from one to the other.

"Ladies! Laaaadies!" Binky tried to restore order to the party, her eyes sparkling.

Suddenly, Sharon smashed the bottle against the far wall, startling them all to silence. White-faced, she said, "It's my turn." She scrubbed tears from her eyes. "You haven't let me have my turn, and you owe me. This is for all of you."

Then she said, "Truth or Dare?" with such authority that they all responded together, "Truth."

Sharon stood at attention. All she needed was a blindfold. "Do you believe it's all my fault Rudi committed suicide?"

Silently, they stared at one another, caught in a common spell, only God knowing what was on each of their consciences. Unflinching, Sharon stood, still waiting for the first shot.

Finally, Lila led her to a chair and eased her into it. Jo brought a brandy. Miriam rubbed Sharon's cold hands. "You all let me do it," Sharon screamed at them. "You did! You did!" She ran for the bathroom.

Jo glared at Binky. "I'll be glad when you're gone." Lila began an asana right there in front of everyone. Miriam said, "I wonder if I could get an earlier flight." Bewildered by this stranger, herself, Maddy turned to

Franny, seeking repentant vindication. After all, Franny had brought something out in the open they didn't want to face either. Franny, who had ushered her into a false new world. Franny turned her back.

The women were arguing now about who-had-done-what-and-when as Maddy slipped by them, heading for where? She heard Sharon throwing up in the bathroom and felt remorse. What had made her do such a dreadful thing? Perhaps this was all some jet lag nightmare. Then the door to the bathroom banged open, and she was facing a shivering, perspiring—yet now serene—Sharon.

"Thanks, Maddy," Sharon said so fervently Maddy knew she meant it from her heart. Something had been exorcised from her. And maybe Maddy had been delivered from something, too. Something she couldn't find words for, something she'd ponder until she understood it.

❀ ᔐ ❀ ᔐ ❀ ᔐ ❀

Next morning, Maddy reclaimed her house joyfully, refusing the Pattersons' suggestion they stay a bit longer. She missed her old servants she'd trained so carefully, but as the day progressed the new servants seemed anxious to please. And there was much to do before Pete got home for Christmas.

She explored the bounty of Hero's and the Gelael, enjoying the smells of rich Dutch cheeses and Indonesian coffee, selecting raisins and nuts and candied fruit for baking. She roamed the aisles choosing French marzipan, Swiss chocolates, English marmalade, and Japanese noodles. She stopped to savor the German words from the loudspeaker, "O Tannenbaum, O Tannenbaum."

December days were the hottest in Jakarta, and Maddy was so uncomfortable she paid what was asked for the tree at the outdoor nursery instead of bargaining for it, which, of course disappointed the Indonesian selling the trees. But at least he sold it to her, which many of them wouldn't do if you spoiled their fun by not bargaining.

By late afternoon, refreshed by air conditioning, she sat down to survey her work. The resplendent tree wore both feathered doves and red velvet bows she'd brought from home and delightful stuffed doll and animal ornaments sewn by Indonesian women. But no matter what viewpoint she took in the room, her tree still looked like a Balinese dance movement, an arm raised on one side, the other side at ease. But all the so-called Christmas trees here were like that. She smiled. Some continuity at last.

Maddy prepared a bowl of eggnog, put a stack of Christmas carols on the stereo, and turned off all the lights except those on the tree. She didn't feel homesick or the least nostalgic for "good old days." She'd sent notes around asking some of the others to join her for eggnog, but they wouldn't come. She'd be the outcast for a while, the topic of every conversation. Eventually, they'd decide to "take her back," but it would never be the same. And she didn't want it to be.

Impulsively, Maddy called for the driver to take her to the Hotel Borobudur, where she relaxed into the elegant comfort of its grand lobby. The mosaic clocks still told the world's time, but she thought now in terms of the elastic rubber time. Someday, it would be five years from now—ten, nothing left from her sojourn here but memories. There was so much she hadn't done—so much of experiencing Indonesia she wanted to cram into her time here—and it wouldn't be the expurgated version mandated by the Franny Wards.

Two Western couples got off the escalator, dragging their carry-on bags, exhausted and dazed to be here at last. Maddy relived that first bedazzlement by the Hotel Borobudur, the bemusement of the mellow, bell-like sounds of bamboo instruments of an *anglung* band playing the unlikely "White Christmas."

Unable to stop herself, she made her way across the great expanse of marble floor to them. "Welcome to Jakarta!" she cried. And she knew she meant it for herself, too, no matter how much life here might change her. A different Maddy walked past them out into the night. Someone who could stretch time and embrace all that the mix of nationalities offered here. Someone who could meet Indonesia on Indonesia's terms and revel in it. Someone who was pure Maddy.

And surely Pete wouldn't object. Not now. Not when she told him what she is definitely certain of now—Maddy *is* home.

EPILOGUE:
And so the story's told

THE DALANG INTONES THE FINAL RITUAL PHRASES OF HIS NIGHTLONG tale, the last tremulous note of a bronze gong dwindling to silence. The amplifier is switched off. The crowd stirs. Bare feet slip into sandals. Sarongs are tightened. Sleeping children are lifted. The puppet master carefully packs his puppets away in their large wooden chest. The cramped musicians stand and stretch. The white screen is folded. The crowd moves out into the dawn of a new day, leaving the shadows to sleep until night falls again.

Javanese believe a *Wayang* performance is inscribed in the world; its consequences surpassing the intentions of the storyteller. Not only is it impossible to know how their experiences will color the return of the Ladies of the Borobudur to their own world, it is just as impossible to know the future of the Indonesian lives touched by them. Nor can we know what the memories of any of them will be when they bring them out again.

Please take along what has meaning for you now and leave the rest for another time.

217

GLOSSARY

anglung: simple rattan musical instrument sounding much like
    a xylophone
apa kabar: "How are you?"

babu anak: nursemaid
babu cuci: laundress
bagus: very good
baik sekali: splendid
banka tin: an alloy of mostly tin, and a little silver, used in goblets,
    candlesticks, etc.
banyak: much, many
banyan tree: East Indian fig tree
Batak: person from Batak province in Sumatra
batik: intricate patterned traditional cloth of Java produced by a
    complex process of waxing and dyeing
besok: tomorrow
bibi: aunt

cuci: wash

disana: there
disini: here
dukun: witch doctor and mystical healer
durian: evil-smelling tropical fruit

gemuk: fat

helicak: motorized tricycle

ikan: fish
ikat: a fabric in which the thread is tie-dyed before it is woven, giving
    a soft, diffused look to the most geometric pattern

jam sepuluh: 10 o'clock
jamu: medicine

kampung: neighborhood
kebathinan: the white magic doctor of the mystical sect
kebatinan: the mystical sect
Kincamani: soft drink vendor, serving from a cart on wheels
kopi: coffee

lakon: story
lular: yellow cream for removing skin impurities

makan: to eat
makan malam: evening meal
mas: sir or Mr.
masuk: to come in
menawar: bargain
muezzin: the crier who, from a minaret, calls muslims to prayer
    five times a day

nama: name

pergi: go (away from)

rupiah: Indonesian monetary unit

selamatan: religious thanksgiving meal
selendang: long, wide shawl worn over shoulder in which a woman
    carries a child
soto ayam: chicken soup
Susannan: Prince

terima kasih: thank you
tidak: no or not
tukang: workman or street vendor

waduh (waktu): this is very bad or woe is me
warung: a small shop, stall, stand

Barbara Haines Howett has been a journalist with the *Atlantic City Press*, co-editor of the *Brigantine Beachcomber*, and freelanced articles for numerous suburban newspapers. As a mature student, she received a Master's Degree in Creative Writing from Antioch University's foreign program in London. Publishing credits include *Chicken Soup for the Woman's Soul, New Millenium Writings, Poets & Writers, Kaleidoscope*, and *Phoebe*. She is an avid traveler, and has lived in Indonesia, Singapore, Nigeria, England, and Canada. She currently resides in Pennsylvania.